RAVES FOR *THE LAST KING OF TEXAS*

"Tres's taste for excess is as ferocious as his addiction to fiery food, and the fearless joy he takes in his roughneck adventures gives a real kick to this colorful series."
—*The New York Times Book Review*

"A winner . . . perfect pacing, expert switching between subplots and an unusually strong cast of supporting players."
—*The Washington Post*

"In Rick Riordan's case, believe the hype. He really is that good, one of a tiny number of authors who can consistently make me laugh out loud. With stylistic talent to burn, characters who jump, fully realized, from the page in a matter of seconds, and an enviable sense of both place and pacing, Riordan's novels rock. *The Last King of Texas* proves Riordan only gets better."
—Dennis Lehane

"You'll almost certainly enjoy the . . . blend of cultural chaos and color-infused action that covers everything from ancient love stories to modern amusement park rides."
—*Chicago Tribune*

"There's a reason this guy keeps winning awards. *The Last King of Texas* is Riordan at his best—razor-sharp dialogue, crisp prose, a wonderful sense of place, and P.I. Tres Navarre, one of the coolest dudes I know. Rick Riordan is a master stylist. I can't wait for his next."
—Harlan Coben,
Edgar Award–winning author of *The Final Detail*

"Rick Riordan has a Texas-size talent for spinning a great story, and *The Last King of Texas* is exactly that!"
—Tami Hoag

THE LAST KING OF TEXAS

RICK RIORDAN

BANTAM BOOKS

New York ★ Toronto ★ London ★ Sydney ★ Auckland

THE LAST KING OF TEXAS

A Bantam Book

PUBLISHING HISTORY
Bantam hardcover edition published January 2000
Bantam mass market edition / April 2001

ISBN 978-0-553-57991-8

Published simultaneously in the United States and Canada

Bantam Books are published by Bantam Books, a division of Random House,
Inc. Its trademark, consisting of the words "Bantam Books" and the portrayal of
a rooster, is Registered in U.S. Patent and Trademark Office and in other
countries. Marca Registrada. Bantam Books, New York, New York.

PRINTED IN THE UNITED STATES OF AMERICA

OPM   10   9

To Lyn Belisle,
first editor and fan, Renaissance woman,
damned good sport,

AND

Rick Riordan, Sr.,
who knows all the rides

ACKNOWLEDGMENTS

Many thanks to the people who helped with the research for this book—Dr. Jeanne Reesman, head of the English division at the University of Texas at San Antonio; Lieutenant Peña, supervisor of criminal investigations for the UTSA campus police; Officer Sandy Peres and Sergeant Cunaya of the San Antonio Police Department media relations office; Lieutenant Quintanilla, commander of the SAPD homicide division; Corporal Mac McCully and Sergeant Marin of the Bexar County Sheriff's Department; Ben and Jim Glusing for the continued use of a fine ranch in Sabinal; Rick Riordan, Sr., for the family history; Dr. John Klahn and Dr. Roderick Haff for medical information. Special thanks to Bexar County Sheriff's Deputy Don Falcon and Sergeants Eddie and Andrea Klauer of the SAPD, who helped shape this book more than a little. On-going thanks to Gina Maccoby and Kate Miciak for their support and invaluable guidance, and to Becky, Haley, and Patrick.

THE LAST KING
OF TEXAS

ONE

Dr. David Mitchell waved me toward the dead professor's chair. "Try it out, son."

Mitchell and Detective DeLeon sat down on the students' side of the desk, the safe side. I took the professor's chair. It was padded in cushy black leather and smelled faintly of sports cologne. Walnut armrests. Great back support.

Mitchell smiled. "Comfortable?"

"I'd be more so," I told him, "if the last two people who sat here hadn't died."

Mitchell's smile thinned. He glanced at Detective DeLeon, got no help there, then looked wearily around the office—the cluttered bookshelves, file cabinets topped with dreadlocks of dying pothos plants, the tattered Bayeux tapestry posters on the walls. "Son, Dr. Haimer's death was a heart attack."

"After receiving death threats and being driven out of the job," I recalled. "And Haimer's successor?"

Detective DeLeon sat forward. "That was a .45, Mr. Navarre."

When DeLeon moved, her blazer and skirt and silk blouse shimmered in frosty shades of gray, all sharp creases and angles. Her hair was cut in the same severe pattern, only black. Her eyes glittered. The whole effect reminded me of one of those sleek, fashionable Sub-Zero freezer units, petite size.

She tugged an incident report out of the folder in her lap, passed me a color Polaroid of Dr. Aaron Brandon—the University of Texas at San Antonio's new medievalist for one-half of one glorious spring semester.

The photo showed a middle-aged Anglo man crumpled like a marionette in front of a fireplace. Behind him, the limestone mantel was smeared with red clawlike marks where the body had slid into sitting position against the grate. The man's hands were palms-up in his lap, supplicating. His blue eyes were open. He wore khaki pants and his bare, chunky upper body was matted with blood and curly black hair. Bored into his chest just above his nipples were two tattered holes the size of flashlight handles.

I pushed the photo back toward DeLeon. "You homicide investigators. Always so reassuring."

She smiled without warmth.

I looked at Mitchell. "You really expect me to take the job?"

Mitchell shifted in his seat, looking everywhere except at the photo of his former faculty member. He scratched one triangular white sideburn.

The poor guy had obviously gotten no sleep in the last week. His suit jacket was rumpled. His rodentlike features had lost their quickness. He looked infinitely older and more grizzled than he had just six months ago, when he'd offered me this same position for the first time.

It had been mid-October then. Dr. Theodore Haimer had just been forced into retirement after his comments about "the damn coddled Mexicans at UTSA" made the *Express-News* and triggered an avalanche of student protests and hate mail the likes of which the normally placid campus had never seen. Shortly afterward, while the English division was still boxing up Haimer's books and interviewing candidates for his job, the old man had been found at home, his heart frozen like a chunk of quartz, his face buried in a bowl of dry Apple Jacks.

I'd decided against teaching at the time because I'd been finishing my apprenticeship with Erainya Manos for a private investigator's license.

My mother, who'd arranged the first interview with Mitchell, had not been thrilled. *A nice safe job for once,* she'd pleaded. *A chance to get back into academia.*

Looking now at the photo of Aaron Brandon, who'd taken the nice safe job instead of me, I thought maybe the whole "Mother Knows Best" thing was overrated.

"We offered you this position last fall, Tres." Mitchell tried to keep the petulance out of his voice, the implication that I could've saved him a lot of trouble back in October, maybe gotten myself killed right off the bat. "I think you should reconsider."

I said, "A second chance."

"Absolutely."

"And you couldn't *pay* any reputable professor enough money now."

Mitchell's left eye twitched. "It's true we need a person with very special qualifications. The fact that you, ah, have another set of skills——"

"You can watch your ass," Detective DeLeon translated. "Maybe avoid making yourself corpse number three until we make an arrest."

I was loving this woman.

I swiveled in Aaron Brandon's chair and gazed out the window. A couple of pigeons roosted on the ledge outside the glass. Beyond, the view of the UTSA quadrangle was obscured by the upper branches of a mesquite, shining with new margarita-green foliage. Through the leaves I could see the walls of the Behavioral Sciences Building next door, the small red and blue shapes of students making their way up and down steps in the central courtyard, across wide grassy spaces and concrete walkways.

Icicle-blue sky, temperature in the low eighties. Your basic perfect Texas spring day outside your basic perfect campus office. It was a view Dr. Haimer had earned through twenty years of tenure. A view Aaron Brandon had enjoyed for less than ninety days.

I turned back to the dead man's office.

Yellow loops of leftover crime-scene tape were stuffed into the waist-high metal trash can between Brandon's desk and the window. On the corner of the desk sat a pile of ungraded essays from the undergraduate Chaucer seminar. Next to that was a silver-framed photo of the professor with a very pretty Latina woman and a child, maybe three years old. They were all standing in front of an old-fashioned merry-go-round. The little boy had Brandon's blue eyes and the woman's smile and reddish-brown hair.

Next to the photo were the death threats—a neat stack of seven white business envelopes computer-printed in Chicago 12-point, each containing one page of well-written, grammatically correct venom. Each threat was unsigned. The first was addressed to Theodore Haimer, the following six to Aaron Brandon. One dated two weeks ago promised a pipe bomb. One dated a week before that promised a knife in Brandon's back as a symbol of how the Latino community felt about the Establishment replacing one white racist with another. The campus had been swept and no bombs had been found; no knives had been forthcoming. None of the letters said anything about shooting Brandon at home in the chest with a .45.

"You have leads?" I asked DeLeon.

She gave me the Sub-Zero smile. "You know Sergeant Schaeffer, Mr. Navarre?"

I said, "Whoops."

Gene Schaeffer had been a detective in homicide until recently, when he'd accepted a transfer promotion to vice. Sometimes Schaeffer and I were friends. More often, like whenever I needed something from him, Schaeffer wanted to kill me.

"The sergeant warned me about you," DeLeon confirmed. "Something about your father being a retired captain—you feeling you had special privileges."

"Bexar County Sheriff," I corrected. "Dead, not retired."

"You've got no special privileges with me, Mr. Navarre. Whatever else you do, you're going to stay out of my investigation."

"And if the person or persons who killed Brandon decides I'm Anglo racist oppressor number three?"

DeLeon smiled a little more genuinely. I think the idea appealed to her. "You cover your ass until we get it straightened out. You can do that, right?"

How to say no to a job offer. Let me count the ways.

"I'd have to talk with my employer—"

"Erainya Manos," Dr. Mitchell interrupted. "We've already done that."

I stared at him.

"The provost is more than agreeable to retaining Ms. Manos' services," Mitchell said wearily, like he'd already spent too much time haggling that point. "While you're teaching for us, Ms. Manos will be finding out what she can about the hate mail, assessing potential continued threats to the faculty."

"You're wasting your money," DeLeon told him.

Mitchell continued as if she hadn't spoken. "The campus attorney's office has employed private investigation firms before. Confidence-building measure. Ms. Manos considered the contract a more-than-fair trade for sharing your time with us, son."

"I bet."

I looked at DeLeon.

She shrugged. "Say no if you want, Mr. Navarre. I've got no interest in your P.I. business. I'm simply not opposed to the campus hiring somebody who can stay alive for longer than three months."

I gave her a *Gee thanks* smile.

I sat back in the late Aaron Brandon's chair, understanding now why Erainya Manos had cheerily let me take the morning off. You have to cherish those open employer-employee relationships.

Mitchell was about to say something more when there was a knock on the office door.

A large young man leaned into the room, checked us all out, focused in on me, then wedged a plastic bin of mail through the doorway.

"You're the replacement," he said to me. "Thought so."

I'm of the opinion that you can categorize just about anybody by the type of vegetable their clone would've grown from in *Invasion of the Body Snatchers*. The guy in the doorway was definitely a radish. His skin was composed of alternate white and ruddy splotches and gnarled with old acne scars. On top of his head was a small sprig of bleached hair that matched the white rooty whiskers on his chin. His upper body sagged over his belt in generous slabs of red polo-shirted flesh. His face had upwardly smeared features—lips, nose, eyebrows. They did not beckon with intelligence.

"Gregory," Professor Mitchell sighed. "Not *now*."

Gregory pushed his way farther into the office. He balanced his mail bin on his belly and stared at me expectantly. "You have my essay?"

"Gregory, this isn't the time," Mitchell insisted.

Gregory grunted. "I told Brandon, I said, 'Man, some people are really late with the grading but you take the cake. You ever want your mail again you get me my essay back.' That's what I told him. You got it graded yet?"

I smiled.

Gregory didn't smile back. His eyes seemed out of focus. Maybe he wasn't talking to me at all. Maybe he was talking to the pothos plants.

"I don't have your essay," I said.

"It's the one on the werewolf," he insisted. The mail bin sagged against his side. I'd disappointed him. "The Marie de France *dit*."

"*Bisclavret*," I guessed.

"Yeah." Unfocused light twinkled in his eyes. Had I read the essay after all? Had the pothos read it?

"*Bisclavret's* a *lai*," I said. "A long narrative poem. *Dits* are shorter, like fables. The essay's not graded and I may not be the one grading it, Gregory."

He frowned. "It's a *dit*."

Professor Mitchell sighed through his nose. "Gregory, we're having a conference . . ."

DeLeon took off her gray blazer and folded it over the top of her chair. Her bone-colored silk blouse was sleeveless, her arms the color of French roast and smoothly muscled. Her side arm was visible now—a tiny black Glock 23 in a leather Sam Browne holster. When Gregory saw the gun, his mouth closed fully for the first time in the conversation, maybe the first time in his life.

DeLeon said, "Dr. Navarre told you it was a *lai*, Gregory. Were there any other questions?"

Gregory kept his mouth closed. He shifted his mail bin around, looked at Professor Mitchell like he was expecting protection, then at me. "Maybe I could check back tomorrow?"

"Good idea," I said. "And the mail?"

Gregory thought about it, checked out DeLeon's Glock one more time, then dipped a beefy hand into the bin. He brought out a rubber-banded stack of letters that probably represented two weeks of withheld mail. He threw it on the desk and knocked over the silver-framed photo of Brandon's family.

"Fine," Gregory said. "Package, too."

The package hit the table with a muffled clunk. It was a manila bubble-wrap mailer, eleven by seventeen, dinged up and glistening at both ends with scotch tape. It had a

large red stamp along the side that read INTRACAMPUS DE-
LIVERIES ONLY.

While Professor Mitchell shooed Gregory out the door,
DeLeon and I were staring at the same thing—the
plain white address label on the mailing envelope. AARON
BRANDON, HSS 3.11. No street address or zip. No return.
A computer-printed label, Chicago 12-point.

I remember locking eyes with DeLeon for maybe half a
second. After that it happened fast.

DeLeon put a hand on Professor Mitchell's shoulder and
calmly started to say, "Why don't we go—" when something inside the package made a plasticky *crick-crick-crick*
sound like a soda bottle cap being twisted off.

DeLeon was smaller than Mitchell by maybe a hundred
pounds, but she had him wrestled to the floor on the count
of two. I should have followed her example.

Instead, I swept the package off the desk and into the
metal trash can.

Nice plan if I'd been able to get to the floor myself. But
the trash can started toppling. First toward my face. Then
toward the window. Then it went off like a cannon.

In the first millisecond, even before the sound registered,
the force of the blast frosted a huge ragged oval in the glass,
then melted it in a cone of metal shards and yellow ribbon
and flames, ripping through the wall and the mesquite outside and shredding the new leaves and branches into ticker
tape.

I was on my butt in the opposite corner of the office. My
ankle was twisted in the walnut armrest of Aaron Brandon's
overturned chair and my ribs had slammed against a filing
cabinet. There was an upside-down pothos plant in my
lap. Someone was pressing a very large A-flat tuning fork
to the base of my skull and my left cheek felt wet and
cold. I dabbed at the cheek with my fingers, felt nothing,
brought my fingers away, and saw that they glistened red.

Except for the tuning fork, the room was silent. Leaves

and pigeon feathers and pages from essays were twirling aimlessly in the air, curlicuing in and out of the blasted wall. There was a fine white smoke layering the room and a smell like burning swimming-pool chemicals.

Slowly, DeLeon got to her feet. A single yellow pothos leaf was stuck in her hair. She pulled Mitchell up by the elbow.

Neither of them looked hurt. DeLeon examined the room coolly, then looked at me, focusing on the side of my face.

"You're bleeding," she announced.

It sounded like she was talking through a can and string, but I was relieved to register any sound at all. Then I heard other things—voices in the plaza below, people yelling. A low, hot sizzle from the remnants of the blasted garbage can.

I staggered to my feet, brushed the plant and the dirt off my lap, took a step toward the window. No more pigeons on the ledge. The bottom of the garbage can, the only part that wasn't shredded, had propelled itself backward with such force that an inch of the base was embedded in the side of the oak desk.

Distressed voices were coming down the hall now. Insistent knocks on neighboring doors.

Mitchell's eyelids stuck together when he blinked. He shook his head and focused on me with great effort. "I don't—I don't . . ."

DeLeon patted the old professor's shoulder, telling him she thought he was going to be okay. Then she looked at me. "A doctor for that cheek. What do you think?"

I looked out the hole somebody had just blasted in a perfect spring day. I said, "I think I'll take the job."

TWO

The bomb-squad guys were a laugh a minute.

After barking orders to the campus uniforms and kicking through the rubble in their storm trooper outfits, sniffing the trash can and measuring lug nuts and screws and other metal fragments that had embedded themselves several inches into the concrete window frame, the squad decided it was safe to stand down. They threw Gregory the mail boy into an office down the hall for questioning by the FBI folks, though it was clear the poor kid knew nothing about the bomb and was already rattled to tears at the thought of his werewolf essay being blown to Valhalla. Then the squad relaxed in the hallway with their Dr Peppers and let lesser individuals take over the investigation.

"Same as that'n last year," one of the storm troopers said. "You remember that kid?"

A blond guy with a sergeant's badge clipped to his belt took a noisy pull on his soda. "Blew off three of his fingers, didn't it?"

"Four, Sarge. Remember? We found one of them later, under the bed."

They all laughed.

Another guy mentioned the lunatic they'd caught last month trying to drop TNT-filled Ping-Pong balls off the Tower of the Americas. He reminisced about how the perp would've blown a hole in the sergeant's crotch except Sarge was such a good catch. Hilarious.

I was sitting in a student desk about thirty feet down the hallway. I would've been happy to move farther away and leave the squad to their fun, but there was a paramedic patching up my face.

The narrow mustard-colored corridors of the Humanities Building were overflowing with SAPD, campus police, ATF, UTSA administrators. With everybody bustling around and the bomb-squad guys hanging out in their flack suits, I had the distinct feeling that I'd been dropped into the Beatles' yellow submarine during a Blue Meenie invasion.

One of the bomb-squad guys glanced down the hall to where Ana DeLeon stood talking with Lieutenant Jimmy Hernandez, the SAPD homicide commander. "Always thought DeLeon'd be a blast."

Another said, "Dyke. Forget it, man."

The sergeant cupped his crotch. "Just hasn't met the right kind of pipe bomb yet."

That got a few more guffaws.

DeLeon was a lot closer to them than I was, but she gave no indication that she'd heard. Neither did the lieutenant.

An evidence tech came out of the blown-up office. He went over to the bomb-squad sergeant and compared notes. I.E.D. Improvised explosive device. A metal pipe joint packed with solid oxygen compound and a few common household baking ingredients, some nuts and bolts thrown in for extra nastiness, a nine-volt battery wired to the package's flap— designed to break circuit when the package was opened. Instead it had broken prematurely on impact with the desk. The whole thing had probably cost thirty bucks to make.

"Gang-bangers," the sergeant told the evidence tech. "Solidox—real popular with the homies. Simple and cheap. Half the time they blow themselves up making it, which is all right by me."

Detective DeLeon was still talking with Lieutenant Hernandez. Another plainclothes detective came up behind them and stood there silently, unhappily. He was about six-one, Anglo, well dressed, looked like he ate rottweilers for breakfast.

DeLeon gestured in my direction.

Hernandez focused on me, recognized me with no pleasure, then said something to the rottweiler-eater. All three of them started down the hall.

" 'Scuse me," DeLeon told the bomb squad.

A few riotous comments appeared to be dancing on their lips until they noticed Hernandez and the big Anglo guy flanking her. The squad managed to contain their humor.

When DeLeon reached my paramedic she asked, "How's he doing?"

"I can talk," I promised.

DeLeon ignored me. The paramedic told her I'd be fine with some painkillers and a few stitches and some rest. DeLeon did not look overjoyed.

Lieutenant Hernandez stepped forward. "Navarre."

His handshake delivered about sixty pounds per square inch into my knuckles.

Hernandez was a small oily man, hair like molded aluminum sheeting. He did his clothes shopping in the Sears boys' department and his wide brown tie hung down over his zipper. Despite his compact size, the lieutenant had a reputation for hardness matched only by that same quality in his hair.

He released my mangled hand. "Detective DeLeon tells me you dunked the bomb. She says you did all right."

DeLeon was scribbling something on her notepad. When she noticed me looking at her, her thin black eyebrows crept up a quarter inch, her expression giving me a defiant *What?*

"Detective DeLeon is too generous with her praise," I told Hernandez.

The big Anglo guy snorted.

Hernandez shot him a warning look. "DeLeon also tells

me you're considering the teaching position. May I ask why?"

A sudden pain ripped through my jaw. The EMT told me to hold still. He dabbed some bandages onto my cheek. The sensation was warm and numb and far away.

When I could move my mouth again I said, "Maybe I resent being blown up."

Hernandez nodded. "But of course you're not under any impression that taking this job might afford you a chance at payback."

"Teaching well is the best revenge."

A smile flicked in the corner of Hernandez's mouth. The Anglo guy behind him studied me like he was mentally placing me in a bowl with the rottweilers and pouring milk on me.

"Besides," I continued, "I was assured the case was already in good hands."

DeLeon's eyes met mine, cool and level. You almost couldn't tell she'd just been through an explosion. Her makeup had been perfectly reapplied, her hair re-formed into severe black wedges, not a glossy strand out of place. The only visible damage to her ensemble was a two-inch triangular slit ripped in the shoulder of her pearl-gray blazer. "This incident changes nothing, Mr. Navarre."

The big Anglo said, "Should fucking well change who's in charge."

Hernandez turned toward him and held up one finger, like he was going to tap the big guy on the chin.

"*We* are in charge, Kelsey. *We* as in a _team_. *We* as in—you got problems with the way I make duty assignments, file a complaint. In the meantime"—he waved at DeLeon—"whatever she says."

DeLeon didn't skip a beat. "Get with Special Agent Jacobs. Cooperate—whatever she wants on the bombing. Help canvass, get statements from everybody who's handled packages on campus, negative statements from everybody who hasn't.

I want timing on the delivery of the package correlated to the time of the shooting. I also want statements from every student in every class Brandon has taught this semester."

Kelsey grunted. "The Feds'll take a pass. You know goddamn well—"

Hernandez said, "Kelsey."

"So I'm just supposed to piddle with busywork while we let that scumbag Sanchez sit out there?"

"*Kelsey,*" Hernandez repeated.

Kelsey's eyes were locked on DeLeon's.

Lieutenant Hernandez's voice broke in as soft and sharp as asbestos. "Are you capable of acting as secondary on this case, Detective?"

After three very long seconds, Kelsey reached into his shirt pocket, took out a ballpoint pen, held it up for DeLeon to see, and clicked it. Then he turned and left.

"One big happy," I noted.

Hernandez's aluminum hair glittered as he turned toward me. "While I'm in charge, Navarre, you can depend on it. You need to speak to anyone concerning the Brandon homicide, you will speak to Detective DeLeon. My advice, however—teach your classes, stay safe, and stay out of her way."

"Two pigeons and a lot of fine essays died in that blast."

Hernandez sighed. "Let's do a story, Navarre. Let's talk about a time one of my top people advised me to—say— de-prioritize a lead."

Hernandez stared at me until I supplied a name. "Gene Schaeffer?"

Hernandez nodded almost imperceptibly, then looked at DeLeon. "There was an aggravated assault case about the time you transferred out to sex crimes, Detective. Local crackhead had been terrorizing a neighborhood of senior citizens over by Jefferson. Everybody knew who was doing it, nobody would testify. Along toward Christmas, this crackhead got a little too excited, beat an old lady almost to death. Again, nobody would testify, nobody saw anything. Then, a week later, said crackhead is found with two broken arms, hanging duct-taped upside down from a railroad crossing gate on Zarzamora. He's about half dead, eyes pounded so bad he looks like a raccoon. We cut him down. He gives a full confession for the assault on the old lady, says please will we put him in jail and let him give some money to the victim's family. Real heartwarming. He also refuses to ID his attacker, so we know we got a vigilante out there. A couple of interesting names came up in the case. Some Christmas cards and goodies from that neighborhood got mailed to an interesting address on Queen Anne Street—jam, preserves, fruitcakes."

"Jellied fruits," I added.

"Jellied fruits," Hernandez agreed. He clamped a very strong hand on my shoulder and didn't seem to mind at all that he was stopping my blood flow. "So what I'm saying here, Mr. Navarre, is, things change. Friends move on, the paperwork keeps coming across my desk, favors get depleted, my patience gets thin. You understanding me here?"

"Clear as Cuervo," I promised.

"Outstanding. I hope the rest of the semester goes well for you, Professor."

Hernandez gave my shoulder one more crush, nodded to DeLeon, and went to see about the media who were gathering outside the police tape by the elevator.

The other way down the hall, the bomb squad was still hanging out, drinking Dr Peppers, talking about the length of their respective pipe bombs and TNT Ping-Pong balls and occasionally weaving in references to DeLeon's legs and her probable lingerie preferences.

"First case?" I asked her.

It took DeLeon a few seconds to focus on me. "I worked agg. assault for a year, Mr. Navarre. Sex crimes for two. I've seen plenty."

"First time primary on a homicide?"

Her jaw tightened.

"Hell of a case to cut your teeth on," I agreed.

"Don't patronize me."

I held up my hands. Even that much movement made the soreness in my left arm flare. "Kelsey seems pretty sure the Feds will take a pass."

She stared down the hallway. "Like I said, Mr. Navarre, you've got no special privileges."

"He mentioned somebody named Sanchez. Who would that be?"

DeLeon almost smiled, thought better of it. "I'll see you around, Mr. Navarre."

The paramedic got up, began packing his kit, and said he should be getting me to the hospital. DeLeon nodded.

She turned toward the bomb-squad guys, who were still leering at her, then took something from her blazer.

She hefted the thing in her hand for a split second—long enough for the bomb squad to register what it was and notice that its weight was too heavy, but not long enough for them to rationalize that DeLeon wasn't really that insane. I'll be damned if I know where she got the Ping-Pong ball, or what she'd filled it with. Maybe she'd lifted it from the student rec center when she went to wash up. Maybe she'd been carrying it in her pocket for months for just such an occasion. Police are nothing if not resourceful.

DeLeon said, "Hey, Hills, catch."

Then she did a fast underhand pitch at the chest of the blond sergeant.

You've never seen a bomb squad scatter with so little room to maneuver and so much Dr Pepper spraying into the air. The Ping-Pong ball hit Sergeant Hills in the chest and bounced harmlessly to the floor.

Hills' face went the color of chalk dust as he looked up at DeLeon. "You crazy fucking *bitch*."

His fingers splayed open. A large Dr Pepper stain was seeping into his crotch and down his left thigh.

DeLeon responded so softly you almost had to read her lips. She said, "Boom."

Then she turned and walked steadily down the hall, toward the news camera lights.

THREE

By the time I got to Erainya Manos' office, the codeine Tylenol from the Methodist Hospital was working fine. My face had softened to the consistency of tofu and I could only feel my feet because in my VW convertible, I can feel everything.

I pulled into the strip mall on Blanco and 410 and found the nearest empty space, thirty yards down from Erainya's office. The agency itself is never busy, but it's wedged between a Greek restaurant and a leather furniture outlet that both draw good crowds.

On the office door, stenciled letters read:

THE ERAINYA MANOS AGENCY
YOUR FULL-SERVICE GREEK DETECTIVE

Inside, George Bertón was sitting at his desk. Kelly Arguello was sitting at mine, reading *Spin* magazine. Between them, blocking the aisle that led back to his mother's command center, Jem Manos was kneeling on the floor, constructing a monstrous triple-decker windmill out of Tinkertoys.

As I walked in, Kelly and George gave me a standing ovation. The phone started ringing.

Behind the huge desk at the back of the office, Erainya said, "Can we answer that?"

From the higher pitch I could tell it was the alternate number, the one Erainya calls her "dupe" line.

As it rang a second time, Jem ran up and grabbed my fingers and told me he was glad I hadn't exploded. He tugged me toward his windmill.

Kelly and George started barraging me with questions.

When the phone rang a third time, Erainya stood and yelled at us across the room. "<u>What</u>—you people can't *hear*?"

Everyone fell silent. Kelly went back to my desk. George went to his and checked the Caller ID display. Jem pulled me toward his Tinkertoys.

On the fourth ring, George waved to Erainya, warmed up his fingers, then picked up the receiver with a flourish. "Pro Fidelity Credit—Collections—Samuelson."

He listened, looked up at me, winked. "Yes, that is correct."

George leaned back. Two wide vertical stripes ran down his golf shirt and made his flat upper body look like a bike lane. He nudged his Panama hat farther up his forehead.

I'd developed this theory about Bertón—the white leather shoes, pencil mustache, Panama hat, Bryl-ed hair. I suspected George only *worked* at the turn of the twenty-first century. Each evening he secretly teleported back home to 1962.

"Yes," he continued. "We can verify that. Let me transfer you to Mrs. Donovan."

He punched a button, held up a finger.

Erainya said, "Go, already."

The phone on her desk rang. Erainya answered in a voice that sounded ten years younger and half as testy. "Donovan. Yes, Mr. LaFlore. I have it right here. Yes. We were interested in seeing if he'd been the same sort of problem for you. Frankly, we're considering a lien."

She then sat back and proceeded to get some poor schmuck's credit history.

Jem whispered to me about his Tinkertoys. Apparently I'd been wrong about them being a windmill. He was trying for a perpetual motion engine.

"Where'd you learn *that?*" I demanded.

Jem grinned up at me. Erainya hadn't cut his hair in a month, so his silky black bangs hung in his eyes like a Muppet's.

"Secret," he said.

Jem is advanced for a five-year-old. Erainya thinks he'll do great next fall in kindergarten. I think he'd do great next fall at MIT if they had a better playground.

George logged in some paperwork. I sat on the edge of my desk and looked at Kelly Arguello. She'd gone back to reading her *Spin*. Her hair was purple-tinted this week, tied back in a ponytail. She was wearing white denim cutoffs and white Adidas with ankle socks and an extra-large black T-shirt that read LIBERTY LUNCH in reggae colors.

Kelly never dresses to show off, but you can't help noticing her swimmer's figure. Even in an oversized shirt and old cutoffs, she has the kind of smoothly muscled body that George, a shamelessly dirty old man, likes to call "Padre Island Spring Break contest-winning material."

Kelly looked over the top of her magazine at me. Her eyes are beer-bottle brown. She focused on my stitched cheek, then wrinkled her nose. "You smell like you're still on fire."

Bertón laughed as loudly as he dared. Any more volume and Erainya would've thrown a crisscross directory at his head. I speak from experience.

"Always nice to have your coworkers' sympathies."

"We're glad you're okay," George assured me. "Tell us about it."

I told them about the bomb, about Detective DeLeon, and about my decision to accept the UTSA job.

"Instead of P.I. work?" Kelly asked.

"In addition to. Erainya seems to think I can make her money at *two* jobs now."

"Professor Tres?"

"Be nice to me, impudent one. Soon I will have access to grades for the entire UT system." I did the mad scientist finger-wiggle in her face.

She said, "Bullshit."

Law students. No sense of fear.

Kelly had been taking classes up at UT Austin this semester on Mondays, Wednesdays, and Fridays. Tuesdays and Thursdays she'd been driving down to San Antonio to help at Erainya's office. My bright idea. UT was giving her credit for it—legal-related fieldwork.

It wouldn't have been a bad arrangement except Kelly's Uncle Ralph thought I was doing him a favor by being Kelly's big brother. Uncle Ralph has a variety of sawed-off double-barrel weapons that I try not to get on the receiving end of. Kelly, for her part, doesn't always buy into the "big brother" scenario.

Back at her desk, Erainya was still playing Ms. Donovan, bemoaning the state of the personal-insurance industry with some cherished colleague.

"I know," Erainya consoled. "They might as well rob us at gunpoint."

"Gunpoint," George Bertón whispered. "That's good."

Erainya glared over at Bertón, twisted her fingers upward in a gesture I could only assume had highly negative connotations in Greece.

George grinned, looked back at me. "She's sending me after your terrorist, you know."

"Terrorist?"

"Whoever. Your death-threat writer. Should be fun."

I studied him to see if he was serious, if he felt at all nervous about tracking down someone who pipe-bombed offices and shot holes in English professors.

George had dealt with worse, I knew. He'd done a couple of tours with the Air Force Special Police in Saudi Arabia in the eighties. During the Gulf War he'd been standing just outside the bunker in Bahrain when an Iraqi missile blew it to hell. After Bertón returned stateside and tested for his P.I. license, his wife had been killed in some kind of camping accident, leaving George ownership of her small title company and a rather sizable life insurance policy. For the past seven years, George had worked investigations only when he felt like it— usually for Erainya, tracking down skips on the West Side when it was clear Erainya and I couldn't get to them ourselves.

In San Antonio, that happened a lot. Anglo investigators could go through the Latino side of town, offering reward money for locating an heir to a big estate, and they'd come up with nothing. Flip it around—a Latino working the white neighborhoods, same thing. You do P.I. work in S.A., you learn quickly you'd better have a partner on the other side. George Bertón was one of the best.

"You know where you'll start?" I asked him.

"Activists, radicals. I can find some. They usually come out from California, stay for a while spouting the *La Raza* stuff. Then they figure out South Texas isn't L.A. and they go home."

"You know anybody named Sanchez?"

"This is San Antonio, man. I know seven thousand anybodies named Sanchez. Why?"

"SAPD let that name drop."

Bertón shrugged. "I'll ask Erainya. She's been making some calls to the police."

"You worried about this at all?"

"Oh, yeah. You know the last time the FBI had something to do in San Antonio besides polish their sunglasses?

They're going to love this. Even if I find this guy first, I won't have time to submit one report before the Feds come in busting heads. UTSA doesn't have much to worry about, Tres. They want to pay us to duplicate efforts, that's fine by me."

"SAPD seems to think the Feds will take a pass."

George laughed.

"That's what they said," I insisted.

George waved the comment away. "Give me a break, Navarre."

Jem kept working on the perpetual motion machine. He had one wheel that turned two others and made the top spin around like a helicopter. He was now trying to figure out how to stabilize the base.

Kelly flipped a page in her magazine. "So, Tres—you still going on that double date tonight? With your face looking like that?"

I flashed George a look to let him know I would murder him later.

He held up his hands. "Hey, Tres, I told her you were doing me an act of charity, man. That's all."

"What a guy," Kelly agreed. "Always giving. Who was the recipient last month—Annie?"

George said, "Yeah. The banker."

Kelly made her lips do a long silent *M*. "If your love life was a disease, Tres Navarre, it would have killed you long ago."

"You prescribe chicken soup?"

"Among other things. Not that you listen."

George cleared his throat loudly. Erainya gave him another look-of-death.

"Hey," Bertón whispered to Kelly, "you get tired of waiting, *chica*—" He curled all his fingers toward his chest.

Kelly actually blushed.

"She did great on the background files for this UTSA case,"

George told me. "Stuff on the professor, his family. Amazing what this girl can pull together in a morning. You know this dead professor, this Aaron Brandon guy—you know he's part of the same Brandon family that was in that thing a few years ago?"

"That thing."

I looked at Kelly for enlightenment. She didn't give me any.

"Yeah, you know." George made a gun with his hand. "Pow, pow."

"Pow, pow?"

"Yeah." George smiled, apparently satisfied that we were on the same page. "Family's got some bad damn luck. Anyway, Kelly pulled up all of that in one morning. Just on the computer. She's something."

"She's something," I agreed. "Speaking of those background files—"

"You're going to want a copy." Kelly opened my side drawer and produced a thick rubber-banded folder, plopped it in front of me. "Erainya got me started while certain other people were out getting themselves blown up. Regretfully, not completely blown up. Was there anything else?"

Her tone was super-sweet.

I said, "Ouch, already."

She batted her eyes.

Erainya hung up the phone, put her hands on her desk, and hoisted herself to a full imposing height of five-foot-zero. She looked across the office at me, her eyes black and piercing.

"So, what—?" she demanded. "You managed not to get yourself killed. You think that makes your morning successful? Come back here."

"Been nice knowing you," George commiserated.

I rapped my knuckles on his desk, then went to see the

boss. I could feel Kelly Arguello's eyes on my back the whole way.

Behind every man, there is a woman whom he's successfully pissed off.

Unfortunately, with me, there's usually one in front, too.

FOUR

Erainya's desk was piled high with manila case folders arranged in precarious spirals like cocktail party napkins. In the valleys between were crumpled balls of legal paper, framed pictures of Jem, two phones, investigative reference books, surveillance equipment, and the disgorged contents of several purses. Multicolored sticky notes were slapped down here and there like stepping-stones through the chaos.

It was difficult to tell, but the project on top seemed to be a spread of brochures, glossy three-folds like mailers for investment companies. The one nearest me read *St. Stephen's. Excellence Is Our Tradition.* A sepia photo of an adolescent boy with glittering braces smiled sideways at me.

Erainya nodded me toward the client's chair.

She had on her usual outfit, an unbelted black T-shirt dress that hung on her body like a handkerchief over an Erector set. No makeup, no jewelry, no hose. Simple black flats.

"This is your idea of a thank-you for the nice job?" she demanded. "You get yourself detonated?"

"I'm ungrateful, I know."

She made a sideways slap at the air, a gesture of annoyance she does so often I'd learned not to sit next to her in restaurant booths. "You're lucky UTSA is keeping us on."

"Totally ungrateful," I agreed. "You arrange a teaching position for me without my knowledge, let me win you an investigative contract with the University, and I don't even say *kharis soi*."

Erainya frowned. "What is that—Bible Greek?"

"Only kind I know. I'm a medievalist, remember?"

"The modern phrase for 'thank you' is *ephkharistó*, honey. Good one to learn, seeing as I keep doing you favors."

She reached toward her spiral files, used her fingers as a dowsing rod, then pinched out the exact slip of paper she wanted. She handed me a printout of classes—medieval graduate course Lit 4963, Chaucer undergraduate seminar Lit 3213, one section of freshman English.

"Three classes," Erainya said. "Wednesday and Friday afternoons. You're a visiting assistant professor, six thousand for the rest of the semester allocated from the dean's discretionary fund. I don't call that bad."

"What's your commission?"

She sighed. "Look, honey, I knew you had some hard feelings when you had to turn down the teaching position last fall."

"Completing the license was my decision, Erainya."

"Sure, honey. The right decision. I'm just saying—this opportunity came up—"

"A man getting shot to death."

"—and I figured it was perfect. You get to teach some classes, keep working for me. They offer you a contract next fall, you'll get full benefits and thirty K a year. Plus what you make for me."

I drummed my fingers, let my eyes weave across the clutter of Erainya's desk. "You're going to send me to boarding school if I say no?"

It took her a second to remember the brochures. "They're not boarding."

"Private school for Jem?"

She scowled, began gathering up the brochures. "I want the best."

"These places have scholarships?"

"Stop changing the subject."

"Most people still do public, Erainya. Kids turn out fine."

"You're telling me Jem is most kids?"

I looked back at Jem, who was now trying to explain to Kelly Arguello how the gears for his Tinkertoy motion machine worked.

"All right," I admitted. "He's exceptional. Still—"

"You worry about your college classes. Let me worry about kindergarten."

"And the Brandon case?"

"Let George take care of that."

"SAPD give you anything?"

"I just told you—wait a—"

I leaned toward the morass of papers on her desk and did my own dowsing job, plucked a phone message slip that was sticking out of a stack of reports.

"Put that back," Erainya demanded.

I read the message. "Ozzie Gerson. *Deputy* Ozzie Gerson?"

"I'm not talking to you."

"Ozzie's about as low in the sheriff's department as you can get without crawling under one of their patrol cars. You're asking him for information. On a city homicide case, no less."

Erainya tapped her fingers. "Look, honey, I know you."

"Meaning what, exactly?"

"Meaning if I tell you details, you're going to decide it's your case. You're going to go poking around when what I really need for you to do is stay safe and make UTSA happy."

"Is this connected with that thing a few years ago?"

"That thing."

"Yeah. You know. That other guy named Brandon. Pow, pow."

Erainya folded her arms. Her black hair stuck out wiry free-style, not unlike Medusa's. "Just do your teaching, honey. Give George a week and he'll have a full report for UTSA. You got an advanced degree. You can read it."

"Gosh, thanks."

"And what I said about the sheriff's department—just because Ozzie's a mutual friend, don't get any bright ideas."

"You know I'll ask him."

"Let me pretend, honey. For my pride, all right?"

"Anything else?"

Erainya picked up the private school brochures again. She shuffled through them, contemplating each, then carefully dealt out three in front of me. "If you were choosing between those, which would you pick?"

I frowned at the brochures. Maroon, green, blue. All very slick. All sported pictures of venerable school facades and happy honors students, grinning and hugging their textbooks like old friends.

I looked up at Erainya. "I know nothing about schools."

"You know Jem?"

"I have that pleasure."

"All right, then. I'm asking you."

I picked up the brochures reluctantly. A weird memory came to me from thirteen years ago, when I'd looked through brochures for graduate schools. The forms, the spiel, the tuitions. These were about the same. "Eighty-five hundred a year?"

Erainya nodded. "Cheap."

"For New York, maybe."

"I want the best," Erainya insisted. "I'm not asking you about the finances, honey. I'm asking you about those three choices."

Hesitantly, I held up the green brochure. "This one. I've heard it's a nice place. Small. Got an arts program. It isn't Catholic."

"I thought *you* were Catholic."

"I rest my case."

Erainya took back the brochure. "I'll get Jem a visiting date. He'll want you to take him."

"Me?"

"You don't know Jem adores you, honey? You blind?"

"We need to work on the kid's taste."

"No argument." Erainya collected the brochures. "Now get out of here and rest. You got class tomorrow. And no poking around in George's case."

"Suggestion noted."

Erainya shook her head sourly. She gazed at the gilded icon of Saint Sophia hanging on the wall next to her desk and muttered something, probably a Greek prayer to deliver the Manos clan from wicked, disrespectful employees.

As I was going out, George Bertón was fielding another call. He covered the receiver long enough to say, "See you tonight."

Kelly looked up from Jem's Tinkertoys. "*I'll* see you Thursday."

I agreed that he would and she would.

Then I ruffled Jem's hair and told him to keep at it with the perpetual motion engine. I anticipated needing one.

FIVE

By the time I got home the painkillers had started to wear off. The delayed shock of the morning's explosion was starting to do funny things to my brain.

As I walked up the sidewalk of 90 Queen Anne, the backward-leaning facade of the old two-story craftsman looked even more precarious than usual. The purple bougainvillea around the awnings seemed fluid and sinister. When I got around the side of the building to the screen door of my in-law apartment, I had trouble making myself touch the latch.

Once inside, I settled onto a stool at the kitchen counter. Robert Johnson leaped up next to me and rubbed against my forearm. I ignored him. I was too busy trying to convince myself that the dots on the linoleum floor were not accelerating.

I pulled down the wall-mounted ironing board and picked up the phone, which is installed in the alcove behind for reasons known only to God and Southwestern Bell.

There was a message from my mom, wondering if I was going to make it for dinner. Another message from Maia Lee in San Francisco, asking if I was okay. Maia apologized for being out of town when I'd called her Sunday.

My finger hovered over the ERASE button for a good five seconds. I punched it.

I called Deputy Ozzie Gerson's cell phone number and

found him working patrol on the far South Side. When I
mentioned the Brandon murder he grumbled that he'd try
to stop by.

Then I went back to the kitchen counter, snapped the
rubber band on Kelly Arguello's files, and started reading.

Professor Aaron Brandon. Born San Antonio, 1960, gradu-
ated Churchill High in 1977. B.A. at Texas A & M, M.A.
and Ph.D. at UT Austin. First full-time teaching job: a
year here in San Antonio, non-tenure track at Our Lady of
the Lake University, 1992–93. Contract not renewed for
reasons unspecified. After that, six glamorous years at UT
Permian Basin, known among the region's academics as
UT "Permanent Basement." Brandon had returned home
to San Antonio last Christmas to accept the emergency
opening at UTSA. He had been killed three weeks before
his thirty-ninth birthday. He had no police record of any
kind. His wife's name was Ines, age twenty-four, maiden
name Garcia, born in Del Rio, also no police record. They
had a five-year-old boy named Michael—older than Jem
by two months.

The curriculum vitae Aaron Brandon had submitted to
UTSA looked mediocre—a minimum of articles, published
in lesser-known journals, a course load that was ninety percent freshman English and ten percent medieval, references
that were no more than confirmations of his past employment status. The only violent edge in Brandon's life seemed
to be the works he studied. He had an affinity for the more
disturbing texts—Crucifixion plays, Crusade accounts of
the Jewish massacres, some bloodier stories from Chaucer
and Marie de France. The theses he'd written looked ade-
quate if not brilliant. It made me feel just dandy to have
been offered the same job as he.

Kelly's search for the name Brandon in the *Express-News*
archives had yielded nothing about Aaron but some about
his family.

A business section interview from '67 featured one Jeremiah Brandon, founder of a company called RideWorks. Kelly had highlighted the last paragraph of the story. This mentioned that Jeremiah had two sons he was raising by himself—Del and Aaron.

According to the article, Jeremiah Brandon was a former printing-press repairman who had made a small fortune repairing and building amusement rides for the many carnivals that passed through South Texas. Now with a permanent workshop and fifty employees, Jeremiah was increasing his profits yearly, and had invented such child-pleasing rides as the Super-Whirl and the Texas Tilt.

I studied the 1967 photo of Jeremiah Brandon.

He looked like a turkey buzzard in a suit—thin, hardened, decidedly ugly. The fierce hunger in his eyes animated his whole frame. I could imagine him descending on a broken amusement ride like so much delicious roadkill, stripping it to its frame and wrenching out the offending gears with his bare hands and teeth.

The next article, dated April 1993, announced Jeremiah Brandon's murder. The details were sketchy. Jeremiah had been socializing with his workers at a West Side bar on a Friday night. An unknown assailant had entered the bar, walked up to Jeremiah Brandon, and fired multiple rounds from a large-caliber handgun into the old man's chest. The assailant had fled. Despite numerous eyewitnesses, the police had no positive ID to work with. Not even a sketch. The witnesses at the Poco Mas Cantina on Zarzamora had apparently been less than model citizens when it came to exercising their memories.

There were three follow-up articles, each shorter than the one before it, each pushed farther away from page A1. They all said the same thing. Police were without leads. The investigation had failed to produce a suspect, at least none that the police wanted to share with the press.

I flipped through a few other pieces of paperwork—
Aaron Brandon's driving records, insurance policies. The
lease for Aaron and Ines' Alamo Heights home was made
out in the name of RideWorks, Inc.

I was still thinking about the murdered father and son
when Deputy Ozzie Gerson knocked on my front-door
frame.

"Can't believe it," he said. "You still live in this dump."

"Good to see you too. Come on in."

He inspected the living room disdainfully.

Ozzie was the kind of cop other cops would like you to
believe doesn't exist. He had a fat ring the size of a mana-
tee slung around his midsection, powdered sugar stains on
his uniform. He wore silver jewelry with a gold Rolex and
his greasy buzz cut covered his scalp as thinly as boar's
whiskers. His face was pale, enormous, brutishly sculpted
so that even in his kinder moments he looked like a man
who'd just attended a very satisfactory lynching.

"You call this an apartment?"

"I tried calling it a love cave," I admitted, "but it scared
the women away."

"This isn't an apartment, kid. This is a holding cell.
You've got no sense of style."

By my standards the in-law looked great. On the futon,
the laundry was clean and folded. Stacks of agency paperwork were tidily arranged on the coffee table. My tai chi
swords were polished and in their wall rack. Stuck on the
refrigerator, like a normal home and everything, was a kid's
watercolor (Jem's) and a postcard (my brother Garrett's, with
the endearing inscription IN KEY WEST WITH BUFFETT—
GLAD YOU AIN'T HERE!!!). The only possible eyesore was
Robert Johnson, who was now lying on the kitchen counter with his feet curled under his chest and his tongue sticking out.

"Track lighting," Ozzie advised. "White carpet. A big
mirror on that wall. Go for open. Light and airy."

"I feel it," I said. "I really do. You want to sit down while I call the decorator?"

He pointed over his shoulder. "We can talk and ride."

I turned to Robert Johnson, who had seen Ozzie too many times to get excited by him or his designer tips. "Lock up if you leave."

Robert Johnson curled his tongue in a tremendous yawn. I took that as an assent.

My landlord, Gary Hales, was now on the front porch of the main house, cracking pecans into a large metal pail. The spring afternoon wasn't particularly hot, but Gary had one of those head-mounted mist sprayers slung across his balding skull. The thing must've been on full blast. Droplets floated around him like a swarm of gnats, dripping off his nose and chin and speckling his Guayabera shirt. Gary looked up apathetically as Ozzie Gerson and I walked by, then went back to his work. Just Tres Navarre getting picked up by the police. Nothing out of the ordinary.

"Last week fucking parade detail," Ozzie told me. "Today I been on duty an hour and already three calls. I need a hot dog."

"Life on the edge," I sympathized.

"Balls." He unlocked the passenger's door of his patrol car, realized he had about sixty pounds of equipment on the seat, then started transferring it to the trunk with much grumbling.

Inside, the unit was about as spacious as a fighter jet cockpit. The area between the seats was filled with cellular phone and ticket pad and field radio. In front, where the drink holder and my left leg should've gone, an MDT's monitor and midget keyboard jutted out from the dashboard. The overhead visors held about a foot of paperwork, maps, and binders. The *big* book, the one with the whole county vectorized, was wedged between Ozzie's headrest and the Plexiglas shield that sealed off the backseat. I had just enough room to buckle my seat belt and breathe occasionally.

Ozzie took a right on Broadway, then a quick left on Hildebrand.

The week after fiesta and the streets were deserted. Over the weekend, three hundred thousand revelers had trickled out of town, leaving the locals drained, hungover, red-eyed, and stiff from a week of intense partying. The pedestrians all moved a little slower. The curbs were still littered with confetti and beer cups. Pickup trucks passed with empty kegs in their beds. Streamers dangled from trees. It would be at least Friday before San Antonio rebounded for another major party. That, for San Antonio, was an impressive period of austerity.

Ozzie took the McAllister Freeway on-ramp and propelled us south at a speed somewhere between the legal limit and the barrier of sound. The city floated by in detached, tinted silence—Trinity University, Pearl Brewery, the gray and brown skyscrapers of downtown.

"So," Ozzie prompted.

"So. The Brandon family attracts bullets."

Half a mile of silence. "You and Erainya. SAPD. The Feds. Suddenly after six years everybody wants to talk to me about the Brandons."

"We just love you, Ozzie."

Ozzie picked up his transmitter and told Dispatch to show him 10-8, back in service.

"Our unit number's twenty-thirteen," he told me. "Case I get shot or something."

"There's positive thinking."

"I tell the detectives six years ago—I say, 'Look out, this guy will be back.' Three weeks ago, I tell them, 'Hey, there's word on the street he *is* back.' But do they listen to me? No. They wait until Aaron Brandon is murdered, then they figure it's time to ask me for help. What is that about?"

"Go figure."

"You don't know what I'm talking about, do you?"

"Nope. You going to enlighten me?"

"I probably shouldn't."

"Probably not."

The downtown skyline receded behind us, the landscape ahead turning to a mixture of tract housing and salvage yards and acres of scrub brush.

Ozzie took the 410 split into the unincorporated South Side. "Jimmy Hernandez down at city homicide, he made it clear he wants a lid on this until his people are ready to move."

"And your career has been a tribute to following orders from the brass."

Ozzie's neck flushed. I thought we'd entered dangerous territory until he glanced over and allowed the corner of his mouth to creep up just slightly. "There's that. You put any of the story together yet?"

"SAPD's got two dead UTSA professors on their hands. Everybody is assuming the Brandon murder at least had something to do with campus politics. Except maybe it didn't. SAPD suspects some kind of connection to the murder of the professor's dad six years ago, something to do with a guy named Sanchez. Until they run down that lead, SAPD sees no reason to tip their hand. They're happy letting everybody think the political angle."

"You're warm."

"What I can't figure out, no offense, is why everybody wants to talk to you."

"You know what I did before this, Navarre?"

Before this. Ozzie-code for the unapproachable subject: *Before I got busted back to patrol.*

"County gang task force," I recalled. "Seventeen years, wasn't it?"

I knew it had been fifteen, but the mistake pleased him. Ozzie let it stand.

"The reason everybody wants to talk to me—I'm the expert on Zeta Sanchez."

Ozzie said the first name *Say-ta,* Spanish for the letter *Z*. He looked at me to see if it rang a bell.

"Nope."

"First part of Zeta's story reads pretty typical—dad died young. Zeta was raised by his mom down at the Bowie Courts, claimed a gang when he was twelve. Head of his set by age fourteen. By fifteen he'd started piecing out some West Side heroin action."

Dispatch crackled a call for another unit. Ozzie craned his ear to listen: 10-59—suspicious vehicle report.

"Over by Lackland." Gerson wagged an accusing finger at me. "Probably some damn P.I."

"You were saying?"

Ozzie frowned at the MDT terminal, then back at the freeway. He took the exit for South Presa.

"I arrested Zeta Sanchez so many times when he was growing up, I feel like I practically raised him. When he was about seventeen he left the small stuff behind—the gang-banging, the drugs—and got a job with Jeremiah Brandon."

"Aaron Brandon's father."

"Yeah."

"He made amusement park rides."

Ozzie laughed. "Yeah. You know anything about the carnival circuit?"

"You mean like candied apples? Duck shoots?"

"The carnies are havens for cons. Smugglers. Thieves. Murderers. Grifters. Name your flavor. Jeremiah Brandon did business with all of them. By the time he died, Jeremiah was calling himself the King of the South Texas carnivals. Had the amusement-ride market sewn up all over the Southwest and northern Mexico. And he wasn't just selling rides, kid. Brandon would fence stolen property for his buddies on the circuit, launder their cash, make problem employees go away. A whole network of people all over the country owed him favors. You wanted some goods smuggled out of state, or you wanted to disappear, or you needed to find some hired guns for a quick job, Jeremiah could help. You worked for him, you could make some big money."

"Which Zeta Sanchez did?"

"For a couple of years, Zeta Sanchez was Jeremiah Brandon's right-hand man."

"A kid from the Bowie Courts."

"Jeremiah always hired from the West Side. He set himself up like a feudal lord down there—bought up the local businesses for his cronies to run, slept with any of the women he wanted to, recruited the meanest talent from the local gangs. Wasn't any accident he was killed at that cantina on Zarzamora. That was where old Jerry held court, bought drinks every night, let his employees grovel to him. He'd lend them money, get them out of trouble—whatever they needed, as long as they remembered who owned them."

"Nice guy."

"I'm probably being too easy on him. The thing was, King Jerry knew talent when he saw it, and he saw it in Zeta Sanchez. He started Sanchez on simple stuff—arm-breaking, fencing, your occasional murder. Pretty soon Sanchez was flying all over the country collecting from RideWorks' delinquent debtors, bringing back attaché cases full of cash. Brandon was so pleased he gifted Sanchez with a gold-plated .45 revolver for a calling card. Beautiful weapon."

"And they lived happily ever after."

"Until the Brandons screwed Sanchez, yeah. Jeremiah's sons, Del and Aaron—they started getting a little jealous about this upstart Mexican getting so tight with their old man. They decided to sour the relationship, turn Dad against Sanchez. Pretty soon the favors toward Sanchez were drying up. Sanchez and Jeremiah argued more and more. Then a rumor got around that old Jeremiah had been boinking Sanchez's wife, pretty little thing about seventeen, eighteen years old. Wouldn't have been the first time Jeremiah did something like that. Most of his mistresses came from the families he employed. Who'd complain? Like I said, you took Brandon's money, everything you had belonged to Brandon. Sanchez forgot that—forgot he was just hired help."

"And when Sanchez heard the rumor about his wife—"

"Sanchez decided to take a little nighttime drive down to the Poco Mas, have a chat with the Old Man. Jeremiah was at his booth like always, polishing off a bottle of Cuervo, hitting on some *chiquitas*. Jukebox was going. Place was packed. So Sanchez walks up to his boss, cool and easy, and draws on him—that same damn gold-plated .45 Jeremiah had given him. Empties every damn round into Jeremiah's chest. Hollow-tipped bullets, filled with mercury. Then Sanchez goes to the bar, takes a shot of tequila, walks out. Course by the time we come asking, nobody saw anything. Nobody remembered what the gunman looked like."

"You were at the scene?"

"You ever seen a man with no chest, kid? I mean, hollowed out like a balloon? You don't forget that too easy. I'm telling you . . ."

Ozzie glanced over in weary camaraderie, his smile pleasant and dead as an open-casket display.

We turned into a worn-down residential area and cruised the streets. Every white person in every yard waved. The Latinos and a few African Americans stared at us. None of them waved.

Ozzie watched the houses go by, his big glassy eyes deconstructing the architecture and the landscapes and the people in the yards with the same dispassionate criticism.

"Not enough trees," he said.

"Pardon?"

"I couldn't live here. Not enough trees. And all the garages in the front. Makes for an ugly facade."

"What happened to Zeta Sanchez after he killed Jeremiah?"

Ozzie's gaze kept sliding over the lawns and garages. "Disappeared. Word was he ran to Mexico to escape a hit by Brandon's older son, Del, who took over the business. Or maybe Sanchez *got* hit and was buried in the countryside somewhere. The manhunt yielded exactly nothing. There never was any hard evidence to connect Sanchez to the kill—no shells. No prints. None of the witnesses would break no matter how hard we questioned, not and risk retaliation from Sanchez's *veterano* friends on the West Side. Sanchez just vanished. Jeremiah Brandon's murder case stayed open—still is, but you know how it goes. Old Jeremiah wasn't exactly a great loss to society. Then about three weeks ago, Sanchez reappeared. Just showed up at the Poco Mas. Walked in after six years like he was a regular guy, ordered a tequila shot, and told the bartender to call some of his old *vatos,* tell them the 'Z' was back in town."

"And a few days after that, Aaron Brandon, Jeremiah's younger son, was shot to death in his living room."

"That's about the size of it."

"Aaron was an English professor."

"Maybe now. But six years ago? Back then he was snarled up good in the family business. My guess, he was helping his brother Del put a knife in Sanchez's back."

"You got anything more than a guess?"

Ozzie's head jerked back in a silent laugh. "You know what the M.E. pulled out of Aaron Brandon's fireplace last Saturday?"

".45 slugs."

"Better than that. Hollow-tipped bullets, mercury-filled. Not many sons of bitches ever used that kind of artillery in San Antonio."

"Still—"

"And there's a witness. The professor's wife and kid were out of town but they got this maid lives above the garage. Everybody else in the neighborhood is pretty much deaf old retirees, but the maid heard the two shots, gave a pretty good description of the guy she saw coming out of Brandon's back door just afterward. She made a positive ID on Sanchez in a photo lineup."

"Two shots with a .45, in a quiet residential neighborhood. Sanchez just strolls out the back door and is nice enough to leave a witness. This after he was smart enough to stay hidden since when—'93?"

"Revenge makes you stupid. Thing about gang-bangers, they're smart only in the ways that they're smart. Kind of like academics."

"Hey—"

"I'm telling you, Navarre. I know Sanchez. He's good for the murder. SAPD looks where I told them to look, they'll nail his ass. Let's get some food."

Ozzie cut across Military Drive and pulled into the parking lot of a Circle K that squatted at the entrance of a particularly bleak subdivision.

When the big-haired cashier saw Ozzie, she rolled her eyes. "Where the hell *you* been all week?"

"Busy, Mabel. Hot dogs warm? Damn near gave me *E. coli* last time."

"Oh, the hell they did," Mabel grumbled. "You wish some bacteria'd eat off that extra flesh of yours, Ozzie Gerson."

"Balls." Ozzie went behind the counter and pulled two foam cups from the special cop dispenser.

I kid you not. There *is* a special cop dispenser. The cups say FOR POLICE USE ONLY.

He tossed me one. "You're honorary today, Navarre. Help yourself."

I got some Big Red. Ozzie went for Pepsi. *For police use*

only. Do not try this at home. We are trained professionals. We know how to pour soda into these special cups.

Ozzie grabbed two hot dogs and offered me one. I declined.

Ozzie began chewing on both of them. He eyed a couple of large Latinos in construction clothes who were buying cigarettes from Mabel.

"What about the pipe bomb at UTSA?" I asked him. "The death threats?"

Ozzie kept chewing. "You mean was that Sanchez? Why not? Solidox bomb is an old gang scare tactic. Lot of the *veteranos* know how to make them."

"They learn how to craft political hate mail, too?"

Ozzie dabbed the ketchup off his jowls with a Circle K napkin. He kept his eyes on the Latinos at the register, who were now asking for a fill-up on number four.

"I don't know, Navarre. Don't waste your time trying to figure out Zeta Sanchez. He's a gang-banger. He passed the exit for humans a long time ago."

"Bullshit."

Ozzie shrugged. "You don't want to hear it, don't. Jeremiah and Aaron Brandon weren't white, we wouldn't even be having this conversation. We'd let Sanchez go on killing his own. Tell me it ain't so."

I tried to control the swell of anger in my throat, the feeling that I was back in my father's patrol car again, arguing social issues until common sense started to bend like light around a black hole. Ozzie was one of the last of my father's generation on the force, the last who could give me that feeling. Maybe that's why I'd kept in touch with Ozzie over the years. A sort of negative nostalgia.

Ozzie met my eyes, tried to soften his look of obstinance. "Listen, kid. It's like I told Erainya—leave this murder to the SAPD. All your friend Bertón's got to do is dig around UTSA a little, talk to some Mexican activist groups, decide they've got nothing to do with the case and UTSA is safe. And I'm telling you—this has got *nada* to do with campus politics. UTSA will be grateful, you'll get paid for doing squat, we'll get Sanchez in custody, everybody will be happy."

"Except Aaron Brandon, his wife, his kid."

Ozzie's eyes were the color of frozen vodka. "So the prof had a family. You become a cop, Navarre, you take that reverse gear and you rip it out of your transmission. You don't go backward. You don't think about what you can't change."

"Like the days before you worked patrol?"

Gerson's doughy face mottled with red.

"Why'd they demote you, Ozzie? You never talk about it."

"Drop it, Navarre. You weren't the son of the guy that hired me, you'd be walking home right now."

The Latinos got their cigarettes and paid for their gas and left. Ozzie looked disappointed. He wadded up his hot dog paper tray and made a basket in the trash can. "Screw it, anyway. I protested some bullshit evaluations from the new chief. It was all fucking politics, okay?"

He started toward the door, waved for me to follow. "See you, Mabel."

"Can't wait," she called.

We hadn't gone half a mile in Ozzie's unit before the call came through, not over the radio but on the cell phone, which meant Dispatch didn't want the media overhearing.

Ozzie said "Yeah" a few times, then checked the information that was clicking across his MDT in glowing orange. "36; P-32. Got it."

The patrol car was accelerating before he even hung up.

"Speak of the devil," he said. "They just got a warrant. Sanchez is bunking at his brother-in-law's house, just off Green Road."

"That's close to here."

He smiled. "Sheriff's jurisdiction. SAPD is requesting uniformed presence from us immediately. You up for this?"

He didn't wait for an answer. We hit eighty mph and subdivisions started falling away, the land turning to farms, rows of ripening watermelons, horse ranches.

"Trees," Ozzie murmured. "I retire, man, my place is going to have trees in the lot."

Then we careened in frightening silence onto Green Road and west toward Zeta Sanchez.

SIX

If you didn't know better, you might think the right side of Green Road is lined with rolling hills—gray dunes covered with worn-out toupees of spear grass and skunkweed and now, in late April, an occasional stroke of wildflowers.

But there are no hills in this part of Bexar County. What lines Green Road are mounds of landfill, compliments of the BFI city dump. When the wind blows in your direction, that quickly becomes apparent.

On the left side of the road were shacks of impoverished farmers, county welfare recipients, Texas backwoods families who'd been there for generations before the dump moved in. Their dirt yards were littered with plastic children's toys bleached white from the sun, stunted chinaberry trees, and patches of wild strawberry. Many had handmade cardboard signs in front that read BFI STINKS! Watermelon fields stretched out behind mobile homes that leaned and sagged at weird angles on cinder-block foundations.

On one front porch, a flock of half-naked toddlers, tanned the color of butterscotch pudding, scampered around, climbing in and out of an old clawfoot tub. Pale hairy adult shapes, also half-naked, moved through the interior of the shack.

Ozzie kept checking the telephone poles for block numbers, only occasionally finding evidence that we were going the right way. The idea of these shacks having mailing addresses seemed about as unlikely as them having Web sites. *Click here for a virtual tour of my hovel!*

After a half mile we got stuck behind a caravan of yellow BFI garbage trucks. Ozzie cursed and blasted his bullhorn, but there wasn't much space for the trucks to go on the shoulderless two-lane. Finally Gerson punched the gas and pulled into oncoming traffic. In the space of eighty yards we came close to smearing three truckloads of migrant fieldhands and ourselves all over the road. We swerved back into the right lane nanoseconds before colliding with a wide-eyed farmer in a Ford.

"Have a nice day," Ozzie grumbled without slowing down. I pried my fingers loose from the dashboard.

The land flattened to field and fence, shacks and farmhouses spaced farther apart. We left the dump behind.

"When we get there," Ozzie said, "we do nothing stupid. If we're the first, we sit on the house and wait for backup. If it gets bad, you stand behind the passenger's door, use it as a shield. Got it?"

"What's the brother-in-law like?"

"Hector Mara. West Side *veterano* like Sanchez. They go way back."

"Dangerous?"

"Everybody's dangerous. Show me a wife in a domestic disturbance call, I'll show you dangerous. But Hector Mara? Next to Zeta Sanchez he's a big old *pan dulce*."

Then we were on top of 11043 Green, and we weren't the first.

The property sat on the Y intersection of Green and another, smaller farm road. Thick tangles of banana trees and bamboo lined both sides. The only visible entrance was blocked by an SAPD patrol car with both doors open and the headlights on. Two more cars, unmarked blue Chevrolets, were pulled off the shoulder nearby. Four people stood in the shade of the banana trees to the side of the driveway—two SAPD uniforms and my good buddies from homicide, DeLeon and Kelsey.

We pulled in behind the SAPD unit.

Through the break in the foliage I could see two houses on the lot. The nearest, about thirty yards up the gravel drive, was cinder block from the waist down and unpainted drywall from the waist up, still decorated with the green tattoos of different building-supply companies. The building made an *L* around a covered cement porch that overflowed with mangled bicycles and broken lawn chairs. Bedsheets covered the windows.

Twenty yards farther out was a small mobile home of corrugated white metal.

The field around both buildings was overgrown with yellow sticker-burr grass and swarmed with gnats. One car was visible on the lot—an old silver Ford Galaxie parked under an apple tree. No signs of life except for three chickens in a coop. Near that, a well-tended garden patch of sunflowers, cabbages, tomatoes.

Ozzie and I joined the SAPD party in the shade. In the afternoon heat the huge banana plants exuded sticky, bubbly goo at the joints and smelled disconcertingly of sex.

DeLeon had changed into new clothes—rust-colored blazer and skirt, a fresh white silk blouse. She leaned calmly against a fence post, gently slapping a folder full of paperwork against her skirt.

Her partner Kelsey had shed his coat. His baby-blue dress shirt had half-moons of sweat around the armpits and his tie and collar were loosened. In the sunlight I could see the fine red network of capillaries in his nose. He glared at me as I walked up.

"What the hell is *this* doing here?" He looked at Ozzie Gerson. "You brought a fucking civilian?"

Ozzie took a pack of Doublemint from his shirt pocket and shook a stick loose, unwrapped it and put it in his mouth. "He's with me, Detective. Don't worry about it."

"I'm worrying."

"Leave it," DeLeon ordered. "What's the twenty on the other units?"

One of the uniformed officers spoke into his field radio, got an answer. "Five minutes, maybe."

"Maybe?"

The uniform stifled a yawn. Probably, like Ozzie, he'd been pulling fiesta duty all last week. "Half the shift called in sick at the substation, ma'am. We're covering the whole South Side today."

DeLeon sighed, turned to Kelsey. "I wanted SWAT here. Where are they?"

"No point," Kelsey said. "I told the lieutenant not to bother."

DeLeon stared at him. "You *what?*"

Kelsey put a piece of spear grass to his mouth. He bit the end and spit it out. "This ain't that hard, partner. We going to bust Sanchez or wait here all day under the poontang trees?"

The second uniformed officer suppressed a smile. Kelsey grinned at DeLeon, waiting for her response.

"Probably be unwise to stay here," I broke in. "Been so long since Kelsey's smelled the real thing."

Kelsey's nose reddened.

Ozzie laughed louder than he needed to, slapped me on the back. "Smelled the real thing. That was good, Navarre. Joke, Detective. You know?"

Kelsey didn't smile. He pointed his middle finger at my chest. "You sign a release to ride in that car?"

"Sure he has," Gerson lied.

Kelsey nodded. "Which means something unfortunate happens in the course of our work, Mr. Navarre, I got no legal liability. With that said, you want to come along, fine by me."

He nodded to the uniforms and they fell in line as Kelsey trudged up the gravel drive. After a resentful glance at me, DeLeon followed. Ozzie and I brought up the rear.

"Kelsey's okay," Ozzie assured me. "First time I had to work with a piece of ass, it was tough on me too."

I told Ozzie that made me feel a lot better. Apparently Ozzie took me seriously, because he patted my shoulder paternally. "Nobody's going to hurt you, kid. Stick with me."

Friends are grand.

We walked toward the porch of the cinder-block building.

Kelsey stopped ten feet from the edge of the porch. He looked at the high grass and sticker burrs and swarms of gnats one would have to tromp through to get to the back of the house, assuming there was even a door on that side.

"This looks like the back entrance," Kelsey decided. He smiled at DeLeon. "I think you should have the honor of taking the front, since you're primary. Don't you?"

DeLeon didn't hesitate. She dropped her paperwork, took her Glock from the holster. "Absolutely."

She made a wide arc around the house, using her gun to part the weeds.

Kelsey grinned at the uniforms, then directed one of them toward the white mobile home farther out in the field. He was about to step up on the porch when Ozzie nudged his arm. "Yo, Detective. Sheriff's jurisdiction?"

Kelsey waved him ahead with an exaggerated flourish. "Be my guest, Deputy."

Gerson pointed at me, then pointed far away. I backed up to the open edge of the porch. Kelsey and the other uniform moved to the other side, where the foot of the L-shaped house jutted out.

Gerson banged on the door. It was a particleboard job, thinly painted white, no window or peephole.

"Hey, Sanchez!"

Shouting erupted from the mobile home across the field. I looked over and saw a dark-skinned man standing in the doorway, yelling at the uniformed officer. The officer was holding up his hands, trying to get the guy to quiet down. The man in the doorway looked like he had been asleep

thirty seconds before. He wore only grimy white boxer
shorts. His upper body was well muscled and his head was
bald and brown as an egg.

"What the fuck *is* this, man?" he yelled. "*¿Otra vez?*"

He looked in our direction. When he spoke again it was
even louder, like he wanted us all to hear. "I got to go to
work in a few minutes, *hijo de puta*. Respectable job. What
the hell, damn *pinche cabrones* on my *chingate* property—"

He kept cursing in Tex-spañol, shifting his weight
stiffly from foot to foot. From the way the uniform was re-
acting, and from the bland look Kelsey gave the alterca-
tion, I got the feeling Baldie was not the man we really
wanted.

Ozzie Gerson banged on the door again. "Yo, Zeta.
Open up, man. Got some friends out here—"

Snap.

The first shot made a splinter-flower in the door. The
second ripped a hole through Ozzie's left shoulder.

Immediately a third shot punched through the particleboard door, a little bit higher, but Ozzie had already turned
and dived full force into the cement. He started scrabbling
away, trailing blood.

Kelsey and the uniformed officer hit the ground on top
of each other, their weapons drawn. The uniform swung
around the corner of the building, firing two rounds into
the door. On the second shot Kelsey lunged out at ground
level and tried to grab Ozzie by the collar, but someone in
the house returned fire and Kelsey fell back to the wall.
Ozzie kept crawling on his own. Time slowed to the consistency of sap.

I remember standing paralyzed by the edge of the
porch, then feeling a sickening momentum build up in my
gut. I ran toward Ozzie, collapsing into a forward roll as
another shot was fired, landing by Gerson, grabbing his
bloody uniform shirt, beginning to pull. Kelsey shouted

curses at me but then he was there too, helping. Together we lugged Ozzie around the corner of the building.

Ozzie made wet sounds of pain.

The uniform next to me was yelling a code 10-11 into his field unit. The uniform at the mobile home was screaming at the bald guy to get on the floor. I looked over in time to see the officer's nightstick flash. Two strikes to the knees and Baldie crumpled awkwardly on the steps. At the count of three, his hands were cuffed in the small of his back.

No more shots came from inside the cinder-block house.

Ozzie Gerson was propped up against the wall, alternately cursing and screaming. There were so many voices I almost didn't hear the other noises coming from around the back of the building.

A door slammed. There was a muffled thud, some rustling. Then a very loud: "Hey!"

It was DeLeon's voice. A single shot ricocheted off brick, followed by more scuffling noises.

I locked eyes with Kelsey and just for an instant I saw what the bastard was thinking, what options he was weighing. Only one of those options was running to DeLeon's assistance. Then he was up and moving but I was already ahead of him, ripping through the brush and stickers.

When we got to the back of the house it was already over.

A second Latino man was kneeling with his chest and the side of his face slammed into the back wall of the house. He wore only jeans and huarache sandals. He was an enormous man, dark-skinned and hairy as a timber wolf. It was hard to tell much else about his looks because they were mostly ruined by the pistol-whipping he'd received. Nearby in the dirt lay car keys and a gun—a long-barreled .38.

Detective DeLeon didn't look much better than her apprehendee. Her skirt was torn and her panty hose reduced to amber cobwebs. Her white blouse was ripped. Her blazer floated in the tall grass nearby like some kind of pointy scarecrow. She had shiny red cross-hatching on her cheek and a line of blood down the side of her mouth.

She also had her Glock 23 pressed decisively under Timber Wolf's ear and was in the process of cuffing him one-handed.

Kelsey looked at her, looked at me, then lowered his weapon. He shouted our status to the officer at the front of the house.

Three seconds later the young uniform came busting out the back door with his gun drawn. He took one look at DeLeon and the apprehendee I assumed was Zeta Sanchez and was so surprised he nearly backed up into the house.

DeLeon got up and wiped her bloody mouth with the back of her hand. She let the uniform take over with Zeta Sanchez, then stumbled toward Kelsey and muttered, "Thanks for the front door."

She stumbled again as she walked past us. Sirens were already wailing in the distance.

Kelsey watched her go. In a tone of grudging admiration he muttered, "I'll be damned."

I turned and punched him hard in the gut.

It was a tai chi upper cut, only slightly less forceful than a pile driver. By the time I regained the feeling in my hand, Kelsey was doubled over, contemplating the pool his lunch had made in the dirt.

Then I walked back around the corner of the house, figuring I should try to help stop the bleeding of another guy I didn't like much either.

SEVEN

That evening after the *Eyewitness News* I owed Andy Warhol a reimbursement check for two and a half minutes.

With a concerned face, KENS anchorman Chris Marrou told San Antonio all about my day—how a pipe bomb this morning had nearly killed a private investigator, a UTSA administrator, and an SAPD homicide investigator; how the incident had spurred police into swift action this afternoon, leading to a bloody standoff and finally the arrest of longtime fugitive Anthony "Zeta" Sanchez. Police would not officially comment on Sanchez's connection with this morning's bombing or the recent murder of UTSA's Professor Aaron Brandon, but unnamed sources confirmed that indictments on both counts were imminent. Rumors had surfaced about Sanchez's onetime employment by the Brandon family and Sanchez's possible role in the 1993 murder of Aaron's father, Jeremiah, none of which the SAPD would comment on.

"But the UTSA campus," Chris Marrou assured me, "is breathing a collective sigh of relief tonight."

Chris seemed mildly disappointed that he couldn't offer a more detailed explanation for Zeta Sanchez's actions, but what the heck. The footage was good. The news cameras kept zooming in on Hector Mara's bloody front porch, the bloody back wall of his house, the bullet holes in the door. Grade A local news. A mug shot of Anthony "Zeta" Sanchez looked a lot better than Zeta had in person—a handsome, sharply angular face, mustache and beard no thicker than marking pen around his jaw and mouth. He had the heavy-lidded eyes and deceptively calm expression of a well-fed carnivore.

Marrou told us that Deputy Oswald Gerson was in critical but stable condition at Brooke Army Medical Center, that Hector Mara of 11043 Green Road had been questioned and released by police, and that the D.A. was praising the efforts of the detectives involved in today's arrest. I turned off the news.

I fixed myself a margarita, took it out to the back patio, and sank into my well-worn butterfly chair.

I sipped painkiller-on-the-rocks while the sun went down over Mrs. Geradino's garage. The webworm patches in her pecan tree glittered orange. Her sprinkler sliced across the yard. The Geradino babies—six Chihuahuas that resembled boiled and shucked armadillos—yapped mutely at me from the other side of their mother's glass patio doors. Your basic romantic sunset at 90 Queen Anne.

I thought about Jeremiah Brandon—the old turkey buzzard with his seedy connections to the carnival circuit and his appetite for underage women that had eventually gotten him killed. I kept envisioning his face from the 1967 photograph, stuck on a body with no chest—a broken piñata thrown into the corner of a West Side barroom, surrounded by stone-faced employees who hadn't seen a thing. I thought about Jeremiah's two sons, Del and Aaron, and what it might've been like growing up in a family that made amusement rides. A kid's dream. Maybe Aaron Brandon had fond memories. Maybe he'd taken his own five-year-old son Michael to Uncle Del's shop from time to time to try out the products.

Or maybe growing up around the carnival business had been an endless series of encounters with people like Zeta Sanchez, carny owners with the same hungry eyes as

Jeremiah Brandon. Maybe that kind of childhood produced an adult who studied medieval gore and monster stories and Crusade massacres. Maybe Aaron Brandon kept his little boy the hell away from that shop.

I took a long hit on my margarita.

The sun had almost disappeared behind Mrs. Geradino's garage. I checked my watch. Two hours before I was supposed to pick up George Bertón for our double date. Enough time to visit my worried mother, maybe make one other stop before that.

I began the almost impossible task of getting out of a butterfly chair with a margarita in one hand. I wasn't making much progress when the back door creaked open and a man's voice said, "Undignified, *vato*. Somebody was to shoot you like that, you'd spout like a wine sack."

I turned my head. "Your perception of the world is overly grim, Ralphas."

Ralph Arguello grinned in my doorway, his knuckles rapping lightly on the frame as if some long-dormant instinct was reminding his body that it was polite to knock.

Ralph's chili-red face was completely clear of life's little worries—self-consciousness, doubt, morality. His eyes floated behind thick round glasses and his salt-and-pepper hair was pulled back in a tight ponytail. He wore an extra-large white linen shirt and black jeans. Several gold rings set with onyx stones glittered on his punching hand. "Sounded like you had a rough day, *vato*. Came by to see if you made it through."

I pointed to my stitched-up cheek. "Most of me."

Ralph stepped onto the porch, took a joint from his shirt pocket, then held it up toward me with a question— maybe *did I want some?* or *did I mind?* He proceeded to light up without waiting for the answer. I didn't want some, and I did mind, but neither of those facts would've fazed Ralph.

He held in the first toke, looked up at the corrugated tin of the porch roof, and let smoke escape through his nostrils. "Just wanted to tell you—when you're ready to mess with these people who blew you up today, come find me."

"You don't buy that the police have it under control?"

Ralph laughed. "Yeah. *Mi amigo* Zeta Sanchez."

"You know Sanchez?"

Ralph stared at me. Stupid question. Ralph knew San Antonians the way Audubon knew birds. The kill-and-study ratio was probably the same.

"Zeta is *sangrón*," Ralph admitted. "He makes a threat, it's going to happen. But pipe bombs at professors? No, man."

"Why so sure?"

"Zeta wanted to kill you, he'd walk up and shoot you."

"Sounds like that's what he did, in the end."

Ralph shook his head dolefully. "You meet Sanchez's brother-in-law, Hector Mara?"

"Bald guy, lives in a trailer home, likes to scream at policemen."

"That's him. Hector and Sanchez—they used to be rivals back at the Courts. Patched things up when Sanchez married Hector's sister Sandra."

"So they were brothers-in-law. So?"

Ralph took a second toke, stared into the backyard. "So nothing. Just that Hector Mara's been doing okay for himself the last six years since Zeta left town. Bought himself a scrap-metal yard on the West Side. Found enough money to pay off the mortgage on his grandmother's old house— that place he inherited out on Green Road."

"All that money from a salvage yard?"

Ralph shrugged. "He does a little fencing, takes away some business from my pawnshops. But the way I heard it, that's not where most of Hector's money comes from. Once

Zeta Sanchez left town, Hector was freed up to do business with some of Zeta's old rivals—one guy in particular, Chich Gutierrez. Chich and Zeta, man—they couldn't stand each other."

"What kind of business?"

"*Chiva,* man."

"Heroin."

"Another thing—I hear Hector's more than a little bit in debt to Chich right now. Like maybe in debt enough to owe some large favors."

"Hector Mara is in debt to a guy who hates Sanchez."

"Mmm. Hector thought Sanchez was gone for good, might be kind of inconvenient if his old compadre showed up again, started asking about his new business connections. Especially if Sanchez had ideas about getting back into the *chiva*. Sanchez, man—he's a war hero. People admire his style. He could take over Chich Gutierrez's business without half trying."

"I'll look into that."

"Just do it careful. Tell George Bertón when you see him tonight—tell him I said to be careful."

"How'd you know I was going to see George?"

Ralph grinned.

"Uh-oh," I said. "Kelly?"

"No, man, I didn't hear it from her."

He was enjoying some excellent, private joke.

"What?" I demanded.

He took a long last pull on the marijuana, then flicked the joint to the ground, crushed it under his heel. He offered me a hand and pulled me effortlessly out of the butterfly chair. "Just remember to deal me in, *vato*, once you're ready."

"You said Hector Mara's salvage yard was taking away some of your fencing business."

"That's right."

"So are you siccing me on Hector because you think it

might help me? Or because you want to get rid of the competition?"

Ralph grinned. "Your perception of the world is overly grim, *vato*. Enjoy your date."

I could hear him laughing quietly all the way through my house.

EIGHT

Aaron and Ines Brandon's house was a driftwood-colored craftsman on Castano, a few blocks east of Alamo Heights High School.

The street was one of those San Antonio gullies that floods in the smallest rainstorm, houses perched atop forty-five-degree yards on either side, the cars on the curb caked with dried flood lines of oak leaves and pecan pollen.

I parked on the street behind a red Fiat and walked up the sidewalk, over a Big Wheel, through a scatter of street chalk.

There was a brass mezuzah on the doorjamb.

I was just raising my hand to knock when the door swung open and a large Anglo man collided with me. He was maybe two hundred pounds, my height, loud yellow shirt, and a square face.

He muttered, "Damn, fricking—" then pushed past in a wake of cheap sports cologne.

I watched him lumber down the unlighted walk. The back of his retreating head looked like gorilla-mask fur, greased and combed. He skidded on a piece of pink street chalk, cursed, kicked the Big Wheel, then kept trudging down the steps toward the Fiat.

Glass shattered somewhere inside the house. A woman yelled angrily.

I took that as an invitation.

The living room was stark white—carpet, walls, sofa,

molding. Against the right wall was the limestone fireplace
I'd seen in Detective DeLeon's crime-scene photo. The
freshly scrubbed bricks still retained the craters of two .45
rounds that had slowed down not at all traveling through
Aaron Brandon's body. Open moving boxes clustered next
to the sofa. Through an archway on the left, in the dining
room, glass shards of a newly broken window dangled from
the frame.

At the far end of the sofa, a woman stood with her back
to me.

She was leaning over an oak end table forested with
framed family photos, her hands clamped tightly on the table corners as if she were contemplating a war map. She was
a light-skinned Latina, tall and slender, her hair shoulder
length and silky red-brown, the color of roasted peppers.
She wore a beige blouse and black jeans. If she'd been any
more earth-toned she could've laid down in a South Texas
oil field and disappeared.

I rapped on the doorjamb.

"Forget something, Del?" Her voice was small and cold.
"You want my checkbook, too, you fucking bastard?"

I cleared my throat. "Wrong bastard."

She whirled to face me.

Her mouth was wide and pretty, her nose slightly crooked,
her eyes so large and brown the color seemed to tint her
corneas like a cinnamon overdose. It was the kind of face that
strikes you as beautiful because of a successful combination of
flaws.

"Who—" She stopped herself, shook her head vehe-
mently. "No. I don't care who you are. What the hell are
you doing in my home?"

I wasn't technically inside, but I remedied that by stepping over the threshold.

"Sorry to disturb you, Mrs. Brandon." I plucked an
Erainya Manos Agency card from my front pocket, held it
up. It was one of the granite-gray executive cards. Somber.

Professional. I tried to make my expression match the card. "I came by to ask you some questions. Your brother-in-law Del ran over me on his way out, then I heard the window break. I got concerned."

She made a little feral noise. "Another goddamn cop. You people think you've been here so often you can just walk in my front door now?"

She picked up the nearest potential projectile—a lead-framed photo. "¡Vete ya! No more questions. No more cops."

The granite-gray executive approach didn't seem to be winning me many points. I tried for a smile.

"There's no need to break things," I assured her. "Actually I'm not—"

The photo banged into the wall two feet to my left. Glass cracked when it hit the floor. Little pieces spiraled into the air.

Mrs. Brandon picked up another piece of ammunition. She motioned toward the front door with the new frame.

"You don't want to throw that," I told her.

In fact, she did. I had to lurch forward and catch her wrist before she could. She tried to hit me with her free hand. I intercepted that too.

We stood in that dance position for a few heartbeats, Ines Brandon glaring up at me.

Her breath smelled faintly of red wine. Close up, the little crook in her nose looked like an old break, probably some childhood accident. She had the faintest white scar across the bridge, about where reading glasses would sit. Whatever she'd run into so long ago, she looked like she'd never quite gotten over the indignation.

"You can goddamn well let me go," she growled.

I released her wrist, took away the photograph she'd been about to throw. Mrs. Brandon stepped back and sank to the edge of the sofa.

Her eyes became hot and vacant, like jettisoned rocket rings.

"Well?" She gestured around listlessly. "Ask your questions. Search the house. What do I care? It's not mine anymore."

I looked at the photo—a wedding picture of her and Aaron, taken in front of a grimy adobe chapel with freestanding pink silk flower arrangements on either side. The setting, and the look of desperate, guilty excitement in the young couple's eyes, screamed bordertown wedding. I set the photo back on the table.

"RideWorks holds the lease on your house," I said. "Del's kicking you out?"

"That's my brother-in-law."

"Quite a human being. How's your son holding up?"

She pressed at the corners of her eyes. "Leave Michael out of this."

"He's here?"

"He's with Paloma. Our—my maid. I couldn't have Michael here with Del coming over. My brother-in-law and I—we aren't exactly cordial."

"Nice guy like Gorilla-Head? Hard to imagine."

She studied my face more closely.

"You were on the news today," she decided. "When they showed that man's arrest. You're with the sheriff's department?"

"Tres Navarre. I'm a private investigator."

She mouthed the word *private*. "A real P.I. You're joking. For UTSA?"

"Yes."

"Ah-ha. The University wants to be sure they're not liable for Aaron's death."

"Something like that."

She laughed without humor. "I'm not going to sue, P.I. Tell them not to worry."

"The man in custody—Zeta Sanchez. Had your husband ever mentioned him?"

"Don't you have someplace better to be?"

"Or Del? Did he ever mention Zeta Sanchez?"

"Del doesn't talk to me unless he's kicking me off his property. Or calling me a Mexican whore. Sorry."

I looked at the fireplace.

"My language embarrass you?" Ines Brandon demanded.

"No. But keep trying if you want to. Your son's not home. You might as well cut loose."

Her face reddened. She made a fist and then couldn't seem to decide what to do with it. She flattened it on her thigh, dug her fingers into the flesh above her knee. "I don't think I like you very much, P.I."

I tapped one of the boxes with my foot. "Where to? Back home to Del Rio?"

She punished me with some silence. I counted to fifteen, sixteen, seventeen. Tres Navarre, tai chi sage. Man with the Patience of Mountains.

Finally Mrs. Brandon glared up at me, annoyed that I had not yet spontaneously combusted. "I can't go home. Too much to take care of here. Michael and I are getting a small apartment for a few months. The police—" She faltered, took a shaky breath. "The police suggested I make no immediate plans to leave town."

"You were away when your husband was murdered, weren't you?"

"In Del Rio with my son, visiting friends. But you never know. I might've—" Her voice broke apart. "I might've paid that Sanchez man. The police can't be too careful. I might've—oh, shit."

She slid from the arm of the couch into the seat, brought up her legs and hugged them, her forehead on her knees.

I waited while she shivered silently. I found myself looking at the mantelpiece, the gunshot holes in the limestone. I stepped back toward the front door, ran my fingers along the doorjamb, then went to the front window, looked at the latch.

"Did your husband have a gun?"

She spoke into her knees. "They already asked. A .38. In the bedroom closet. I hated Aaron keeping it in the house with Michael."

"And it's still in the closet?"

"It was. The police took it."

"No forced entry. Your husband answered the door wearing nothing but his jeans. He let his killer in, made no attempt to get his own gun. They talked in the living room, standing up, your husband here in front of the fireplace. The killer shot him twice. If your husband didn't know his killer, it would've played out differently."

Mrs. Brandon gathered her knees closer to her. "My maid will be back with Michael in a few minutes. I want you gone."

"Had Aaron and his brother been arguing recently?"

"I don't want another stranger in the house."

"Had they?"

She exhaled. "They hardly ever spoke—no more than two or three times since we were married. They hated each other."

"Because of the family business?"

"Because of everything."

"But your husband never mentioned Zeta Sanchez."

"No."

"What about a man named Hector Mara?"

It was a blind shot, but it hit something. Ines Brandon's face clouded. She seemed to be casting around for some context. Maybe she just remembered the name from today's newscast. Maybe it was something more.

Then her face shut like a blind. "Sorry."

"It could be important, Mrs. Brandon."

"What's important is that my son not have to deal with any more strangers."

"Mrs. Brandon—"

"Good night, Mr. Navarre."

It bothered me that she remembered my name. It meant she'd been paying a lot more attention than I'd given her credit for. But her eyes made it clear that our conversation was over.

I decided to honor that.

When I looked back from the front door, Ines Brandon was still curled in a ball on the sofa, her arms hugging her knees, her eyes fixed on the fireplace like there was something blazing there.

NINE

My old teammate from Alamo Heights varsity, Jess Makar, opened the door at my mother's house. This shouldn't have been a surprise since Jess lived with my mother, but it had been a long time since I'd seen him anywhere except seated at the kitchen table, beer in hand, watching ESPN.

Jess scowled at me. His boyish good looks had, over the last three or four years, begun to settle like cement along with his midsection. His blue eyes had become permanently stained with capillaries. Tonight he wore sweatpants and a Dallas Cowboys tunic streaked with motor oil.

"Tres," he grumbled. "Might as well join the party."

His cologne was stronger than usual. It didn't mix well with the usual scents of my mother's house—vanilla incense, shrimp steaming in the kitchen, the dusty aroma of old curios, Indian blankets, spicewood carvings.

In the main room, Christmas lights were blinking in the exposed rafter beams. Folk music was playing. Over at the pool table, the normal coterie of young rednecks was breaking setups and pouring each other shots from my mother's liquor cabinet.

I'm not sure where she gets the guys. Her liquor supply and pool table have just always attracted tan, muscular men between the ages of twenty and thirty-five, three or four a night ever since my mom got her divorce. As near as I can tell, Mother doesn't know these guys, never calls them anything but "dear," has no recollection that most of them went to school with me. The man pouring the shots at the moment had once traded lunch boxes with me in third grade. His name was Bobby something. Or at least it had been. Probably Bob, now. Mr. Bob.

Every piece of furniture had been removed from the center of the living room. Mother's Guatemalan-patterned sofas were piled in the entrance of the den. Her pigskin chairs were lined up on the back porch by the hot tub. The upright piano had been pushed into the hallway. In the middle of the now-bare floor, Mother was kneeling on her twenty-by-twenty Persian carpet, folding large pieces of marbleized paper into origami hats.

Jess stepped over several of the finished products and retrieved a Lone Star longneck from the fireplace mantel. "Tell your mother she's obsessed."

Mother carefully made a fold in the paper, pressing out a long isosceles triangle. "*Please,* Jess."

She was dressed in jeans and black turtleneck under a red-and-orange dashiki. Her Birkenstock clogs were nearby on the carpet. Mother's Cleopatra haircut had been newly frizzed in what was either a perm or the aftermath of an electrical storm.

She pressed another triangle into the paper. "The Crocker Gallery sold *two* yesterday, Tres—*Samurai Moon* and *Plum Dragon*. The buyer owns a hotel in *Florida*. He wants to see five more that match the color schemes of his suites by the end of the week. I'm simply swamped."

Jess mumbled some obscenities about Florida, looked at me to share his disgust. "I told her let's just hire some Mexicans, get 'em folding the damn things in the backyard. Set up a damn art factory."

My mother sat on her haunches and glared at him. "This is my *art,* Jess."

Jess plunked his beer back on the mantel. "They're fucking paper hats, Rachel. Get over it."

Before she could respond, he stormed off toward the

bedroom hall. It's difficult to storm properly when one has to squeeze sideways past an upright piano, but Jess did his best. I heard seven more heavy footfalls, then the door of the master bedroom slammed.

Over at the pool table, billiard balls clacked. New beers were opened. Joni Mitchell sang softly on the stereo behind the rednecks, telling them all about Paris and flowers and Impressionism.

My mother stared into the empty hallway, her face stony with anger.

"He's learning to take time-outs all by himself," I said. "That's encouraging."

The comment didn't even get her attention, much less a rise.

"Mother?"

The creases in her origami unfolded slowly, the paper trying to find its original shape. Mother closed her eyes.

She reassembled her composure—a weak smile, chin higher, wisps of black hair pushed away from her face.

Then she stood and gave me a hug. "I'm sorry, dear. You shouldn't have to see our little squabbles."

Their little squabbles. As if she hadn't been married to my father. "It's okay, Mother."

She pushed me away gently, wiped something out of her eye. "Of course it's okay."

She stared down the hall.

"Isn't it?" I asked.

"Of course! Or it would be if you wouldn't keep scaring your poor mother to death. Look at your face."

She ran her finger down the three new stitches on my cheek.

"The day picked up after that," I told her.

"I don't want to hear it."

"Okay."

She glared at me. "Of *course* I want to hear it, Jackson. Kitchen. Now."

I followed her down the Saltillo-tiled steps. The smell of boiling shrimp was overpowering—brine and allspice and Tabasco. Mother stirred the pot, reset the timer, then sat me down at the butcher-block table with a beer in my hand and a fresh red wine in hers and commanded, "Tell."

Several times during the story her eyes drifted toward the sliding-glass door that looked across the patio to the master bedroom. The curtains on the other side stayed shut, blue TV light flickering behind them.

I told Mother about the UTSA job, the police assurances that the Brandon case would be wrapped up quickly, the arrest I'd witnessed this morning. I told her about my double date tonight.

She stared into her wine.

I waited for half a Joni Mitchell verse. I found myself studying Mother's hands, the way they cradled the glass, their raised veins and faint age spots the only real indications this was a woman in her mid-fifties. "You missed your cue."

She refocused on me. "What, dear?"

"Your cue. For pestering me about my date. Asking me how soon I can quit P.I. work now that I've got a real job. Lecturing me on why I shouldn't go riding with Ozzie Gerson. Stuff like that."

She plinked a fingernail against the blue-tinted rim of the Mexican glass. "Please, Jackson. I am *never* that bad."

"What's up with you and Jess?"

"I don't want to talk about it."

"Did you hear my story at all?"

"Of course."

"And?"

Mother's eyes drifted away. "I remember Ozzie. Your father and he hunted out at Sabinal many times—Jack used to say that Ozzie's hobby was collecting bad luck."

"Apparently that hasn't changed."

"He also said Ozzie was one of the few deputies he'd

trust with his life. If Ozzie advised you to stay out of this matter—"

The patio door slid open and Jess entered the room, an army-green duffel bag over his shoulder. He swiped his Cowboys cap off the television. "I'm going."

Mother stood, unlacing her fingers from the wineglass. "Jess?"

He trudged up the steps into the living room.

"Jess?"

The front door slammed. Over the Joni Mitchell and the poolroom chat and the bubbling of shrimp we could just barely hear Jess' truck engine start in the driveway.

Mother turned, sank back into her chair. Her eyes had gone blank.

"I could call off my plans," I offered.

"Don't be silly. Everything's fine. Go on your date, dear."

"You're sure?"

She stared at me, daring me to contradict her. "I'm sure." Her voice was tin. "You go on."

I looked at my watch. George Bertón was on the South Side, our dates back in Monte Vista, reservations at Los Barrios for eight-thirty. I could stay here maybe another ten minutes. Safer if I just canceled.

Mother reached over and patted my hand, tried for a smile. "Don't *worry*."

"Jess will probably just drive around awhile, blow off some steam."

"Yes," she agreed.

When I met her eyes, I realized how completely clueless I was about their relationship, about what they were like the ninety-five percent of the time I wasn't around. I'd never wanted to know before. Now I felt about as useful as a paperweight in a wind tunnel.

I left Mother at the kitchen table with a refilled glass of cabernet and the new *Texas Monthly*. The kitchen timer was still going next to her, ticking off the minutes until the shrimp were boiled. I followed the smell of Jess' cologne all the way through the house and into the front yard, where it finally dissipated.

I tried to convince myself that it was only my shitty day, my strung-out nerves that were giving me the urge to ram my VW into Jess Makar, if I could've found the bastard.

Cultivating that sense of well-being, I got in my car and started the engine, heading out to be a lucky lady's dream date.

TEN

George Bertón stood in his front yard looking like an extra from *Dr. No*. His Panama hat brim cut a black ribbon across his eyes. His pencil mustache was newly trimmed. He wore a pink camp shirt with the obligatory Cuban cigar in the pocket, black slacks, polished white shoes, and a tiny gold cross in the V of hairy chest at his open collar. He carried a bouquet of wildflowers wrapped in cellophane.

I pulled the VW up to the curb.

"For me?" I asked.

George leaned into the passenger's-side window. "I been standing here so long I got three other propositions. I was starting to think you'd chickened out."

"That would've been the smart choice," I agreed.

George dropped the flowers on the seat. "Reminds me. I *do* have something for you. You want to wait or come in?"

"You think we have time?"

"Not my fault."

"Hey, you could've picked *me* up, Bertón. *I* was on the way."

I pointed to the carport, where George's restored red '70 Barracuda convertible sat enshrined.

George looked appalled. "*Drive* her? I spent all last weekend on that chrome, *ese*. It's supposed to rain tonight. I'm talking mud and everything."

"I'll come in."

George's front lawn was a quarter acre of colored fish-tank gravel lined with aluminum edging. Pyracantha bushes made perfect cubes underneath the windows. The cottage itself was white stucco with blue-and-white awnings, white drapes on the picture windows. Like George, it could've shifted back in time forty years and no one would've been the wiser.

I followed Bertón into the living room.

"Hang on a sec," he said. "It's in the back."

There wasn't much to look at while I waited. The walls and floors were bare, the furniture consisting of two papasan chairs, a TV on the floor, and a glass coffee table with nothing on it. George's only clutter was carefully confined to a coat closet by the front door—a space that held the altar for his wife at Dia de los Muertos, and the rest of the year held George's Sinatra CDs, his car magazines, his gothic novels, his cigar box, and everything else dear to his heart. It was a space he could close off quickly and make it seem, to the casual visitor, that he was a man living in complete austerity.

The closet was open tonight. I peeked inside. Unpainted Sheetrock was pinned with photographs of George and friends. One showed George and me on our trip to Corpus last Christmas. George was grinning and pointing at the marlin he'd goaded me into catching. Another showed George and the kid he was Big Brother to on the weekends—Sultan, I think his name was, eleven years old, already flirting with gangs. Another photo showed George's forty-third birthday party at Pablo's Grove, where I and about five hundred other well-wishers had shown up chewing Cuban cigars and wearing Panama hats and the loudest golf shirts we could find. Interspersed with these photos were years of thank-you letters from the Elf Louise program, the local charity that collected Christmas toys for poor kids.

"Close that damn thing," George said behind me.

I turned.

George handed me a brown bag with something rectangular inside.

"You're a damn saint," I said. "Why do you care if the closet is closed?"

"Just open the bag."

Inside was a paperback novel—Wilkie Collins' *The Woman in White*.

I asked, "Do I get to choose between this and the flowers?"

"You're missing out on the greats, *ese*. And you a damn English professor now."

"Doesn't mean I've read everything the Victorians ever wrote. Like some people I could name."

George grinned. "I spend enough time waiting around for you, I need long novels."

Having taken the book as a gift, I couldn't very well throw it at him. I said thank you. Then we closed up the house and walked back out to the VW.

I had the convertible top down and the night had cooled off pleasantly, smelling like rain. We drove south from Palo Blanco onto Jefferson. The business strip was bright with car dealership lights and taqueria neon, the air rich with blooming mountain laurel from every South Side yard.

I waited until we turned onto S.W. Military before broaching the subject of our dates. "So—Jenny."

George smiled. In the nighttime illumination his skin glowed like whipped butter. "Don't get nervous on me."

"I'm just wondering why *I'm* the one dating her. I had you and her figured for a pair a long time ago."

"She's worked at the title office since before Melissa died, man. Going out with her would be like going out with my sister."

"But why me?"

He laughed. "Is it *that* bad a favor? Didn't you say Jenny was nice? Don't you guys joke around every time you come over?"

"Sure."

"And you think she's pretty?"

"Sure, George. It's just—" I stopped. "Who's *your* date?"

Bertón wagged his hand, palm down—the burned-on-an-oven gesture. "Jenny's got this friend. *Ay que rica.* Seen her at Jenny's house a few times and I started asking about her—like is this girl single or what? Jenny said yes, and maybe she could set me up but it had to be a double and it had to be with you. So here we go."

"Jenny said me specifically?"

"Don't ask me why. I reminded her what an ugly bastard you were, unlucky with women, but she still said she wanted to give it a go."

"Who's her friend?"

"Wait 'til you see her, man. Not that Jenny is a pig or anything."

"I'll tell her that. 'George said you weren't a pig.' "

We drove a few more blocks, listening to the wind crinkle the cellophane on George's bouquet.

"I talked to Ralph Arguello this afternoon," I said.

George raised his eyebrows, looked over.

I told him how I'd spent my afternoon.

George slid a cigar from his shirt pocket. "Wish somebody had clued me in sooner. I spent all day talking to some very pissed-off Latinos, all the radical groups I knew of, a couple more I got from a buddy at *La Prensa*. I'm talking about people who spend all day field-stripping AK-47s and reading Che out by Braunig Lake. Complete wackos. None of them gave me anything on the UTSA bombing. Nobody knew any new players in town. Nobody targeting the local campuses. Nobody even knew the name Brandon."

"So you buy the personal vendetta story? Sanchez came back with an old score to settle, decided to finish off the Brandon brothers the way he finished the dad?"

"I talked with an ATF guy I know. They've already passed on the bomb investigation. FBI likewise. Officially, they're still standing by to advise, but basically they're turning it back to SAPD. Bomb is too obviously a local make. The hit looks personal. They like Sanchez for it just fine."

"You don't sound convinced."

George lit his cigar, puffed on it thoughtfully. "Hector Mara running heroin, huh?"

"Ralph suggests being careful," I said. "It's usually a good idea."

"Mmm."

We turned north onto I-10 and skirted downtown, finally exiting into the palatial dark hills of Monte Vista. The sound of the wind and engine died sufficiently for conversation.

"Maybe we should listen to Ozzie," I continued. "Just tell the University what they want to hear—that the murder had nothing to do with them and their faculty is safe. We could close out the case and bill them for a day's work."

George looked over, his eyebrows raised.

"Nah," we said together.

We turned onto Mulberry and rode west, heading toward the address George had given me for Jenny's condo.

George's cigar smoke collected in front of his face each time I changed gears, then evaporated as I accelerated again. His eyes squinted almost shut.

After a while I noticed that he seemed to be muttering to himself—counting, or praying maybe.

"You all right?"

He removed the cigar, licked his lips, then laughed. "Yeah, fine."

"The case?"

"No. Just thinking—you know this is my hundredth date? You think I should get a door prize or something?"

"You keep track of every date?"

"Oh, yeah."

"One hundred exactly. You mean since—"

"Since Melissa. Yeah."

I opened my mouth. Closed it again. Nope. Don't ask, Navarre. Remember, this man liked his closet closed.

Bertón said, "You really want to know?"

Another block, then morbid curiosity got the best of me. "I heard—it was some kind of accident, right?"

George touched the tip of his cigar to his mouth. His tilted hat brim swamped his face with shadow. "We were camping up by Garner State Park, way up in the hills by the Frio River. At dawn 'Liss was still asleep in the tent, so I figured I'd go down to the Frio to do a little fly-fishing. This was our first vacation since I'd gotten out of the service, you know? A little time to get away, we figured. I came back to the tent about noon and found her."

"Found her."

"Raped," he said. "Then murdered—chopped up with my camping ax."

My hand tightened on the wheel. "George—"

" 'S'okay," he said. "Really. Seven years later, you know, and it's okay. But . . ."

"They ever catch who did it?"

He shook his head. "They suspected me for a while—I couldn't blame them. But it still keeps me awake at night— the fact that this monster got away. That and the guilt. I'm not careful—it's like one of those balloons of coke the drug mules swallow to get across the border, you know? I'm always wondering if it's going to pass through my system eventually or maybe rupture, explode my heart."

I looked over at him, met his eyes briefly in the streetlight, looked back at the road. What do you say to a story like that—sorry?

George sat up and tried to lighten his tone. "So anyway . . . now you know, huh? A hundred dates later. Maybe this'll be the special one."

He smiled frailly at me, looking suddenly, as we passed under another streetlight, like a very old man, someone who'd come from 1962 the hard way.

Jenny's condo building was a new high-rise behind Trinity University, designed for young professionals or students with rich daddies. It was the kind of place where the condos cost as much as the older two-story homes around them but with half the maintenance and none of the charm.

We buzzed Jenny's number in the lobby. Ninety seconds later she came down the elevator alone.

"I'll be," she exclaimed. "Two handsome men! Hey there, stranger!"

She squeezed my arm, noticed and decided not to comment on the new facial scar, then decided to get a little bolder and fold herself around my elbow.

Jenny was a nice-looking woman—maybe twenty-seven, her skin so smooth and shining with health it looked like air-mattress plastic. Her hair was floofy blond, teased to the consistency of cumulus cloud, and her dress just as light— willowy white layers of cotton. The only things of any hardness about her were her black boots and her large earrings shaped like fish skeletons.

George fiddled with his flowers. "Where's your *comadre?*"

"Oh." Jenny sighed, brushed her hand against my chest. "Ana's on her way down. Her pager went off right when you buzzed and she had to call the office. She's always— well, here we go."

The elevator doors opened again. The woman who stepped through was about five-nine, a dark-skinned Latina. Her red sleeveless dress was mid-thigh length and showed off well-muscled legs and arms. Her black hair was wedge-cut at the jawline and done in bangs on top—a style that might have made another woman's face look babyish, but not hers. Hers was serene, softened with amber and blue highlights but not enough to dilute the stern set of her eyes and her mouth. She came out of the elevator trying to fit something into her small black purse.

She looked up and gave us an economic, careful little smile, took two steps, then took another look at me and froze.

She continued forward, her smile a little more forced. As she got closer I could see crisscross abrasions under the makeup on her cheek.

"George," Jenny said, "Tres, let me introduce Ana."

"Ana," I repeated, greeting Detective DeLeon for the third time that day. "Nice to meet you."

ELEVEN

The ride to the restaurant was a long one.

Not that I had to avoid conversation with Ana DeLeon. The detective and George were isolated in the backseat by the wind and the roar of the VW engine, but in front Jenny was bending my ear about her day, her week, her month. She must've been used to people tuning her out, too, because she double-checked my attentiveness with annoying frequency.

"And so I was telling George we shouldn't be using a check-writing service," she said. "There's really just four of us at the title office and that didn't justify the cost, you know?"

"Mm-hmm."

"Right?"

"Right."

"And so I started doing the bills myself and we saved *so* much money. I just went to this seminar on Peachtree and I mean I can't understand how I got along without it. I mean you must have to do that kind of thing with Erainya's agency, right?"

"Right."

"Yeah?"

"Uh-huh."

And so forth.

I liked Jenny. Intelligent. Good sense of humor. George was right that she and I joked around whenever I visited

his title office. But the mean-spirited truth was I had night-
mares about the man Jenny would marry, what he would
look like after thirty years. I pictured him sitting in his
easy chair with the game shows on and his nose buried in a
magazine, a bright-faced geriatric Jenny standing over
him chirping about her day and his responses of "uh-huh"
that were once politely upbeat now reduced to inured
grunts. It was not an image I wanted to have in my head on
a first date.

When we got to Los Barrios the dinner rush was in full
swing. The restaurant's green exterior walls were floodlit,
its pink neon sign glowing. The surrounding two blocks
on Blanco were lined with cars and people crowded into
the brick entryway.

"You can sometimes find parking in the back," Jenny
advised. "This place has gotten so busy since it expanded
it's unbelievable, even on a Tuesday night. You know?"

"Sure."

"Hasn't it?"

"Oh, yeah."

She was right about the parking. We were able to wedge
the VW between two Cadillacs in front of a house halfway
down Santa Rosa. I held the door as George and Ana extracted themselves from the backseat. As DeLeon passed
me she whispered, "Great car."

I made a snarly face at her but she'd already brushed
past and was asking Jenny something about her shoes.
George helped me put the top up on the Bug as the first
splatters of rain started falling.

We had to wait for our table. The foyer was full of cou-
ples in evening wear, families with children, some college
kids. Through the arched interior windows you could see
into the restaurant's different sections, each crammed with
diners. The decor was nothing fancy—plastic tablecloths,
pseudo-Aztec art, fake plants, cheap wood paneling. The
smell, however, promised great things.

While we waited we were again spared the problem of communication by the rockin' svelte sounds of Rod "the Rod" Rodriguez and his electronic mariachi band. Rod was doing a number somewhere between "My Way" and "Gracias à la Vida"—kind of a black velvet, Hammond-organ-salesman sound with a Tijuana twist. A couple of young drunk women were dancing. There were quite a few dollars in Rod's jar.

We finally got a booth in the oldest section of the restaurant, the part that had once been a Dairy Queen.

George grinned nervously and called Ana DeLeon "princess" and insisted on ordering for her—the *chile relleno.* DeLeon allowed the order to stand, though she didn't look dazzled by George's manly charge-taking. Jenny had a long conversation with the waitress about different sauces and finally decided on the green enchiladas, only with red sauce, and refried beans rather than *borrachos,* and no MSG in the rice and a couple of other changes on the clauses and sub-paragraphs of the menu that probably should've been initialed when it was all agreed on. I ordered the quesadillas, regular, with a kid's order of cheese enchiladas on the side.

Jenny looked across the table at me, her fingers lacing a cradle for her chin. "A kid's order?"

"For Robert Johnson."

Jenny frowned. "Who?"

"A hungry mouth to feed at home."

She thought about whether she wanted to follow up on that, apparently decided it might spoil the evening. She turned to DeLeon. "So, girlfriend—tell them what you do."

DeLeon glared at her.

Jenny glanced at me meaningfully, preparing me to be impressed.

"Jenny," DeLeon complained.

George sat forward. "What? What do you do?"

DeLeon shot me a warning look. "I work for the city. It's nothing."

George waited for more. Jenny nudged DeLeon but she nudged right back.

"It's not that interesting," DeLeon promised. Then to me, coolly, "What about you, Mr. Navarre? How do you come to know George?"

"George and I work together."

She frowned, trying to make a connection. "You mean with the title company?"

She would've run George's name through TCIC, of course, just to make sure she wasn't going to be socializing with a felon. That's standard procedure for any cop who dates. But the system wouldn't necessarily have told her about George's less reputable line of work.

"George is a private investigator," I told her, smiling.

"Like Tres," Jenny put in, hoping to impress.

DeLeon stared at George, who was still grinning nervously. She looked back at me and mirrored my amused little smile. "How nice. Must be fun work."

George shrugged. "Better than what I did before. Police work."

DeLeon raised her eyebrows, nodded cool encouragement. "Oh?"

Just as George was about to explain himself, the food arrived. I thought we'd been saved. Jenny found a few small faults with her specialized order, and then the rest of us had to do the obligatory "Yum" comments and make remarks about how many doggie bags we would need.

I put Robert Johnson's to-go order aside and admired my entree.

Los Barrios is one of the few restaurants that does quesadillas right—making the cornmeal into thick, triangular pastries, deep frying them with the cheese and slices of poblano pepper inside. Crispy and spicy. Heaven, once you put a little garlic *chimichurri* sauce on top. I concentrated on the food, on my excellent margarita, on the blissful momentary silence.

Then, just as Jenny was about to redirect us toward some innocuous new topic, DeLeon said, "You were saying something about police work, George?"

She had a good voice for interrogations—detached yet encouraging, almost big-sisterly.

George dabbed his napkin against his mustache. He'd taken off his Panama hat and his hair glistened in neatly Bryl-ed rows. "Used to be in the Special Police. Air force."

"Really," DeLeon said. "I considered SP."

Bertón jerked his head back. "You were in the air force?"

"One tour, spent mostly at Lackland. Decided against reenlisting and went to college instead."

"I'll be damned." He looked at me, amazed.

"They have women at Lackland these days," I confirmed. "I've seen pictures."

He blew air, looked back at DeLeon. "Well, princess, don't cry for missing SP. Damn near killed me, that job. A lot of my friends got out and went straight into civilian police work, you know, because it's all they could do. Not me. Way I see it, to survive in police work you've got to have some kind of overactive testosterone problem."

Jenny was silently moving her lips as if she were trying to jump-start her voice to break in.

"Damn good quesadillas," I said. "Anybody want some?"

Jenny yelped, "Yeah!" a little louder than she needed to.

DeLeon told George: "Go on."

George shook his head. "Most of the cops me and Tres have met on the job—back me up here, Tres—"

I smiled at him, then at DeLeon, who smiled back.

"—most of the cops get high on the authority thing, the boots and the sunglasses, you know? The detectives are even worse—complete hot-shit complex. They treat P.I.s like dirt. Am I right, Tres?"

DeLeon looked at me, rapt with attention. I took a bite of *borracho* beans and mumbled, "Yum."

"Really," she said to George. Her beeper went off. She checked the number and said, "Geez."

"What?" George wanted to know.

DeLeon smiled. "It's my work."

"At this time of night?"

She laughed with all the warmth of rattling aluminum foil. "Well, it isn't P.I. work, George, but it does keep me busy. I've been sort of waiting for word that I could get to this one particular witness, and they just gave me the 'come on in' signal. I should really—"

Bertón's fork had dropped slowly to his plate. "Witness?"

Jenny chewed her lip nervously.

DeLeon reached over and patted George's hand. "I hate to cut out, but I should catch a taxi. You remember how it is, George, you get an arrest case and the clock starts ticking for the indictment."

"You're a—"

"Cop, honey. Homicide detective. The hot-shit variety."

"Oh, hey, I didn't—"

She smiled. "Not a problem, George. I sympathize. Really, we should do this some other time. It's been great, and really—" She slid her plate over. "You guys have some *chile relleno*. Looks terrific."

She gave Jenny a silent, unequivocal order with her eyes, a *we need to talk* command that made Jenny grab her purse before she even knew she'd done it.

"Oh—you shouldn't go alone, I guess," Jenny gabbled. Then to me, "Maybe I should—I could just take a rain check or—you know?"

"Sure," I said.

"Okay?"

"Yeah, sure."

"I'll—"

Jenny wavered, looking at me apologetically, then saw something she hadn't expected, the beginnings of a smile I'd been trying to suppress.

Her face got a little colder. "Well—maybe another time."

George and I stood and mumbled sureties that we'd all be sitting around the table again real soon, and then the women left to catch their taxi. Rod "the Rod" Rodriguez oozed into the mambo version of "The Long and Winding Road."

George deflated into his seat. I sat next to him and started laughing.

"What the hell are you so cheerful about?" George snarled. "You *knew* who she was, didn't you?"

"The food is really good," I told him. "Isn't it?"

"Uh-huh."

"Yeah?"

"*Yes,* already!"

I grinned, then waved down the waitress and told her to bring two more margaritas for the bachelor master detectives.

TWELVE

After dropping off George that night, I should've gone straight home to bed.

Of course I didn't.

The abbreviated dinner date had left me wired. My mind was still spinning from getting nearly blown up and shot at and gainfully employed all in one day. Most of all, I'd allowed myself to slip into case mode. Too many years of missing-persons traces, peripheral work on homicides—training myself to work in forty-eight-hour sprints before the statistical window of success slammed shut in my face.

I decided to swing by Erainya's, see if she was awake. *Just for a minute,* I told myself. *Just to get back in her good graces and promise to be a good little teacher from now on.*

That plan changed as soon as I pulled in front of Erainya's house. Her door opened instantly. Erainya stomped down her front steps with Jem in tow and an armful of gear. She was wearing her commando clothes—black drawstring pants, long-sleeved T-shirt, black sneakers. With her black hair, in the dark, she looked like a pale, floating, pissed-off face. Jem was wearing scarlet *Rugrats* pajamas and new white Reeboks only slightly brighter than his smile.

Erainya let Jem into the backseat of the VW, then lowered herself and her stuff into the passenger's side and slammed the door. "Shoot me if I ever let you out of my sight again."

"Look, about Ozzie Gerson—"

"You ain't been home making lesson plans, honey."

"The call just happened to come in while we were talking and—"

"Wherever you go tonight, you're taking me."

"I'm going home."

"I brought my 9mm. Stop now and I might not use it."

I shut up. Jem squeezed me around the neck from behind and told me he was glad we were going to have fun together tonight. I mumbled my halfhearted agreement, then started the engine.

We did a U on Garraty and headed south through Terrell Hills.

Erainya said, "Full story."

The full story took us all the way to Broadway. Erainya loved it. She asked me where I wanted to go now and when I told her, she loved that even more. She muttered Greek words of disgust all the way to the Hildebrand intersection.

Jem asked where we were going.

I glanced at Erainya for guidance.

Having the mother he did, Jem had been on excursions that most kids would've found boring or nightmarish or both. His nap and sleep cycles were completely unpredictable, much like his mother's verdicts on what was safe and appropriate for him. At the moment he seemed happy, ready for anything. The place I wanted to go, however, might not be so kid-friendly.

"He's fine," Erainya promised. "I got to baby-sit you and him at the same time, I can do that. Uncle Tres is taking us somewhere, honey."

"I am?"

"Tell the boy."

I tried for a smile as I looked back at Jem. "You want to see where they make amusement-park rides, Bubba?"

Jem hit the roof shouting hurray.

We continued south on Broadway toward downtown.

Jem talked about the latest Sega games. We passed underneath I-35 and into an area of repair shops and used-car dealerships.

A couple of hookers stood on the corner of North Alamo outside a vacuum cleaner repair shop. The hookers had seen better days. Something about their garish makeup, the black stockings and yellow dresses, the drug-enhanced fiery smiles—that display in front of the grimy windows filled with aging Hoovers and Electroluxes—there was probably a joke in there somewhere, but tonight it seemed a little too pathetic to make.

I took a right on Jones.

The buildings were dilapidated warehouses, long and low, nothing on the horizon but palm trees and the blinking spikes of radio towers.

We followed the old Southern Pacific tracks past the Brewery Art Museum, then over the river and right on Camden. The address we wanted filled the 300 block. A dimly lit sign out front said RIDEWORKS, INC., with the R and the W drawn like roller-coaster loops. Underneath, smaller letters proclaimed: KING OF THE SOUTH TEXAS CARNIVAL BUSINESS.

At the near end of the lot was a long portable building, facing in toward a cement yard fenced off by ten-foot-high chain link. Beyond that was a corrugated-metal warehouse the size of a small airplane hangar. Lining the side of the street, four insanely tall palm trees cut black silhouettes against the sky at gravity-defying curves, like Dr. Seuss trees.

I pulled across the street from the yard gates. A single light glowed behind the white-paned side window of the RideWorks office. One floodlight on a telephone pole threw a yellow oval of illumination on the closed hangar doors of the warehouse. Other than that the place was dark. Several cars lined the side of the street next to the warehouse—a Pontiac, an old Chevrolet, a Ford double-wide pickup.

Jem stuck his head over the front seats.

"They make rides?" he asked me excitedly.

"Yep."

"Can we go in?"

"Not right now," Erainya said. She was watching the buildings, getting impatient. "Honey, if you were thinking we could just . . ."

She stopped. We both focused on the same thing—the tiny flame of a lighter flaring up in the cab of the pickup truck across the street. The flame briefly illuminated a cigar, shadowy red jowls, the brim of a cowboy hat. Then it flicked out, replaced by the fainter glow of the cigar tip.

Before I could comment, a new set of headlights cut in directly behind us, coming up Camden. Del Brandon's red Fiat convertible glided up to the RideWorks gates and stopped.

"Someday, honey," Erainya told me, "I'm gonna decide whether you got the best timing in the world or the worst."

Del Brandon got out of his sports car. He looked the same as he had that afternoon, storming out of Ines' house—same greasy wedge of gorilla hair, same yellow shirt, now snagged on a side-holstered gun. His face was large and washed out and marked with a terminal heartburn scowl.

He looked warily at my VW.

Then the Fiat's passenger's-side door opened and Del's companion got out.

Erainya said, "Mother of Jesus."

Del's friend was a boulder of a man with incongruously girlish hair—tight blond cornrows curled up at the bottom and tied off with little blue rubber bands. Bo Peep on steroids. His facial features were thinly applied to a block-shaped head—his eyes shallow, dull dents; his smile an accidental mark. Gray running clothes. Height maybe six-five, density three or four tons. I didn't see any gun, and I didn't have any illusions that it mattered. Bo Peep was not a man who would bother with, or be bothered by, weapons smaller than a ballista.

They were both still staring at us when the cigar smoker in the truck opened his cab door and called, "Del."

In the sudden illumination of the dash light, the man in the truck appeared weathered and dour, maybe sixty years old, rough and thick as a granddaddy oak. He resembled any number of Texas ranchers from here to Brownsville, his mouth mostly lower lip and cigar.

The rancher planted his boots on the street, glowered in our direction, then walked toward the sports car, where Del and Bo Peep were waiting. The three men stood together, looking at us. They didn't talk. That was a bad sign. It meant they had no disagreement about us.

"Are they going to show us the rides?" Jem asked. He was bouncing now, a well-placed fifty pounds on bad shocks, and the VW was bouncing with him. The three guys across the street didn't frown at us any less.

"Maybe we should drive on," I suggested.

Erainya opened her door, got out, and leaned across the car's roof. She hollered, "One of you guys Del?"

"Or," I mumbled, "maybe you have another idea . . ."

The three guys glanced at one another.

Del Brandon stepped forward. "Who's asking?"

"Who's asking? Come on, honey. You want to come closer, see we aren't monsters or anything?"

Something about the way Erainya talks—I've seen it a dozen times and I've never quite gotten the magic of it. It makes even the most hardened guys red around the ears. They check their zippers, check that their ears are washed, try to remember if they ate a good dinner. They get uncomfortable and deferential. Erainya immediately becomes the hard-assed mother from the Old Country they never had.

Del walked toward us, stepping carefully through the dark maze of crisscrossed railroad tracks. He stopped about five feet away from my window. From there, he could probably see Erainya's face, Jem's pressed against the glass behind me, my face in the driver's window. If Del recognized me from our brief encounter at Ines', he didn't let it show.

"What'd you want?" he asked.

"Look, honey," Erainya told him. "I didn't know you had another deal to take care of tonight. It's just I thought you'd be expecting me."

Del shook his head slowly, fishing around for some possible explanation. After almost a minute, when I was sure he was going to decide Erainya was bullshitting him, he seemed to come up with an idea. "You mean *you're*—"

"Sure," Erainya agreed instantly.

Del's large mouth opened, then closed. "Southwest Carnival? The buyer from Arno?"

"I don't want to mess up your deal," she said. "You go ahead with whatever."

Del came a step closer. He peered in at me, then back at Jem. "You've got a kid with you."

I was getting the feeling Del had never scored real high on those standardized achievement tests.

"That's Jem," Erainya agreed. "He's mine. What—you make kiddie rides, you've never seen kids?"

Del held up his hands, immediately defensive. "I'm just asking—I mean, if Arno sent you—"

He faltered, then gestured to where the human boulder and the old rancher stood waiting. "It's just that we didn't—"

"You think you can give us a few minutes afterward?" Erainya asked.

Del shifted, looked back at his two *compadres*. "It's kind of late."

"My five-year-old, he's still up. You got an earlier bedtime than a five-year-old?"

Del looked chastised. "What kind of unit do you need?"

"I won't know that until we talk."

"You're prepared to do business tonight?" He gestured toward the VW. "You ain't going to haul nothing in *this*."

"I am *always* prepared to do business."

Del thought about that, then nodded with a little more certainty. "I'll try to wrap things up. Wait here. You damn near screwed my deal."

"Manners," Erainya warned him.

He held up his hands defensively again, patted the air a few times, then retreated to his two friends.

The men talked. It took some doing, but Del apparently got the old rancher to ease up, to go ahead with whatever business they were planning.

Once the transaction started it went fairly fast. Bo Peep opened the gates and the rancher backed his truck in. The three of them opened the hangar doors and walked out a trailer—about the same size as the truck but twice as tall. We couldn't see much of the amusement ride on the trailer, since it was covered in yellow tarp, but the shape was like a giant tulip.

Once the men got it hooked up, the rancher handed Del a grocery bag. Del sat on the bumper of the truck and counted bricks of cash while Bo Peep and the rancher waited. Apparently Del was satisfied. He gave the bag to Bo Peep, shook hands with the rancher. No smiles anywhere. The truck pulled away with its huge trailer and disappeared down Camden. Del wiped the sweat off his brow, then looked across the street at us and waved big, indicating we should drive the VW in.

Erainya got in and closed the passenger door.

"I want you to notice something, honey," she told Jem. "I didn't lie to that man. Not once."

Del and Bo Peep stood in front of us, their faces yellow and stern in our headlights. As we came in Bo Peep walked behind us, very casually, and closed the gates. We wouldn't be leaving quickly. And we didn't have any bags of cash to offer Mr. Brandon.

"Honesty," I told Jem, "is good in small quantities."

THIRTEEN

"It's been a crazy day," Del Brandon said.

He opened Erainya's door for her. Jem clambered out first, did a beautiful tight-end run around Del, then headed for the old-fashioned carousel animals that flanked the steps of the office.

Del raised a finger and said "Don't" about the time Jem launched himself onto the blue elephant's saddle and started bouncing. Del put his finger down, giving up.

I got out on my side and found myself in rock-climbing position against Bo Peep's chest.

I looked up into his nostrils. "Howdy."

He receded a step. Gravity stopped pulling my arm hairs toward his body.

Del sized me up, gave Erainya an amused "my-bodyguard's-bigger-than-your-bodyguard" kind of smile. "You want to take a look around the shop?" he asked her.

He led us through the open hangar doors. Bo Peep trailed about twenty feet behind, Jem doing tight fearless orbits around him and asking what PlayStation games he liked.

The tour was quick. Del waved in different directions, said a few words, snuck occasional glances at Erainya to see if bags of money were forthcoming.

The corrugated walls of the warehouse were lined with workbenches and machine tools, welding equipment, scrap metal shavings heaped in corners. In the middle of the room were three carnival rides in various states of assembly—a

Super-Whirl with the multicolored base attached but the seats scattered around the cement floor like massive wobbly Easter eggs; an eight-armed Spider Rider stripped to just the hydraulic mechanisms; a miniature carousel that looked pretty much complete.

"I can have the two ready in a few hours if I call up some of my boys," Del promised. "The carousel's cash-and-carry."

Del led us over to the Super-Whirl and started pointing out the hydraulics underneath. "Forty-five-degree lift-and-twirl action. Thirty rpms. You don't get any better on a trailer-mounted unit. It's a classic."

Erainya nodded sagely. "How much?"

"Very reasonable. Thirty thousand."

Erainya managed to keep any reaction off her face. I set my mouth hard, thinking about the few people I'd known in my life who dealt in cash amounts that large and were fearless enough to tote it around in grocery bags. None of them were nice people.

Jem had been jumping on the balls of his feet, anxious to try out everything. Finally he broke loose and ran toward one of the disassembled carriage units on the ground. Del lifted his finger, thought about the last time he'd told the kid "Don't," then turned to Erainya instead. "That's not safe."

"Jem," Erainya said. Jem scootched to a stop, reined himself back to his mom's side. He didn't stop grinning.

"It's late," Del reminded us. "Let's talk business."

Erainya said, "So this is all you got?"

"Right now. We can also repair any old units you got." She nodded toward the Cro-Magnon man looming behind me. "You always need him in the room?"

Del glanced at Bo Peep, then at me. He apparently decided the security risk was not high. "Get a Nehi, Ernie. We'll be in the office."

Bo Peep drifted away. The rest of us followed Brandon out of the warehouse.

"You got to understand about Ernie," Del said as we crossed the yard. "Guy's gone state-to-state with the carnies so long, on the lam, he's just about fanatical to me for giving him a settle-down job, no questions asked. You worked the road long?"

"I know Ernie's type," Erainya assured him.

We walked up the office steps between the plaster horse and the blue elephant. Both glistened with hysterical smiles.

Inside, the reception area was no more than seven feet square, rafter beams lower than a miner's cabin, walls so old and dim and brown it was impossible to tell what they were made of. Whatever it was, it was solid enough to accept nails, which is how the majority of things were posted—an old Hung Fong's calendar, some company notices, photographs of workers at the shop, pictures of the rides. Up along the top of the walls were ripped fragments of old party decorations in several different colors. A truly impressive collection of gimme caps hung on more nails behind the receptionist's desk.

The receptionist, in fact, was about the only thing that wasn't nailed to the wall. She was flat on her back on the desk, snoring. After what I'd already seen of Del Brandon's business practices, it somehow didn't surprise me to find his receptionist in this condition, still in the office at midnight. She was Latina—minute size, frizzy red hair, improbably large bosom, and much spandex. In sleep, her little pointy face twitched and slanted like the drunken dormouse from *Alice in Wonderland*.

Brandon walked past her and swatted her knee. "Jesus Christ, Rita."

She stopped snoring instantly. "Yeah, Del, like you don't want me horizontal."

Brandon glanced back at us, his face pained. "She's got a lousy sense of humor. I got a wife."

Rita snorted. She sat up, rubbed her eyes, then focused on Jem and grinned. "Hey. A cutie." She groped in the drawer behind her and came up with a smushed box of Mike and Ikes. "Want some?"

Del grumbled something about Rita getting to work, then led us down a short hall into a somewhat larger office. The carpet was threadbare sulfur. The fluorescent lights gave everything a greasy hue. Lined along the floor next to Del's desk, like luminarias, were leftover Taco Cabana bags filled with aluminum foil wads and smelling of old *carne guisada*.

Behind the desk was a framed, poster-size black-and-white photograph of *Jeremiah Brandon, Our Founder* as a young man, leaning against a half-dismantled printing press. The shot looked straight out of a World War II-era *Life*—the happy industrial worker laboring for Democracy. Except for the youthful softness in his cheeks and neck, Jeremiah looked not much different from the other picture I'd seen of him in middle age. Still the buzzard's face, crooked smile, a merciless light in his eyes that spoke of past poverty and a determination to avoid it in the future. Jeremiah's fingers were long, resting on the rubber-coated rollers and steel gears of the printing press like they were keys of an organ. His arms were black with machine grease up to his elbows. Grease speckled his collarless white shirt, his trousers, his cap. I had a feeling the liquid could've been blood and Jeremiah would've smiled just the same way.

I looked from the photograph to the real-life Del Brandon.

You couldn't miss the contrast. Del looked like his dad after twenty years of Prozac and éclairs—a fatter, duller version of the original, the ferocious hunger in his eyes watered down to a kind of unfocused discontent.

Del sat down at his desk, which was absolutely empty— no pens, no paper, nothing. The desk of an untrustworthy man.

He spread his arms. "Well?"

Erainya patted Jem's head. "Why don't you go play with Rita, honey?"

Jem ran fearlessly into the other room—a lot more fearlessly than I would have if someone suggested *I* play with Rita. Erainya shut the door behind him, then sat in the only free chair. I leaned against the wall by the desk.

Del sat back in his chair, waiting.

"Mr. Brandon," Erainya said, "we're private investigators."

Del had been about to prop his boot up on the desk. He missed, dropped the foot to the floor, and sat up. "Come again?"

"I'm a private investigator, honey. I need some information about your brother."

Brandon's eyes got very small. "Did Arno tell you to fuck with me like this?"

"I don't know Arno."

"You said—"

"No, I didn't. You assumed."

Del opened his mouth, looking back and forth between me and Erainya. When the color came back into his face, it came a little too quick.

Maybe he wasn't really planning to go for his side arm, but when his hand started slipping toward the edge of the desk both Erainya and I had the same idea. Erainya pulled her 9mm from her purse. I walked around the desk, lifted Del's hand, and removed his .38 semiauto from its holster.

Del didn't object. He took the intrusion calmly, like a man who was used to being disarmed. When he spoke again, he addressed Erainya.

"You think this is a good idea? You think you can treat me like this?"

"We don't want you getting stupid, honey. That's all."

I ejected the gun's magazine into the trash can. I checked the desk, found no other weapons, then nodded to Erainya.

She put her 9mm back in her purse.

"I yell now," Del warned, "that kid of yours will be Ernie's lunch. What are you thinking?"

"All we want is to ask a couple of questions, honey."

"You tricked me."

"I do what's easiest. Tell me about your brother."

"He's dead. What's to tell?"

"You sound real broken up about it," I noticed.

Del shrugged.

"You looked broken up this afternoon," I added, "kicking Aaron's widow and kid out of their home."

Del's eyes got even smaller. "That's where—on the porch, yeah. What the fuck is this about?"

"We're working for UTSA, Mr. Brandon," Erainya said. "The University wants to make sure their professor didn't get shot full of holes through any fault of theirs. You heard the police are holding a suspect in your brother's murder?"

"I didn't know that, you think I'd be out at night conducting business? Years I've been waiting for them to catch that fucker. He killed my father."

"You believe Zeta Sanchez had a grudge against you?"

"Fuckin' A."

"Your brother too?"

Del's gaze slid down to his empty desktop, then back to Erainya. "Look, lady, the police already asked me all about that. I told them I don't know."

Erainya nodded sympathetically. "And the truth is?"

Del licked his lips. "You just want to know so UTSA will relax."

"That's right, honey."

"Then you'll get out of here?"

I gave him the Scout's honor.

"Just so you understand," he started, "Zeta Sanchez—Anthony—he should've been grateful to us. Nobody else would've given him the kind of chance we did."

He looked at Erainya for support.

She said, "Absolutely."

"Sanchez's folks worked for us for ages. His dad was a metal welder. His mom worked in the office." Del nodded past me, toward Rita's reception area. "I remember her pretty well. I was about fifteen when Anthony was born. Sanchez's dad died not too long after that but his mom worked here a few more years before quitting. The thing about my dad, though—once your family worked for him, he kept track of you, tried to help out any way he could. So he kept tabs on the Sanchezes. When Anthony started getting into trouble with gangs, Dad offered him a job here. Dad did that for a lot of the employees' kids."

"Heartwarming," I said.

"Everybody got a chance in Dad's business. Even Zeta Sanchez. Even my stupid fucking brother. Everybody."

From out in the office, Rita's voice exploded with laughter. Jem was singing her something.

Erainya said, "Why would Sanchez want you and your brother dead?"

"We shut the bastard down, that's why. Zeta was moving drugs through RideWorks. Using *our* fucking company to move heroin for his friends on the West Side. If he'd been found out, we would've been closed down. Everything my dad built, everything Aaron and I were going to inherit— gone. I got Dad to see what was going on. Aaron didn't have much to do with it, but Sanchez didn't know that. He blamed us both, told us we were just jealous he could run the company better than we could. Dad had it out with him after that—threw Sanchez out on his ass. You know what Sanchez did to retaliate."

"And the rumor about your dad sleeping with Sanchez's wife?" I asked.

"That story's bullshit."

"The girl's name was Sandra," I recalled. "Her brother's still around—Hector Mara. You wouldn't happen to know him?"

"I don't have to convince you two of shit," Del blustered. "I told you what you wanted to hear. Now you can get the hell out."

In the reception area, Jem kept laughing along with Rita. They both said "Whoops!" in unison.

Del nodded toward the door. "Ernie'll be coming back about now, checking on things. My transactions don't take this long, miss."

Erainya took a card from her purse, slid it across the table toward Del. "You think of anything you forgot, honey, call us."

"I got other things to do, lady. Either you got thirty thousand dollars to spend or your time is up."

"Your wife awaits?" I asked. "Or Rita?"

His face reddened. "I'll remember you, asshole."

"Good night, Del," Erainya said. "Thanks a million."

We went outside to collect Jem, who was giggling at Rita trying to balance a beer bottle on her forehead. Jem asked if we could come back here tomorrow. He said it was fun even without the amusement rides working.

Erainya told him probably not.

We left Rita still trying to do the beer bottle trick, Del Brandon glaring at us while he reloaded his gun.

FOURTEEN

Wednesday morning came way too early and it brought along a friend named Margarita Hangover.

I sweated through an hour of the Yang sword form, then showered until Gary Hales banged on the wall to let me know his bathtub was backing up. The plumbing at 90 Queen Anne is fun that way.

I shaved carefully around the gash on my cheek. The discoloration and puffiness had gone down since yesterday. I could see the shape of the new scar—a little smile, half an inch long.

I read my morning battery of E-mail reports from Erainya, breakfasted, dressed in coat and tie, and got on the road by nine. Most of Robert Johnson's hair went with me on the coat, since he'd used it as a bed the night before, but when you have exactly two nice outfits and one of them smells like a bomb blast, you make do.

I drove northwest on I-10 until the real estate developments and strip malls began falling away to the natural topography of the Balcones Escarpment—crumpled folds of land thickly covered with live oak and prickly pear. Just inside Loop 1604, the UTSA campus rose from the woods in an isolated cluster of limestone cubes. The area around it had begun to urbanize over the last few years, but occasionally in the early morning you still see deer, armadillos, roadrunners at the edges of the parking lots.

I'd lived in the Bay Area for ten years before moving

home to San Antonio. My California friends would not have called this a particularly beautiful place. Those brave enough to visit me in Texas complain of the boring vista, the oppressive storm clouds that frequently rolled in, the harsh flat prairie ugliness.

I try telling them that it's a matter of perspective, that San Francisco is like a Monet—any idiot can appreciate it. San Antonio, on the other hand, takes time, patience. It's more like a Raymond Saunders, put together with muddy strokes and scraps of handwriting and broken stuff. But it's beautiful, too. You just have to be more perceptive.

Of course my Bay Area friends counter that, by my logic, all the truly perceptive Mensa types should be living in Allentown, Pennsylvania, appreciating the completely sub-liminal beauty there. At that point in the argument I usually order more tequila and tell my friends to screw themselves.

I turned onto Loop 1604 and drove across the dusty ac-cess road to the north entrance of campus. I parked in the faculty lot and tried not to feel strange about it.

After twenty minutes filling out paperwork for the pro-vost's secretary and the dean's secretary and the campus police lieutenant's secretary, I was back in the late Aaron Brandon's office—my office.

The hole in the window had been covered with clear plastic tarp. Odds and ends and half-burned essays from the floor had been heaped onto the desk. Unfortunately, many of the essays were still readable, thus gradable.

I sat down in the black leather chair. Outside, the spring morning looked glazed behind plastic. The picture of Aaron Brandon with his wife and child had been replaced upside down on the desk.

My graduate medieval seminar started in three hours.

I began sorting through my predecessors' files—syllabi, lecture notes, grade sheets, highlighted readers, personal ef-fects. It didn't take long to learn what belonged to Brandon and what belonged to old Dr. Haimer, the office's original occupant. Haimer's materials were the tried and true and dusty—the General Prologue, Gawain, the Wakefield plays. Brandon's syllabus, as I anticipated, tended toward the flashy and gory—Crusade narratives, miracle plays, fabliaux. The Middle Ages according to Stephen King.

I'd stacked about a foot of paper into two piles, *Brandon* and *Haimer,* when I hit a thin folder labeled RIDEWORKS stuck to the back cover of Brandon's *Riverside Chaucer.*

Inside was an eight-by-ten photograph of Aaron with father Jeremiah and brother Del. All three stood on the running board of an old-fashioned carousel. Jeremiah must've been in his sixties by the time this shot was taken, not long before his murder. His hair had turned greasy white, his face thinner with age, but his eyes still glittered with the same fierce intensity. I tried to imagine this man making advances toward a seventeen-year-old married girl named Sandra Mara-Sanchez, and I decided with a cold certainty that Jeremiah Brandon would've been capable of it.

The brothers Del and Aaron looked strikingly similar to each other but hardly like Dad at all. None of the three men looked particularly happy.

Under the photo was a Xerox copy of an article from a Texas business journal, dated three years ago. The story announced that a settlement had been reached between the IRS and a drill-bit manufacturing company in the Permian Basin. An insider at the company had tipped IRS investigators about cash transactions the company owner was conducting with wildcatters. A sting operation had been launched. Once caught, the owner had bargained his way out of jail time for tax evasion by agreeing to massive fines and relinquishing control of the company to a board of directors made up of other family members.

I read the article again. I looked at the photo.

When knuckles rapped on the door, I closed the folder and set it aside.

"Tres?"

Professor David Mitchell looked better than he had the day before—his jeans and dress shirt freshly pressed, white sideburns trimmed, face hinting at a good twelve hours of sedative-assisted sleep. He sawed a piece of paper against his thigh.

"I've asked my secretary to delay her," he told me. "We have about five minutes."

"Come again?"

He looked behind him nervously, then came all the way in and closed the door. "Ines Brandon."

"Aaron's widow. She's here?"

Mitchell sighed. "Mrs. Brandon needs to collect some of her husband's things. I wasn't sure how you'd—Perhaps we could talk in the hall?"

"Talk about what?"

He stared over my shoulder for a few seconds, then shook his head, coming out of his reverie. He held up the folded paper in his hand. "I'm sorry. The first report from Ms. Manos. You've seen it?"

"Have a seat."

"But—" He pointed behind him. "You're sure?"

I waved him toward the student's chair.

Mitchell checked his watch. He sat down reluctantly, probably remembering what had happened the last time he sat there, then unfolded Erainya's report and frowned at it. "Ms. Manos seems to be urging us to end the investigation."

"Erainya would love to keep taking your money. She's just trying to be clear with you. The State Licensing Board takes a dim view of investigators who churn cases, string clients along for more hours than necessary. If the police are right, UTSA has nothing to worry about. Brandon's murder was some kind of personal matter between Aaron and the man who killed him, Zeta Sanchez. Sanchez is a former employee of the Brandons. He might've murdered Aaron's father back in '93. If that's all true, you may wish to discontinue your investigation."

Mitchell's frown deepened. "The death threats, son. The bomb—"

"—could've been sent by Zeta Sanchez."

Mitchell studied my face. Apparently I didn't do a good job looking convinced.

"You don't believe that," he decided. "The letters started coming before Dr. Brandon was even hired. You know that."

"One letter came to Dr. Haimer. A month or so later, six more like it came to Brandon, then the bomb."

Mitchell rubbed his jaw. "You're saying someone could've copied the style of the first threat."

"It's possible. When did Dr. Haimer report it?"

"He didn't. He merely threw it in his file cabinet with all the other hate mail. Dr. Brandon came across it when he took over the office, but he didn't report it to us until after he received the second and third letters, addressed to him. That was the first time we knew we had a credible threat. That was in February, about five weeks into the term."

"So conceivably, anyone who saw that first letter to Haimer could've decided to copy the style and continue the death threats. A person who was after Aaron Brandon for another reason might've found the UTSA controversy a convenient cover."

"This man, Zeta Sanchez, would go to such trouble?"

"Doesn't seem likely," I admitted. "But the police already have a lot of other evidence pointing to Sanchez."

Mitchell shook his head. "The only people who could've seen that letter were University people, Tres. If something happened as you described, I can't imagine it was done by a—" Mitchell faltered.

"Gangster?"

"Yes."

"You want us to keep looking into the matter."

"I want Ms. Manos to look into it."

"That's what I meant."

Mitchell smiled faintly, checked his watch again. "Are you sure you wouldn't rather—"

"One more question." I pulled out the eight-by-ten carousel photo, held it up for Dr. Mitchell to see. "You know these men?"

Mitchell shook his head. "Aaron's relatives?"

"This one is his dad, Jeremiah. The other is Del, Aaron's brother. You ever seen the brother around campus? Maybe visiting Aaron's office?"

"Not that I recall. Why?"

I was thinking about whether to mention the business journal article when someone else knocked on the door. Professor Mitchell looked at me with a silent warning. He mouthed the words: *She's drunk.*

"It's okay," I promised.

Mitchell looked dubious, but he got up and opened the door. He stuck his head outside, mumbled something to the person waiting, then turned and said to me by way of reassurance, "I'll be just down the hall."

He was replaced in the doorway by Ines Brandon.

Today she wore jeans and an army-green silk blouse with a basket purse slipping off one shoulder. Her red-brown hair was tied back in a stubby ponytail.

When she saw me, anger filled her like compressed air. "I don't believe this."

"You say that with such joy."

"Put it away," she demanded.

When I didn't immediately get her meaning, she walked to the desk and tore the photo of the Brandon men out of my hand.

She ripped the photo in half, carefully aligned the halves, and ripped them again, letting the pieces flutter to the singed carpet.

"It's away," I said.

There was a leaden quality in her eyes, as if the thoughts beneath were moving sluggishly. "Get the hell out."

"Can't. I've got a class in three hours."

Her hands worked into the smallest possible fists. "You came into my house. Now you're sitting at my husband's desk. You goddamn prying—"

"Mrs. Brandon—I work here."

"I don't give a—"

"As an English professor."

Her thin black eyebrows knitted into tilde marks.

She looked uncertainly around the office—the hole in the window, the scorched papers, the stacks of files I'd been sorting through. "I thought—"

"I told you I was a P.I. That's still true. So happens I'm also—"

"You're Aaron's *replacement*?"

I nodded.

Ines Brandon studied my tie. She looked at the upside-down family photo on the desk. The woman in it looked nothing like her—hair longer, lighter-colored; body ten pounds heavier and healthier; her smile sincere and warm.

"You can take whatever you need," I told her. "I'm sorry."

Ines Brandon's fingers touched the glass over the photo, trailed to the edge of the desk, and slipped off. "Everybody's sorry," she said.

She swayed, then sank into the chair that was, fortunately, right behind her. She curled forward, pinching her hand over her eyes. Her purse tumbled into her lap.

The office got intensely quiet. The plastic on the window ballooned inward with the breeze. The mesquite rustled. Outside the door, two male voices approached and then receded down the hallway.

Ines' fingers massaged small circles at the corners of her eyebrows.

When she focused on me again, her eyes couldn't target quite right. "Your name was Navarre?"

"Tres Navarre. Yes."

She mouthed the word *Tres* a few times, let out a sour laugh. "The third. How perfect."

"I'm trying not to dwell on that."

She shut her eyes. "This isn't your fault. I'm sorry. I don't have a box. I don't even know what things are his."

"Let it wait. His things don't have to go anywhere."

Her expression didn't change, but a thick tear traced its way down the base of her nose.

She tried to stand and couldn't quite make it.

She frowned, looked into her purse, then fished out an orange prescription bottle and stared at the label accusingly.

"How many?" I asked.

"They insisted. I broke a window."

"I remember."

"The doctor said the sedatives—" She stopped, still frowning. "Two pills. I think I took two. I don't remember."

She tried to put the bottle back in her purse and dropped it on the floor instead. "I need to go."

"You're not doing so great. Is there anyone who could—"

"Take me home?" she interrupted.

"Yeah."

She looked up at me wearily, her expression a mixture of resentment and plea.

I suddenly realized I had just made an offer.

FIFTEEN

I had to wake Ines Brandon when we pulled in front of her house on Castano. With some effort, I extracted her from the VW, got her up the five steps, navigated her around the Big Wheel and the street chalk.

Before I could ring the bell on the front porch, a scowling woman opened the door.

"I *tell* you," she scolded Ines.

The woman's arms were beefy slabs. Her upper body was stuffed into the world's largest black Papal Visit souvenir T-shirt, the faded picture of John Paul II on the front unflatteringly distorted by the bulges of the woman's breasts. Her stubby legs threatened to bust out of turquoise sweatpants and her hair was pulled back in a painfully tight bun. Her feet were bare. Her face was as brutally sculpted as a Mayan pedestal—weathered and wide and flat, designed to withstand several thousand tons. She smelled pungently of cloves. She took Ines' arm and guided her into the house.

"This is Mr. Navarre," Ines mumbled. "I didn't have a box."

The woman cursed at her gently in Spanish, then looked back at me and said in a stern voice: "Stay."

"Arf," I said.

The woman didn't react. She and Ines disappeared down the hallway. I heard the sounds of minor protests, chastisements, orders to take off shoes. Miniblinds were snapped shut.

There was even less to see in the living room than there had been before. Most of the boxes were now taped closed. All the framed photographs had been removed from the end table. The broken window in the dining room had been covered with a piece of cardboard.

The Pope-shirted woman reappeared from the hallway, wiping her palms on her turquoise pants. Her squashed, disapproving eyes zeroed in on me. "Thank you, go."

"You're Paloma?"

The woman gave me a grudging nod, then brushed past and went to the front door. She opened it, looked at me expectantly.

I pointed down the hallway where Ines had disappeared. "You get her to sleep all right?"

"No *Ingles,*" Paloma suddenly decided. She glared at me obstinately.

"No problema," I assured her. Then, still in Spanish, "We had to leave Mrs. Brandon's car at UTSA. The north visitors' lot. It'll be all right for this afternoon, but someone should pick it up by tomorrow morning."

Paloma continued glaring at me, letting me know that nothing could have insulted her sensibilities worse than a fluent gringo.

"Thank you, go," she tried again, in English.

"I bet you're great with solicitors. Those aluminum-siding guys from Sears."

She shoved the door shut, irritated. "You won't go. Why?"

"I'm curious."

"La policia." She scowled. "They were curious. The reporters, *también.* No more. Señora Brandon needs sleep."

"You've been with the family long?"

"Five years. Since Miguel."

"Since Michael was born—their son."

"Sí."

"Is Michael here?"

"No."

As if on cue, a whirring toy sound wailed from one of the back bedrooms, then died. It sounded like one of those sparking ray guns.

Paloma's stone face darkened.

"*Mira, Paloma,*" I told her. "I don't mean to pry. I've been hired to take Dr. Brandon's job. I'd like to know how he got himself killed. I don't want to follow in his footsteps."

Paloma's eyes drifted away from me and fixed on the fireplace. She scowled at the bullet holes in the limestone, as if remembering exactly where she had scrubbed, and how hard, and what the color of the water and the soap foam had been afterward.

"We're leaving this place," she mused. "For now, an apartment. Maybe later, out of town."

"And will that return things to normal?"

Paloma made a sound deep in her throat, like stone grinding. "You wish to see normal?"

She grabbed my wrist and tugged me down the hallway, past a closed door on the right, past an open bathroom, to a door on the left that was papered with foldout animal posters from various scholastic magazines.

Paloma pushed me into the doorway and held me there, her fingers digging into my shoulders. I was expecting to see your basic boy's room, like Jem's—buckets of Tinkertoys and Legos, miniature furniture, piles of little clothes and shoes. Everything in primary colors.

What I saw instead were sheets. At least ten of them—white, blue, daisy-patterned, brown—draped waist-level wall-to-wall, covering everything. The cloth sagged in canyons, rose here and there to peaks that were probably chairs underneath. Square outlines hinted of tabletops, a bed. Where the sheet corners met, they were weighted down by heavy books to keep them together. In some places they were tied off or safety-pinned. There seemed to be talcum powder everywhere—sprinkled liberally over the tops of the sheets, gathered in thick drifts where the cloth sagged, hanging in the air with a cloying scent. The room looked like it had been commandeered for a Christo art event.

Three feet from the bedroom door was a small triangular opening in the sheet tent. A toy ray gun lay on the carpet next to an empty plastic Lunchables tray and a Toys "R" Us circular with all the coupons cut out.

Paloma pushed past me and managed to lower herself enough to scoop up the trash.

"Miguel," she grunted. *"Ahí."*

Nothing moved.

Outside the bedroom windows I could see the backyard— about twenty feet of grass, a barbecue pit, swing set, pecan tree. In the corner a wooden garage was topped with a second-story apartment. The day was sunny, but it felt miles away outside the gloom and the powder and the dust.

"Miguel!" Paloma called again.

This time sheets rustled in the corner. A little spherical dent appeared in them, slid toward the entrance, then emerged at the opening as the head of a five-year-old boy.

If I had not known he was half Latino, I never would've guessed it. His skin was paler than mine, paler than damn near anybody's. His eyes were blue like Aaron Brandon's, his hair reddish like his mother's.

He was wearing a T-shirt and underwear and nothing else. He peered up at me with mild curiosity.

"Miguel," Paloma said, "this is Señor Navarre. Señor Navarre is a college teacher like your papa."

Michael seemed to be trying to reach some conclusion about my face, as if he weren't quite sure if it was real or a pretty good mask.

"Hey, Michael," I said.

"This is my cave," he informed me.

"I can see that. It's a real nice cave."

Michael suddenly developed a keen interest in picking the skin off his knuckle.

"He needs to clean it up," Paloma grumbled, but not like she expected any action.

"What's with the powder?" I asked.

"It's fog," Michael said to his knuckle. "Makes you invisible."

"That's good," I said. "But just in case they get through, you zap them, right?"

He snatched his ray gun, gave me an upward glance.

Paloma receded in the doorway and gestured for me to follow. I told Michael I'd see him around.

The last I saw of him he was digging the muzzle of his ray gun into his bare knee.

"This," Paloma said, "is *normal*."

It took me a few steps before I could speak. "Since his father's death?"

"Before. Since the fights. Now will you go?"

We stopped in the living room, Paloma once again holding the front door open for me. Her face seemed even more compressed, her eyes almost slits, her mouth flattened into a hard amber line. The irreverently stretched Holy Father smiled up at me from Paloma's shirt, one papal eye bigger than the other.

"I'll go," I promised. "But the apartment in back, above the garage—is that yours?"

She stiffened.

"You were the witness—the one who ID'ed Zeta Sanchez for the police."

"*Madre de Dios,* if you don't leave now—"

I didn't make her finish the threat. I said good-bye and went out to my car.

When I looked back, Paloma stood motionless in the

doorway—her eyes dark, her face hard and impassive, as if she'd turned back into red Texas granite. I couldn't blame her for that. Anything as soft as human flesh could never have supported the weight of the Brandon household.

SIXTEEN

Sometimes necessity is the mother of invention. Sometimes necessity is just a mother.

All the way back to the University, I brainstormed ideas for the graduate seminar, knowing I would have just enough time to stumble into the classroom with none of Brandon's backlogged papers graded and no prepared lecture notes.

I kept trying to come up with some brilliant game plan to make a good first impression. At ten past one, sitting on a table in front of eight graduate students in HSS 2.0.22, I was still without that plan.

"So." I tried to sound enthusiastic. "I thought we'd start by going around—tell me your names, a little about yourselves. Ask whatever you want about me. Who wants to start?"

No hands shot into the air.

I waved encouragingly toward a couple of mid-fiftyish women by the door. They were crocheting from a shared bag of pink yarn.

"You ladies?"

They introduced themselves as Edie and Marfa, escaped housewives. Marfa told me she wanted to read some medieval romances. Edie smiled and gave me the eye.

"Ah-ha," I said. "And you, sir?"

The elderly man cleared his throat. He wore a mechanic's jumpsuit and a buzz cut. "Sergeant Irwin, USAF, retired. I'm still in this class because the military is paying every penny, and so far I'm damn glad of it."

I thanked him for sharing, then waved toward the next man—a young Anglo in a Men's Wearhouse Italian suit.

He looked up from his organizer long enough to say, "Brian. I run a small carpeting business and I'm probably going to drop the class. Don't mind me."

Behind Brian was Gregory, the giant radish mail boy who delivered pipe bombs.

"Always nice to see a familiar face," I told him.

Gregory mumbled something. He didn't meet my eyes.

Next to him sat two guys in Nirvana T-shirts and jeans and plentiful chains clipped to their belt loops. Simon and Blake. They asked me how it was hanging. I asked them how they'd come to choose a medieval literature class and they shrugged and grinned like *Class? We're in class?*

The last student, in the far corner by the window, mumbled hello but didn't give a name or any other firm indication of gender. He/she looked like a Morticia Addams drag queen.

"Great." I looked at the clock. We'd managed to burn four whole minutes. "So—any questions?"

After some awkward silence and pencil fumbling, one of the grunge guys, Blake, raised his hand and asked about class hours. Would he still receive full credit for the first three months of the semester even though What's-his-name had gotten bumped off?

"Yes," I said. "Full credit, even from What's-his-name."

That emboldened the others.

Morticia asked if their essays had ever been graded. I said that most of them had been salvaged from the bomb blast and were currently on my desk. They'd be graded soon.

Marfa lowered her knitting needles and asked Brian the carpet salesman if he'd really be able to drop the course. Wasn't it too late in the semester? Brian told her she would need special permission from the dean's office, but he was pretty sure she could get it if she raised enough hell. Marfa looked at me to see if that was true.

I tried to look sympathetic. I wrote down the question on my notepad. "I'll find out. Something else?"

Simon, the second grunge boy, raised his hand and complained that Dr. Brandon had been, well, a psychopath, and was I one too?

Gregory the mail boy broke in. "I *liked* those stories."

Morticia groaned. "Oh, man, you're nuts. I was all like— I don't want to know how it feels to be *impaled,* okay?"

I wrote on my notepad, NO IMPALING. "You're talking about the Crusade narratives?"

Several heads nodded. Edie informed me that Dr. Brandon had been obsessed with violence. More heads nodded.

Sergeant Irwin, USAF, retired, raised his hand. "The Marie de France stories. We bought this whole book and only read one. Some of the others aren't quite so, well, offensive. Maybe we could read them."

Edie agreed. She wanted to know if there were some romances in the book, some without werewolves.

"I *liked* that one," complained Gregory.

Edie and Morticia started to argue with him.

Blake hollered, "Come on, man! It's this guy's first day and stuff."

The grumbling died down. Morticia and Gregory and Edie kept glaring at each other. Marfa was giving me the eye now, wiggling her eyebrows in time with her knitting needles.

"Great," I said again. We'd now ripped through twelve minutes. "I noticed the old syllabus was a little heavy on the gore. Maybe the Marie de France book would be a good place for a fresh start. How about the first three *lais* for Friday? We'll revisit *Bisclavret* and move to *Lanval* and *Guigemar.*"

There was some general mumbled assent.

That gave me an opening to lecture a little bit about Marie de France, about the courtly love debate and the Anglo-Norman world. I kept stopping to ask if my students had heard all this before. They looked amazed. A few of them even bothered taking notes.

I was just wrapping things up when George Bertón came in, dressed in his usual sixties leisure clothes and Panama hat. He held Jem by one hand and an enormously full brown paper bag in the other.

I kept lecturing about the difficulties of translating Anglo-Norman alliteration.

George and Jem tiptoed around the back of the room and quietly took two desks next to Gregory. Jem waved at me, then pulled a new action figurine out of his OshKosh overalls and held it up for me to see.

George looked at me seriously and pantomimed straightening a tie. My hand started to go up to my collar, then I stopped myself. George grinned.

"Well," I concluded. "That's probably enough for the first day. We'll look at those first three *lais* on Friday. I'll keep the same office hours as Dr. Brandon. Anything else?"

Edie the housewife raised her hand. "I read in the newspaper yesterday—"

"About the bomb blast," I interrupted. "Thank you, but I'm fine."

"No . . ." She frowned, as if my assumption that she'd been interested in my welfare had confused her. "I just wanted to ask, is it true you're a private investigator?"

I looked back at George, who was slicing his hand horizontally across his throat, mouthing: *No. No.*

"It's true," I said.

The class shifted in their seats. Nobody followed up with questions. Nobody asked my trench coat size.

"Well—" I said. "Okay then. See you Friday."

At that, Jem put down his action figure and began clapping for me. The students looked back uneasily and began collecting their things. Jem kept clapping until the room was empty except for him, me, and George.

George grinned. "Bravo, Professor."

"What are you guys—"

George held up his bulging paper bag. "Join us for lunch?"

SEVENTEEN

"You want the special or the beef?"

The question was a mere formality. George nudged the Rolando's Special my way, grabbed the *carne guisada* for himself, then leaned back in his chair and crossed his legs at the ankles.

He unwrapped the end of the mega-taco and took a bite, staring thoughtfully across the UTSA *patillo*.

The white patio tables were abandoned this late in the afternoon, the sunken courtyard quiet except for the flutter of pigeons and the sound of the stone monolith fountain sluicing water off its slanted top into the pool below. Overhead, reflected light from the water pulsed across limestone pillars, up the two-story roof of opaque plastic bubbles. Lines of wooden slats hung from above like weird, Mondrian stalactites.

According to UTSA folklore, the campus had been laid out following an ancient Aztec city design, which put the *patillo* in the center of the community and the fountain right where the altar would've been. Jem, who had already taken two bites of his kid's taco and pronounced himself full, was now tightrope-walking his Captain Chaos doll around the rim of the pool, right about where the bloody heads of the sacrificial victims would've rolled.

I looked down at my Rolando's Special—a giant flour tortilla stuffed with eggs, guacamole, potato, bacon, cheese, and salsa. Normally it would have been enough to elevate me into Taco Nirvana. Today, all I could think about were sheet caves, the desolate interior of the Brandon home, and the things George Bertón wasn't saying.

He'd offered no comment on my morning's activities. Without expression, he read the short article I'd found in Aaron Brandon's desk about the IRS investigation in West Texas, then tucked it into his olive-green shirt pocket along with his cigars. He'd been animated enough talking about my classroom performance, the virtues of Rolando's, the great things Jem had been making with his Tinkertoys, but when the conversation had turned toward the Brandon case, George had closed up.

Not that George didn't sometimes close up about his cases-in-progress. Every investigator does. But after our free conversation last night, his remoteness today made me uneasy.

"The IRS article," I prompted. "Mean anything to you?"

"You mean like was Aaron Brandon interested in drill bits?"

"No, doofus. I mean like was Aaron Brandon getting ideas about turning his brother Del in to the IRS. If so, and if Del found out about it, Del might've wanted to stop him."

"I don't know."

"Okay," I said. "Hector Mara. What about him?"

"I don't know."

"What do you mean, you don't know?"

"I talked to some people, heard pretty much the same thing Ralph told you. Mara's been doing business with Chich Gutierrez—maybe running some heroin, though nobody could tell me exactly how or where or to whom. Maybe Zeta Sanchez coming back would cramp Mara's style. Maybe it would cut into Chich Gutierrez's business. Doesn't necessarily mean Hector and Chich would set Sanchez up for a murder."

"Whatever happened to Sandra?"

George peeled back some tinfoil. "You mean Hector's sister. Sanchez's wife."

"Yeah. The girl Jeremiah supposedly slept with. Whatever happened to her?"

George hesitated. I could see a change in his eyes—a distance that hadn't been there before. "Jeremiah Brandon had a reputation, *ese*. The young girls who worked for him, or were family members of men who did—Jeremiah liked making them his conquests. He'd always win. Eventually the men would find out, but they usually did nothing. What could they do? If they complained, they lost their jobs. If they threatened, somebody like Zeta Sanchez would come visit them in the middle of the night. Jeremiah had all the power."

"Lord of the manor."

"What?"

"Something Ozzie Gerson said. Go on."

George stared past me. "Jeremiah would get a girl pregnant, or maybe the affair would just go on long enough where the family couldn't tolerate it anymore—Jeremiah would solve the problem by making the girl disappear. He'd give her a nice wad of cash, put her on the next bus to somewhere, or hand her over to his carnival buddies on their way out of town. She'd be gone to a new life, anywhere in the country. Jeremiah would be on to his next conquest."

"And Sandra?"

"A couple of days before Zeta Sanchez killed Jeremiah Brandon, Sandra Sanchez disappeared."

"Ah."

"Yeah. Suddenly all these trips Jeremiah Brandon was sending Sanchez on—all these collections Sanchez was making all across the country, they started to have a new meaning for Sanchez. His boss had been using that time to get friendly with Sandra."

"Bad."

"Unforgivable. A loss of face like that for a guy like Sanchez—unforgivable, *ese*."

"Maybe for Hector Mara, too. Sandra was Hector's sister. Jeremiah Brandon used her and threw her away. Hector had as much reason to hate the Brandons as Zeta Sanchez. If Hector needed to get Sanchez out of the way and was looking for somebody to kill for the frame-up, what more logical choice than a Brandon?"

George was quiet for a count of five. "Possible."

"But you've got something else. What is it, George?"

"What do you mean?"

"You started to tell me something a minute ago, then decided against it."

Slowly, George put together a grin. "I'm thinking of a number between one and twenty, Navarre."

"Screw you."

George laughed. "Ask me tomorrow. I've got an aversion to talking about leads before they work out."

"It's damn irritating."

"It's exactly the way you operate."

"Rub it in."

We finished eating in silence. George worked on the *carne guisada*. I got through about half of my special. Nearby some pigeons fought over an old popcorn box while Jem walked Captain Chaos around the fountain, Jem's forearms getting speckled with water.

George crumpled his aluminum foil wrapper into a baseball-sized wad and began flipping it up and catching it.

"At some point we're going to have to talk to the SAPD again," I told him. "You find out anything more about Ana DeLeon?"

George raised his eyebrows, did an overhand catch. "Don't even think about it, Navarre."

"I'm only asking—"

"Yeah, I know." His eyes glittered. "I met your old

girlfriend from San Francisco last Christmas—remember? Maia Lee?"

"What's that supposed to mean?"

"That Ana DeLeon's just your type. And knowing that should be enough to warn you off."

"You're so far off base—"

" 'S'okay, man." George flipped his aluminum foil ball. "You like the fortress women, the unapproachable ones. You like the challenge. Try to settle for somebody who can't outthink you *and* beat you at arm-wrestling—you're disappointed, can't stick with it. Annie, Carolaiyn, how many others didn't make the cut since Maia Lee, man? I've lost count."

There was no bitterness in his voice, no criticism. His smile was even a little wistful.

"I won't dignify that with a response," I told him.

"Don't need to."

He turned the aluminum ball in his fingers. His smile disintegrated.

"What?" I asked.

George shook his head. "Old Jeremiah Brandon. It's just that the more I hear about him, the stories, the way Sanchez brought him down—"

"I know."

George shook his head. "I don't think you do, *ese*. What Brandon could do to the people who worked for him, the young women especially, the things he got away with—it hits me in a place I don't want to be hit. I start feeling glad somebody shot the old man, start wishing I'd even been there to see it. I begin thinking of Zeta Sanchez as a hero. That scares me, *ese*. It scares me a lot."

We sat listening to the water sluice into the fountain, the pigeons pecking at a potato chip under a nearby table.

I looked over at Jem, who was circling the rim of the water fountain, his arms out like an airplane, his Captain Chaos clenched in one fist.

The sight of Jem made me smile, as it always did. Thank God for that kid. I looked over at George. He was apparently thinking the same thing.

I said, "You bought Jem that damn figurine, didn't you?"

George put his fingers on his chest. "And break Erainya's *no-toy* rule?"

"Affection-buying bastard. What can I do while you're out chasing leads?"

George smiled, a little sadness still in his eyes.

"You can teach your classes, Professor. What else?"

EIGHTEEN

"Full name," Detective Kelsey demanded.

"A guy hits you in the stomach," I said, "and you don't remember his name?"

The detective pushed back from his desk. His big Irish nose turned brake-light red. "Did I ask you here, asshole?"

"Jackson Navarre. You want me to spell it?"

"Give me your license."

He propped it on his keyboard and began clacking the information into the computer, using index fingers only.

I scanned the corkboard on his cubicle wall. There were pictures of Kelsey in camouflage next to a dead ten-point buck; Kelsey in bowling clothes; Kelsey in a TCU football uniform; Kelsey in SWAT black with an H&K 94 carbine. Lots of pictures of Kelsey. Lots of sports equipment and guns and deceased animals. Zero other human beings.

Down the central walkway of the SAPD homicide office, foot traffic was light. It was Wednesday evening but could just as easily have been three A.M. Monday or one P.M. Friday. No windows gave away the time, no change of lighting, no clocks. To the left and right, gray walls and gray carpet and gray five-foot-high dividing walls stretched out, the colorlessness punctuated here and there by a troll doll goggling over someone's cubicle, a sad ivy plant, a buzz-cut head asking something of the buzz-cut head next door. The space was devoid of noise and smell and temperature, designed like an emotional sponge to suck all the passion out of the events the investigators handled every day.

Kelsey's cubicle was not in a position of privilege. He was next to the case files closet, close to the interrogation rooms, within ear-pulling distance of Lieutenant Hernandez's office.

Kelsey stopped typing. He put his index finger on my license, looked back and forth between it and the screen to make sure he got everything right. His finger hesitated over my middle name. "Tray?"

"*Trace.* You know—Spanish. *Numero tres.*"

Kelsey grunted, hit RETURN. "Statement."

I went through what I'd seen yesterday during the apprehension of Zeta Sanchez at Hector Mara's farm. I didn't mention Kelsey's hesitation responding to Ana DeLeon's call for help. Kelsey did not type in how I had punched him in the gut. We were fast friends that way.

While Kelsey finished composing, I looked through the big glass window of the commander's office. Lieutenant Hernandez was having a deadly serious conversation with a well-dressed Anglo who had the reddest hair and the whitest skin I'd ever seen.

"Who's the leprechaun?" I asked.

Kelsey followed my gaze. He thought for a second, probably debating whether or not he had anything to lose by answering. "Canright. ADA on rotation to homicide this week. Lucky us."

I looked again through the window. Canright was holding up gold-ringed hands and shaking them, like he was showing the size of an imaginary fish. Hernandez leaned on the edge of his desk, his hands pinched tightly under his armpits. The lieutenant's face had its usual metallic hardness.

"So what's the argument?" I asked.

Kelsey pointed behind me with his chin. Down the side corridor, I could just see the doorway of the first interrogation room. An armed, uniformed deputy stood outside.

The face of Ana DeLeon passed briefly behind the tiny one-foot-square window—mid-pace, mid-conversation.

"Celebrity guest," Kelsey said. "Zeta Sanchez stonewalled the ATF for twelve hours yesterday. Now DeLeon's giving it a try. Guess Canright was expecting we'd have a confession by now. We're holding up his political career."

At that moment, the commander's door flew open. Canright stormed out, Hernandez right behind him. Their argument re-formed around the doorway, five feet away from us.

Down the other way, the interrogation room door opened too. Ana DeLeon led Zeta Sanchez out by the upper arm. The surprised guard lurched into formation behind them.

DeLeon wore a khaki Lands' End trench coat over the red dress she'd had on the night before. From her eyes and makeup and hair it was clear she'd never gone to bed.

Sanchez was dressed in orange prison scrubs and plastic sandals. His wrists were clamped together in plastic cuffs, the kind they reserve for the most violent offenders. The side of his face was swollen from DeLeon's pistol-whipping yesterday, and he sported an even newer injury—a busted lower lip that was stitched up and oozing on the left side like a bisected caterpillar. The mustache and beard made a cursive *W* around his lower face, a shape mirrored by his high hairline. His eyes were calm, sleepy. The undamaged side of his mouth crept up in a little smile that made my stomach go cold.

DeLeon walked him in our direction until Hernandez and District Attorney Canright intercepted her, right in front of Kelsey's desk. Kelsey and I stood up, making the walkway mighty cozy.

"Where are you going?" Canright demanded.

DeLeon raised her eyebrows. "The bathroom."

"The *what*?"

"He needs to pee, sir. You know—the little boys' room?"

Canright's face erupted in strawberry spots. He looked at

Hernandez, whose expression stayed neutral. Zeta Sanchez, for his part, had his eyes on DeLeon. He kept pushing the tip of his tongue suggestively against the busted side of his lip.

"Detective—" Canright started.

"We're crossing our legs here, sir." DeLeon looked at Hernandez for a green light. "My interview, my suspect, and he really needs to pee. Okay, Lieutenant?"

After a moment of silent deliberation, Lieutenant Hernandez gestured toward the exit.

"Thank you." DeLeon looked at me for the first time, dispassionately, like I was an overdue stenographer. "Walk with us."

ADA Canright's face turned even redder. "Wait just a goddamn—"

DeLeon was already pushing past.

I was almost too surprised to move but fell in line behind DeLeon and Sanchez and the deputy guard. The four of us went out the reception area of homicide, past two secretaries and a group of crying women, into the hallway.

The outer corridors of the department were tiled in green, fluorescent lit, with metal rolling equipment carts abandoned here and there and windows looking into dark rooms. It reminded me of a hospital delivery ward. We walked to the end of the hall where the vending machines and restrooms were, our heels clacking against the tiles.

When we got to the men's room door, DeLeon let loose of Sanchez's arm. "Go ahead."

Sanchez looked from her to the door, calculating.

DeLeon asked, "You need one of the guys to help you find it?"

Sanchez gave her a mildly surprised smile, as if the insult pleased him. He went inside.

The deputy started to follow but DeLeon stopped him. "That's okay."

The restroom door closed.

DeLeon leaned against the vending machine and let her posture deteriorate, her weariness have its way. She rubbed her eyes, then the back of her neck. Finally she focused her bloodshot eyes on me. "Your job is to be silent."

"Not my best role."

"You visited the Brandons, didn't you? Saw that little kid and his mom?"

"I did."

"It shows in your eyes when you look at him. The anger. Tone it down."

I hadn't even realized it until she said it, but she was right. Two minutes in Zeta Sanchez's company had eroded any doubt that the man was a murderer, that he could have walked with smugness bordering on stupidity into Aaron Brandon's home in Alamo Heights, plugged him twice with a .45, and walked out, expecting complete impunity. Looking into Sanchez's face, I stopped wondering about motive and connections and possible frame-ups. The man was loosely packaged, industrial-grade violence.

When I thought about the sheet cave in Michael Brandon's room, about Ines Brandon's tears, I wanted to wipe that little smile off what was left of Sanchez's face.

The door of the restroom opened. Sanchez came out. He looked around uncertainly, like he himself couldn't believe he hadn't tried to make a break for it.

DeLeon clucked her tongue disapprovingly. "I didn't hear water running."

Sanchez took a moment to focus on her and register the comment. "What?"

"You didn't wash your hands."

The hardness in his eyes diluted with confusion. "*What?*"

DeLeon sighed, looked at me, then back at Sanchez like a mother with strained patience. "I might have to shake your hand later, Anthony, and I know where it's been. Go back and wash your hands."

He stared at DeLeon, then at the bathroom door. Then

he went back in. This time we heard water running. The shudder of pipes as the faucet shut off. The printing-press sound of the towel roll dispenser being pulled down to fresh cloth.

Our deputy guard looked at the floor, shook his head, muttered something about a waste of time.

Sanchez came back out. He showed DeLeon his clean hands, the webbing between his fingers still glistening with water and soap foam. He looked at DeLeon with intense curiosity, as if he was really interested in what she'd say.

"Okay." She started to lead us back down the hall, then stopped abruptly, turned back, and almost ran into Sanchez. "You want a Snickers?"

Sanchez hesitated, shook his head cautiously.

"No?" DeLeon looked at me with the same question, but her eyes were giving me a dead courtesy, an act. I shook my head.

She tried again with Sanchez. "Peanuts? M&M's? You got to be hungry."

Sanchez wavered. "Peanuts."

DeLeon held out her hand to the deputy and tapped her fingertips against her palm. The deputy grumbled, then fished around in his pockets until he came up with some quarters. DeLeon bought Sanchez some peanuts.

We walked back down the hall and into the homicide division. As we passed Hernandez's office a new, calmer conversation was taking place inside—Hernandez, Kelsey, Canright. The three men's eyes fixed on us like sniper sites as we walked past. They noticed the peanuts.

When we got to the interrogation room, DeLeon waved Sanchez and me inside. She told the deputy to stay by the door.

The room was the size of a closet, walls painted the same homicide gray as outside. There were two hardwood chairs and a little desk with a computer terminal, some manila folder files, a tape recorder. Zeta Sanchez sat in one chair. At DeLeon's insistence I took the other, next to the terminal. My chair had one leg that was slightly shorter than the others. When I moved it went *bimp-bump* like a wooden heartbeat.

Sanchez strained his wrists against the plastic cuffs, trying to get some circulation. With difficulty he opened his peanuts and emptied the bag into his mouth.

DeLeon reached over and punched RECORD on the cassette machine. She gave today's date and all of our names, then leaned back against the door frame. "So, where were we?"

Sanchez chewed his peanuts. DeLeon hugged the elbows of her khaki coat, pushing the side of one red pump against the tile floor. I found myself shifting in my uneven chair. *Bimp-bump.*

Finally Sanchez swallowed. He crumpled his peanut bag, let it drop. "We weren't nowhere."

DeLeon nodded. "That's right. You know who this is here, Anthony?"

Sanchez avoided looking at me.

DeLeon waited.

When Sanchez finally met my eyes I tried to suppress any emotion. I went blank, the way I do in tai chi, forcing my thoughts to sink into my diaphragm.

Sanchez's eyes were gold. They had an unreal quality to them—a brilliant and completely merciless sheen. I suddenly understood why his old boss Jeremiah would've gifted this man a gold-plated .45.

"This is Dr. Navarre," DeLeon said. "He's the new English professor out at UTSA, replacing Aaron Brandon. I want you to apologize to him."

"You want me to what?"

"Navarre thinks you want to kill him. He's been losing

sleep over it. Guy's an English prof—figures you scared one of his predecessors to death already, blasted the second one. He figures you've got a thing against UTSA and now you've got it in for him."

Sanchez's eyes drifted up to the ceiling. The thin beard line around his jaw, trimmed under his chin, looked like some kind of black bird. He had a scar across his neck that I hadn't noticed before—a beige line the texture of jute. His smile started to re-form. He tried to control it, then broke out in a laugh.

He looked at both of us, sharing his cold mirth. "Say what?"

"Apologize for scaring him so bad," DeLeon said. "That's all. Tell him it's okay."

Sanchez shook his head, grinning in a dazed kind of way. "You want me to say I'm sorry. For a bastard I didn't kill."

"You want a lawyer present yet?" DeLeon asked.

"I don't want nothing."

"Just checking. Apologize, Anthony."

He laughed, looked at her for several seconds to see if she would keep the straight face. She did. That just amused him more. He looked at me and his golden eyes sparkled. "Yeah, man. Sorry."

He bent over, the laugh bordering on the hysterical now. He shook for a while, wiped his eyes with the backs of his bound hands.

I sat perfectly still.

"That's fine," DeLeon told him. "Now let's see if we can clear away some of these details, just so Professor Navarre feels better. We've agreed that you didn't kill Aaron Brandon, right?"

Sanchez sat up, laughed a little more.

"Right?"

He nodded.

"Okay. So last night we found a .45 three blocks away from Brandon's house, stuck in a drainage ditch. We got a match to the bullets that killed Aaron Brandon. The gun has one of your thumbprints just inside the revolver chamber. We got a witness who saw you coming out of the Brandons' house the night of the murder, after she heard two shots . . ."

DeLeon shook her head, like she was annoyed with the evidence, then looked at Sanchez for help. "You make sense of any of that, seeing as you didn't kill anybody?"

His gold eyes kept their amusement. "Nobody saw me there, 'cause I wasn't. You plant a gun, say it's mine—I can't do shit about that."

"It was a revolver, Anthony. A gold-plated revolver."

Sanchez's face darkened. "You fuckers couldn't—"

He stopped himself.

DeLeon waited. "We fuckers couldn't what, Anthony—have that revolver? The one you killed Jeremiah Brandon with six years ago? And why would that be?"

No answer.

DeLeon stepped over to the table and grabbed a folder, slid a piece of paper out of it and dropped it onto Sanchez's crotch.

"I was wondering why you came back now, Anthony, why you waited so long—at least now we got the answer to that. How was prison in Mexico?"

Sanchez looked down at the discharge document. I could read the words *Nuevo Leon, Sistema Penitenciario Federal,* Mexican state seals on either side.

"I show you sometime," Sanchez offered to DeLeon.

"That throat-slitting just about heal, did it? I hear the other guy looked even worse."

Sanchez just smiled.

DeLeon retrieved the paper with two fingers, slid it back into the folder, and tossed it onto the table. "Why'd you go to Hector Mara's, Anthony?"

Sanchez licked his lips. "We're friends, man. Old *compadres*."

"And relatives. Oh, sorry. Ex-relatives. I mean, until that little thing between your wife and Jeremiah Brandon. What was her name—Sandra? What is that legally, when your wife skips town because she's been sleeping with your boss, then you go and kill the boss? Does that constitute a legal divorce?"

Sanchez's neck muscles worked into knots, but he said nothing.

"You knew we'd be looking for you, Anthony, right? Even before you killed Aaron. Why stay with your old buddy Hector, visit your old hangouts, talk to old friends like you've been doing? Why keep such a high profile?"

"Just wanted to settle some things, man. That's all."

"Like killing the Brandons?"

Sanchez didn't respond.

"Hey, Anthony, you know, I'd like to think you weren't stupid. I'd like to think you didn't shoot Aaron Brandon. I really would. I mean it's embarrassing—using a weapon you fucking well know will get traced back to you, ditching it so sloppy, leaving a witness. I'd like to think somebody set you up for this to get you out of circulation—somebody who's been holding on to your gun all this time and found it a lot easier to shoot an English teacher than to shoot you. Tell me that's the way it is, Anthony. Maybe I can help."

"Fuck you, missy."

"You're not helping me believe you're smart, Anthony. You shot a cop when we tried to bring you in. Even without the Aaron Brandon murder, you're not making much of a show for brains."

"I hear that fat fuck Gerson's voice, I'm gonna empty a few clips at him. That's the smart thing."

DeLeon held up her hands in exasperation. "You're not

helping at all, Anthony. Look at Dr. Navarre—he's practically peeing in his pants."

Sanchez looked at me and we locked eyes a second too long. There was nothing I could do about it. The signal went out. A moment of clear, silent hostility passed between us as hotly charged and unintentional as a thousand-volt arc through a squirrel.

Detective DeLeon tried to get his attention back. "Yo, Anthony. How did Dr. Brandon get dead with your gun if you didn't kill him?"

Reluctantly, Sanchez's eyes drifted away from mine. "*No mas,* missy. That's all I'm saying."

"You were set up?"

Sanchez shook his head noncommittally.

"But you're innocent."

"Fuckin' A, missy. *Por vida.*"

"Well shit." She looked at me. "So they're going to put Mr. Sanchez away for murder—but I can't tell you for sure he's the man that killed your predecessor. Might still be somebody out there, laughing their ass off that Mr. Sanchez was willing to take the rap. Sorry, Dr. Navarre. Conclusion of interview."

She reached over to the machine, punched STOP.

"That it?" Sanchez asked.

DeLeon nodded. "Why're you letting them do this to you, Anthony?"

Sanchez brushed his fingers over the stitches on his busted lip. "I ain't letting nobody do shit." He focused on me again. "So you a professor?"

"That's right."

He grinned. "You know how they say, you got blood on your hands once you kill somebody?"

"I know how they say that. Yeah."

"Let me see your hands."

It would've been a mistake to look at DeLeon. Or to

hesitate. Never mind that we were in the middle of SAPD with an armed guard outside and Sanchez in plastic cuffs. The moment was dangerous.

I extended my right hand. Sanchez took it, turned it over, traced my life line. My skin crawled. His thumb was warm and callused and his frayed cuticle scraped against my palm. The fingers of his other hand tightened around my knuckles.

"It ain't in the hands." His breath smelled of peanuts. "You kill somebody, it shows in your eyes—eyes like you got. You really scared of me, Professor?"

He moved quick. Almost too quick. His cuffed hands clamped on my wrist like a vise grip and yanked me down, my face toward his head. If I'd tried to pull back I would've gotten a broken nose. Instead I dropped sideways out of my chair, flipping Sanchez over me in a somersault. He tumbled, slammed into DeLeon's legs, and I back-fisted Sanchez's busted mouth with my free hand as he went down.

I got up slowly. DeLeon had Sanchez's neck in a lock. The deputy was there, his gun in Zeta's face.

Sanchez had trouble coughing with his jaw clamped shut. A long string of saliva and blood swung from his lip.

DeLeon moved away while the guard pulled Sanchez roughly to his feet.

Sanchez managed a grin. "Feel good, puhfeffoh? Tell them they ain't getting ffit from me, okay? You tell them."

The guard dragged Sanchez out of the room, the felon's mouth a bloody, smiling piece of wreckage.

DeLeon sighed wearily as the door clicked closed. She rubbed the side of her face. "Thanks."

"*Thanks?*"

"That was more than they got out of him in twelve hours yesterday. He needed an audience, someone to show off for. For him, that interview was a major success."

I looked at the back of my hand, where Zeta's saliva was

still wet, matting my hair to the skin in dark slick trian-
gles that smelled of peanuts and blood. My skin crawled. I
felt as if I'd just gotten a big sloppy lick from a mastiff
who could just as easily have ripped my throat out.

"Happy to help," I told DeLeon.

NINETEEN

"You got evidence," Assistant D.A. Canright said. "Solid witness, ballistics, prints. You got a suspect any jury in their right minds would convict. You did great, Ana, okay? Be happy."

DeLeon did not look happy.

I was sitting at a desk about fifteen feet away, pretending I wasn't paying attention and still needed to be there with the ice pack on my hand. Lieutenant Hernandez had met my eyes several times, but I think he was already so disgusted with me he'd stopped caring.

DeLeon said, "I want to follow up."

Canright ran skinny white fingers through his red hair, shot a look at Hernandez. "Am I not being clear? Ana, honey, am I not being clear?"

"My last name is DeLeon."

Canright made a cup with his hands. "This guy shot an innocent man in his home, Ana. A college professor, husband, father. Then he shot a cop. I don't need a 'why' to nail his ass in court. You took him down. Your first homicide case—you did great. Now it's mine."

"Let me explain it another way, sir." DeLeon took her notepad and pen from her overcoat. She wrote as she said, "I'm. Not. Done. Honey."

She underlined the words, tore off the sheet, and tried to tuck it into Canright's coat.

The ADA stepped back, brushing her hand away. "All right, Ana. That's it. That's *it*."

"Mr. Canright—"

"Detective," Hernandez intervened. "You're up for cold-case duty. Starting Monday we rotate you in for three months. Between now and then you should get some rest."

"Lieutenant—"

Hernandez turned toward Kelsey, who was leaning against a nearby partition. "Take care of what Mr. Canright needs for court. Follow up."

Kelsey smiled. "My pleasure." He drifted back toward his cubicle.

Canright nodded with dry approval. He turned to say something else to DeLeon, probably something appeasing.

Lieutenant Hernandez said, "Good-bye, Mr. Canright. We'll keep you apprised."

Canright closed his mouth, nodded. When he got to the doorway he couldn't stand it. He turned and called, "You did an excellent job, Ana, honey. I mean that."

The homicide office sucked up the sound of his voice. Everything returned to quiet neutral gray as soon as the door swung closed.

DeLeon crumpled her note and dropped it at Hernandez's feet.

"Ana," Hernandez said, "they want a quick resolution. They smell blood. You're a district attorney, you don't see a two-plus-two case like this and beat your head against a wall trying to figure out how you can make it come up five."

"God damn it, Lieutenant—"

"You don't wait for the media to tear you apart for inaction. You prosecute."

"It's incomplete. Canright knows it. You know it."

"It's open-and-shut. Even if it wasn't—you really want to fight for a douche bag like Sanchez?"

She turned to go.

Hernandez said, "Wait."

DeLeon looked back at him icily.

"Between now and Monday, you get no new cases. I stand by what I said—Monday it's the cold squad, before then it's some rest. That doesn't preclude wrapping up your present caseload. As long as it's low-key and quick. Not too taxing on you. I want you fresh for Monday. You understand me?"

The intensity in DeLeon's eyes eased up a bit. "Yes, sir."

"Discreet. Low-key. Nothing that might give Mr. Canright apoplexy."

DeLeon allowed herself a tired smile. "I understand, Lieutenant."

As DeLeon walked away, Hernandez looked around to see who was watching. He met my eyes again, pretended he hadn't, then returned to his office.

I found DeLeon's cubicle at the end of the room, next to one of the sergeants' offices. The sergeant was apparently on vacation. His glass door was closed, the lights off, a woodcut GONE FISHIN' sign hung over the shade.

DeLeon was sitting in her task chair, the Lands' End trench coat shed over it like melted Swiss, her pumps kicked onto the carpet. She stared momentarily at something taped to her computer screen, then bent forward and buried her face in her forearms.

I leaned against the side of her cubicle.

The back of DeLeon's red dress had unzipped itself about an inch at the collar. Three tiny lines of soft hair ran down her neck from the sharp wedge-cut, like jet trails.

"Buy you some dinner?" I asked.

She opened the top eye and peered at me wearily. "Don't you ever go away?"

She sat up, rubbed her eyes, then refocused on the thing taped to her monitor. It was a Polaroid of a stuffed longhorn doll—Bevo, the UT mascot. An anonymous white male

•

hand was holding the muzzle of a .38 against its head. A little handwritten sign under the longhorn's chin said PLEASE MOMMY BRING THEM DOUGHNUTS OR THEY'LL VENTILATE ME!! The writing was intentionally childlike and the bull's goofy cartoon grin didn't fit his predicament. On top of DeLeon's monitor, a circle of dust-free space marked the spot where the longhorn had probably sat.

DeLeon yanked the Polaroid off the computer screen. "Bastards."

"Locker-room humor."

"Oh, yeah. Me and the boys—we're tight. We snap each other's butts with towels all the time."

I tried not to picture that. "Be a lot worse if they just ignored you."

"You're just the expert on everything, aren't you, Navarre? You and your friend Mr. Air-Force-Special-Police."

"About last night—"

"Save it."

She began shuffling papers with a vengeance, clearing her IN box, taking down little stickie notes and division memos that adorned the fabric walls.

As the first layer of paper came down, personal stuff was unearthed—a photo of DeLeon getting awarded her detective's shield, a framed B.S. in criminal justice from UT, a picture of her as an air force cadet.

Two things surprised me. One was a photocopy of a Pablo Neruda love poem, *"Te Recuerdo Como Eras."* The other was a tiny framed picture of a female police officer who looked like a heavier, lighter-skinned version of Ana DeLeon. By the color of the photo and the style of the woman's hair and uniform, I placed the photo circa 1975.

"Your mom?"

DeLeon glanced at it, then shoved another folder across her desk. "Yes."

She kept sorting papers, her eyes glassy.

"You okay?"

She glared at me, then pulled a color photo out of a case file and flicked it up at me with two fingers. "This is how okay I am."

All I saw in the photograph at first were glaring browns and reds. Then my mind made sense of the shapes and I pulled back, repulsed. It was a young child, African American, murdered and displayed in a way my mind comprehended but refused to process into complete thoughts.

"Jesus."

She slid the picture back into the file. "Good thing I was called away from our wonderful evening. Between the Brandon case and a couple of other things the Night CID couldn't handle I got *that* lovely call. Girl was three."

I swallowed, closed my eyes. The image wouldn't go away.

"No mystery," DeLeon said. "What was it the lieutenant said, a two plus two? Stepdad was a crack addict. Started yelling at the mom because she was stealing his money. It went downhill from there. Young victims. That's why I got out of sex crimes. Now here I am again—*otra vez.*"

DeLeon focused on her blank computer screen. "So what am I supposed to do? I'm supposed to get things in order and take a couple of days off. Simple."

"Hernandez is in a tough spot. Sure you don't want to catch some dinner?"

"Hernandez does what he can. And yes, I'm sure."

"If you needed a little help on the Sanchez follow-up—"

"I'd what? Share information with you? And every damn private investigator in town would be knocking on my door anytime he needed help. The newspapers would be screaming about how we couldn't handle our own cases. No thanks."

"We want the same answers."

"Great. You find out something on your own, come in and make another statement. That's all you are, Navarre: another witness with a statement."

"That why you brought me into the interrogation room?"

She paused. "It was a gamble."

"Gamble again. I have a friend who might help. People don't like talking to cops, they might talk to my friend."

"I don't like your friend."

"I don't mean George Bertón."

"Neither do I. I know about Ralph Arguello."

I'd heard police officers speak Ralph's name many times, never lovingly, but DeLeon's tone held a lot more poison than I would've expected.

"You've had the pleasure of Ralph's acquaintance?"

She shot me another cold look, but underneath something was crumbling, eroding. "Will you get out of here, please?"

"Here's an idea. I'll ask if you're giving me a firm 'no' on poking around about the Brandon murder. You don't respond. I'll take that as a silent, completely off-the-record consent and we'll go from there. I'll keep you posted. So how about it—can I look around on the Brandon murder?"

"No."

"You're not getting the subtle innuendo routine, here." She raised her voice a half octave. "Just go."

"Get some sleep one of these days, okay?"

"Leave."

I left her at her desk, shuffling through files and photos with what looked like aimlessness. A shudder went through my nervous system, the aftershock from the photo of the murdered child. I found myself reviewing lines from the Neruda love poem on DeLeon's cubicle wall, wondering how it had made its way there amid the paperwork of violence—"I Remember You As You Were."

I made a beeline out of the neutral gray and the fluorescents of SAPD homicide, heading toward the outside—toward smells and color and moving time. I wanted to see if it was nighttime yet. I had a feeling it might be.

TWENTY

Drifting along the sidewalk in front of police headquarters was the usual parade of undesirables—cons, thugs, derelicts, undercovers pretending to be derelicts, derelicts pretending to be undercovers pretending to be derelicts.

They collected here each evening for many reasons but hung around for only one. They knew as surely as those little white birds hopping around on the crocodile's back that their very proximity to the mouth of the beast made them safe.

Patrol cars were parked along West Nueva. Inside the barbed wire of the parking lot, in a circle of floodlight, five detectives in crisp white shirts and ties and side arms were having a smoke. Outside the fence a couple of cut-loose dealers were trading plea-bargain stories.

I walked across Nueva to the Dolorosa parking lot, got in the VW, and pulled onto Santa Rosa, heading north. I made the turn onto Commerce by El Mercado, then passed underneath I-10—over the Commerce Street Bridge, into the gloomy asphalt and stucco and railroad track wasteland of the West Side.

Ahead of me, the sunset faded to an afterglow behind palm trees and Spanish billboards. Turquoise and pink walls of icehouses and bail bond offices lost their color. On the broken sidewalks, men in tattered jeans and checkered shirts milled around, their faces drawn from an unsuccessful day of waiting, their eyes examining each car in the fading hope that someone might slow down and offer them work.

I turned north on Zarzamora and found the place where Jeremiah Brandon had died a mile and a half up, squatting between two muddy vacant lots just past Waverly. Patches of blue stucco had flaked off its walls, but the name was still visible in a single red floodlight—POCO MAS—stenciled between two air-conditioner units that hung precariously from the front windows.

The building was tall in front, short in back, with side walls that dropped in sections like a ziggurat. Tejano music seeped through the hammered tin doorway.

Two pickup trucks, a white Chevy van, and an old Ford Galaxie were parked in the gravel front lot. I pulled the VW around the side, into the mud between a Camry with flat tires and a LeBaron with a busted windshield, and hoped I hadn't just discovered the La Brea tar pit of automobiles.

The rest of the block was lined with closed *tiendas* and burglar-barred homes. Crisscrossed telephone lines and pecan tree branches sliced up the sky. The only real light came from the end of the block across the street—the Church of Our Lady of the Mount. Its Moorish, yellow-capped spires were brutally lit, a dark bronze Jesus glaring down from on high at the Poco Mas. Jesus was holding aloft a circle of metal that looked suspiciously like a master's whip. Or perhaps a hubcap rim.

At the entrance to the cantina, I was greeted by a warm blast of air that smelled like an old man's closet—leather and mothballs, stale cologne, dried sweat and liquor. Inside, the rafters glinted with Christmas ornaments. Staple-gunned along the walls were decades of calendars showing off Corvettes with bras and women without. The jukebox cranked out Selena's *"Quiero"* just loud enough to drown casual conversation and the creaking my boots must've made on the warped floor planks.

I got a momentary, disapproving once-over from the patrons at the three center tables. The men were hard-faced Latinos, most in their forties, with black cowboy hats and steel-toed boots. The few women were overweight and trying hard to pretend otherwise—tight red dresses and red hose, peroxide hair, large bosoms, and chunky faces heavily caked with foundation and rouge designed for Anglo complexions. Long neck beer bottles and scraps of bookie numbers littered the pink and white Formica.

On a raised platform in back were two booths, one empty, one occupied by a cluster of young *locos*—bandannas claiming their gang colors, white tank tops, baggy jeans laced with chains, scruffy day beards. One had a Raiders jacket. Another had a porkpie hat and a pretty young Latina on his lap. The girl and I locked eyes long enough for Porkpie to notice and scowl.

Then I recognized someone else.

Hector Mara, Zeta Sanchez's ex-brother-in-law, was talking to another man at the bar.

Mara wore white shorts and Nikes and a black Spurs tunic that said ROBINSON. His egg-brown scalp reflected the beer lights.

Mara's friend was thinner, taller, maybe thirty years old, with a wiry build and a high hairline that made his thin face into a valentine. He had a silver cross earring and black-painted fingernails, a black trench coat and leather boots laced halfway up his calves. He'd either been reading too much Anne Rice or was on his way to a *bandido* Renaissance festival.

A line of empty beer bottles stood in front of the two men. Mara's face was illuminated by the little glowing screen of a palm-held computer, which he kept referring to as he spoke to the vampire, like they were going over numbers.

I climbed onto the third bar stool next to Mara, and

spoke to the bartender loud enough to be heard over Selena. *"Cerveza, por favor."*

Mara and the vampire stopped talking.

The bartender scowled at me. His face was puffy with age, his hair reduced to silver grease marks over his ears. "Eh?"

"Beer."

He squinted past me suspiciously, as if checking for my reinforcements.

Hector Mara just stared at me. Huge loops of armhole showed off his well-muscled shoulders, swirls of tattoos on his upper arms, thick tufts of underarm hair. He had an old gunshot scar like a starburst just above his left knee. The vampire stared at me, too. He clicked his black fingernails against the bar. Friendly crowd.

"Unless you've got a special tonight," I told the bartender. "Manhattan, maybe?"

The bartender reached into his cooler, opened a bottle, then plunked a Budweiser in front of me.

"Or beer is fine," I said.

"Eh?"

I made the "okay" sign, dropped two dollars on the counter. Without hesitating, the old man got out a second beer and plunked it next to the first.

I was tempted to put down a twenty and see what he'd do. Instead I slid one of the Buds toward Hector Mara.

"Maybe your friend could go commune with the night for a few minutes?" I suggested.

Mara's face was designed for perpetual anger—eyes pinched, nose flared, mouth clamped into a scowl. "I know you?"

"I saw Zeta today."

Mara and the vampire exchanged looks. The vampire studied my face one more time, memorizing it, then detached himself from the bar. He flicked his fingers toward the *cholos* in the back booth and they all lifted their chins. The vampire walked out.

I watched him get into the white Chevy van and drive away.

"Yo, gringo," Hector Mara said. "You got any idea who you just offended?"

"None. Much more fun that way. Although if I was guessing, I'd say it was Chich Gutierrez, your business partner."

Mara's eye twitched. "Who the fuck are you?"

"I was at that party you threw yesterday out on Green Road. The one where Zeta blew a hole in the deputy."

Mara's eyes drifted down to my boots, then made their way back up my rumpled dress clothes, my face, my uncombed hair.

"You ain't a cop," he decided.

"No."

"Then fuck off."

He pushed the beer back toward me and returned to his PalmPilot, started tapping on the screen with a little black stylus. On the jukebox, Selena segued into Shelly Lares.

I looked at the bartender. "*Donde esta* the famous spot?"

"Eh?"

"The place where Zeta Sanchez killed Jeremiah Brandon."

The bartender waved his hands adamantly. "No, no. New management."

He said it like a foreign phrase he'd been trained to speak in an emergency.

Mara pointed over his shoulder with the stylus. "Second booth, gringo. The one that's always empty."

The bartender mumbled halfheartedly about the change of management, then retreated to his liquor display and began turning the bottles label-out.

"The D.A.'s going to prosecute," I told Mara.

"Big surprise."

"They figure ten to ninety-nine for shooting the deputy, life for Aaron Brandon's murder, maybe federal charges for the bomb blast. Quick and easy. That's before they even consider the Old Man's murder case from '93."

"*Hijo de puta* like you gonna love that."

"And who am I?"

A stripe of green neon drifted across Mara's forehead as he turned toward me. His eyes burned with loathing. "Reporter. Got to let those nervous gringos see the right headline, huh? *Mexican Convicted for Alamo Heights Murder.*"

I pulled out one of my Erainya Manos Agency cards, slid it across the counter. "What if I thought Sanchez was framed?"

Mara's bad-ass expression melted as soon as he saw the card. He looked from it to me. "The guy in the Panama hat."

"George Bertón."

Mara pushed the card away, then leaned far enough toward me so I could smell the beer on his breath.

"I told your friend," he hissed. "I said I'd *think* about it. All right? Don't push me."

I tried to stay poker-faced. It wasn't easy.

"Sure," I said. "I was just in the neighborhood. Thought I'd check back."

Mara sniffed disdainfully. He gestured toward the back of the room and the screen of his PalmPilot flashed like mercury. "You see the *locos* in the corner? No, man, I don't mean *look* at them. They'll think you want trouble. Those are Chich's boys. His younger set. You think I'm going to sit here and talk friendly with them watching us, you're crazy."

"Make small talk. Were you in this place the night Jeremiah Brandon got shot?"

"I—" Hector looked down at the bar. "No. I missed it. Most righteous thing that ever happened in this place."

"I can understand why you'd think that."

"Oh, you can."

"The old man had an affair with your sister."

"Affair, shit. Raped, used, sent Sandra away when she was so shamed and scared there wasn't no choice. Like a whole bunch of girls before her. I never even saw her—not a good-bye, nothing."

"Hard."

"You don't know about hard. Now you need to leave."

"Tell me about Sandra."

Hector Mara hefted his PalmPilot. "I got a salvage yard to manage, gringo. Books to balance. Don't help when the fucking police keep me tied up the whole day, neither. Why don't you leave me alone?"

Hector tried to ignore me. He started writing.

I drank my beer. Behind us, Shelly Lares sang about her broken *corazón*.

"Was Sandra happy married to Sanchez?"

Hector's PalmPilot clattered on the bar. "*Chingate.* What the fuck you want, man? Why do you care?"

"I like annoying you, Hector. It's so easy."

Hector stared at me.

I pointed my bottle at him and fired off a round.

"You fucking insane, gringo."

"Tell me about your sister and I'll leave."

Hector glanced across the room. The men at the tables were bragging about greyhound races. One of the *locos* at the back booth laughed and the pretty Latina squealed in protest. They didn't seem to be paying us much mind.

Hector Mara curled his large brown fingers into his palm one at a time. Tattoos of swords and snakes on his inner arm rippled. "You want the story? I claimed a rival set to Zeta Sanchez when I was fourteen. Chich Gutierrez, he was one of my older *vatos*. We were a shitty little set but we thought we were bad. Then one night Zeta and some of his homeboys cornered me at the Courts, said I could die or switch claims. If I switched, I could tell them where to shoot me."

"Your leg," I guessed.

He nodded, traced his fingers over the scar tissue above his knee.

"I did that for one reason, man. I looked at Sanchez and I knew he had the kind of rep I needed for me, my family. Once I was down with Zeta, I got respect. My kid sister Sandra got respect. People left her alone. That was important to me, gringo. Real important."

Hector looked at me to see how I was taking the story so far, maybe to see if the gringo was laughing at him inside.

Apparently I passed the test.

"Sandra wanted to be a poet," Hector said. "You believe that? She never claimed no girl posses when we lived in the Courts. Couldn't stand up for herself. Me claiming Sanchez was all that saved her. Then when we were about sixteen, our mom got busted for dealing. Me and Sandra moved out to my grandmother's place."

"The property on Green Road."

Mara nodded. "For a couple of years I had this stupid idea maybe Sandra was going to make it. Farm life. New school. Perfect for her. She never got into trouble. Made it all the way through high school. Even started college before Zeta got interested in her, you know—in a new way. Zeta decided it was a good match."

"And was it?"

Hector turned his beer bottle in a slow circle. "Zeta was old-fashioned. Didn't want his wife going to college. But he was good to Sandra. Looked out for her."

"You believe that?"

More silence. "She and Zeta would've worked things

out, wasn't for the Brandons. After the Old Man caught her, she didn't have no choice but to take his money and run. Sanchez would've killed her for what she did, her fault or not. But, man—it could've been different for her. She almost made it out."

"And you?"

"What about me?"

"Did you make it out?"

Hector smiled sourly. He dabbed his finger in the circle of sweat at the base of his beer, smeared a line of water away from the bottle. "I'm a man. Ain't the same for me."

"You decided to keep living on your grandmother's property. Those chickens in the coop, the garden—those things require maintenance. Somebody cares about that place."

"Go home, gringo. Quit while you're ahead."

"Zeta's gun—the gold revolver. He left it with you."

The sour smile faded. "Say what?"

"The gun didn't go south with Zeta. He should've ditched it, but for some reason he couldn't throw away that gift from Jeremiah Brandon. He left the gun in San Antonio with somebody—I'm guessing you. The fact that police found it near Aaron Brandon's house is important. You see?"

Mara's eyes darkened to a dangerous shade. "Be careful, gringo."

" 'Cause the thing is, Hector, if somebody was to frame Zeta, you'd be in a good position to do it. What with Zeta staying at your place and all, and you doing business with Sanchez's old rival Chich."

"I told your friend in the goddamn Panama hat—"

"Yeah, I know. You told George you'd think about it. All I'm saying is maybe you should think a little harder. Let us hear from you."

Hector studied me for another stanza of Shelly Lares,

then reassembled his cold smile. "You'll hear from me, gringo. Now *lo siento,* eh? I got to do this now to keep appearances."

Then he got up and pushed me off my stool as hard as he could.

I went toppling backward and on the way down managed to connect just about every part of my body with something hard and wooden. I landed with the seat of the stool in my gut, my left leg laced through the spokes. The floor was sticky. A beer bottle cap was pressed into my palm.

Mara stood over me. The crowd was silent, waiting for a fight.

Mara disappointed them.

"Be cool to the homies, gringo," he told me. "Stick around. See how long before they drag you out with the trash."

He grabbed his PalmPilot and walked toward the exit, the old gunshot wound making his gait only slightly stiff. The *locos* in the corner laughed at my expense.

I got up, dusted myself off.

In the reflection of the hammered tin, I watched Hector Mara getting into his old Ford Galaxie and pulling out of the lot.

When someone humiliates you in a bar, you don't really have a choice. You've got to sit back down and finish your drink, just to prove you can. So I did.

I listened to another Shelly Lares tune. I thought about George Bertón, tried to remind myself that George was a big boy who knew what he was doing, and he'd just yell at me for interfering if I called him now. I thought about Hector Mara's initiation to Zeta Sanchez's set until my leg started to ache. I looked at the little red circle the beer bottle cap had bitten into my palm and thought about a hundred other places I would rather be than the Poco Mas.

Then another round of laughter erupted at the *locos'* table in the back and I decided I might as well add insult to injury.

I grabbed the Budweiser that Hector Mara had refused and went to talk to a girl I knew.

TWENTY-ONE

Her name was Mary. The last time I'd seen her, just before Christmas, Ralph Arguello and I had rescued her from an underage prostitution ring by throwing her pimp off the Navarro Street Bridge. Her liberation had been one of the only good by-products from my search for a rich client's runaway daughter.

Mary was wearing tonight what she'd worn back in December, which was a bad sign—partially unbuttoned denim dress, black hose, thick-soled pumps, way too much makeup in an effort to conceal her fifteen years. Her hair poured down either side of her pretty face like slow-motion loops of caramel in a candy bar commercial. Her ankles were crossed and her shoulders tensed as she sat on the young man's lap and watched me walk up to the booth.

I looked at the guy in the porkpie hat. "I need to talk with your lap-warmer for a minute."

Porkpie stared at me, his mouth spreading into a dazed grin, like he'd just gotten a much bigger birthday present than he expected. "That a fact?"

His three friends in the booth watched, waiting for some kind of cue. The one with the Raiders jacket could've been carrying just about anything underneath. I tried not to dwell on that.

I set my Budweiser on their table, then held out my hand for Mary. "That's a fact."

Mary's face was deadly calm except for her eyes, which

kept trying to warn me off. She didn't want to come with me, but she knew better than to stay between me and Porkpie. She took my hand, slid off the guy's lap and onto the floor next to me.

"The bar," I told her.

"Hey, *chica*," Porkpie said. "You figure he'll take a whole minute?"

"Push him off his stool," one of his friends suggested.

The others laughed.

Mary brushed past me, her eyes still trying to give me a warning. I took back my beer and started to follow.

To my surprise, the boys didn't make a move.

I kept walking, the skin on my back tingling, my feet sensitive to any bump or dip in the floorboards behind me.

Mary perched on the stool where Hector Mara had sat, her legs crossed, her fingernails resting upright like talons on the stained oak counter. When I sat down next to her she leaned forward and whispered harshly, "Jesus, Tres. You trying to get me killed?"

"What are you doing out here, Mary? You told Ralph—"

Mary hissed: "Shut up!" then pursed her lips, closed her eyes tight like she was trying to retract the statement.

The skin below her eyes was dotted with extra mascara. Her babyish cheeks were clown-red, her lips pouty and slick with lipstick. "I got a little behind with some payments, is all. Don't make a big deal out of it. Buy me a beer, at least."

"You're fifteen."

She burst into a laugh as brief and violent as her anger. "So? Come on, Tres. You're cool."

"You want me to get you out of here?"

"I was fine until you messed me up. You know them guys—"

As if on cue, Porkpie slid out of the booth. He swaggered in our direction, pushed with needless force past a couple of the older guys at the tables, then came toward me. His friends threw out encouraging comments.

His arms were lean and smooth, his face round. The wispy black fuzz around his chin was the only testament to his graduation from puberty. He walked in an imitation of the joint walk of ex-cons, a gait he had neither the weight nor the muscles for.

"Yo, *pendejo,* minute's up. Little mama got to put out more better than that for me, man."

He leered at Mary, gestured for her to come away.

"Go back and sit down," I told him.

He gave me vacant eyes, a wide smile, his thoughts already retreating into his chest in a prebattle mode I recognized well. I saw the tension in his left hand, knew that he was about to impress me with a weapon-draw he'd probably practiced in his bedroom mirror a thousand times.

When the switchblade came out of his back pocket, flashing up in an arc toward my nose, I already had the rhythm of the move. My hand followed his wrist, caught it from underneath halfway, then pulled it toward me, dragging his arm across the counter between Mary and me.

Porkpie's armpit slammed against the bar. With my free hand I pressed his cheek down onto the sticky oak, crumpling his hat into a felt wad. My other thumb dug into the nerves of his wrist until the knife clattered free, falling somewhere behind the bar. The old bartender started waving his arms at me, protesting about the new management.

I let go of Porkpie's head and fished the gun out of his huge pants pocket before he could get to it. I flipped him around so he was facing his friends. I had his hand twisted up between his shoulder blades and his own Taurus P-11 pressed against his ear.

His friends were half standing, half crouching in their booth seats. All three had guns drawn—a nine, a .38. The guy with the Raiders jacket had drawn something that looked like a miniature AK-47. Nice kids.

"It's the need to show off," I said in Porkpie's ear. His

face smelled like an autoshop. "You got this nice ten-shot and you have to scare me with the switchblade routine first. That won't earn you the big money from Chich."

"Fuck you." His voice was tight as a rivet.

Mary sat completely frozen. So did three tables full of patrons between me and the kids with the guns.

"Tell your homeboys to put their pieces down," I said, a little louder.

Porkpie said, "You're fucking *dead.*"

I looked at the guys across the room. "I heard him say *put the guns on the table.* Did you hear that?"

Enough time passed for a line of sweat to snake its way between my shoulder blades, for Porkpie to exhale his sour breath on me six times.

His friends put their guns on the table.

I told Mary, "Outside."

"I ain't leaving," she said hoarsely.

The fear in her voice told me otherwise—that she knew who the young *locos* would take their revenge on once I was gone. I slid off my bar stool and side-walked Porkpie toward the door, his playmates' eyes drilling holes in me the whole ten feet. I waited until Mary was out the door behind me, until I heard her steps crunching over the gravel. She knew my car. I waited until she'd had enough time to find it.

Then I pushed Porkpie into the cantina, toppling him against a table and into the lap of a large woman in red. I backed out the door, dropped the P-11, and ran.

No shots rang out. No one followed. In a way, that just made me more nervous.

Once we were in the VW, driving north up Zarzamora, Mary exhaled more air than I would've thought possible for her small body to contain. "You're a fucker, Tres. Messing me up like that."

"You're welcome, Mary."

"They'll *kill* me, they see me again!"

"Sounds like a good reason not to see them again."

"You're *such* a fucker."

"How much do you need?"

"What?"

Her caramel curls were coming undone in the wind.

"I don't have much. I can give you maybe thirty in cash."

She drew her knees up on the seat and hugged them, a move a larger girl, a woman, couldn't have done. "I don't want your money."

"You wanted fuzz-face's instead?"

"Man, just lay off. Okay? You're not my dad. You're not even old enough."

Her real dad, I knew, had not been old enough to be her dad either, but I didn't bring that up.

We turned on Woodlawn and started east. "Your stepsister still live on Agarita?"

"They kicked me out, man. I don't stay there no more."

"You got a friend to stay with?"

She hugged herself a little tighter. Finally, mumbling into her knees, she gave me the address of a girl she knew near Jefferson High, a girl who was still living with her parents and going to school. "But they put me up already this month. I don't know if they'll go for it."

"They'll go for it. Call your social worker in the morning."

"Social worker don't do shit, Tres. My old man came back three times and she don't do shit, no more than my mother."

"Call Ralph, then. Promise me you'll do that."

Mary mumbled some unflattering and untrue things about why Ralph Arguello liked to help wayward girls. I chose not to respond.

Finally Mary's shoulders deflated. "Yeah. Okay. I'll call him."

We drove back toward Jefferson, into the old neighborhoods of tiled porches and palm trees and once-majestic Spanish homes that had long ago been divided into units, fitted with burglar bars. Their front yard patches of nopalita cactus were carved with gang graffiti on the oval blades. In my headlights the sidewalks and curbs glowed with spray-painted gang symbols. Pitchfork up, one block. Pitchfork down the next. Make a pitchfork hand gesture the wrong way on the wrong block and you died.

"Tres, why were you at that place tonight, talking to Hector?"

"You know him?"

She poked at her lip, then looked at the greasy spot of lipstick on her finger, wiped it on her knee. "I see him there a lot. Sometimes with Chich. Week ago he was in with this big guy with a beard and ponytail and shit—looked like a big-time dealer. Scarier than Chicharron."

"Zeta Sanchez."

She nodded hesitantly. "I didn't mess with them. The Sanchez guy was all talking about his wife, looking to find her. And the other guy, Hector, he was saying like, 'This ain't going to get you nowhere, man.' I wouldn't have talked that way to Ponytail, the way he looked."

When we got to the address on Jefferson Drive where Mary's friend lived, Mary insisted on going in by herself.

She got out of the car, then turned and leaned back in. "Hector's badder than he looks, Tres. I think you should watch it."

"What makes you say that?"

"He nearly killed this other guy I saw him talking to in the Poco Mas. Couple of weeks before. A white guy."

My throat tightened. "Who?"

The porch light of the house came on behind Mary and she said, "I gotta go."

I reached over and caught her wrist gently. "This Anglo. Describe him."

"Chunky. Dark hair. One of those orange tropical shirts. I don't know."

"You hear a name?"

"B—Branson?"

"Brandon?"

"Maybe that was it."

A woman called Mary's name from the porch and Mary winced apologetically. She leaned all the way into the car and gave me a sticky kiss on the cheek. She smelled of at least three different kinds of cheap perfume.

"Call Ralph," I told her.

She tried for a smile, then trotted up the sidewalk to meet her friend. With her back turned, without the conscious effort in her walk, she almost looked fifteen.

I pulled away from the curb, hoping the wind would push the scent of her perfume away.

TWENTY-TWO

I woke up Thursday morning in a sweat, shaking off dreams of Erainya looming over me, chastising me for not holding a Taurus P-11 correctly.

When I opened my eyes, the only one looming over me was Robert Johnson. He sat on the window ledge above the futon, the morning sun cutting across his face and making his whiskers glow like fiber-optic threads.

"Row," he announced.

"I know, I know. Breakfast."

At the magic word, he did a trampoline dismount from the window to my stomach to the floor, then showed me where the kitchen was.

Once I'd served him his Friskies, properly fried with cheese and taco meat on a bed of flour tortilla, I started some coffee and eggs for myself and pulled down the ironing board to make a call.

The answering machine was flashing again. I had no memory of the phone ringing the night before, but that was not unusual for Tres Navarre, zombie sleeper. The first message was from my mother, letting me know that everything was fine, though she had not in fact seen her insignificant-other Jess since the night they'd argued and if I wasn't too busy, did I want to go to an art opening tonight? The second was from George Bertón. George said he was sorry for not returning the calls from me and Erainya last night but he thought he might have something and he wouldn't be reachable today. Could we meet him at his house tonight?

I called George's number. Sure enough, he wasn't reachable, though his answering machine did give me a great recipe for *sopa de ajo*.

I sat down at the kitchen counter with my coffee and eggs and my stack of essays. I put on some early B.B. King to help me concentrate. This was my day to grade.

As I ate, I read the first paragraph of the first essay four times. I made one mark in the margin that said *Good point*. B.B. sang about his woman and his guitar. Robert Johnson ate his Friskies taco noisily.

I looked at the phone.

"To hell with it."

I went back to the ironing board and called SAPD. Ana DeLeon's number in homicide rang five rings, clicked, then a man's voice said, "Kelsey."

I tried to contain my excitement. I told Kelsey who I was and asked for DeLeon.

"She's not here right now, Navarre. She's getting her beauty sleep. You want to send her flowers or something, I can give you the address."

"It's about the Brandon case, Kelsey. It's important."

"So talk to me."

I tapped my red pen on the essays. "She's going to want this information, Kelsey. I mean today."

"I'm not hearing anything important yet, Navarre."

I told him about my evening at the Poco Mas, about the connection between Del Brandon and Hector Mara.

Kelsey was quiet long enough to write the information down. "Mary what?"

"Ramirez, maybe. Or Rios."

"Maybe?"

"There's about five surnames in the family. I don't remember. You can try the sister's address and the friend's. There's no guarantee she'll be at either place."

"Assuming it's worth looking. Fifteen-year-old witness, a runaway who'll do anything for a few bucks. Probably drunk when and if she saw anything—Hector Mara with some white guy with a B name and you planted the idea the name might've been Brandon. Even a public defender will laugh his ass off."

I didn't like admitting that he was right. "Substantiate the link another way."

"You don't think we've looked at Hector Mara? We spent the day together on Tuesday, Navarre. You don't think we've looked at Del Brandon? We had Del down here days ago—him and three of the best Jewish lawyers money can buy. They knew the drill, made it pretty clear we wanted to stick any shit to Del, we'd have to mix it with superglue."

I looked down at my unfinished eggs, pushed them away. "Just tell DeLeon. Mara's the key. Break him the right way, he'll talk."

"Damn, Navarre, let me write this all down. Can I share your pointers with the other guys down here in homicide? Is that okay?"

I hung up the phone.

I looked at Robert Johnson, then at the essays.

"I shouldn't go out," I told Robert Johnson.

Smack, smack. Carnivorous head shake.

"You're right. Better me than you." I put my red pen down next to his food dish. "Try to have half of them graded by the time I get back, okay?"

I got my car keys and went out to see a sick friend.

TWENTY-THREE

Ozzie Gerson's apartment was everything mine wasn't—modern, stylish, devoid of character. It sat off Thousand Oaks Drive and Highway 281 in a housing development still new enough to have the plastic multicolored pennants flapping out front and the banners that said NOW LEASING and MODEL UNITS and IF YOU LIVED HERE YOU'D BE HOME RIGHT NOW. That last had always sounded like some kind of Zen threat to me.

The neighborhood was about as far from the West Side and the Poco Mas as you could get—wide boulevards cut from the hill country, glistening with Lexuses and SUVs. New upscale strip malls with Starbucks and Le Boulanger, the Texas elements of cactus and limestone and live oak neatly carved down to median strips and parking lot entrances.

Ozzie's apartment was on the third floor of Thousand Trails Villa, overlooking the street. There was a hibachi grill and a pair of muddy police shoes on the landing and a Bexar County Sheriff's Department sticker below the door knocker. I rapped loudly, called out my name, then let myself in.

"Bedroom, Tres," Ozzie hollered. "Take off your shoes and come on back."

I looked down. Three pairs of boots were lined up neatly on a linoleum strip by the door. The rest of the living-room floor was pristine white carpet—not a grease mark or spill or streak of dirt anywhere. I put my present for Ozzie down momentarily, pulled off my boots, and left them next to Ozzie's.

Walking across the living-room carpet was like walking across marshmallow. There was a cream-colored couch and matching love seat placed at a V in front of the fireplace, a neat stack of *Handloader* and *Police Ammo* magazines on the glass coffee table next to a vase of fresh-cut bluebonnets. On the mantel were years of photos from Ozzie's ex-wife and two kids in California. The ex-wife, Ozzie'd once told me, was very dependable about sending photos every Christmas, but each one had her in it, too, along with the kids. Every year, Ozzie carefully cut her out with an X-Acto knife and inserted a picture of himself instead. The photos were odd to look at—Ozzie floating between his kids, slightly off in color and size and resolution, overlapping their Christmas Day like some alien beaming in from *Star Trek*.

The dining room was dominated by a state-of-the-art, polished oak-and-glass gun locker filled with every manner of hunting rifle and handgun. Around it were more gold-framed pictures—Ozzie with my father at our family ranch in Sabinal, standing on either side of a dead buck; a much younger, slimmer Ozzie receiving his detective's shield from my dad; Ozzie with his latest girlfriend Audrey, the large redheaded manicurist who Ozzie swore "had a shot at Miss Texas once."

I walked back to the bedroom.

Gerson was propped up in bed amid enough down comforters and pillows to break a free fall. There were two prescription bottles, a TV remote control, and a can of Sprite on the bedstand. The drapes were open and sunlight flooded in, making the daytime soap opera on TV almost impossible to see.

Ozzie looked pretty good for a man who'd recently come out of the ICU. His color was back. His upper body was bare—Buddha-belly and flabby tits and massive arms swirling in coarse black hair, an old Marines tattoo on his right biceps. His left shoulder was heavily padded and taped, but there was no hint of bleeding. Ozzie's face was its usual brutish slab of pink—a bull's visage, shaved and smiling.

"You ever watch these shows?" he demanded. "Audrey likes them. She tells me they're good—I don't know."

On the screen, a doctor was talking to a woman in a low-cut evening dress.

I placed Ozzie's present on the bedstand. "Hope you're feeling better."

His smile widened. He turned the little bonsai plant around. "What's this?"

"A tree. You said you wanted a place with trees."

He laughed. "Nicest fucking gift I've gotten so far. Not counting what Audrey gave me last night. Thanks, Navarre."

"One can't outdo Audrey."

"One sure as shit can't. Pull up a chair."

Ozzie filled me in on his condition—how he'd survived an infiltrated IV and bad hospital food, survived his first phone call from his kids in three years. How he planned on going back to light duty tomorrow over the doctors' objections. Ozzie said he'd be damned if he'd lose field hours toward his next salary review over a scumbag like Zeta Sanchez.

I was almost convinced Ozzie was really doing fine until he tried to sit up and the blood drained from his face.

"Can I help?"

"Nah. Nah." He took a few careful, slow breaths. "How about that medicine bottle though? The bigger one. Yeah. Thanks."

He downed a couple of painkillers with some Sprite, then stared at the TV. After a minute the glassiness cleared from his eyes again. "So. You screwing up the Brandon case yet?"

"Who, me?"

Ozzie gave me a crooked grin. "Your daddy would kill you. Let's hear what you've got."

I filled him in on the last two days. As he listened, Ozzie's smile faded into a hard line. His eyes drifted back to the television. "You tell Kelsey about Del Brandon and Hector Mara?"

"I told him to tell DeLeon. Kelsey didn't seem to think they could do much to establish the connection."

"He may be right."

Two feminine hygiene commercials played through.

"You worked with Kelsey before—"

"Before I got demoted," Ozzie supplied. "Yeah. Kelsey used to be on city vice. I was county gang task force. We crossed paths."

His voice was less than enthusiastic.

"You trust Kelsey?"

Ozzie worked his mouth like he was tasting the question. "This guy you saw with Hector Mara, the guy with the black fingernails and the trench coat. You know who that was?"

"Chich Gutierrez."

"Kelsey told you that?"

"No. I'd been hearing things about Hector Mara buying heroin from a guy named Chich Gutierrez. I guessed."

Ozzie didn't seem to like that. "By himself Chich would be nothing—a joke. Look at the way the guy dresses, for Christ's sake. But the fact that he's always compared himself to Sanchez, always tried to act that bad . . . it makes him unpredictable. Chich goes the extra mile to prove he's got what he hasn't got, you know? You chew on an inferiority complex like that long enough, it turns you dramatic."

"Two nights ago, Del Brandon told me Zeta Sanchez had been trying to move heroin through RideWorks back in '93. Del said that's why he was so anxious to push Zeta out of the business. You ever hear anything about that?"

Ozzie's eyes fixed on the woman in the low-cut evening dress. She was weeping and the doctor was comforting her. "You wanted to know how I got demoted. You going to get sore now if I tell you the truth?"

"Probably."

He sighed, then rested his head back in the pillows. "Fall of '92, I started having some ideas along the lines you just described. I figured you take a guy like Zeta Sanchez, with connections to the gangs, big-time access to the heroin pipeline, you put him together with a guy like old Jeremiah Brandon who's got a ready-made distribution network—things are going to happen. You use the carnival circuit, you could move a good amount of stash pretty much anywhere in the nation with very little trouble. So I started asking around."

"And something went wrong."

He looked over at me, anger simmering in his eyes. "About the same time, there was a big internal affairs bust going down. Some of the deputies working at the jail were smuggling in drugs for the prison gangs. Others were getting paid to look the other way. Sixteen deputies were fired. Five criminally prosecuted. A few higher-ranking people in the department were implicated, too, but there wasn't enough proof to fire."

"You were one of the ones implicated?"

"Forced reassignment. Three scumbag cons came forward and fingered me. Guys I had never even heard of, but you can bet your ass they all knew Zeta Sanchez. They got reduced sentences for their cooperation. I went down in the departmental housecleaning. After that, nobody listened to me much on the subject of Zeta Sanchez and RideWorks."

"There was no truth to the allegations against you?"

"I'll pretend you didn't need to ask that question."

On the television, two men in cardigans were lighting

each other's cigarette. Ozzie flicked his thumb against his forefinger, mimicking them.

"You think it's still happening?" I asked.

"What—smack running through RideWorks? Del Brandon couldn't think his way off one of his own merry-go-rounds, kid. He couldn't handle something that big."

"Hector and Chich were worried about Zeta Sanchez coming back to town. Del Brandon was too. He was also real worried about his brother Aaron, who was reading articles about how to sic the IRS on your relatives to take over a family business. Maybe Del and Hector and Chich got together and killed two birds with one stone—framed Sanchez for Aaron Brandon's murder."

Ozzie laughed. "Mr. Navarre."

"Sir?"

"You really want to get Zeta Sanchez off the hook, don't you?"

"I don't think he killed Aaron Brandon. Call me old-fashioned. I think that means we should look for whoever did."

"Guys like Zeta Sanchez—you can't go soft for them. They're Attila the rat."

"Attila the what?"

Ozzie held up the TV remote and punched the volume down to zero. "Something from when I was a kid in the fifties, down in Harlingen. I never told you this story? My mom was a waitress, worked a lot at night so she wanted to get me a pet. Only she couldn't afford a dog or anything, so she came home one night with these two dime-store rats—the little kind, one black and one white."

"Rats?"

"Yeah. Only we found out pretty quick they weren't both males. A week went by and they had a litter of little pink things, looked like grubs. My mom said we'd have to drown them, but we never did. They grew into gray adult rats, then had babies and pretty soon the babies had babies. I woke up one morning and the original two rats were gone. Nothing left but little patches of hair in the wood shavings. Their kids had eaten them. My mom didn't know what to do. The rats kept having babies, and eating them, and eating the weaker adults. Most horrible time in my childhood, waking up every morning and dreading to look in that cage, wondering what I'd find. Finally, there was only one rat left—he must've been fourth or fifth generation—and he'd eaten all the other rats. This fat, mean little fucker had made a bed out of their fur. I'm not kidding you. I named him Attila. My mom said we had to let him go, that Attila was big and mean enough to survive in the world, so we let him loose in the alley."

"That's pretty intense for a young kid."

"You won't see me keeping pets, Navarre. The thing is—every time you look at a *veterano* like Zeta Sanchez or Hector Mara, somebody who made it through the gang life and got past the age of twenty, you're looking at Attila the rat. You're looking at the end product of generations of truly efficient cannibalism. They've made themselves a bed out of all the weaker ones."

"It's not that simple."

Ozzie shook his head sadly. "What do you hear from George Bertón?"

"I'm seeing him later tonight. I get the feeling Hector Mara might be trying to tell him something."

"How do you mean?"

I told Ozzie about Hector's comments at the Poco Mas—how Hector seemed to be considering some kind of offer George had made.

Ozzie thought about that. His eyes closed. They stayed that way for half a minute before opening again. "I got to get some sleep."

"Okay."

"Let me know how it goes with George. You mind getting the drapes?"

I got them. The room dipped into cool darkness. Ozzie turned the television off.

"Thanks for the tree," Ozzie said.

I told him no problem.

"And, Tres—I owe you. Pulling me out of the line of fire the other day. Don't think I've forgotten that."

"It's okay, Ozzie."

"It's not." He shifted, tugged the covers over his bare belly. "It's not. You need anything—you need anything at all, you come find me."

"Thanks, Ozzie. I'll do that."

Gerson mumbled something I couldn't make out.

I left him in the dark, swathed in downy beige comforters, the bedroom quiet except for the ping of carbonation in his Sprite can.

I went into the living room to reclaim my boots.

TWENTY-FOUR

I wasn't planning on meeting the SWAT team at Hector Mara's farmhouse that afternoon. I just got lucky.

When I pulled over at the Y in the road where Hector's property sat, the shoulder was already crowded with police vans, lights flashing. SWAT members with black flak suits and assault rifles milled around in the road.

With typical April fickleness, the sunny morning had turned into an overcast afternoon—fiberglass-yellow clouds, air as moist and warm as dog's breath. Ana DeLeon and Kelsey were having a chat with a squad sergeant over by the banana trees as I walked up.

"Remembered the reinforcements this time, did we, Kelsey?"

Kelsey pointed at me without speaking, balled his other fist, then gestured to the SWAT sergeant to follow him. The two men walked toward the nearest patrol unit.

"Navarre." DeLeon's voice was weary with the sound of recently jettisoned adrenaline. "What do you want?"

I looked up the drive at the Mara property.

The door of the L-shaped cinder-block house had been busted off its hinges. Several of the windows were broken. SWAT members stood on the porch, a uniformed officer leaning in the doorway writing up a report. There was a similar scene at the white mobile home. They must've smashed open Hector's chicken coops, too, because the fields were now overrun with poultry. Wild bantams were pecking around the base of the apple tree. A Rhode Island Red was perched on a broken tricycle seat. There was even a rogue peacock strolling down the driveway, dragging a strip of pink toilet paper in its plumage.

"Let me guess," I said. "You followed up on my message. Mara was gone."

DeLeon wore a navy blazer and skirt and a cream blouse. In the afternoon light, her face seemed softer, her eyes not quite so severe.

"Don't flatter yourself, Navarre. What got us out here was some work by the ATF. They finished tracing the Solidox in the pipe bomb—got it down to the exact hardware store, got an ID on the buyer from one of the clerks."

"Hector Mara."

"We just got through busting up his mobile home—found some things we missed on the first search. Or maybe they just weren't there the first time—some wiring. A timer."

"Pretty clear, then."

"The one thing we did not find is Mr. Mara."

I pointed toward the cinder-block L. "Can I take a look?"

"Nothing there. We went through it pretty thoroughly."

"May I take a look?"

DeLeon considered, then let her dissatisfaction with me collapse in a kind of tired apathy. "With me present, I suppose."

We walked up the drive, past the peacock, past a couple of uniformed cops complaining about the humidity and the woes of polyester uniforms.

"That friend we spoke about," I told DeLeon. "He could maybe track down Mara. If Mara's still in town."

"I'm not dealing with Arguello."

"You figure Lieutenant Hernandez will give you more time?"

DeLeon kept walking, occasionally slipping on the gravel in her heels. "Not likely."

"Because nothing here points away from Sanchez. It just means Hector was helping him out."

"Something like that."

"Nice and simple," I said. "And it stinks."

DeLeon stopped at the porch. The SWAT team had moved on. The bullet-riddled door lay flat across the entrance like a broken drawbridge.

DeLeon pushed her hair behind her ear, turned slowly, and looked out across the fields.

"You doing all right?" I asked.

She raised her eyebrows, gave me the little head shake women do when they're addressing a man who's acting like a three-year-old. "Just fine. And you?"

I watched two SWAT guys out in the field, trampling Hector Mara's tidy garden. They were kicking the heads off cabbages.

DeLeon smoothed her skirt. "I'm sorry. I'm on edge."

"Understandable."

In the main room, bedsheet curtains had been ripped down. Shafts of dust-moted light sliced across an old television set, a bare plywood bookshelf, a beanbag chair that had been cut open, its polyfoam guts spread across the cement floor. The tiny kitchen had been ransacked. Bathroom likewise, even the top of the toilet tank removed.

The first bedroom was filled with antique furniture too solid to destroy. Against one wall was a teak sideboard with the glass removed. A sewing table charred from the long-ago fire, an old foot-pedal Sears machine on top. A stripped bed frame. A basket of faded quilt remnants. Hung on the wall was a small cross studded with silver *milagro* charms. Men's clothing was heaped in the corner—sweats, tank tops, running shorts, the kind of clothes Hector Mara wore. The room smelled of old perfume and sweat. Neither the clothes nor the smell of sweat went with the rest of the room. It looked as if Hector had moved in after his grandmother's death and never bothered to redecorate.

There was a second bedroom down the hall at the end of the L.

Despite the police ransacking, I knew whose room it was the moment I entered—Sandra Mara's.

A young woman's clothes that hadn't seen the light of day in years were now disgorged from a closet in the corner—Jordache jeans, fuzzy sweaters, moccasin shoes, the kind of pastel tourist T-shirts you get from Solo Serve and La Feria. The upturned dresser drawers had spilled silver bangles, random stud earrings, a few sparse items of makeup. Not much for a teenage girl. There were no CDs, no magazines, few personal effects. Most notable was the ankle-deep pile of books and loose papers that had been swept off the shelves against one wall.

I toed through some of the book titles—Heller, Marquez, Vonnegut, Brontë. An African American poetry anthology, a Latin American one, Sylvia Plath. Good assortment. Very good for a high schooler.

I picked up the Sylvia Plath. The library pocket pasted to the inside cover said JUDSON ISD. The book had been due May 12, seven years ago. Hell of a late fee. Of course, before Sandra Mara had checked it out, the book had been borrowed exactly once, in 1975. Probably JUDSON ISD hadn't missed it yet.

The loose papers looked like pages of high school essays—double-spaced cursive, most dated spring, 1992. One was on "The Wife of Bath." I scanned half a paragraph and was depressed to find it better than most of the college papers I'd been looking at that morning.

I picked up another book—this one with a gold marbleized cover, no title. A writing journal. The first half of the book was filled with tiny cursive handwriting, distinctly feminine. I read a line or two.

When I looked up again, Ana DeLeon was standing at the window.

On the sill next to her were three porcelain mugs, all shaped like grotesque sailors' faces with long noses and cherry cheeks and glazed rum-sodden smiles. Ana DeLeon was circling her finger absently around the rim of one.

"Mind if I check this out?" I asked.

It took her a while to focus on me. "What?"

"This journal. Hector's sister's. I thought I would borrow it."

"Let me see it."

DeLeon flipped some pages. She looked at the words without reading them, traced the edges of the cover.

She handed the journal back to me. "I should tell you no. But I can't see that it'll be missed."

"No photographs."

"What?"

"No photographs anywhere," I told her. "None of Sandra. None of anybody else, for that matter. Did you find any during the search?"

"I don't recall any."

I looked out the window. Under a stand of cedars, half a dozen chickens were clucking and pecking around the feet of some SWAT guys.

One of the men, an assault rifle on his knee and greasepaint under his eyes, glanced in my direction. I smiled. He didn't smile back.

I looked down at the grinning sailor's-head mugs. The mugs didn't offer any advice.

I looked toward the closet.

"What?" DeLeon asked immediately.

I walked over to the closet, crouched down, tugged the tiny glinting piece of red and gold paper from the crack in the cement.

DeLeon stood over me. "What is it?"

I kept the paper wrapper curled in my palm while my

finger traced the almost invisible seam on the closet floor—
the square outline I would've missed if not for the paper.
"Trapdoor."

DeLeon said, "Stand back."

DeLeon yelled out the window for some assistance,
somebody with a crowbar.

Thirty seconds later the little room was filled with cops.

A minute after that the excitement was over. DeLeon
and I were alone in the room again, staring down at a crawl
space that smelled of cool damp earth and was absolutely
empty.

"So much for that," she said.

"Let me call Ralph."

"No."

"In another twenty-four hours, Mara will be gone. An
APB won't accomplish anything and you know it."

"I said *no,* Tres."

The use of my first name caught me off guard as much
as the tone of her refusal.

"Ana, I want to see you win on this. Let me help."

She turned away. After a ten-count she surprised me.
She said, very softly, "Let me think about it."

I didn't push it. I walked to the window and looked out
at Hector's smashed garden, the apple tree with the muddy
tracks of his Ford Galaxie still fresh underneath, the white
mobile home in the field of spear grass. I tried to imagine a
young woman, Sandra Mara, at this bedroom window
every day—looking up from a book of poetry or from a
journal she was writing in, being surprised every time that
the scene outside was not the asphalt-and-brick housing of
the Bowie Courts.

I flicked a slip of paint off the window ledge, watched it
helicopter into a sailor's-head mug. "I could maybe get
used to it here. The quiet. The country."

DeLeon met my eyes. She looked surprised, momentarily vulnerable, as if I'd intercepted one of her thoughts.

I said, "If I grew up where Hector and Sandra grew up, I might not want to leave this place once I'd dug in."

She nodded. "I suppose."

"You want to plant tomatoes this fall?"

Grudgingly, Ana smiled.

Then Kelsey's voice called her name from down the hall. My reward evaporated. Ana kept my eyes a moment longer, then left without a word, leaving me in Sandra's room, staring at the hole in the closet floor, crumpling a red and gold George Bertón cigar seal between my fingers and wondering about a lot of things.

TWENTY-FIVE

I spent the rest of the afternoon by the phone at 90 Queen Anne, waiting for calls back from my contacts with the local press. I wanted anything on the heroin trade from the last seven years, any articles that might mention the Brandons, the Maras, Zeta Sanchez, Chich Gutierrez, or Detective Thomas Kelsey of the SAPD.

By the end of the day, my contacts hadn't returned my calls, and I'd been forced to actually grade a set of papers for UTSA. Robert Johnson, the lazy bastard, helped not at all.

Over dinner of homemade *dolmades* and *spanakopita,* my weekly allotment from Erainya, I read Sandra Mara's journal.

Sandra's cursive was flawless—delicate loops, perfectly slanted, page after page written in the same golden brown ink. It was the kind of cursive that would drive handwriting analysts crazy because it was completely devoid of anomalies.

Sandra didn't believe in beginnings. No *Dear Diary* or *I haven't written in a while* or *Today I have something special to tell you.* No dates on the entries or signatures at the end. It was difficult to tell where one entry started and the next stopped. Sandra merely indented for the next paragraph and started writing.

This to Sylvia Plath.

I want to cut your thumb a few more times. I want to leave off

*the gauze and make you squeeze limes instead. A thrill? Look at
my brother's leg. Tell me what part of him is white. Only what
the gun splashed open, melted into a star, smoothed out by a year
with demons so that I could live. Don't impress me with your slip
of a knife. Don't talk to me about soldiers. No one ever bought
your life with an open wound.*

Your typical light verse from a seventeen-year-old girl.
Several pages later.

*I should have stayed inside this afternoon. The letter came.
Acceptance. Full scholarship. Grandmother and I set a jar of
raspberry sun tea under the apple tree and we danced. Grandmother with her cane and all. We laughed at the chickens. I
thought of college. And then the car in the gravel drive and Hector
walked up with Him. After two years. He was only larger, no less
or more frightening. A devil like that can have only His fixed
amount of horror, never more or less than 100%—as a child, as a
man. I should have stayed inside. I knew His look, the weighing
He did. I was naked on a scale. I took my letter and I went inside.
My grandmother became old again, hobbling alongside and muttering encouragement about college, but I just felt His eyes on my
back. I knew what He was thinking. I should have stayed inside.*

The other entries were equally intense. Tiring to read,
unsatisfying. They told me about Sandra Mara like an intra-
venous feeding.

I skipped to the end and read the last paragraph.

*How could a few minutes in a hallway shake me so much?
He's so unexpected. I still can't write about it without catching my
breath. Recognition in a dozen words, maybe less. He'd been
standing in the same shadows as I, knew them instantly.*

He kissed me today.

I closed the journal. Then I sat watching the light die in
the crape myrtle outside the kitchen window.

When the light was gone, I went out to my car.

Fifteen minutes later I was pulling up in front of Ride-
Works, Inc.

It wasn't any prettier than it had been two nights before,

but it was a hell of a lot more crowded. Rusted pickup trucks and low-rider Chevies lined the curb. The chain-link gate was open and the Super-Whirl Erainya and I had seen in pieces in the warehouse on Tuesday was now fully assembled in the yard, workers buzzing around it. The ride's giant metal arms were fully extended, lit with purple and yellow bulbs like dingo balls.

I walked through the gates, one hand in my pocket, the other slapping Sandra Mara's journal against my thigh. When I caught the eye of a worker, I smiled amiably, pointed toward the office door. "Del?"

The worker had a Fu Manchu mustache and a grimy face. On his head was a metal welder's visor the size of a snowboard. He considered my question, shrugged, then went back to his cigarette.

I went up the office steps, past the carousel animals, into the Room of Infinite Gimme Caps. No one was passed out on the secretary's desk this time. Del's office door was open. The restroom door at the other end of the reception area was closed and muffled thumping noises were coming from behind it.

I poked my head into Del's office.

Empty. Jeremiah Brandon smiled coldly at me from the 1940s photograph on the wall, daring me to trespass, double-daring me to sit at his son's desk.

"Screw you, Jerry," I told him.

I made myself comfortable and waited.

A few minutes later, I heard water running in the bathroom. Del's voice muttered something. Then the bathroom door opened and Rita the secretary came out, followed by Del.

Rita had her purse on her shoulder and trotted straight out the door, dabbing her lipstick as she went. Del walked toward the office. He didn't see me until he got in the doorway. Then he turned a lovely shade of magenta. "What—"

"Hey, Del."

He was wearing jeans and a red shirt with parrots on it. His unruly mat of black hair was flat on one side.

He drew his .38 from his side holster. This time I didn't stop him. He said, "Get the hell out of my chair."

"Wearing your gun in the bathroom with Rita. You're inviting embarrassing accidents."

"Get out of my chair."

"There's another right there. Sit down."

Del Brandon had apparently been hoping for terror.

He shifted uneasily, squeezed the gun's grip a few times for reassurance. "I warned you."

"You sure did, Del. Now sit down and put away the gun. We need to talk."

"What makes you think you can just—"

"Sit down," I repeated.

He seemed to be thinking of options. Apparently he couldn't come up with any. His gun hand sagged. He lowered himself into the chair across from me.

"Hector Mara," I said. "I was about to look him up in your personnel files but maybe you could save me some time. You got him listed under *M* for Mara or *H* for heroin?"

Del's face paled. "What?"

"You remember. Hector Mara. The guy you were arguing with at the Poco Mas a couple of weeks ago."

"I wasn't—" Del's eyes tried to latch on to something in my face, some toehold of doubt he could push up from. "Who told you that?"

"That would be smart," I said, "telling you."

"It isn't true."

"Of course not, Del. So set me straight."

Del glowered at the empty desk. He seemed to have forgotten he was holding the .38, which would've been all right if it hadn't still been pointed at my gut.

"Hector Mara does some accounting work for me from time to time. But I wasn't at that bar. I don't go there and you should know why. My father died there."

"Accounting work," I repeated. "Hector Mara. The bald *veterano* with the snakes tattooed on his arms. He's your accountant."

Del licked his lips. "Sometimes—you know. We deal mostly in cash. It's a hassle to just drop it in the bank."

"Mara launders money for you through his salvage yard."

"I didn't say that."

Del had developed this cute little tic in his right cheek that was doing a 2/4 beat—DUM-duh, DUM-duh. It made me laugh.

"You know Ozzie Gerson, Del?"

The tic kept up its little rhythm.

"Deputy," he mumbled. "Used to give my dad a hard time."

"Ozzie Gerson told me you weren't smart enough to find your way off a carousel, much less run heroin out of your company. Was he right?"

His face slackened to putty. "Wait a goddamn minute. You got no right to talk about me that way. Ozzie Gerson . . ."

His voice trailed off. He sat there on the visitor's side of his desk, suddenly staring at nothing. His shirt was misbuttoned, longer on one side than the other—probably from his armed restroom encounter with Rita. Looking at Del Brandon, I felt tired.

"Forget it," I told him. "Let's talk about your brother. You and he had been arguing over the company, right? Watch your muzzle, Del."

Del managed to focus on his .38, which had been slowly tilting its little black eye up toward my forehead. Del frowned, like he was wondering where the gun had come from. He clunked it on the desk.

"Aaron and me always argued," he told me. "Doesn't mean I shot him. You can ask the police—I got an alibi."

I whistled. "An alibi."

Del didn't seem to catch the sarcasm, if indeed sarcasm

was something Del ever caught. With some effort, he hauled himself out of the chair. He drifted over to the file cabinet, rummaged around until he came up with a bottle of Chivas Regal, still in the little purple sack. Then he came back over and sat down.

"Stuff gives me gas like you wouldn't believe," he grumbled. He uncapped the bottle and took a long hit.

I braced myself.

Del's eyes watered immediately. He tried to rub his nose off his face, then blinked at me through the tears.

"You want to know about Aaron?" Del sloshed his bottle around, pointing at things in the office. "Aaron never wanted this damn company. Growing up, me and him, Aaron could always figure the numbers faster. He could've worked the deals, no problem. If he'd shown even a little interest, Dad would've handed him the whole company, shut me out. I'm sure of that. But God forbid Professor Aaron should ever get his collegiate hands dirty. Never wanted to touch the business. Me, I had a hard time learning the ropes. Dad used to beat the shit out of me when I'd screw something up. 'Why can't you think on your feet like Aaron?' Then he'd get pissed off that Aaron wasn't around, and he'd beat the shit out of me some more for that. I took thirty years of that kind of crap for Aaron and me both, because I was the one who was always in the office. So you tell me—who deserved this company?"

"You, Del," I sympathized. "Obviously you."

"Damn right." Del took another swig of liquor. "Even then Dad didn't leave me the whole business. Couldn't bring himself to cut out Golden Boy completely. RideWorks was split sixty-forty, with me named president. But there were ways to get around that."

"Such as?"

As if to demonstrate, Del shifted in his chair, grimaced, then glared accusingly at his Chivas bottle. Brandon: the very name connotes charm and grace.

"You were saying?" I prompted.

"What?"

"How you got the whole company for yourself."

"Oh. Yeah. According to Dad's will, I was supposed to turn over Aaron's share of the profits when the profits showed up. Only I made sure none ever did on the books. After a few years of that, I finally got Aaron's approval to sell. I sold RideWorks to a paper corporation, mine, gave my brother half the selling price—about twenty dollars. Then I bought the company back from myself and kept operating it."

"Cute. Who helped you think up that trick?"

Del shrugged. "Like I told you, Aaron wasn't interested in the business. He didn't deserve it. Me, all I ever wanted was to run this company. I love the rides. A good one, well made—" He shook his head in admiration. "It's the most beautiful thing you'll ever see. Some of the old classic carousels I've been restoring for this society downtown— I'm telling you."

Del picked at the knee of his pants. His face suddenly reminded me of a little boy with the same sad, vacant expression, sitting cross-legged at the entrance of a sheet cave, digging at his knee with a toy ray gun. I didn't like seeing the family resemblance.

"Aaron ever threaten to take the company back?" I asked.

"Nothing that would've stood up in court. You think I was worried enough to kill him over something like that, you're crazy."

"How about Sandra Mara? Were you worried enough to kill her?"

A little color seeped back into Del's cheeks. "What is your thing with Sandra Mara?"

"My thing with her is simple, Del. I've spent a long time doing missing persons cases. I pay attention to the people who aren't around. They're usually the most interesting."

Del scowled. "Maybe my dad screwed her. Maybe it got him killed. She's just a girl. Who cares? She got shipped out of town, just like ten or eleven before her."

"Like ten or eleven before her," I agreed. "Which makes it easy to believe the same happened to Sandra. I'm starting to wonder."

I opened Sandra's journal, read the last paragraph aloud, the one where Sandra got kissed.

Del's face stayed blank. "So?"

"I think that describes Sandra's lover. And I'm having trouble fitting your father into the role."

"Maybe she was screwing somebody else. It happens."

"Maybe. But I'm starting to put myself in your place, Del. That's a scary thing. I'm starting to wonder what it would be like if I hated my dad, and I kept playing the devoted son so I could eventually inherit the business that I loved, and then somebody like Zeta Sanchez moved in on my turf and threatened to cut into my inheritance. I'm starting to wonder exactly what I'd do."

Del's eyes fixed on the wall behind me.

"Maybe I'd stage something," I decided. "A scenario I was sure Sanchez would believe, something that would drive a permanent wedge between Sanchez and my dad. Then I'd make sure Sanchez found out about it. Hell, I'd tell Sanchez myself and offer to help smuggle him out of town when the poor guy got so understandably irate he pumped six hollow-tipped bullets into my father. 'Too bad, Zeta. No hard feelings. Here's your ticket to Mexico. Thanks for handing me the company on a plate.'"

"Get out," Del croaked.

"Tonight I'm going to compare notes with a friend of mine, Del. I'm hoping that between him and me, we'll have enough to give you to the police in microwave-safe packaging. My best to Rita, okay?"

"Get out," Del said again.

I got up and walked around him to the door. Del made

no effort to stop me. His eyes stayed fixed on the portrait of Jeremiah Brandon behind the desk, the hatred in Del's gaze as he looked at his father a clearer message than anything he'd said aloud.

I walked out through the reception area. Rita's cheap gardenia perfume was still lingering in the air.

You go into conversations with people like Del hoping to shake them up, not quite sure what pieces will fall out of their pockets. Sometimes you pick up little shards of guilt, or surprise, or complicity that can tell you everything. Having shaken up Del, though, the main thing I came away with was the feeling that I'd just bullied a kid. An ugly, obnoxious, fat kid, to be sure. One who would push you off his carousel if you tried to take his seat in the flying teacup. But a kid.

In the yard, Del's workers were breaking down the Super-Whirl, forcing its huge lighted arms flat like the carcass of a particularly obstinate bug. I silently wished them luck, then walked out onto Camden Street.

TWENTY-SIX

At nine-thirty, I drove to Erainya's house to pick her up for our rendezvous at George's.

Jem came along, too, but this time inexplicably fell asleep in the backseat as soon as we hit the highway.

We drove toward the South Side on the upper deck of I-10, the VW top down, the wind skin-temperature, the lights of downtown receding behind us. Down below, dark little houses sped by, tiny fenced yards, miles and miles of laundry lines, tableaus of beer drinking on back porches, cars with headlights on and hoods up, shreds of heavy metal music.

I filled Erainya in on my day.

She stared straight ahead, her index finger stroking her lip. "Kelly came down today."

"How're things in Austin?"

"She says fine. She's dyed her hair kind of yellow this time. Looks good."

"Ah, the rites of spring."

"She worked the county courthouse most of the morning—got a little bored sitting around the office with both you and George gone."

"She find anything?"

"Turns out Aaron Brandon filed a civil suit against Del about three years ago for control of RideWorks. Aaron claimed Del had swindled him out of his share."

"And?"

"And it never went to court. Aaron dropped the suit a couple of months after he filed."

"Out-of-court settlement?"

Erainya shrugged. "I guess. The question is, what kind?"

I fixed my eyes on the road and thought about the red-and-gold cigar seal I'd found in Sandra Mara's bedroom closet. If George had something to tell us, something that would sew up the holes, I swore to God I'd buy him the world's largest Cuban cigar.

We exited on Roosevelt and turned south. The Tower of the Americas swung behind us like a compass needle. On either side of Roosevelt were closed-up car dealerships, their sale banners flapping apathetically. The side streets were dark and deadly quiet.

I must've been driving on autopilot, because the next thing I remember is Erainya shoving me and saying, "Heads."

We'd turned onto the broken asphalt of Palo Blanco. Up ahead, George's well-kept little house was dark. Its porch light was off. Even the carport light George used to showcase his 1970 Barracuda was off.

Next to the curb, a white van idled. Dark shapes of men moved across the gravel lawn.

My insides froze.

We were at the end of the block, still too far away to make out anything more, when the dark shapes melted into the van and its brake lights flared. Doors slammed. The van accelerated away from us.

I stopped in the middle of the street. There was no need for Erainya or me to speak. She got out, trundled Jem from the backseat, and carried him still sleeping to the sidewalk, already fishing for the gun in her purse. I punched the gas.

The white van took a hard left on Mission Road and careened out of sight. I tried to match its speed on the turn and found myself skidding sideways, nearly slamming into the gates of the old Catholic orphanage across the street before second gear took hold and fishtailed me forward again.

The van was now a hundred yards ahead, speeding south on the straight stretch of Mission Road. I pushed the VW faster. On the left, the dark wooded boundaries of the public golf course raced past; on the right, picnic areas, sports fields, tiny homes and graffitied bus stops. I tore through two intersections that were mercifully empty of traffic but the van kept pulling farther ahead.

I waited until third gear was about to explode, then shifted to fourth. The underbelly of the VW rattled like aluminum foil.

The golf course fell away on the left and the road widened and zigged, aligning itself with the edge of the San Antonio River basin. Fifty yards down on my left, the river made a dark, glittering streak through the center of what was basically a glorified drainage ditch. Lit by moon and city night glow, the grassy earthen walls sloped down from the guardrails to the wide marshy banks, the underbrush fleeced with paper trash from thousands of upriver polluters. I floored the accelerator, slashed through potholes of standing water as the van pulled ahead of me on Mission.

The van turned hard on the Southcross Bridge and crossed the river, doubling back north on Riverside.

I slowed for the bridge, lost some time in the turn, then followed across and up Riverside. I got the VW back into fourth gear, taking the curvier east bank at an insane sixty-five and still losing my prey. Another minute and they would be gone.

For the last time in our sixteen-year relationship, I cursed my VW.

The white van swung wide for a right onto Roosevelt. I tried to follow, feeling the arc of the turn getting away from me, the VW going sideways with its own force toward the guardrail, my feet starting to skid back and forth of their own accord like a novice ice-skater's. Then there was the crumple of metal and a tilt in the horizon and the sickening feeling of weightlessness.

I expected sound—a blast or crunch or tear of metal and bones. I was wrong. There was no sound—just free fall, followed by a cold, slick blackness all around me, the feeling of tumbling, of being compressed into a smaller and smaller somersault until something that might've been my spine went *snap.* Somewhere far away, I heard the rush of a large animal through grass—a rhino, perhaps.

My eyes opened. Through a smear of Vaseline, I saw the river off to my left, a huge orange-and-black beast rolling slowly and convulsively toward it. The thing heaved itself up on end when it reached the bank, poised there as if contemplating a drink, then decided it had just enough momentum to topple forward one more time. It hit the water with a resounding hollow *galoosh,* the wheels still spinning.

I was afraid to move, afraid any effort might cause what little life I still had to leak out. I didn't want to know how bad off I was.

I stared at the water glistening in moonlight, the dark marsh weeds and bare branches globbed with paper pulp. I smelled like someone had stirred rotten meat into a fish tank and dumped the contents on my head. Far away I thought I heard sirens. Lights of the houses on Riverside blinked on. I watched the upturned back wheels of my VW spin for one rotation. Two rotations.

I decided I was not dead yet. I tried to move my arm. I found that my sleeve was snagged on some kind of bush. In fact, all of me was snagged on some kind of bush. I'd been forcibly grafted onto a large chaparral.

I tried a foot, found it suspended from a branch by a ripped jean leg. Slowly, I managed to extract myself, then to pick the larger gobs of thick wet river garbage off my body. I inspected what I could of myself in the dark and realized with infuriating certainty that I was fine.

I cursed loudly and creatively. That felt good so I did it again.

Fueled by anger and probably a fair amount of shock, I started walking.

At least, the police told me I was walking when they found me. I was half a mile or so from George's house. I don't remember talking to the uniforms, or changing into the moth-eaten but dry spare set of clothes the police kept in their trunk, or getting a ride with them back to Bertón's.

I do remember my reunion with Erainya in George's graveled front yard. She was crouching down, holding Jem, trying to answer a detective's questions and Jem's at the same time.

Jem was still sleepy-eyed, pointing at the house and saying he wanted to see George.

Erainya kept saying, "Honey. Honey."

When she saw me, she closed her eyes for three seconds, muttering some kind of prayer. "Take Jem, honey. Please. Take him away just for a few minutes."

I did nothing.

I was staring into George's front door, into the living room now blazing with light. I could see a left foot—a single white Nike shoe sticking into view. Police were moving around the shoe. Cameras were flashing.

I locked eyes with Erainya. Her glance was black as ever, harder than ever, but starting to erode. Her voice trembled a little when she repeated, "Take Jem for a few minutes, honey. Can you do that?"

I looked at the detective, who nodded. "There's hot chocolate in my car—down there, third one."

I told Jem to come with me, and when he wouldn't or couldn't, I picked him up and carried him.

I found myself hugging him tight, trying to get reassurance from the breaths that expanded his little warm chest, the smell of sleep and child sweat in his rumpled hair. I carried him down Palo Blanco and tried to keep talking in gentle tones so he wouldn't focus on the sound behind us of his mother crying.

TWENTY-SEVEN

Policemen's faces and questions blurred together. At some point Erainya reclaimed Jem. Then I was separated from both of them. A field sergeant came by and took my statement. Halfway through, he finally corrected my understanding of the situation. He pulled me back from total despair with a frown and a matter-of-fact "I thought you knew."

George Bertón was not dead.

George's ambulance had been long gone by the time I'd arrived on the scene. The body in George Bertón's house, the body SAPD wasn't in any hurry to move, wasn't George's.

The sergeant told me George's condition was critical. And no, I could not leave immediately to see him. The sergeant insisted on taking the rest of my statement, refused to answer further questions, then left me locked in the backseat of the patrol car with the detective's thermos of hot chocolate.

I didn't want any hot chocolate, which was just as well. My hands were shaking too badly to unscrew the cap.

I smelled of mothballs and wet garbage. My hair felt shellacked. The throbbing in my head synchronized itself to the pulse of siren light from the unit across the street.

I closed my eyes.

After a few minutes the car dipped from the weight of someone sinking into the front seat.

I looked up expecting to see the night CID detective. Instead I found the Bexar County medical examiner.

As usual, Ray Lozano looked way too nice for your average dissector of dead people. His hair was a huge well-plowed field of black, thick but immaculately trimmed around the edges. He wore a dark blue silk suit covered in a lab wrap. Surgical gloves covered his wedding band and his Swiss Army watch.

Normally Lozano would've been smiling way too much for an M.E., too. But not tonight.

"Hey, *ese.*" He didn't offer his hand, just a very long look of shared anger that glowed like the belly of a furnace.

"Ray," I said. "Lucky call for you tonight."

Under his breath, Lozano swore. "They tell you about it yet?"

I shook my head.

"You want to know?"

"What do you think?"

Lozano looked strange without a laugh ready to burst out. For the first time, he looked his age.

"I can't tell you much about George. He was already en route to BAMC when I got here. As for inside, there's a dead guy named Hector Mara lying faceup in the living room. Any idea why?"

"The shooting was between him and Bertón?"

"No. No way. Shooter was a third person. Signs of forced entry on the back door. They lifted half a boot print in the alley. Shooter came in and interrupted Bertón's and Mara's conversation. Mara drew a revolver but never got a chance to fire it. Caught one round in the chest, close range, I'm saying a .357."

I closed my eyes, tried to concentrate on my breathing.

"You sure you want to hear this?" Lozano asked.

I nodded.

"We don't have George here, so it's hard to reconstruct the whole story unless—" Lozano stopped, then went on.

"Until he gets out of surgery. I know he was shot twice in the back, probably same caliber that hit Mara. My guess, we're looking at one shooter. The guy plugs Mara when Mara draws his revolver, then turns on George. George is armed but he doesn't try anything. I don't know why. The shooter tells George to turn around, or maybe George turns to run. When he does, the shooter fires twice. Bertón goes down in the kitchen doorway. Shooter walks back over to Mara, makes sure Mara is dead with a shot to the head, contact wound. Then, for some reason, he doesn't take the same precaution with Bertón. Most likely he's scared off the scene before he can."

"When Erainya and I arrived."

"Maybe. The timing is good. This didn't go down very long before you two showed up. Both entrance wounds on Mara were atypical, disproportionately large for the tissue damage and exit wounds. I was wondering about the caliber until I noticed the muzzle imprint on the head wound— erythematous rather than abraded."

"Which means in English?"

"Which means in English a silencer. A .357 semiauto handgun with a silencer. Our shooter came in prepared to do some killing."

"You keep describing one person. One shooter."

"Based on what *you* saw—the van, multiple people— there must've been more guys at the scene, right? But I'm still saying one shooter went into the house. And why the back-door entry? I don't know. It just seems things would've played differently if there'd been a crowd in the room."

I closed my eyes again, tried to squeeze out the burning sensation in them.

"You look like shit," Lozano said. "I heard about your car, man. You're crazy not letting them take you to the ER."

"I'm fine."

"Like hell," Lozano said. "Look at me."

When I didn't he grabbed my jaw and twisted my face toward his, took a penlight from his pocket and shined it in my eyes. He grunted, put the penlight away, and dug his fingers around my scalp at various points.

"Ouch," I said.

"Relax. My patients never complain." He withdrew his hands. "You start feeling dizzy or nauseous, get your ass to the hospital. Otherwise go home."

"I got to see—"

"Don't even try seeing George, *ese*. Not tonight. I told Erainya the same thing. Brooke Army Medical Center won't let you close to him even if you go down there. Best-case scenario he'll be in surgery until dawn, ICU for at least two or three days. You want to see him tomorrow, go home and rest tonight."

He made me promise.

"There's one other thing," Lozano said. "Got a message for you from one of the homicide dicks. Lady named DeLeon."

"Yeah?"

"She said to tell you she couldn't be here tonight. It's not her call. But she also said you should phone her. She said it might be time to talk. That make sense to you?"

"Yeah. Maybe."

The paramedics were now moving a full body bag down the front steps of the house. The crime-scene photographers were wrapping up their work on the peripheries, taking down the floodlights from around Hector Mara's Ford Galaxie where it sat parked at the end of the block. There was still no media on the scene. Just another West Side homicide, I thought bitterly. What's the hurry?

"Whoever did this," Lozano said softly, "these same people have any reason to be pissed off with you?"

I looked at him and didn't see a friend. I saw a whole lot of deaths in his eyes, a whole lot of scalpels cutting impersonally through cold muscle. It was somehow reassuring.

"If they don't yet," I told him, "just give me a couple of days."

Twenty-Eight

Erainya knows best.

She will often tell me this. The fact that it is frequently true does nothing to help my annoyance level.

The next morning I decided she was truly insane. She called me at eight-thirty, succinctly gave me the update that George was in a coma from blood loss, his condition still critical. Then she insisted I stick with our original plans—Jem was going to his kindergarten visit today and by God I was going to take him.

"Jesus Christ, Erainya. George—"

"—is the reason you're taking Jem," she finished. "I'll be down at the hospital. Me and Jenny from the title office already got the rotation list worked out for a vigil, two people at a time. We've already got more help than we need, honey. You and Kelly go tonight, ten to midnight. Just be ready for kindergarten in half an hour."

After I'd growled yes and hung up the phone and spent a few minutes wondering why I'd given in, I realized maybe her request wasn't so crazy after all. Maybe the annoyance she'd succeeded in provoking was better than other feelings I might've been consumed with. Maybe taking Jem to kindergarten the morning after we'd all been up until two, attending the possibly fatal shooting of a mutual friend, was better than anything else I might've spent the morning doing.

By nine Jem and I were driving through Monte Vista in a

car that was even more absurd than our situation—George
Bertón's precious baby, his '70 Barracuda.

That too had been Erainya's idea. After my accident last
night, she'd pointed out, I needed a car, a temporary
loaner, and Erainya just happened to know where George
kept his spare keys. She didn't offer her own car to me. Go
figure.

I'd never driven the 'Cuda before—never done more than
glimpse it while Bertón performed his holy rituals under
the hood with a chamois cloth and a lug wrench and an oil
can.

The car had nothing in common with the VW except
color, age, and ragtop. The dash was polished oak. The
stick shift and bucket seats were covered in black leather.
A gilded Virgen de Guadalupe statuette hung from the
rearview mirror. The disc brakes responded to the lightest
tap and the monstrous 440 motor purred like a tigress under the shaker hood. I couldn't drive the thing without
hearing War's "Low Rider" in my head.

We pulled over at the corner of East Craig and
McCullough, outside the private school that swallowed
up most of the block. The campus was a series of reno-
vated mansions on a hill, shaded with live oaks, the thick
green lawns immaculate. The kindergarten building was
a plantation-style carriage house on the corner, directly
above us.

Jem and I watched kids on the playground—scampering
over the jungle gym, swinging, playing on the monkey
bars. The kids all looked happy. The teachers in the yard all
looked happy. I felt like I should look happy too but I knew
I damn well might start screaming any minute.

"You might like it here," I told Jem. "Nice play struc-
ture."

Jem nodded.

He was dressed in khaki pants and a little green polo
shirt that made his dark skin glow. His hair was newly cut

into a bowl of black. He pressed the creases in the top of his lunch bag over and over. He hadn't said much on the way over—a short treatise on breakfast-cereal toys, a few questions about the Barracuda. Those questions stopped as soon as George's name came up.

"You ready?" I asked him.

Jem nodded again, with no enthusiasm.

We walked up to the white-columned porch of the carriage-house kindergarten building and did a lot of handshaking with a pale blond woman in a willowy dress. Mrs. Something-or-Other. Her name started with *T* and had about seven syllables and I felt very inadequate when I heard the kindergartners rattling it off effortlessly. She wore a lot of perfume. Jem was mostly interested in her necklace—one of those primary-teacher specials with little ceramic animals and multicolored alphabet letters designed to capture the attention of twenty kindergartners at a time. Even I had an overwhelming urge to fondle it.

"We're so pleased to have you here today," Mrs. T. told us.

She called over a sandy-haired kid named Travis and introduced him to Jem. Thirty seconds later Jem and Travis were in line to play wall ball.

"See you at one-thirty?" Mrs. T. asked me.

"I'm supposed to *leave* him?"

She smiled patiently, like she was used to hearing that question. "Well, it's better for him, to interact with the children, you know—"

"I knew that."

She smiled some more, then excused herself to go greet another pair of visitors—an ample redheaded woman with an equally redheaded, overweight child.

I stepped back against the fence and watched Jem play. It was the first time I'd seen him with a group of his peers. He'd never been in day care, never had anybody at his birthday parties who was under thirty, yet he seemed perfectly at home. Ten kids were now involved in his wall ball game. Jem and Travis were rewriting the rules so more could play.

"It's hard," a woman said.

I looked over. It was the redheaded woman who'd just dropped off her kid.

I tried to match her sympathetic smile. "What's hard?"

"Leaving your child—it's hard, isn't it?"

I opened my mouth, tried to form an explanation about my non-relationship to Jem, then just nodded. The mother patted my arm in camaraderie and drifted away.

I looked over at the kindergarten teacher. She was crouching to talk face-to-face with yet another visitor, a pale child with messed-up hair and an untucked shirt. My stomach twisted when I recognized him. It was Michael Brandon, Aaron and Ines's kid. His mother was standing over him, trying to fix his cowlicks.

Ines wore her usual earth tones—a tan and chocolate quilt jacket over white blouse, khakis, cord sandals. Her ancho-colored hair was tied back in a butterfly clasp.

The teacher tried to coax a smile out of Michael. When that didn't work, she called a kindergartner over. Neither Michael nor the other kid looked thrilled about the pair-up, but Michael reluctantly allowed the boy to lead him onto the playground.

As Michael approached the wall ball game, Jem zeroed in on him and came over grinning. Jem knew a fellow newbie when he saw one. He took Michael's hand and started explaining the rules of the game.

Ines Brandon saw me as she turned to leave. She hesitated, then continued walking.

I followed her down the steps, past a few other parents. Halfway to the curb, I caught her arm.

She turned with a prepackaged smile. "If it isn't the P.I. Don't tell me—you happen to work at the kindergarten, *too*."

"Whoa. I'm just dropping off."

She pulled her elbow away. "Oh, *por favor.*"

"Seriously. Kid in the green shirt."

I pointed out Jem, who was now whacking the ball against the wallboard. Michael was on his team.

Ines appraised me skeptically. She held up one hand to block the sun, her fingers making shadow bars across her nose. "I'm trying to decide whether you'd rent a kid just to have an excuse to follow me."

"He's my boss's son. And don't give her any ideas about renting him out."

Ines let her shoulders relax just a little, dropped her hand. "I'll assume you're telling the truth. I don't know why. But don't expect an apology."

"My expectations in that department are low. How's your move coming along?"

She gazed past me, toward the playground. "Del was generous—a whole three days to pack. I've leased an apartment on"—she stopped herself—"near Woodlawn Lake."

"Why this school?"

"The public schools in this neighborhood . . ." She shook her head. "I went through a poor school system like that. No way my son is going to. I want to be out of San Antonio by next fall, but if I can't . . ."

"What'll you do for money?"

"That's my problem." She tugged the sleeves of her quilt jacket over her wrists. The right cuff had a black smudge on it—maybe mascara. "As long as I find Michael someplace safe."

"Safe." I thought about Michael's sheet cave.

"*Exactly.* Now if you'll excuse me. It's been a treat, but—"

"You must have a lot of packing to do."

"Yes."

"Packed the sheet cave yet?"

Her eyes heated to the temperature of espresso. She stepped forward, put her hand on my chest, and gave one hard push.

"*Basta ya,*" she hissed. "I've let you into my house twice. That doesn't give you the right—"

"Speak softly," I warned.

From the back fence, Mrs. T., the kindergarten teacher, was watching us, smiling nervously, probably making mental notes for the boys' admissions files.

The kindergartners continued to play. Swings creaked. The ball pounded off the backboard in Jem and Michael's game. A little girl at the top of the blue and beige play-structure tower was pounding her feet on the metal, yelling that she was the queen and nobody could get her.

"You don't have any idea," Ines told me. "You don't know what it's like keeping a routine for my son's sake. Getting him up every morning. Getting him dressed and fed. You don't know how hard it was just getting him here today."

"Asking for sympathy?"

"You fucking better know I'm not."

"Because I could sympathize. It was hard getting Jem here today, too, Mrs. Brandon. You know where he and I were last night? You remember that man I asked you about—the one you didn't know, Hector Mara? He went over to my friend's house last night. Good friend of mine—George Bertón. The two of them were talking, probably about your husband's murder, when somebody came in and shot them both."

Ines' face had turned chalky. "I don't . . ."

She took a step sideways toward a small live oak tree and steadied herself against the trunk.

"Mara's dead," I told her. "My friend's not quite—yet. Jem, his mom, and I walked in right after the shootings, stayed at the scene until almost two."

"What do you want me to say?" Ines asked me harshly. "That I'm sorry?"

"Somebody with a .357 put my friend into a coma. That person is still out there."

"I didn't ask your friend to get involved, Mr. Navarre. Or you, for that matter."

"That's right. You're right. Forget the shootings are connected to your husband's murder. I don't know why I thought you'd care."

"Don't you *dare* presume to know what I care about."

"Look, Ines—"

"Go *away,* goddamn you. Leave Michael and me alone."

I pinched the bridge of my nose, tried to remember I didn't have a reason to be arguing with this woman. "I need some help."

"I don't want any part of it."

"My guess is that your brother-in-law Del is behind the shootings somehow. He and a heroin dealer named Chich Gutierrez. You're telling me you wouldn't like a chance to nail Del Brandon?"

"I can't help."

Mrs. T. rang a handbell. Kids dropped off playground equipment and started forming lines in front of the classroom doors. Jem was in the middle, walking with his fingers pinched to the shirt of the boy in front of him. The teacher glanced uneasily in our direction one more time, then followed her charges inside.

"The kids get out at one-thirty," I told Ines. "What are you doing until then?"

She was silent, her lips thin and angry.

"You have other plans?"

"The move—"

"Yeah," I said. "Michael's room. Come with me instead. Help me dredge my car out of the river."

She stared at me, then laughed uneasily. "What?"

"You heard me. How often do you get an offer like that?"

Her mouth quivered, formed a fragile smile. "I don't even like you."

"So come watch me be humiliated. It'll be a blast."

She looked down toward the street, her mouth hardening again. "Would we be even?"

"What?"

"You drove me home from Aaron's office Wednesday. If I drive you today, would we be even?"

She held out her hand. I shook it.

"Charm and diplomacy win again," I said.

"That," Ines Brandon said, "and the fact I never want to owe you anything, Mr. Navarre. Never."

Then she turned and started down the sidewalk toward her car, leaving me to follow or not.

TWENTY-NINE

"At least your VW knew when to quit," Ozzie Gerson said.

We were standing in the drainage channel on the banks of the river, watching the tow-truck guys connect their winch hooks to the carcass of my VW. Ines Brandon sat nearby on the hood of Ozzie's police unit.

The VW lay on its back, half submerged, bashed to hell on the passenger's side and smeared with toilet paper and river garbage. During the night some adventurous kids had come by and spray-painted *PUTA!!* in white across the VW's exposed underbelly. *Whore.* The final indignity to an old, unappreciated dame.

Up on the rim of the ditch I could see the flattened section of guardrail the Bug had smashed through, the path of destruction it had made rolling down the muddy slope through the bushes. The chaparral I'd been thrown into was about thirty feet from the first point of impact on the slope. I was trying to figure out how I'd ended up there in one piece.

"You got lucky." Ozzie's pale blue eyes were cold with anger and frustration. "Luckier than Bertón, anyway."

"You offered to help," I reminded Ozzie. "I need to know where to find Chich Gutierrez."

The mechanics attached the first hook to the VW's fender and pulled the line tight. Metal groaned. I think maybe I did, too.

Gerson lifted his left arm stiffly, testing the muscles.

The bandages under his uniform shirt crinkled. "You sure that's your job—taking revenge?"

"Anything I needed, you said."

"I don't want you getting killed on my watch, Tres. Your father'd haunt me forever."

The tow-truck guys started their winch motor. More groaning metal. The motor bellowed like a wounded sea lion but made no discernible progress getting the VW out of the muck.

"Tell me everything," Ozzie said.

I told him about the SWAT raid at Hector Mara's house; the George Bertón cigar wrapper in Sandra's closet; the white van I'd chased down Riverside. I told him, too, about Ray Lozano's read of the crime scene at Palo Blanco.

"George found out something about the Brandon murder," I said. "Something that bothered him enough to try solving it quietly, on his own. He talked to Hector Mara at the Poco Mas on Wednesday. Then he had another meeting with Mara last night. He and Hector were coming to some kind of agreement. I don't know what it was, but George intended to have the case wrapped up with Mara's help by the time Erainya and I showed. The guys in the white van didn't let it happen."

Ozzie moved his arm again, swore softly. "If George was trying to get Hector Mara to sell out Chich Gutierrez, you can bet Chich would get wind of it. Chich would've had men shadowing Hector. They would've seen him go into George's house and known it was time to hit."

We were back where we started. "So where do I find Chich?"

"Leave that to SAPD. You gave them enough to work with, kid. Don't repeat George's mistakes."

I looked over at Ines, her arms hugging her chocolate-and-beige coat. The wind coming down the drainage ditch made her red hair flicker.

"Aaron Brandon's widow?" Ozzie asked me.

"We met by accident."

"The lady doesn't belong here. And you're not in any shape to be helping each other."

"The lady doesn't want any part of the investigation."

Ozzie nodded, eyes still on Ines. "She's the smart one, then. You been to see George yet?"

"I'm supposed to go this evening."

"I just called the hospital an hour ago," Ozzie said. "His left lung was removed."

"He'll make it."

"A ventilator's breathing for his right lung. He's got a fever from the infection and the antibiotics can't kick it. He's dying, kid."

"He'll make it," I repeated.

Ozzie gave me a weary look. "There's one more thing I thought I'd tell you. I'm resigning from the department."

The winch motor cut off. The VW hadn't budged. The tow-truck guys broke out a pack of cigarettes and stared resentfully at the VW's underbelly as they lit up.

"Early retirement for disability," Ozzie continued. "Half pension." He raised the arm. "The doctor's pressuring me about this. I'm beginning to think he's got a point."

"That's not how you felt yesterday."

"Yesterday was a long time ago, in a comfortable bed. This thing with George, after me getting shot the same week . . . I started thinking about me and Audrey in Cancun, how we could be there sipping margaritas this time next week. We both got a little money saved up. It's starting to sound real good, kid. What'd you think old Sheriff Navarre would say?"

" 'You got an extra seat on the plane?' "

Ozzie laughed.

One of the mechanics yelled to him to come help with the cables.

"Idiots should've brought a mobile crane," Ozzie grumbled. "When I get this heap of yours out of the river, kid, I'm slapping a big-ass ticket on the windshield."

"There is no windshield."

Ozzie muttered some more colorful observations about life, then walked down to the tow truck.

I picked my way downstream to Ines.

"Your friend doesn't like me," she said.

"He likes you fine. He thinks you're the smart one."

"Really."

"Sure. Compared to me."

Ines gazed up at the flattened section of guardrail. In full daylight, the tiny scar on the bridge of her nose was whiter. I found myself wondering how she'd broken it, how she'd look without that slight bend.

She said, "Mr. Navarre—"

"Tres."

She paused, seemed to be mentally tasting my name. I guess it didn't taste that good. "Mr. Navarre. I've already told you. I can't help you."

"The dead man I told you about, Hector Mara, the fact that he might've known your brother-in-law Del—that doesn't bother you?"

"¡Hostia! Everything about my ex-brother-in-law bothers me. Talking about him doesn't help."

She pulled herself up onto the hood of the police car, crossed her legs at the ankles. Peeking out the tips of her cord sandals were scarlet toenails, with flesh-colored smiles around the cuticles where the nails had started to grow out.

I tried to imagine what color Ana DeLeon would paint her toenails. Steel-gray? Black?

I mentally slapped myself. "The first time we spoke, you recognized Hector Mara's name."

Ines' fingertip inscribed something in slow cursive on

the hood of the car. She stared down resentfully at her own invisible message. "I suppose if I denied that—"

"I'd only wonder why you were lying."

A sour smile. "It would never occur to you that I'm lying because I hate you, would it?"

"Never in a million years."

"I remembered the name," Ines conceded. "Aaron mentioned Hector Mara once, in a phone argument he was having with Del. Months ago, before we moved to San Antonio. I don't remember the context."

"Did you know Aaron in the spring of '93?"

She scowled. "What does that . . . You mean when Aaron's father was killed?"

"Yes."

She started to ask a question, then apparently changed her mind. Her eyes refocused on the rim of the basin. "I'd come up from Del Rio in fall '92. To enroll at Our Lady of the Lake. It was my first semester."

"Aaron Brandon's first semester teaching there."

"I was in his undergraduate class. We . . . started having a relationship."

"And Our Lady of the Lake didn't renew his contract."

"Not because of me. Aaron was struggling. He didn't have any confidence. To tell the truth, he wasn't a very good teacher. Halfway through the spring semester, he knew the university wasn't going to ask him back. Aaron wanted to give up, go crawling back to his father for a job at RideWorks. I couldn't just watch Aaron give up and go back to the family business. I convinced him to stay with his teaching, to take another job for the following year even though it wasn't the best—"

"At Permian Basin."

She nodded. "In April, I found out I was pregnant with Michael. That's why we got married."

"In Laredo?"

One sandaled foot kicked me not-so-gently on the thigh. "What did you do, P.I.—ferret out my marriage certificate?"

I reminded her about the wedding picture I'd seen in her living room. She pursed her lips—maybe a gesture of contrition. It didn't make my thigh feel any better.

"Our marriage was a secret, of course," she told me. "Jeremiah was still alive then—he would've disowned Aaron for marrying a Mexican. Never mind Jeremiah's paternalism for the South Side 'locals.' That didn't include his son marrying one."

"But Del knew you were married."

"He gave Aaron a terrible time about me, but he kept our secret."

"Del doesn't strike me as the type to keep secrets. Especially Aaron's."

She laughed dryly. "Maybe he just didn't have time to tell. Jeremiah was killed a few weeks later."

"And how did Aaron take that?"

"Aaron hardly talked about what he was feeling, Mr. Navarre. Not even to me. But the murder had one good effect—it resolved Aaron on going to UT Permian Basin, to get out of San Antonio. That's what we were doing in the spring of '93. We were getting ready to move. Getting ready to have our first child. I don't know about his brother, but I'm sure my husband never crossed paths with people like Hector Mara or Zeta Sanchez. An acquaintance like that would've shown on Aaron like a bruise, he was so sensitive. In a lot of ways, fragile."

I thought about the papers and lecture notes I'd seen in Aaron Brandon's files—all of them obsessed with the violence of medieval life. I thought of Aaron in the photos I'd seen—a large man, thick-boned, dark-haired, bred from blue-collar stock, a face as dour as his brother's. I tried to think of him as fragile. I said, "When did things become strained between you and Aaron?"

Ines squeezed her palm until it turned mottled. "Christmas—when he went for his final UTSA interview. Aaron insisted on moving back to San Antonio. I hated him for being so stubborn. I hated him for dragging us back to San Antonio. He wasn't ready for the UTSA job or for facing his brother again. But I'd followed him to West Texas. I'd stood by him for five years. I loved him. He was the father of my child and he would've been a good teacher one day. He was learning so much before we came back . . ."

The winch motor started up again.

I looked at Ines and believed what she said, that this woman had what it took to sustain her husband's career on life support those five years in the Permian Basin, until Aaron had insisted on moving back into his family's orbit, insisted on committing emotional suicide. I found myself growing angry at Aaron Brandon for that.

And maybe deep down, I was jealous. Maybe part of me was wondering how far I would've gone after graduate school if I'd had someone in my life like Ines Brandon.

Ozzie shouted something. The tow-truck men gave the winch another go. They operated it in short bursts until finally, on try number four, the VW lurched forward. The wreckage of the beast emerged reluctantly out of the muck.

"You were back home in Del Rio the night Aaron was killed?"

Ines nodded. "Michael and I were staying with friends. Paloma called us immediately, but—I still don't remember how I made it back to town safely. I don't remember the drive at all."

"And you'd never heard of Zeta Sanchez before?"

"And never want to again."

"What about justice?"

She slammed her hand against the hood of the police car. The metallic *pop* was like a hunter's rifle, half a mile distant.

"Justice? Justice is something you get only after your life has gone to hell, Mr. Navarre. It doesn't make anything better. You can criticize me for packing up and running, if you want, but running is the first thing I think of when I wake up in the middle of the night—my son having night terrors down the hall, hiding under a bunch of blankets, crying, calling for his daddy. I just want to run, take Michael, and get the hell away from this place. I want the past to go out with the trash. Do you blame me?"

I watched as the tow truck dragged my upside-down VW onto dry land, the ragtop ripped loose and trailing behind like a mud-stained cape. I found myself thinking about Ana DeLeon in her blue business suit, standing at the window of an abandoned house, looking out over the untended fields of Bexar County.

"Time to pick up the children," Ines said.

For one brief, guilty instant, I let myself fantasize that the words *the children* had some relevance to my life. Then I turned and trudged back up the slope toward Ines Brandon's car.

THIRTY

The closer Jem and I got to the office, the less Jem spoke. His excitement about the visit to school, his stories about Michael Brandon and the other new friends he'd made started to drain away, replaced by the dread of what was waiting for us back at Erainya's. I had to force myself to turn into the parking lot.

It was Friday, but Kelly was in town anyway, sitting at my desk. She'd washed all the purple dye out of her black hair. Her clothes were black, too—slacks and a tank top and Doc Martens. Her face had the freshly scoured look of recent crying. She was on the phone with some client, telling him there would be a slight delay in our next report.

Jem ran back to his mother's desk and climbed into Erainya's lap. Erainya was also on the phone, talking to the hospital. She looked up and gave me a shake of the head. *No change.*

Jem put his head on her shoulder and his body went limp.

The toys had been carefully collected off the rug and put to the side in a huge plastic bucket, making the center of the office strangely empty. On George Bertón's desk, the Styrofoam hat holder was bald. His paperwork had been removed and added to the stack on my desk.

When Kelly finished her call, she sat staring at the empty space in the middle of the office. Then she looked away, sniffling.

"We're out of Kleenex," she told me. "Wouldn't you know it?"

I reached over and pulled one of George's silk handkerchiefs out of his drawer. "George would probably say, 'You can wipe your nose on my hanky anytime, *chiquita*.'"

Kelly laughed brokenly, pinched her nose into the handkerchief. "God, I hate this. I *hate* this."

"I know."

She took my hand, squeezed it hard, tried telling me details, lists of things she'd done since she'd gotten in this morning. She told me about her long phone conversations with Jenny at George's title office, about scrambling to find names of George's kin and coming up with nothing. Friends—hundreds of them. But family? The little information anybody could volunteer was slim and contradictory— an aunt in Monterey, a half-brother in El Paso, a niece in Chicago. Nobody really knew. A dead wife, everybody knew.

I let her talk, only cueing into the words occasionally.

Then the doorbell chimed and Ralph Arguello came in.

In the two years I'd worked at the office, Ralph had come by exactly once, on an evening when he was certain Erainya would be out. Ralph knew how Erainya felt about him and he'd always chosen to respect her feelings. At least until today.

Ralph had forgone the usual XXL Guayabera and jeans for a raw silk suit—milk white, with a black bolo and black ostrich-skin boots. Under the loose cut of his jacket he could've concealed enough weapons to arm his own cult.

His hair was braided into a tight cord. His thick round glasses shimmered as he examined the office—Bertón's cleared desk, Erainya and Jem. He zeroed in on Kelly's hand in mine, then after a very long half second seemed to dismiss the sight.

"*Vato.*" He acknowledged me.

He picked off his glasses. This in itself was a rare event, and his naked eyes looked huge and dark, as if the lenses had somehow contained them. Ralph might've been close to legal blindness, but his stare revealed a fierceness you never saw through his glasses—an honest warning of the kind of violence he was capable of.

He held out his arms. Kelly went to him, tried for a stiff, perfunctory hug, but Ralph wouldn't let her pull away. He held her until she melted against him in earnest and started crying.

He looked at me over her shoulder. There was one question in his face, a calm demand that I'd seen before and understood perfectly. *When?*

Back at her desk, Erainya said a few weary "thank-yous" to the ICU nurse and hung up the phone.

She ruffled Jem's hair, then stared across the room at us. Surprisingly, she did not throw anything at Ralph to drive him from the office. She merely said, "Mr. Arguello."

Ralph nodded, acknowledging the truce. "Ms. Manos. *¿Qué pasa?*"

"You have to ask?"

He shook his head, then disengaged from Kelly. "And you, *mi chica?*"

"I'll be okay," Kelly whispered.

He gathered the back of Kelly's hair in his fist—a gesture that would've seemed threatening, proprietary, from anyone else. From Ralph, the gesture was still proprietary, but the tenderness and affection for his niece was unmistakable. He let the glossy black hair fall through his fingers, then nodded at me. "Let's talk."

Erainya said, "Wait."

The silent demand in her eyes was as clear as Ralph's. *We will not do anything rash. We will not make things worse.*

I nodded assent. "It's okay, Erainya."

She closed her hand around Jem's small fingers, hugging his shoulder tight with the other arm. "Honey, nothing is okay," she told me.

Outside, the afternoon was heating up, the air scented

with roasting lamb and pepper from Demo's Greek restaurant next door.

Ralph said, "Sorry about your car."

"The car is nothing."

He looked at me dubiously. Ralph knew about me and the VW. He'd known me when I'd first gotten it from my mother, my third year of high school. He'd driven in it with me drunk, sober, in danger, on dates. He'd teased me about it mercilessly while he went yearly from luxury car to luxury car and I continued clunking along in my mother's hideous orange hand-me-down. And he knew that the car had been part of who I was.

"Tell me the score," Ralph said.

He listened while I told him of my last few days.

When I was done he took a joint and a lighter from his shirt pocket and lit up. He took a long toke before speaking. "I don't know much about the *chiva* business, *vato*. Some things, I got no desire to learn. But I got some ideas where we can find the guy you want."

"Chicharron?"

He nodded.

"And Chich will happily give us a confession?"

"Shit, no, *vato*. That we *take*."

The ferocity in his eyes made me shudder.

Through the office window, Kelly and Erainya were standing by my desk now, talking. Jem was making sure all his toys were still there in the bucket.

"I want to keep things legal, Ralphas."

Ralph stared at me.

"I want DeLeon in on what we're doing," I explained. "I don't want to blow her case."

For once, Ralph seemed at a loss for words.

"Ana, huh?" He flicked some ashes toward the pavement.

"You know her," I said.

"Did you ask Ana about that?"

"She said about as much as you are. You object to her coming with us?"

He shrugged. "You want Ana to come along, *vato*—good luck. You know the rules of association. How you figure she's going to want to spend time around me?"

I tried to read his tone of voice, failed. "You've got no criminal record."

"On the books—no. You figure that matters?"

"I'll tell her we're going to ask around. She wants any control over the process, she'd better come along."

"Should be fun."

"You and DeLeon used to date, or what?"

Ralph took one last hit from his joint, then pinched the end out with his fingers. "How you getting around town these days, *vato*?"

I pointed to George's red Barracuda.

Ralph put on his glasses, then nodded approval. "Step up. George would appreciate you keeping her company."

"George would shit."

Ralph chuckled. "We meet at the Boots, say four o'clock?"

"I've got classes. Let's make it five-thirty. And you didn't answer my question."

"Tell Kelly good-bye from me, *vato*. And you understand, you get to hold her hand today only. After that, I got to kill you."

I looked into those Coke-bottle lenses for a few uncomfortable decades before Ralph said, "Kidding, *vato*. I'm kidding."

The tone of his voice did not comfort me at all.

He went out to his maroon Cadillac, whistling something that sounded oddly like a funeral dirge.

THIRTY-ONE

I was two-for-two at walking into class without lesson plans. I hoped that passing back the essays would make up for it, especially since I'd asked my grad seminar to be ready to discuss three Marie de France *lais* that I hadn't read in ten years.

Passing back the papers took all of five minutes. Everybody got a *B* and nobody had any questions. Then I was stuck in front of my eight favorite people with absolutely no clue what to do next.

They'd all come back for more—Sergeant Irwin; Gregory the mail boy; Brian the businessman; Edie and Marfa; the Morticia Addams drag queen; the grunge twins Simon and Blake. None of them had dropped the class. They'd even brought their Marie de France books with them. Shit.

And of course, my department head Professor David Mitchell had come to observe the class. Double shit.

I resorted to that ploy of the desperate—small group work. I broke the class into pairs and had them talk to each other about the *lais*—to compare *Guigemar* and *Lanval* to *Bisclavret* and look at attitudes toward women in the three stories. Hardly original, but hey.

I circulated from group to group, listening, occasionally asking a question. I hoped that the tightness in my face would be mistaken for keen academic interest rather than weariness and anger and the intense desire to throw up.

Every once in a while I'd sneak a look at Dr. Mitchell in

the back of the room. His face was alert, his dress clothes ironed, silver hair neatly combed. Each time he caught my eye he smiled encouragingly, then looked down, frowned, and scribbled something in his notepad.

After milking the group discussion trick for about twenty minutes I got the class back together and acted as scribe for their ideas on the blackboard. I drew bubbles and lines and tried desperately to remember the spelling for *misogyny*. I am, unfortunately, only a mediocre speller, to the complete glee of everyone who knows I hold a Berkeley Ph.D. in English. I long for a blackboard with a spell checker.

"She's a schemer," Gregory told me. "Woman is a schemer."

I tried to spell *schemer*. "Why?"

"Jeez—the way the women trick their men. I mean even in *Lanval* and *Guigemar*, it's the woman who manipulates. Especially in *Bisclavret*."

Morticia Addams rolled his/her eyes. "Not that damn werewolf story again. You think that chick was wrong? Like, what would you do if you found out your husband ran off into the woods and turned into a wolf every night?"

I was secretly thinking Morticia might find it cool, but I didn't say anything. I waved my chalk invitingly. "Any response to that?"

The businessman's cell phone rang. He muted it and smiled at me apologetically.

Sergeant Irwin sat forward. "I think we've talked about *Bisclavret* enough. A woman finds out her man's secret, uses that power to destroy him. End of story."

I widened my eyes. "It is?"

Edie looked up from her knitting needles. Her yarn today was powder-blue. "I felt sorry for the wolf."

She looked at Marfa, who nodded sympathetically. "Poor wolf has his clothes stolen, has to stay out in the woods, the faithless wife goes and marries someone else."

I turned and wrote *faithless* on the board. "Can you relate to her desire for a more . . . human husband?"

Marfa frowned at her knitting. "I suppose."

"Nothing excuses her betrayal," Sergeant Irwin insisted.

I looked at Professor Mitchell. He was following the conversation, which was perhaps a good sign. Perhaps not. I asked Simon and Blake, "Do you guys feel sorry for the woman at the end?"

Simon grinned. "Oh, man, the nose thing was tight."

I looked at Professor Mitchell. We'd definitely lost him.

I gestured at my class. "Somebody want to recap the nose thing?"

Gregory raised his hand. "The werewolf is saved by the king and kept as a pet. The wife and her new husband come visit the king and Bisclavret recognizes her. He can't talk so he bites her nose off, kills her new husband, leaves her offspring bearing noseless children for the rest of time."

Blake made a fist. "Totally *tight*."

"The wife reneged on her marriage commitment," the sergeant said. "She was the villain. She got punished, Bisclavret got his humanity back. Happy ending."

"From the wolf's point of view," Morticia said.

Sergeant Irwin shrugged. "You cross a wild animal, you get what you're asking for."

"Anybody else feel sorry for the wife?" I asked.

Apparently nobody did. I steered the conversation back to Lanval and Guigemar, took some more notes on the manipulativeness of women, tried to avoid gagging.

Then, hoping to balance things out, I gave a little lecture on the theory of women as the "fourth estate"—on the woman's voicelessness in medieval society and the ways a woman writer might subtly combat that problem. I got blank looks from Simon and Blake and Brian. A suspicious scowl from Sergeant Irwin. Edie and Marfa didn't take any notes but they did manage to finish knitting two booties.

Finally, mercifully, the period was up. We agreed to continue the discussion on Monday and the class filed out.

Professor Mitchell smiled at me. "Do you have a minute, Tres?"

"Sure."

Actually I had fifteen. Which I desperately needed to use getting ready for the undergrad Chaucer class, but I sat down next to Mitchell.

"That seemed to go well," he said.

"Oh—thanks."

"Getting Brandon's papers back to them quickly was an excellent idea."

"I'm a pretty fast grader. You know—the throw-them-down-the-stairs method."

Mitchell nodded absently. He was drawing little circles on the corner of his notes.

"I was kidding," I added.

He looked up, his focus a hundred miles off. Then he came back to the present and smiled. "Of course."

"Was there something else?"

Professor Mitchell's eyes tightened at the corners. "I heard on the news about Mr. Bertón. Is he—"

"He's stable. He's got friends with him around the clock. That's about all we can do for now."

"I'm sorry. It makes it hard for me to say—"

"That the University wants to terminate the investigation?"

Mitchell twirled his pencil. "How would you feel if that were so, Tres?"

"It's understandable. Would Erainya have a few more days to finish up on some loose ends?"

Mitchell let his shoulders relax slightly. "I'll arrange it with the provost."

"Good enough."

Some of the heaviness lifted from his face. He pointed

toward my brainstorming on the blackboard. "How is the teaching going so far? How do you feel?"

I wanted to answer *like shit,* but instead I heard myself say, "I'm enjoying it. It's a change of pace, a way to exercise a different part of myself for a while."

I think Mitchell was surprised and pleased by my answer. Not half as surprised as I was—especially when I realized that I meant it. At some level, I was enjoying it. For a few moments in there, I'd actually managed to get into the technicalities of Marie de France, of sexism and romance in the 1200s. It had momentarily let me forget about George Bertón.

"They say a change is as good as a rest," Mitchell offered.

"But not as good as a beer."

The old man laughed. "When this term is done, son, when the grades are in—I'm buying."

The offer warmed me, made me feel almost confident in my new position. Then Mitchell got up, patted me on the shoulder, and leaned closer to my ear. "But son, you misspelled *commitment.* Things like that count. I'll see you Monday."

He left me staring at *commitment,* wishing not for the first time in my life that the damn *C* word would just go away.

THIRTY-TWO

The Bexar County Jail/Sheriff's Department complex sits just north of the Commerce Street Bridge, its back to the railroad tracks and its face to the West Side.

If the cons ever got to look out the arrow-slit windows of the upper stories, they'd see the parallel one-way streets of Commerce and Buena Vista stretching west, through two miles of the worst heroin dealing and prostituting and gang-banging in the city. In other words, they'd see home. Commerce-Buena Vista was a conveyor belt, moving people from street to jail to street in regular, recursive cycles. Plenty of men spent their whole lives on that two-mile path.

I parked in the empty visitors' lot and looked up at the huge orange block of jailhouse. Different levels of roof were topped with black mesh boxes—workout areas for the prisoners. The sounds from up in the blocks were high-pitched and echoey and unreal, like some kind of gigantic aviary.

I went through the north entrance, past the metal detector into the sheriff's office foyer where I'd spent a lot of time playing as a kid.

Finding a deputy who knew me and would arrange a visit with Zeta Sanchez was no problem. Finding a deputy who thought it was a good idea would've been impossible.

I was led through the silvery bulletproofed doors into the sheriff's offices—hallways filled with men in soft uniform jeans and blue polo shirts, the sounds of phones and printers and fax machines.

Past the guards' entrance to the jail, I stopped at the desk so another deputy could go over my clothes with a metal detector wand.

The security doors clanked open. We passed down a long hallway, glassed-in guard stations at every intersection, then left into the visiting area.

The room was bisected by a Plexiglas wall that cut through the center of a long wooden table. The table was marked off into three sections by black tape, black letters on the Plexiglas above. My guard escort waved me toward "B," then left.

I was the only person in the room.

I sat down and studied the empty chair across from mine.

I'd just about memorized it when Zeta Sanchez was buzzed through on the opposite side.

Some people look like walking corpses after one night in jail. Then there are people like Sanchez, who actually seem to thrive on incarceration—who look more robust in prison than they ever did out in the real world. Jail is a world guys like Sanchez engineered, one that fits their sensibilities.

His ponytail had been shorn off and the hair that was left had been combed back and oiled. His once-thin line of beard had spread like watercolor ink across his cheeks and neck.

He sat down in front of me, his eyes a brilliant gold. His mouth was still swollen and stitched, but he managed a smile. He looked like a man who had just punked his cellmate out of smokes and dessert and was looking forward to more fun after dinnertime.

"Professor," he said. "You pulled me out at yard time, man. I was playing some B-ball."

I said, "Hector Mara's dead."

Sanchez's sated expression didn't change. He sat back, crossed his arms. "Yeah?"

"My question to you," I said, "is why are you still protecting Del Brandon?"

"I was shooting three-pointers, man. You pull me out for this?"

"Del lied to you, Zeta. There was no affair between Jeremiah Brandon and Sandra. I think you know that now. I think that's why you were asking around about your wife before you got arrested. Hector Mara was going to say something to a friend of mine last night—maybe something about what really happened six years ago. Now Hector's dead and my friend is dying. Chich Gutierrez saw to that."

Sanchez's eyes were gold ice. "I'm listening."

"Del wanted his father out of the picture. He decided he wanted him dead. He gave you the bait about Sandra and you made his kill. Del helped you out of town with a big thank-you handshake and the hope that you'd stay gone forever. Guy with your temper, it was a pretty safe bet you'd end up in prison somewhere. So when you came back, Del got a little nervous. He'd been striking up some business with Hector Mara and one of your old enemies, Chich. None of them were sure they wanted you finding out about that, or asking questions about what really happened to your wife. You wouldn't feel good learning that you'd gone into exile for six years for the murder of an old man who never even touched Sandra. Kind of make you feel stupid, wouldn't it?"

Sanchez put his large hands on the table between us and tapped his fingers slowly, as if trying to remember a keyboard routine. His eyes stayed fixed on me. "You know something for a fact?"

"Not yet."

"Then you got nothing to sell."

"You could help me along. Or you could keep sitting there behind bars, quietly taking the rap, trying to convince yourself that your old revolver just got into the police's hands by some weird accident. Surely good old Del couldn't have set you up."

Sanchez's face darkened. "I'm a patient man."

"You're waiting to be sure of things before you open your mouth. It bothers you, doesn't it—wondering if Sandra's dead, or with somebody else in some other state, or maybe laughing at you right here in town."

He sat forward an inch.

"You want a deal, *pendejo*?" he said calmly. "Bring me the bitch. Or tell me where she's buried. Then we can talk. Until then, you've got nothing I want."

Zeta stood. He strolled to the barred door, rapped against the window, and told the guard he had a basketball game to get back to.

THIRTY-THREE

Fifteen minutes after I'd decided she wasn't going to show, Ana DeLeon walked into my apartment.

She wore boot-cut jeans, the hems tucked into black Justins, her white collarless blouse overlaid with a denim work shirt, the sleeves rolled up. Her short black hair was tied with a red bandanna, the triangular flap hanging loose in the back. She looked like a *Sandinista* poster girl.

"I'm here," she said, like she was trying to come to terms with the fact.

I was sitting cross-legged on the floor between the futon and the coffee table, the final stack of undergraduate papers in front of me. I'd saved the freshman-comp gems for last. I had my trusty red pen in one hand and a Shiner Bock in the other and Robert Johnson draped across my shoulders like a fox stole—a habit that was somewhat cute when he was a kitten but many years and twenty-one pounds later had become chiropractically unsound.

On the kitchen counter, my aging Sears boom box was blaring out Son Becky's blues band, live from a San Antonio roadhouse in 1937.

I sized up DeLeon's outfit. "You look—"

"Different," she interrupted. "That's the point. Anybody asks who doesn't need to know otherwise, I'm your girlfriend."

"My girlfriend."

"That's right."

I started to laugh.

Her eyes flashed me a warning. "What?" she demanded.

"Sorry," I said. "You just don't seem like the girlfriend type."

"Oh really."

She came over and sank next to me on the floor. Robert Johnson evaporated from my shoulders. DeLeon calmly grabbed my neck with hard, warm fingers and pulled me forward. I figured my neck was going to snap like a twig.

It was a rough kiss, meant to cut off circulation rather than show affection. Her face smelled like apricot scrub. The force of her mouth left me seeing black spots, left my lips doing funny things for several seconds after she pulled away.

"What's the problem?" she asked. Her face was completely dispassionate, freezer steel.

I tried to say, "Wow." What came out instead was a muted honk.

"Sex crimes division, Navarre. Two years. I learned to play a lot of roles. A woman with her own identity, not belonging to anybody—people remember her. But somebody's girlfriend? Girlfriends are invisible."

"Invisible. Sure. Just don't ask me to stand up for the next ten minutes."

She tried to backhand me with her fist. I caught it.

"I'm your girlfriend," she repeated.

"Far be it from me to mess up a woman's cover."

I pushed her fist away.

On the boom box, Son Becky started pounding out eighth notes on his barrelhouse piano with enough gusto to put Jerry Lee Lewis to shame. "Black Heart Blues."

DeLeon looked down at my paperwork. "What are you working on?"

My body kept circulating blood around at unnatural speeds. Parts of me were just now feeling the punch of

DeLeon's kiss, notifying my brain that she was still sitting there, shoulder to shoulder with me, and what the hell was I going to do about it? With effort, I focused on the stack of essays. "Grading."

Her lips pursed in a controlled smile.

"What?" I asked.

"Nothing. You just don't seem like the grading type."

I showed her a hand gesture.

She picked up the paper I was halfway through, flipped back to the title page. She raised her eyebrows at me. " 'The Symbolism of the Boiling Pot in Three Medieval Plays'?"

"Aaron Brandon had a taste for the violent. I suppose it got the better of him in the end."

She pressed her mouth into an *M*. "I didn't tell you— I'm sorry about George. Kelsey caught the Hector Mara murder from the night squad this morning."

"That makes me feel tons better."

"Don't underestimate him, Navarre. Kelsey's dedicated."

I let it pass. "The shooting changed your mind about coming with us?"

"My mind hasn't changed. It's still a shitty idea."

"Then why?"

She got up from the floor, offered me a hand, then pulled me into standing position. "Besides the fact it beats you and Ralph Arguello on the loose by yourselves? Maybe if I had a few more months, I wouldn't do it. I'd keep picking away. But since I have exactly three days before they throw me to the cold-case squad, I feel the need to get inventive."

"Just let me get my baseball bat."

I capped my pen, threw it on the essays, then went to get my car keys and wallet off the kitchen counter. Son Becky's "Black Heart Blues" segued into "Midnight Trouble."

DeLeon walked over to the tai chi swords on the wall, dismissed them, then checked out the books on my shelf. She pulled a title—Marquez's *Cien Años de Soledad*. Colombian first edition. DeLeon's eyes fixed on the bookplate on the inside cover—Ralph Arguello's inscription.

"Are you going to make me ask you again?" I asked.

She looked up at me, caught my meaning, then looked back at the book, flipping a few pages. "There's nothing to tell."

"How serious was it?"

"Ralph and I went out together. Once."

I stared at her.

"Go ahead and laugh. I'd never heard of him before. I ran his name and license plate through TCIC, came up with nothing. I was stupid. I didn't look any further."

"You wouldn't have had to look far—pawnshop detail, theft, vice."

If I hadn't spent some time around her the last few days, I probably wouldn't have noticed the hesitation.

"Ralph lied to me," she said. "I bought it. When I found out, I wanted to kill him. End of story."

I still couldn't get an image of DeLeon and Ralph together. I wasn't sure I wanted to.

DeLeon flipped the Marquez novel shut. "I told you that because now that we're about to see him it's less awkward to tell you than not."

"Of course."

"Now can we drop it?"

I held up my house key and locked my lips with it.

DeLeon put the book back on the shelf. She looked over at the futon, where Robert Johnson was kneading himself a sleeping spot. "My mother was a cop for twenty-seven years—one of the first women in the department to do something besides youth services. You know that? She expected me to follow in her footsteps, wanted me to be the first daughter to inherit her mother's shield number."

"And did you?"

DeLeon nodded.

"Must've made her proud."

Ana's face stayed blank. "If she'd lived that long, I think she would've been proud. I've never ignored a lead, Tres. I've never backed off anything because it was risky or unorthodox. But I'm not lying—going anywhere with you and Ralph could end my career."

"You want me to tell Ralph to forget this?"

"You'd do that?" DeLeon locked eyes with me.

"I'd try. The thing is, it's personal now. Ralph knows George Bertón."

"That's worse," she said. "Personal makes it worse."

Son Becky kept singing—"Mistreated Washboard Blues." Robert Johnson reclaimed his place on the futon, sniffed it cautiously, then curled into a ball. DeLeon kept looking into me, trying to assess how serious my offer to call our expedition off was. I could see what she was thinking, and in the end I don't know what disturbed her more—the realization that I was serious, or the realization that she wasn't going to take me up on it.

She glanced over wistfully at Robert Johnson, now sound asleep.

Her face hardened. "Are we going or what?"

THIRTY-FOUR

Tell any San Antonian, "Meet me at the Boots," and they'll instantly know what you mean—the three-story-tall pair of white-and-brown shitkickers standing outside North Star Mall at Loop 410. It's a popular place for radio announcers to do live broadcasts, or occasionally for P.I.s to use as an easy rendezvous point. This afternoon we were lucky enough to have both.

Those crazy folks from KJ97, "all kinds of country," had set up a trailer platform next to the right heel. Two scraggly DJs with beards and black KJ97 T-shirts and headphones were bantering with each other into the mikes, making vapid jokes and promising fabulous giveaways and otherwise trying to lighten up the homeward commute of all the schmucks fifty yards away, crawling down 410.

Ana parked her Miata in the covered mall lot and we walked across the driveway to the asphalt island from which the Boots rose.

About fifteen people had gathered to watch the DJs. As we skirted the crowd, one of the DJs introduced a new song by rising local star Miranda Daniels. "This is—what, Joey, the *third* cut from her debut album to hit the charts?"

"That's right, Bear."

"Man, this girl is hot. We're talking about 'Tell Me Something,' right here on your country station, KJ97."

I clenched my fists and kept walking. It was the fourth time I'd heard the song that week, and I didn't even listen to country stations. Never do an investigation for a singer, especially an investigation that goes bad. I'm sure I'll be sixty years old riding in a department-store elevator someday and the Muzak version of "Billy's Señorita" will come on, and I'll see the blood and hear the shots in that warehouse all over again.

We pushed by a couple of ladies who were asking the soundman for freebies.

Ralph Arguello was waiting for us just between the tips of the Boots. He was still in his milky suit, the black shade overlays on his glasses giving the impression that someone had shot him cleanly and bloodlessly through the eyes.

He gave me a cross-thumbs handshake. "Glad you made it, *vato*. I had to listen to one more *pinche* redneck song, I was going to shoot somebody." Then he sized up Ana DeLeon. "Long time, *chica*."

"Not long enough."

He spread his hands. "She loves me, *vato*. We got to excuse the lady's broken heart."

"Fuck you, Ralph," DeLeon said.

The last time I'd heard someone say that to Ralph, in a barroom on South St. Mary's, the resulting scene had not been pretty. This time Ralph's razor stayed in its sheath. Ralph gave DeLeon his standard demonic grin.

"Sure, Ana." He held up his pinky, touched between his eyes, then pointed toward DeLeon's head. "But *we* know, eh?"

DeLeon said, "Let's get to business."

I agreed.

Ralph said, "Chicharron."

"You know where he is?"

Ralph looked at me.

"Of course you do," I corrected.

"Hector's salvage yard. Hector's dead, guess who's minding the store, tying up some loose ends before the cops come by. And taking whatever he can get."

"First," Ana cut in, "we need to lay some ground rules."

Ralph turned his palms up. "Such as?"

"I'm only here to watch. I hear anything worth following up on, I'll do so later, legally. I'm not condoning anything illegal. I'm not participating in anything illegal."

"Then you'd better wait in the car," Ralph said evenly. "That's legal."

"Not good enough. And unless I have to, I don't have a name."

"She's my girlfriend," I explained helpfully.

Ralph looked back and forth between us. He chuckled. "Okay. You a little paranoid, *chica?*"

"I want to find out what I can," DeLeon told him. "I don't intend to lose my job."

Ralph chuckled again. "Ana, *chica,* you think cops don't do this shit all the time? I know a detective—the brass have known for years he's associating with the Mexican Mafia. He gets the busts on their competition, uses intermediaries, does business with people worse than me. Nobody can prove shit. You should see the car this guy drives to work, man. I know another guy—"

"There's always scum at the bottom of the barrel," Ana interrupted. "I'd expect you to know them all. You don't know the majority of the SAPD and you don't know me."

I'd never seen Ralph take words like that so calmly, but he just smiled. "She's fine when she's mad, *vato.* Ain't she?"

I suggested, "How about we go?"

The Miranda Daniels song ended, and KJ97 started raving about the Vince Gill number coming up. Ralph looked over at them with distaste. "Yeah, *vato.* Let's go. Your car or mine?"

I glanced at Ana. "We go with Ralph, you're liable to see him do something illegal."

"I'll make some U-turns, *chica.*"

"And he'll smoke," I warned her. "Not Marlboros, either."

"On the other hand," Ralph said, "that sweet little Miata

of yours only got two seats, Ana. Right? Guess somebody could sit on my lap."

"Don't look at me," I objected.

Ana DeLeon looked back and forth between us.

"I have no intention—" Then she faltered. Moral dilemma.

Ralph grinned, waved with a flourish toward the curb where his maroon Cadillac El Dorado was parked in a red zone.

"The road to hell is paved with that shit, *chica,*" he consoled. "Right this way."

THIRTY-FIVE

The U-Best Scrap Yard on Southeast Military was a fine example of Early Apartheid architecture. Razor wire topped the fence. Sheets of corrugated metal lined the inside of the chain link so you couldn't see in to contemplate stealing the proprietor's countless riches. Dandelions choked the base of the fence and the sidewalk glittered with broken beer glass.

Beyond the entrance, narrow lanes twisted between mountains of electronics scraps, broken appliances, car fenders, road signs from defunct businesses.

Sitting in folding chairs by the gate were two large Latino men who resembled lounging sea mammals. They were playing dominoes on a three-legged card table.

"*Mira,* affirmative action," Ralph said. "Yard used to belong to this gringo named Sammy L. He retired, sold the place to Hector, now it's an equal-opportunity fence spot. Hector got North Side kids, West Side kids—whatever. Didn't tell the kids what to steal—just took anything they brought. Paid by the pound, I hear."

Ralph's tone was disdainful, like this was a business arrangement seriously below his caliber.

As we watched, a couple of kids strolled out past the human walruses. One kid was Anglo, the other Latino—both about sixteen, both thin and hard-bodied, greasy hair and baggy clothes. Both were counting money from wads of cash.

"Looks like somebody's still minding the store," Ana DeLeon said.

She opened the back door and got out. We followed suit.

One of the walruses nudged the other as we approached. They watched, sleepy-eyed, their slightly buck-toothed mouths slack under bristly spots of mustache. The guys must've weighed about two-fifty apiece. Their arms were slick, hairless brown slabs; their faces had the apathetic look of men who'd never had to move for anyone.

They barely blinked when Ralph drew his .357. The one on the right didn't even show expression when Ralph pistol-whipped him across the side of the face and sent him sliding to the ground.

The struck walrus slumped there on the pavement, his eyes glazed and stupid, the skin split open in a Z along his cheekbone. Even his blood ran slow, like it too was not used to being picked on.

His friend stayed frozen in his chair, gaping up at us.

I glanced at Ana. Her hands were in her back pockets. Her expression hadn't changed.

Ralph told the walruses, "That's how we say hello, *eses*. We're going in to talk to Chicharron now. You keep playing your little game, keep an eye on my car. You do anything else, anything stupid, we teach you how to say good-bye. *¿Comprendes?*"

They stared at us in complete silence, amazed. Then, real slow, both nodded.

We went inside.

"That was unnecessary," DeLeon grumbled.

"What's more," I said, "do you really think they're just going to sit still?"

Ralph grinned at me, and with a little discomfort I realized he didn't care in the slightest.

In the center of the scrap yard stood a stilted clapboard office that resembled a henhouse. Its exterior was covered with airbrushed graffiti—faux-cursive names outlined and colored to neon illegibility, scenes of violence and clusters of guns like bouquets, Spanish slogans, gang symbols from a dozen different neighborhoods. The windows were ragged squares made with a power saw. One of them held a large electric wall fan. A running board led up to the uncovered entrance.

Inside, Chich Gutierrez was sitting behind a metal desk, tapping a purple felt-tip pen against some paperwork that fluttered in the breeze of the fan's high-speed setting. Chicharron was sporting the same vampire look he'd had at the Poco Mas two nights ago—ponytail, silver cross earring, black leather boots, black jeans. He'd shed the trench coat in favor of a white tux shirt with the sleeves rolled up to the elbows. With a quill pen, the fashion statement would've been perfect.

Instead, there was a .38 revolver on his desk, but Ralph walked in and knocked it to the floor before Chicharron could even register our faces.

The room could comfortably hold two. With four of us, the floor sagged.

Ralph pointed his .357 at Chicharron. He said, "Get up."

The hum of the fan made Ralph's voice sound submerged. Chich studied us with black eyes. He looked at the gun, then at Ralph.

"You know who I am, Chich?" Ralph asked.

"Arguello."

"Then you know to get the fuck up."

Chich's eyes slid to Ana DeLeon. They dismissed her, then focused on me. I smiled.

Slowly, Chich stood.

His face was dead still except for his mouth, which kept twitching at the corners—from fear or amusement, I couldn't tell which. He said, "You going to make this a small mistake or a big one, Arguello?"

Ralph motioned for him to move to one side. I frisked him, removed two switchblades and a tiny 9mm from his pockets. Ralph found some keys and a cash box in the desk. We threw it all in the corner with the .38.

"You can sit down now," Ralph told him.

Chich sank back into his chair.

"You ice Hector?" Ralph asked.

Chich's mouth twitched. "That supposed to be a joke?"

"You the man in the white van, Chich. You better start telling me some things about last night."

"Fuck off, Arguello."

Ralph moved to the wall fan. He ran a fingernail thoughtfully along the plastic grill, then slid his .357 back in his belt. "I knew a guy once, got his hand stuck in one of those old metal fans. You know the round ones? Nowadays everything is fucking plastic, man. Look at this."

Ralph put his left hand on top of the fan, worked the fingers of his right into the holes of the grill, and pulled. The top wasn't fastened very well and bowed out. On Ralph's second pull, the grill ripped away with a watery *zing,* exposing the white circular haze of spinning fan blades. Ralph dropped the grill to the floor. He had little bloody lines on the pads of his fingers.

Ana stood in the corner of the room, her black Justin boot resting on Chich's .38.

"Cheap Taiwanese shit," Ralph said. "You think it'd do much damage, Chich?"

Chich tried for a smile. "You're full of it. Fuckin' pawnshop man."

He wasn't so chatty when Ralph picked up the open-faced fan and heaved it at him.

The spinning blades caught Chich's upraised forearms, grinding into him. The sound was like an outboard motor hitting a sandbar. Metal and plastic shuddered and Chich screamed. He lurched backward out of his chair, flailing, cursing, brushing himself violently like he was covered with fire ants, dragging the fan with him, a blade snagged on his tux shirt, the cord ripped free from the outlet. The fan clattered at his feet.

"You fucking lunatic!"

Chich held up his arms. They were ridged from wrist to elbow with smile-shaped contusions, some merely deep welts, a few ripped open and bleeding.

Ralph walked over to Ana, smiled at her, then bent down and picked up the .38 he'd knocked off Chich's desk. He pointed it at its owner. "Get up."

"I'm bleeding!"

"That was just an icebreaker, man. Get us through the posturing shit. Now sit in your chair."

Chich stood. He wiped his clothes, wiped his mouth. He didn't seem to notice he was smearing blood. Finally he got back into his chair.

Ana said, "Ralph—"

Ralph raised his hand, gesturing for patience. "So, *ese,* you want to tell us what you been up to?"

Chich crossed his forearms, pressed them against his stomach to stop the bleeding. The gesture didn't hide the fact that he was shaking. "I'll fucking kill you, man."

Ralph checked the revolver's chamber, spun in a round, aimed the gun at Chich's head.

"Me and some of my men," Chicharron started, "we were following Hector around. We were there last night. We didn't kill nobody."

"Uh-huh."

"I'm telling you. Hector and me done business together for years. I had some questions over the last month or so, but I wasn't looking to kill him."

Ralph kept the gun leveled. "What kind of business?"

Chich's look of hatred dissolved momentarily in pain. He chewed his lip, pressed his bloody forearms against the cloth of his shirt. "Jesus, man, put the damn gun down. Four or five years, Hector's been a steady customer—a key or two a month. Mostly black tar."

A kilo of black-tar heroin, depending on how it was cut, how far north it went, could bring anywhere from $20,000 to $50,000.

"Hector moved the stuff through RideWorks?" I asked.

Chich glared at me, then squeezed his eyes shut, rocked a little bit. "You're that asshole from the Poco Mas."

"Answer his question," Ralph said.

"I don't know how Hector moved the smack," Chich said. "I got my suspicions about RideWorks, but Hector's a friend. He pays on time, wants his privacy, I respect his business."

"Which is why you were following him in your white van, why you're here the day after he died, going through his desk."

"Hector'd been doing some strange shit. I was getting a little curious. Last month, he doubled his order—got two extra keys of heroin, wanted it on credit. Man's money's never been a problem before, so I said sure. He's an old friend. But that was four weeks ago and I ain't seen no money yet. Then I see him at the Poco Mas Wednesday night with *this* asshole—" He nodded courteously to me. "And I'm starting to get a little nervous. Last night, I shadow Hector and watch him make this meet out on Palo Blanco. While me and my boys are waiting, thinking about what to do, boom—gunshots inside. By the time we get inside and check it out, there's two bodies. Mara's dead. Your buddy Bertón's bleeding like a pig. Looks like they got in a little discussion that went bad, I figure maybe it's over my stuff. But there's no heroin, no money around that we can see. Then you drive up, and we decide it's best to hit the road. So you tell me. You answer *my* question—where's my fucking stash?"

Ralph grinned, looked at me. "I ain't happy yet, *vato*. You happy?"

Chich made a shaky sound that might've been a laugh. "I'm going to tell some of my friends in the big league, Arguello. I'm going to mention that an asshole named Arguello's been threatening me, throwing fans at me. What do you think my friends would do, man?"

Ralph jacked the hammer on the .38. "I think they'd have you replaced in twenty-four hours."

Chich's eyes went blank. "I don't know nothing else."

Ana DeLeon asked, "You see Sanchez since he was back in town, Chich?"

He shivered, trying a little too hard to focus on her. "Once. Nothing to do with the *chiva*. Him and me were cool. Zeta was just looking for his old lady, you know?" Then Chich looked at DeLeon more closely. "W-wait. I recognize you. You're—"

"This is my girlfriend," I told him. "You recognize her, we're going to have us a problem."

Chich kept looking at DeLeon, probably wondering if he had a card he wanted to play. Apparently he decided against it. "I didn't have nothing to do with Mara getting drilled. That's the truth."

"You're making me sad, *ese*," Ralph told him.

Chich raised his bloodied hands, placating. Whatever he was going to say was interrupted by footsteps, crunching in the dirt outside. An African American kid, maybe fifteen, stopped at the bottom of the running board and looked up into the shack, surprised to find a crowd. The kid's hair was long and nappy, his eyelids tattooed in blue like an Egyptian's, his clothes ripped camouflage and black heavy-metal gear. He had his hands full of car stereo parts.

Ralph said, "Come on up."

The kid got to the doorway, saw there was no room to go farther, then noticed Ralph's gun. The kid looked at Chich.

Chich mumbled, "This ain't a good time, Paul."

Ralph stepped toward the kid, tapped the stereo parts with the .38 barrel. "The man's right, Paul. How much you figure for all this?"

Standing next to Paul, I caught the distinct smell of aerosol fumes on his clothes. Looking into Paul's eyes I could see where those fumes had gone. His pupils had a bleary but steady glow, as if whatever brain cells still worked behind them had fused into one singular, misshapen energy source.

Paul said, "Twenty-five dollars."

Ralph laughed, then said to Chich, "Big spender. No wonder you and Hector such big leaguers."

From his coat pocket, Ralph took a business card and a few folded twenty-dollar bills and offered them to Paul. Paul dropped his stereo parts instantly and took the money.

"Next time come visit my Culebra location, *vato*," Ralph told him. "We do you right. In the meantime, hold this."

Ralph handed the kid Chich's .38. "Point this at him and count to a hundred, okay? You remember how to count that high? He moves, shoot him, come find me, I give you a bonus."

Paul nodded enthusiastically. Chich tensed.

"Good kid," Ralph commented. "See you around, Chich."

We left. Chich was trying to convince the kid that Ralph didn't really mean for him to shoot, not really. Paul was counting aloud.

We walked out the entrance of the scrap yard.

The walruses were back to playing their dominoes. Except for the crusted blood on the right one's face, the bloodstained bandanna he was sometimes using to dab it with, the men didn't look at all different.

They tried very hard not to look up as we walked out, across the street to Ralph's maroon Cadillac, which had miraculously had its windows washed.

"Life kicks ass," Ralph told us.

THIRTY-SIX

It wasn't until we were several blocks away that Ana DeLeon pounded her palm against the back of Ralph's headrest, jolting the joint out of his hand.

Ralph cursed. "What's the matter with you, *chica*?"

"You didn't have to do *any* of that back there, you asshole."

Ralph couldn't look back at us and stay on the road. He squinted indignantly at the traffic on Zarzamora. "Do what?"

"Draw blood. Play *machismo*. If you were trying to impress me, you failed."

Ralph's face darkened to a dangerous red. "You think I did that to impress somebody?"

"Either that or you're too stupid to ask questions another way."

Ralph and Ana started cursing at each other in Spanish— the usual names, the usual insults. I considered opening the car door and rolling onto the pavement. I figured my chances of living might be better.

Instead I yelled, "Knock. It. Off!"

The insults died down. Ana held up her hands, then dropped them, like she was throwing her disgust on the floor.

Ralph retrieved his joint, lit up, blew the smoke thoughtfully at the windshield. *"De volada."*

"Bullshit," DeLeon spat.

"That's how you got to live, Ana. I'm telling you—*from the will*. You think about things, plan them out too much, do them for reasons like impressing people—shit, you last maybe three days on the streets. You been out too long. You've forgotten."

"The hell I've been out. I've been right there, you shit-head. I've seen your *de volada*. I see it about six times a week, every time one of the homeboys gets shot to death."

Ralph waved the comment aside. "They froze up—the ones who stay loose, live."

"More bullshit."

"You see me breathing here, *chica*?"

"Yeah. And for how much longer?"

"Sour grapes, Ana. You still mad at me for the wrong reasons."

She started to respond. I took her hand and clamped it, hard.

Ana fumed, called Ralph some more Spanish names under her breath. We drove for a few blocks.

"Were you prepared to kill Chich back there?" she asked, more subdued now.

Ralph blew a line of smoke. "You don't get it. I didn't think that way. It wasn't like—okay I'll do *uno, dos, tres*. I feel what I got to do first and I do it. Then I see what happens next."

"You're saying you can't control yourself."

Ralph laughed, glanced back at me. "*Vato,* I shouldn't have tried, should I? No point explaining."

I didn't answer. Ana's hand in mine was as tense as a coiled snake.

"Where to next?" I asked Ralph, hoping to steer us somewhere else, someplace that might not lead to a gun-fight in the car.

"I got a few more ideas," Ralph said.

"More ideas like Chich?" Ana put as much disdain into the words as they could hold.

"What?" Ralph growled. "You afraid of finding out more about me, *chica*?"

"Not anymore."

"If I'd told you at the start—" Ralph began.

"You would've saved me a *lot* of time." Ana sank back in her seat and turned her hand so that it was gripping mine. Her fingernails dug into my knuckles.

Ralph's face stayed a block of sandstone for a good five minutes—which is, I think, the longest I'd ever seen him go without emotion.

Then he spoke in a voice that was cut from the same hard material.

"Twenty-eight and a half days," he told the windshield. "That ain't a lot of time. It ain't even enough."

THIRTY-SEVEN

There's just no stopping the momentum of a perfect day.

None of Ralph's other leads worked out. There was no word on the street about who had shot George and Hector Mara. No white vans. Nobody willing to confess. Nobody demanded that Ana kiss me to prove she was truly my girlfriend.

After riding in complete silence back to the North Star Mall Boots and mumbling good-byes to Ralph, Ana DeLeon and I drove back to my place in her car.

It was dusk, and the facade of 90 Queen Anne was losing definition. You could almost imagine the house in its heyday, back in the 1940s, when the wooden trim had been unbroken, the paint new, the bougainvillea clipped around the eaves. It had probably been one of the finer places in Mancke Park—the home of a banker, perhaps, or a prosperous merchant. The only thing that spoiled the illusion was the backward slant of the building, the way it had succumbed over the decades to gravity and bad foundation work. There were many days, like today, when I could relate.

On the curb was a black Honda Accord I didn't recognize, but I didn't think much of it. The Suitez family across the street was throwing a party, as they often did, and there were plenty of cars I didn't recognize. It wasn't until Ana looked at the Accord, cursed, then looked at my front porch and cursed some more, that I noticed Detective Kelsey.

He was sitting alone on the main porch of 90 Queen Anne, sipping a glass of iced tea that had probably been provided for him by my landlord, Gary. Gary is quite hospitable to people who come by to abuse me.

Kelsey was dressed in khakis and a denim shirt. His ruddy Irish face looked no friendlier than it had the day before.

As we approached the porch steps he said, "You two got some explaining to do."

I looked at Ana. "You want to stomp on him or should I?"

Ana had done away with the red bandanna. Her hair was disheveled. She fixed Kelsey with a look of smoldering hatred. "Go home, Tom."

"What the fuck were you thinking, Ana?"

"Kelsey," I said, "if you really have to, come inside and you can yell at us some more in there. But I need a drink."

"God damn it—" he started, but I was already walking around the side of the house toward my apartment, Ana behind me. After a few steps I heard Kelsey's chair creak.

I was just getting the chilled margarita pitcher from the refrigerator when Kelsey appeared in my doorway. "You're something, Navarre."

I handed a margarita to Ana, who had climbed, a little stiffly, onto the kitchen stool. Robert Johnson was sitting next to her on the counter, his eyes half-closed, mortally unimpressed. I tried to imitate his expression.

"You want a margarita, Detective? I assume you're off-duty."

Kelsey kept his eyes on Ana. "You think Lieutenant Hernandez wants to hear about the company you kept today?"

DeLeon took a sip of margarita, looked up at me with raised eyebrows. "Not bad, Navarre."

"*De nada.*"

Kelsey took a step farther into the room. "You're going

to lose your goddamn badge, Ana. What the fuck was that stunt you pulled at the salvage yard?"

"Interesting you heard about that so fast," Ana said. "You and Chicharron got some kind of relationship, Tom?"

"Fuck you. I know Chich from when I was on vice. He's a scumbag, but he knows when to talk."

Ana took another sip of her drink, then scratched the base of Robert Johnson's tail. He lifted his backside farther into the air for her. "What do you think, cat? You think this margarita is good enough to make Kelsey seem like less of an asshole?"

Robert Johnson closed his eyes, pleased by the attention to his tailbone. Ana said, "No, you're right. Probably not."

"I'm not kidding, Ana." Kelsey was just warming up. "If I find *anything,* anyone who tells me they were coerced into giving you information pertaining to the Brandon homicide—"

"Chicharron file a complaint?"

"You know damn well he didn't."

"Then go home, Kelsey. It's after hours. I don't need to listen to your shit."

Kelsey smacked the drink out of her hand. Robert Johnson disappeared before the first drop of margarita splattered on the counter. DeLeon shoved Kelsey backward.

I started to come around the counter and Ana snapped, "*No.*"

"You're a fucking disgrace, Ana," Kelsey said. "You'd think you'd be a little more careful, try to set some kind of example. What are we supposed to think, for Christ's sake? You screw up, you're screwing it up for every damn—"

DeLeon had a hell of a slap. Kelsey's face jerked to one side with the force of the strike. Ana's ring made a cut on his cheek—a small, bright ruby of blood.

Kelsey stepped back, rubbed his cheek, and smiled. "I wish it were that easy. I wish we could go at it for a few rounds and make things better. We can't. You know I'm right."

"Get out," Ana rasped.

Kelsey retreated, turned once in the doorway as if thinking of a final comment, then decided against it. He closed the screen door quietly on his way out.

"I'll get you another drink," I told Ana.

THIRTY-EIGHT

I filled our margarita glasses from my pitcher, came around the counter, and pulled up the stool next to DeLeon. We sat shoulder to shoulder, drinking silently.

When her drink was gone I refilled it.

She stared at Robert Johnson, stroked his fur. I found myself watching her fingers.

"It's too much," she said.

"What is?"

"Being a model for every other damn Latina detective for the next three generations. I won't accept that."

"It's too much," I agreed.

"I have enough trouble being responsible for myself."

"Sure."

She pressed her eyes closed, then held the margarita to her mouth.

We sat there until the Herradura tequila in my special recipe was starting to knit its way into my joints, turning my limbs into giant hot-water bottles. After a while Ana started focusing on the things in my kitchen. She asked about the Bay to Breakers poster on the cupboard door, Jem's watercolor pictures on the refrigerator. I even managed to get a faint smile from her when I told her about my brother Garrett and his postcard from Key West.

She glanced at the half-written lesson plans on the counter. "I'm not helping you get those done."

"Tomorrow. I've got the whole weekend now. I'm still supposed to visit George Bertón in the hospital tonight."

"I didn't tell you the truth about Ralph."

I plinked the rim of my glass. "It was a little more than just one date, wasn't it?"

She didn't say anything.

"So . . . you two used to be—" I searched for the right word. Thinking about Ralph Arguello and Ana DeLeon, no word seemed applicable. In fact, the whole idea seemed so absurd I started to laugh. Or maybe it was the Herradura.

Ana scowled. "Oh, screw you."

"I'm sorry. It's just—I've never seen anybody get under Ralph's skin the way you did today. At least not somebody who lived to tell about it."

"He tricked me," she said. "He left me feeling more betrayed than anybody I've ever known. If I got under his skin—good."

My smile faded. "He really hurt you."

"He's your friend. You don't want to hear it."

"Ralph is my friend," I agreed, "in spite of things that sometimes make me want to lock the door when he comes over, or not answer his phone calls. Some of the things I know about Ralph—"

I stopped. Ana didn't seem particularly surprised by what I was saying, but I reminded myself somewhere under the tequila buzz that I was talking to a homicide detective.

"Why do you keep him as a friend?" she asked softly.

"Because he's the most fiercely loyal person I've ever met. In some ways, he's also the most honest."

She made a sour laugh. "Honest."

"Ralph never lets me get away with anything. I get deluded, Ralph is the one who brings me back to reality every time. Ralph is never anything but Ralph. No pretense."

"For six weeks he convinced me he operated a retail chain."

"His pawnshops. They *are* a retail chain."

She gave me a withering look. "And what do you call the rest of it? Throwing electric fans at people. Pistol-whipping them. Where the hell does that come from—that side of him?"

It was my turn to be silent.

Ana swirled her drink. Between us, on the counter, Robert Johnson had his feet tucked under his chest and his eyes closed and his motor on full outboard purr. Life was good with Ana DeLeon's fingers in your fur. The bastard.

"You must've guessed he had that side," I told her. "You're a detective."

She scowled. "But he didn't—Ralph wasn't like that. Intense, sure. Kind of crazy. Relentless when it came to having fun. Like everything was on fire all the time with him. He kind of—he took my breath away. But violence . . ."

She stopped herself, searching my face. I think she realized she couldn't explain to me what she was thinking. She was probably right. Ralph as a lover of women was not something I *wanted* to understand. Especially not with this woman.

"I can see why Ralph would be loyal to you," she said.

"Are you insulting his intelligence?"

She smiled thinly. "No. You two have some things in common."

I got a sudden intrusive image of Ralph outside the U-Best Scrap Yard. He was grinning, checking out his newly washed Cadillac, his thick glasses circles of gold.

Ana looked at her empty glass. "Never mind. The tequila is talking."

"Let it talk. This week sucked."

She leaned toward me, clicked my glass with hers. "Amen."

We were shoulder to shoulder again, the way we had been this afternoon in my living room when she'd introduced me to my make-believe girlfriend. Maybe it was the similarity in scenes, or the killer margaritas, but the next thing I knew I was leaning toward her and kissing her— tasting lime and triple sec, my vision reduced to her temple and a sweep of glossy black hair.

We touched at the mouths only. Our arms stayed where they were—mine, at least, too paralyzed by disbelief to take further liberties. Finally, when I felt dizzy from oxygen loss and the margarita buzz that mixed very well with the scent of Ana DeLeon, she put her hard, long fingers gently on my chest and pushed me back.

She blinked slowly, sleepily, pulling her lips inward as if to reclaim them. She shook her head, then laughed as if she'd just caught herself doing something extremely silly.

"Mm-mm," she mumbled. "Not a good idea."

"You want to try again, just to be sure?" I was astonished my voice still worked.

She was still close enough that when she turned her head and sighed, her breath made a cool path across my arm. "No—listen, I need to go. You need to go visit your friend George."

"Ana—"

"Really, Tres. I've got to."

Deliberately, slowly, she slid down from the stool. She retucked her T-shirt into her jeans, brushed off her denim shirt, pushed the strands of hair out of her eyes.

"I'll call you tomorrow," she said. "About the Brandon case."

I nodded.

"You'll let me know if Ralph calls?" she asked. "He won't call me."

"I will. If he's speaking to me."

She reddened just slightly. "Good night."

"Night."

When the sound of her car engine faded down Queen Anne, drowned out by the sounds of *conjunto* music from the Suitez party across the street, I looked at Robert Johnson, who was still sitting on the counter. His eyes were contentedly half-closed and his fur still raked into furrows from Ana's fingers. He was purring.

"Don't gloat," I told him.

Then I went to get the margarita pitcher and see about emptying the damn thing.

THIRTY-NINE

My body refused to get drunk. At least not drunk enough to forgo visiting Brooke Army Medical Center later that night. Definitely not drunk enough to handle the sight of George Bertón.

Kelly Arguello was waiting for me outside the private room. We relieved two of George's friends from the Elf Louise program, then took their still-warm and very uncomfortable chairs next to his bedside.

No nonrelatives should've been allowed in George's room, of course, but the nursing staff seemed to have caved to Erainya and Jenny's vigil plans as docilely as George's friends had. Two of us would be with Bertón at all times until he woke up—if he ever did.

Kelly and I watched the lights on the bedside monitors, the glow from nighttime fluorescents reflecting on George Bertón's Bryl-ed hair, the moisture that was crusting around his unblinking eyelids. His chest rose and fell with the ventilator's beat.

George looked like an insect half-chrysallized—small desiccated patches of his old self just barely recognizable under white swells of bandages, tubes, tape, and sheets. The skin of his face, what was visible beneath the breathing apparatus, looked thin as rice paper, streaked with capillaries. His hands lay at his sides palm up, curled, and motionless.

We listened to the ventilator. The accordion pump went

up and down in its clear plastic tube, filling George's lungs and deflating them with dispassionate efficiency.

"I want to bolt out of this room," Kelly whispered. "Do you feel like that?"

She'd changed into jeans and a man's white button-down, probably Uncle Ralph's. The sleeves were rolled up and I caught the mixed scents of Ralph's bay rum on the linen and chlorine from Kelly's skin and hair. I imagined she'd made time this evening to visit the Alamo Heights pool, done a few hundred laps. Her hair was tied back in a ponytail and the roots were still slightly damp. She looked at me, her eyes soft and brown and gently pulling as Gulf Coast surf.

"Put on a brave face," I said. "Sound happy. Tell George he's looking good."

"He looks terrible, Tres. It's like he isn't even in there."

"He's not a corpse."

"I know. It's just . . . Sorry. I'm talking like a wimp."

I stared at a photo someone had put on George's bedstand—a silver-framed picture of Bertón, perhaps ten years younger, and a pretty woman that I decided was his wife Melissa. They were standing on a curve of granite overlooking the hill country—probably the summit of Enchanted Rock. I'm sure the photo was meant as a nice "get well" gesture for George, but somehow the smile of that woman murdered so many years ago, the image of her with her arms around George, made me uneasy.

When I looked again at Kelly, she was staring at my chin—maybe tracing the network of tiny cuts there I'd received from my tumble into the drainage ditch last night.

"What are you thinking?" I asked.

She gave me a small, sad smile. "It's nothing."

"Look, if you really want to leave—"

"No, no. I'm staying with *Tío* Ralph overnight. I should be glad to be out of the apartment. He's in a pretty black mood."

"About?"

"Oh—some woman."

She waited for a response. I didn't give her one.

"I was hoping Ralph had done himself a favor and forgotten this lady. Apparently they ran into each other today. You wouldn't think a woman could affect Ralph very much, would you?"

"I wouldn't know."

"Mmm."

The monitor lights continued blinking green. I found myself watching the digital numbers of George's heart rate wavering between 51 and 52. Occasionally the beat faltered and the numbers blinked off completely, then came back on. After a few minutes of watching this, I had to look away.

Kelly took something out of her pocket. "Before I forget. Maybe this is nothing. We found it when we were sorting George's files."

She handed me a carbon copy of a *While-you-were-out* message from Erainya's phone record book, written in George Bertón's immaculate cursive, dated Wednesday. The note said, *Poco Mas. Brandon. Mami called back.*

"Make any sense to you?" Kelly asked.

"No, but I'll follow up."

Kelly nodded. With what was obviously great force of will, she leaned toward the bed and touched George's forearm in the free space between the hospital wristband and his IV plug.

She blinked, then withdrew her fingers, apparently satisfied that Bertón was really there.

"You think all George's friends balance out?" she asked me.

"Against what?"

"Melissa. I was thinking about something Jenny told me—how different George was before he lost his wife. You didn't know him back then?"

"No."

"Apparently not many people did. Jenny made him sound like a completely different person—tender with Melissa but arrogant with everybody else. Very few friends. Heavy drinker. A hell-raiser. According to Jenny, George used to act like this air force hotshot and a lot of people hated him. Can you imagine?"

I admitted that it didn't sound like the George I knew.

"Then he lost Melissa and it just—made him gentle. Charity work. New friends. Always time for anybody. Most thoughtful guy you'd ever—" Kelly stopped, exhaled a shaky breath. "So do you think it balanced out, Tres? You think the friends ever made up for losing that one person?"

"I'd guess it doesn't work that way."

"Kind of scary that one person can count for so much. I hear about a couple like George and Melissa and I don't know. Maybe I'm jealous, or maybe I'm scared as hell and thankful that I don't have somebody that important. Does that make sense?"

I didn't answer.

She smiled sadly, examined my face some more, then reached up and rubbed her thumb against my lower lip, along the side of my mouth.

Her thumb came away tinted red from Ana DeLeon's lipstick. Kelly wiped the color off on her jeans.

We stayed next to George until two of his friends from the Big Brother program came to relieve us.

FORTY

The Poco Mas Cantina was a different place on Saturday morning. Only one battered pickup truck sat in the front lot, and the music coming from inside the bar was subdued, a soft instrumental *corrido*. In the daylight the bar's facade showed its age. Pastel stucco walls were bleached and cracked like a grandmother's makeup; the air-conditioner units whined asthmatically as they dripped condensation onto the gravel.

Inside, one customer, a muscle-bound Latino man in T-shirt and shorts, was sleeping at the center pink Formica table amid wadded-up dollar bills and empty beer bottles. The old bartender with the silver grease-mark hair was placing last night's dirty glasses into a washer rack. A younger assistant stood at the liquor display with a clipboard, doing inventory. At the back booth, where I'd encountered Mary and the armed *locos* three nights before, a chubby, fiftyish Latina woman was counting money into a cash box. She was one of the women I'd seen Wednesday evening, lap-hopping at the bookies' tables. She still wore the same uniform—tight red dress, red hose, smeared peach makeup, hair like a blowtorch.

Neither of the bartenders looked thrilled to see me. The older man reminded me about the new management, then told me the bar was closed.

"I'm looking for Mami," I told him.

His right eye developed a tic. He glanced nervously over at his assistant, then back at me. "Closed. Eh?"

"No Mami?"

"Closed all day."

I slid one of my Erainya Manos Agency cards across the bar. "When you see Mami, tell her I'm a friend of the man she talked to earlier in the week—the man with the Panama hat. Tell her I need to talk."

The old man gave no sign of comprehension. He scooped his hand toward the door, like he was bailing water, then told me a few more times how new the management was and how closed the bar was.

I stepped outside into the graveled lot. Across the street, two women in sack dresses trudged down the sidewalk, lugging plastic La Feria bags. A man in a filthy butcher's apron smoked a cigarette in front of a little meat market. Down on the end of the block, the yellow-capped towers of Our Lady of the Mount rose up against the gray sky. The clouds moved just fast enough so that the iron Jesus seemed to be pushing through the gray like the masthead of a ship.

I crossed the street and walked toward the church.

At the steps of the main sanctuary, I looked back. The old bartender was a tiny figure in the cantina doorway. He was looking in my direction.

I walked inside the church entry hall, past marble columns, oil portraits of archbishops, and polished oak tables neatly stacked with bilingual Catholic newsletters.

Beyond the lacquered interior doors, the sanctuary opened up into a cavern of gilt and air. Angels laced the domed ceiling. Candlelight glittered in every recess, and far up ahead the altar was bedecked for Sunday service.

I walked up several pews and sat down, my eyes fixed on the distant central crucifix.

I didn't know why I wanted to be in a Catholic church after an absence of over fifteen years. Maybe it was my visit to George Bertón's bedside the night before. Maybe it was just something Kelly Arguello had said.

In the pew rack was a Bible, a folded program adorned with doodles by some bored child. A broken pencil. A single rosary bead.

I closed my eyes and the sanctuary doors sighed open behind me. Steps clicked down the aisle—two sets. The pew across from mine creaked.

I looked over and saw the old bartender, kneeling stiffly. He crossed himself with a bony hand. Five rows back, the woman from the bar was settling into a pew. Her face was blotchy from new crying. She frowned straight ahead, then forced her eyes shut and started mumbling a silent prayer.

I looked at the bartender.

His smudges of hair glowed like candle glass. He had leathery skin, deeply wrinkled. He looked frail—probably no more than a hundred pounds. His green slacks and black-striped shirt reminded me of something George Bertón would wear.

"You are Catholic?" he asked me.

The broken English was gone, replaced by beautiful Castilian Spanish, the kind you rarely hear in Texas.

"I used to be," I answered, also in Spanish. "I suppose I still am."

He slid back from his knees onto the pew cushion. The effort made his leathery face tighten. He laced his hands over his belly as if holding in an appendix pain. "That red car on the street. The man you mentioned . . . he was driving it Wednesday night."

"You've got a good memory."

"It's a nice car. His name was Bertón, sí?"

"Did you speak to him?"

The old bartender gestured toward the woman behind us. "I didn't say anything. He spoke with Mami."

I looked back at the middle-aged woman in red. She was still praying in a long, continuous whisper, her eyes and hands squeezed tight. The way the old bartender had spoken her name . . .

"You two are married?" I asked.

The bartender gave me a slight smile, like he was used to hearing that question, spoken with the same amount of disbelief. "Ten years."

"What did Mami tell my friend George?"

The bartender winced. "Mami is foolish enough to sit on the porch most afternoons—at the house, there behind the bar. She was an easy victim for conversation."

He probed his belly gently with his fingers, trying to relocate the source of the pain. "She wants to know if your friend is all right, you see. She heard he was shot, and she had told him things that might get him into that kind of trouble. She has a big heart, and is foolish about talking."

Mami's plum-meat-colored lips kept moving to the *Ave Maria.*

"What things did she tell Mr. Bertón?" I asked again.

"About the man Hector Mara met in the bar—two weeks ago. *Rey Feo.*"

Rey Feo, the "ugly king," was a title for one of the rulers of San Antonio's fiesta week, but I had a feeling that wasn't what the old man meant.

"A nickname," he explained. "I don't know the man's real name. He only came to the bar that once. I asked Mr. Mara about him—*Rey Feo* is what he said."

"A heavyset Anglo," I guessed. "Dark-haired."

The old man shrugged. "I only tell you all this because Mami already made the mistake of talking. Mami's got a big heart. There isn't much lying in her."

"Did she tell my friend anything else?"

The bartender stared at the crucifix over the altar. The gilded-wood Christ looked centuries old, his face as stoic and emaciated as the Mission Indian who had probably carved him.

"Do you understand how this could be bad, me talking to you?"

"But here you are."

He massaged his belly, sighed. "I love her, you see. I can't give her much—not my body, most nights not even my time. I want to at least give her some peace. She wants to know she didn't get your friend killed with what she said. She gets like this over things."

"What did she say?"

"That she recognized a woman. A woman in the photograph your friend had."

My blood slowed to syrup. "Who?"

"There is a man called Zeta Sanchez. This was a picture of his wife. It was a bad photo, but Mami said yes, it was the right woman. Is your friend healing, mister? I want to tell Mami."

I got up, didn't answer him, then walked down to Mami's pew. I knelt next to her. I could hear a faint tremble in the prayer she was whispering.

"It's okay," I said. "The man you spoke to will be fine. He told me to say thank you. To you and your husband, he said to say, 'God bless you.'"

She shuddered, but kept her eyes closed, still praying.

When I looked back from the doorway, the old man was kneeling where I'd left him, facing the altar now, still five rows ahead of his young wife. They both looked at peace, completely unaware of each other or any purpose other than communion with God.

FORTY-ONE

It was six that evening before I went out again.

I'd promised Erainya I'd pick up Jem from his first formal play date, which Erainya with her usual unorthodox parenting had arranged. Jem had come away from the school visit talking about Michael Brandon, and Erainya had followed up on the dubious assumption that a play date would do both kids some good.

I pulled in front of the Brandons' soon-to-be-former home on Castano. A battered blue Camry sat in the driveway. Ines' car wasn't there. The house's front door was open.

I went to the doorstep and yelled hello into the living room. The sound echoed. The brass mezuzah plaque had been pried from the door frame. The fireplace was now sandblasted to unpainted stone, the craters from the gunshots cemented over. The white carpet had been stripped, leaving the floor raw wood with carpeting tacks and glued bits of padding.

I picked my way through the rest of the house. There was a box of Arm & Hammer on the kitchen counter, a yellow sock with a red toe in the hallway closet. The rubble of Legos in the dining room was the only indication that Jem and Michael might've played here recently.

In the second bedroom, only the smell of talcum powder still lingered. Michael's sheet cave was gone. There was one tiny, crumpled ball of paper in the middle of the floor. I unraveled it—a cutout photo of an artificial Christmas tree from an advertisement circular. I recrumpled the paper and dropped it where I'd found it.

The master bedroom was empty. Out the window, in the backyard, a young Latino guy was coming down the steps of the little apartment above the garage, carrying a moving box. Paloma stood in the doorway above, calling instructions down to him.

The guy with the box stopped as I walked into the backyard. He frowned at me, leaned backward, and balanced the box on his belly. "Mister?"

The resemblance to Paloma was striking. He had the same chunky build, the same dark squashed face. He was maybe twenty-five. Khaki shorts, red Chris Madrid's T-shirt.

I told him my name, and that I had come to pick up Jem.

"Mrs. Brandon took the boys out to get some food," he said. "410 Diner."

"That was nice of her." I looked up at the tiny balcony above the garage door. Paloma was clutching the railing, her arms straight, her face a stone scowl. "*¿Cómo esta, señora?*"

She looked down at her son. "Juan, don't stand there. *¿Dos más cajones, eh?*"

She disappeared back through the doorway.

Juan took one more uneasy look at me, then gravity decided the matter. He hefted the box farther up on his gut and lumbered down the driveway toward the Camry.

I went up the stairs and ducked through the tiny doorway of Paloma's apartment.

The room was a triangular attic—the ceiling no more than eight feet high at the apex. The window on the back wall looked out onto the alley. Windows on either side of the front doorway gave a good view of the main house, the backyard, the driveway.

Paloma was stuffing wads of newspaper into a box. Next

to her on the floor was a line of assorted ceramics. To the left, a few packed boxes were piled on a stripped twin-bed frame. By the front window, a fruit crate was covered with a lace doily and decorated like an altar—framed photos, Native American fetishes, candles.

"May I come in?" I asked.

"You're here," Paloma grunted, without turning around. "I say no, you will still be here."

She wadded up another sheet of newspaper and stuffed it in her box.

I knelt to look at the fruit-crate altar. The largest photo, yellowed, showed a younger Paloma with a man. Standing between them were five boys and a girl, their ages ranging from toddler to teenager.

I picked up an object next to the photo—a thin, irregular loop of bone embroidered with lace. "Deer's eye?"

She turned toward me. Her lower lip stuck out, her expression decidedly masculine. Suddenly she reminded me strongly of Winston Churchill. *We shall never surrender.*

"My children's," she mumbled. "They wore it during their first year. Miguel also."

"To protect the wearer from evil," I said. "That's an old custom."

Her face softened. "My grandmother made it for my mother, from a deer my grandfather shot in 1910. We are an old family."

"These are your children in the photo? Your husband?"

That question seemed to shut down any social progress we'd been making. Paloma looked away, picked up a ceramic goblet. The handle was crudely fashioned in the shape of a dragon. She stroked its wings gently, then wrapped the goblet in newspaper, placed it in the box.

"She would throw all these things away," she grumbled. "Such a waste."

I straightened up as much as I could against the slanted

ceiling. Down in the driveway, Paloma's son Juan was trying to figure out how to wedge one more box into the Toyota's trunk.

"Must've been hard," I said, "seeing what you saw the night of Dr. Brandon's murder."

Down below, Juan was looping rope around the trunk lid of the Toyota. Through the shadeless windows of the main house, strips of afternoon light cut across the bare hardwood floors.

When I turned, Paloma was right behind me. She'd moved with a silence I found frightening in a woman so large. There were deep trenches under her eyes, a streak of flour along her jawline.

She took the deer's eye from my hand. "What is it you want, señor?"

"I want to understand what you really saw that night, Paloma—it doesn't make sense to me."

"I do not want to talk to you."

"Someone else fired those shots into Aaron Brandon. Zeta Sanchez was merely set up for the kill."

Her face flattened. "You call me a liar?"

"Nobody else saw Sanchez that night. Nobody else heard the shots. Only you. A man's life rests on what you say."

Footfalls on the steps outside.

"*La policia* believe me." Paloma said it evenly.

"The police are licking their lips to put Sanchez away. What really happened, Paloma? Why are you willing to lie?"

From the doorway, her son said, "Leave her alone, mister."

I turned. Juan's face was hard. His red Chris Madrid's T-shirt was untucked from his shorts. His fists were balled.

Paloma kept turning the deer's eye around in her thick fingers like a tiny steering wheel. She darted her eyes at Juan and said, "*La caja, mijito.*"

Juan hesitated, then saw the sternness in his mother's

expression. He got the box, hefted it, then carried it out, his dark eyes still cracking the whip at me as he passed.

When he was gone, Paloma sighed. "I saw what I saw, señor. *Es todo.*"

"Somebody put two bullets into Hector Mara. If you think silence will keep you safe, it won't."

Her expression hardened. She picked up another ceramic mug, this one shaped like a man's head with a battered blue hat and grizzled beard and a drunken grin. Paloma wrapped its face in newspaper.

"I keep everything, señor." Paloma set the mug in her box, picked up an ashtray. "My children's things. My husband's photograph. Ines' things too, now. Where I go, these things all go with me. Even the bad is important."

She gave me a wary look, as if she hoped but did not anticipate that I would follow her reasoning. "You understand, señor?"

I stared down into Paloma's half-packed box. I took a deep breath, trying to control the desire to kick myself. "Maybe I do, Paloma."

I headed back down her rickety stairs, past her glaring son, down the driveway to George's red Barracuda. I had a meeting to make at the 410 Diner.

FORTY-TWO

Sunset was a good time to hit the 410. The luminous strips of blue and orange sky went well with the neon trim on the *nuevo moderne* diner. Its long oval windows glowed with light and the bar inside glistened green and black. Even the menu board exuded a kind of oily class—black acrylic inscribed with Day-Glo colors that made the words *mashed potatoes & meatloaf* seem chic and trendy.

In the main room, booths were molded from enough chrome to refit several '57 Chevy Biscaynes. Along the walls hung neon-laced portraits of Jimmy and Marilyn and the other Hollywood regulars.

By the front window, three middle-aged Anglos were drinking margaritas and talking about a cattle auction. Midroom, at one of the black Formica tables, an older couple ate in silence—the man with grizzled beard and ponytail, leather cowboy hat, pastel Apache-print Western shirt; his date an enormous pasty woman in a denim dress.

Ines and the kids sat at a back booth. Del Brandon, my favorite person, sat in a chrome chair at the end of the table. Del was talking to Ines, tapping his finger on a set of documents. Jem and Michael were playing with packets of Sweet'n Low.

I grabbed a menu from the waitress station, then slid into the booth beside the kids. "Sorry I'm late."

Jem shrieked with delight and gave me a crushing hug. Nobody else did.

Ines' hair was loose around her shoulders, her face washed clean of makeup. She was dressed for moving—jeans, no jewelry, an oversized Fiesta '98 T-shirt with a glistening crumple of packing tape stuck to one sleeve.

Del's Hawaiian shirt and slacks were disheveled. His wedge of black hair had started to crumble. His expression was equal parts anger and weariness. "What the fuck are you doing here?"

"There are children present, Del. Behave. I'm just picking up my amigo Jem. You remember Jem."

Jem waved hello by flapping a Sweet'n Low packet.

Del glared at Ines. "You invite this jerk?"

I picked up the three-page document in front of him. "Something from your lawyers?"

Del tried to swipe the papers.

I kept them away.

The document seemed to be an agreement between Ines and Del. It recognized Del's ownership of RideWorks, Inc., and renounced all future claims by Aaron Brandon's estate. Ines had already signed it. Her signature—

I looked up at her. "Why?"

Del said, "That's none of your goddamn business."

"Tres." Ines looked protectively at Michael, saw that he and Jem were occupied with saccharin and Captain's Wafers. "Del's right," she said firmly. "This isn't your business."

I flipped the document into Del's chest. "Won't do you much good in jail, partner."

He tried to grab the front of my shirt.

I intercepted his wrist, forced it down on the Formica tabletop. "Temper," I said softly.

Ines hissed, "Stop it! Both of you."

Del yanked his hand away. "You want to see something from my lawyers, Navarre? You'll get it."

"Del," Ines said. "You have what you wanted. Now leave."

Del kept glaring at me. He folded the papers, pocketed them. "Don't fucking come near me again, Navarre. You understand?"

"Good-bye, Del," Ines insisted.

Brandon shoved the metal chair back, gave me one last drop-dead look, then pushed past the waitress who was just bringing the food. The waitress called after him, "But . . . sir—?"

I tapped the table for her. "Right here, please."

Ines and Michael and Jem accepted their meals without a word. Low-cal chicken breast salad for Ines. Hot dogs and corn on the cob for Michael and Jem. Del had ordered the Sonora casserole platter with black-eyed peas and buttered squash and enough corn bread to construct a small toolshed. That was fine by me.

At the next table, the older couple sawed into their chicken-fried steaks. The geezer with the cowboy hat looked away quickly when I caught his eye.

Ines poked at her salad. Jem ate his hot dog. Michael sat frowning at his.

"Michael, eat your food," Ines said.

"Not hungry."

"Try the corn. You like corn on the cob."

Michael picked at the corn skeptically.

Jem got halfway through his dinner and announced himself full.

"Tell you what, guys," I said. "I've got some quarters. How about you check out the sticker machines by the entrance. See if you can get me a Betty Boop, okay?"

Jem negotiated for a Felix the Cat, too. I told him he drove a hard bargain. Then I fished out as many quarters as I had and handed them over. I got out of the booth and let Jem and Michael scramble past.

When I scooted back in, I tried to concentrate on Del's Sonora casserole—corn tortilla, cheese, squash, tomato, a hint of salsa and sour cream. Eating was easier than what I needed to say.

"I didn't expect Del," Ines told me. "I wouldn't have brought the boys."

"Why did you sell out?"

She stabbed her fork into the salad. A strip of mirror set into the black wall tiles by Ines' shoulder gave back her reflection, hazy with grease specks.

"I don't want any part of RideWorks," she said. "What's the difference?"

"You really think signing the company over will keep Del silent about you?"

Her hesitation was almost imperceptible. She brought the fork to her mouth, took a bite, only then glanced up. "What are you blathering about?"

"You're Sandra Mara."

She tried to maintain her look of cold annoyance, but something in her eyes spiraled downward. She lowered her fork, arranged it parallel to her plate. "No. I'm not."

At the entrance of the diner, Jem and Michael scrutinized the toy vending machines, looking for just the right investment. Behind them, the second hand on the pink neon bar clock ticked its way between the only two numbers—4 and 10.

Ines managed a small, bitter laugh.

"You don't know . . ." she started. "You can't possibly know how many times I've anticipated this conversation. I've imagined facing a cop. Or a *veterano* with a gun pointed at me. Now I'm sitting across from a pissant private dick who's a closet English teacher and his boss' baby-sitter, and the best I can come up with to save myself is, 'No, I'm not.' "

"I wouldn't call it baby-sitting."

She crumpled her napkin, threw it against the A.1. steak sauce in disgust.

"Well"—her voice dry as a West Texas creekbed—"what now?"

"Wish I knew."

Cheers from across the room. The three Anglos by the window were applauding the waitress as she brought them fresh margaritas.

Ines said, "Tres, I can't lose my son."

"Don't you think I've considered that?"

"The police would find reasons to take him away. If Zeta knew, he'd have me killed. You haven't—"

"Not yet. I wasn't sure until tonight. Paloma has some of your old things, some mementos you meant to get rid of. One of them was a sailor's-head mug. There's three just like it in the farmhouse on Green Road. Something from your grandmother?"

Ines pushed her salad away. "What do you want?"

"Tell me you didn't know about your husband's murder. Tell me you're innocent."

"Why? So your report will be more complete?"

"Come on, Sandra."

"Don't call me that."

"Ines, then. Let me help."

"Zeta will have me killed. Michael will have no one."

"Talk to me. We'll figure it out."

"Ha."

I dropped my fork into the casserole. "You're right. You should be having this conversation with someone else."

I started to slide out of the booth.

Ines said, "Wait."

She studied me, her hands pressed together, fingertips to her lips. She looked like she was weighing a lot of options she didn't like.

"You want to know about Sandra Mara?" she asked. "Let me tell you about Sandra Mara."

She sat forward, tapped the scar on the bridge of her nose. "Sandra Mara got this when she was eleven, trying to fend off her drunk stepfather. She didn't do a very good job. He broke her nose with a beer bottle. If he hadn't scared himself so bad with the amount of blood coming from her face, that would've been her first experience with sex."

"Ines—"

"Just listen," she insisted. "You think that was unusual for a girl in the Bowie Courts? My point is, most girls would've fought better. They would've had their own razor blades by then and known how to use them. At least they would've screamed, raised hell with their mother or their brothers, told somebody the truth about what had happened. Sandra did none of that. She was too afraid. She spent the next five years in the Rosedale Library, every afternoon and evening, reading books, trying to avoid going home. By the time she was thirteen, when the neighborhood *locas* threatened to kill her if she didn't join a gang, Sandra had read *Jane Eyre, Great Expectations,* fifty other books—but she had no survival skills. She would've died if her brother Hector hadn't joined Zeta Sanchez's set, got himself shot in the leg so his little sister would have the right connections to be left alone."

Jem and Michael had scored their first purchase from the sticker machine. Michael was prying open the plastic capsule while Jem watched impatiently.

"You're pretty hard on yourself," I said.

Ines picked a toothpick from the dispenser, rolled it between her thumb and finger. "Sandra Mara couldn't have been a mother, Tres. Her idea of heaven was her grandmother's farm, where she and Hector moved when she was sixteen. No homeboys running through the house. No strung-out mother or drunk stepfather to avoid. Nothing to keep Sandra from losing herself in books. She even got a college scholarship her senior year. But you don't get away from the South Side without a fight. The same afternoon Sandra found out about the scholarship—"

"—was the afternoon Hector brought Zeta Sanchez out to visit," I said. "I read your journal."

Her mouth hardened with distaste. "When you dig into somebody's past, you really dig, don't you?"

"It wasn't hard to find."

Ines snapped her toothpick, flicked the pieces away. "If you read it, you know. Sandra and Zeta hadn't seen each other in two or three years, since back at the Courts, when Sandra hadn't been much to look at. But Zeta looked at her that afternoon, and you know what? Sandra couldn't fight it. Hector couldn't help her. She let herself get *claimed*. Zeta and Sandra got married two months later. A few months after that, Zeta said, 'You stop college.' Sandra went along with that, too."

"Zeta Sanchez wouldn't be an easy person to fight."

Ines stared at me as if her perspective were shifting, as if she were suddenly aware that I was much farther away than she'd thought. "*Maldición*. Always an excuse, eh? Always a reason to give in. You and Sandra Mara would have gotten along fine, Tres. Sandra might've had five or six of Zeta's babies after quitting school, waited for Zeta to get tired of her and leave, or start using her as a punching bag. Sandra saw her mom go through all that. Would've been easy to follow tradition. But that fall while I was at Our Lady of the Lake, something happened that made me want to stop being Sandra Mara."

"You met Aaron," I said.

"I told you the truth. I was in his class that fall. I didn't know Aaron had any connection to Zeta's employer, Ride-Works. I don't think Zeta *ever* made the connection. He never realized Aaron had been one of my teachers. Aaron was . . ." She laughed fraily. "Aaron was a lousy lecturer. The other students used to gripe to each other before he came into class each day. Aaron's face would twitch whenever he talked about violent scenes in a book, which of course were the scenes he focused on most. So one time before class, this idiot P.E. major behind me joked that Professor Brandon must've been abused as a child. The other students just laughed. I didn't say anything, but I was furious. I promised myself that I was going to be on Dr. Brandon's side after that. I started going to his office hours, discussing books, having coffee with him in the cafeteria. We understood each other almost immediately. Aaron and I could finish each other's sentences from the first day we talked. By the end of the semester, we'd fallen in love. In the spring, after Zeta had forced me to quit school, Aaron and I still found excuses to cross paths a lot. . . . Things just took their course."

"Aaron got you pregnant in April, and you had to make a choice. You chose to invent a new life."

There were color variations in the deep brown of her eyes that I'd never noticed before—jagged yellow and amber lines, as if her irises too had been fractured in the distant past.

"Sandra couldn't have broken away from Zeta," she said. "Sandra couldn't have protected her child. Weeks before Del ever arranged an ID for me that said I was Ines Garcia from Del Rio, I'd already started thinking of myself as that new person. And I promised myself Ines would do whatever she had to for her baby."

I studied the woman across from me—the fierce sincerity in her face, the disheveled hair, the little crumple of packing tape on her sleeve, and the incongruous explosion of colors on the front of her Fiesta T-shirt.

I tried to reinvoke the chill I'd felt a few minutes before, when she'd first referred to herself in the third person. I couldn't do it. The fact that I'd been accepting her story, starting to understand the way she described herself in two distinct layers, scared me.

"Del knew about you and Aaron," I said.

"Of course. He warned us our lives were in danger if Zeta or Jeremiah ever found out. He was probably right. He offered to arrange a new ID for me, a few other papers, and get me safely out of town. That was easy for Del—he'd done it often enough for his father's cronies. In return, Aaron was supposed to hand over his share of RideWorks when the time came to inherit. What did Aaron care about that damn company? He loved me and we wanted to be together. He agreed. He'd already lined up his Permian Basin job for the following fall, so I disappeared into West Texas to wait for him and have our baby."

"And you got married. Again."

"Fuck 'again.' That was Sandra. That wasn't a *marriage*." She spat the word.

"The law wouldn't see it that way. Del knew that—knew your secret could be used as leverage against you and Aaron in the future. You played into his hands."

Ines was silent.

"After you left," I said, "Del went to Zeta. Del convinced him you'd left town because you were having an affair with Jeremiah."

"It was total fiction."

"Of course. But your husband didn't know that, and the fiction suited Del perfectly. Zeta knew all about Jeremiah's reputation with young women. Del didn't have to do much convincing. Zeta shot Jeremiah. Then Del helped Zeta leave the country. Del inherited Jeremiah's company and got rid of all his competition at once—Aaron, Jeremiah, Zeta."

"We had no idea," Ines said. "Del was horrible, but we never thought he was capable of anything like murder. Aaron—it destroyed him when he learned about his father."

"And Del wasn't even done. Afterward, he hit up Aaron for RideWorks. After all, wasn't that Aaron's side of the bargain? Only Aaron had never counted on his dad being gunned down as part of their deal. So Aaron refused. Del took matters into his own hands again. He stole the company from Aaron in a legal maneuver. That pissed Aaron off. He filed a suit, but the minute he did, Del threatened to expose your identity."

"Yes."

"The police would want to talk to you, of course—a woman who'd fled town with the victim's son and a new identity right after her legal husband had committed a murder. At the very least the investigation would ruin your chances at a new life, nullify your second marriage, make Michael a—" At the look in her eyes, I stopped. I folded my napkin, tossed it over my Sonora casserole. "At worst, it would attract the attention of Zeta and his pals. Del had something to worry about too if the story got to the police, but he must've been fairly sure no one could prove anything on him, especially with Sanchez gone. You, on the other hand, had everything to lose. Aaron had no choice but to drop his claim to RideWorks. How old was Michael at the time? Two months? Three?"

"Two months. We had our first terrible argument, Aaron and I. His father's death was entirely my fault."

"Then Del paid a visit to your brother Hector, who also knew the truth about your disappearance. Del used the same leverage with Hector that he'd used on Aaron—'Do some business with me or I'll see that your sister gets crucified.' "

"I don't know what Del told Hector."

"Del was just following up on Zeta's good idea—to move heroin through the carnival circuit. Hector arranged the purchases from a friend of his, Chich Gutierrez. Del distributed the heroin, keeping the amounts small so as not to attract too much attention, but large enough to make RideWorks a nice fat supplementary income."

She raised her hands slowly off the table. "I—don't—know. I don't know anything about that."

I looked at the kids. They'd each gotten another plastic egg from the machine and were prying them open.

"You take it for granted," Ines said hoarsely.

I refocused on her. Her face was hard as copper.

"What?"

"That you can have a child like Jem someday," she said. "Raise him without seeing him shot in the crossfire, without having him go on lookout for the *locos* at age five. You can be in a place where they don't keep the needles and the baby bottles in the same cabinet, have a spouse who isn't in jail for murder or dealing. You take that for granted."

"I take it for granted you'd kill to protect Michael from your past."

"Oh, you're right. You're absolutely right. That's the difference between me and Sandra Mara. I would kill to protect my son."

"How's your batting average so far?"

Ines shook her head, as if she were disappointed in me. "I won't lie to you. I didn't feel guilty that Jeremiah Brandon got killed, or that Zeta had to flee the country. In fact, I was disappointed Zeta didn't get shot in that barroom, too. I can't say I care much if Hector and Del were moving heroin through RideWorks, either, if it bought me and my son some extra years of anonymity. None of that matters. But you think I killed my husband? Or had him killed?"

"That was my original question."

"You're wrong. Aaron was putting Michael and me in terrible danger—that's true. When Aaron wanted to move back here to San Antonio, I told him it was too much of a risk. Too many people here who might recognize me. Aaron insisted. He had all these ideas about challenging Del—getting back that damn company. He seemed to forget what Del would do if he tried. I was desperate, but I'd never—"

"You wrote those threats to the University."

"I—" She faltered. "All right. Yes. I wrote them. Aaron had brought the first letter home, the one addressed to Dr.

Haimer. It wasn't hard. Before I knew it I'd sent six of them."

"You thought if things got unpleasant enough, Aaron would agree to move away again, out of San Antonio."

"There had been two other offers, Tres—one in Iowa, one in Connecticut. Not wonderful jobs, but we should have gone there. We would've been safe there. But Aaron was so damned determined to come home."

"And the bomb?"

"Hector's idea, before we even knew Zeta was back in town. Hector was sure the University police would discover the bomb before it ever went off, that they'd blame it on campus radicals. Hector just wanted to convince Aaron the threats weren't idle. He didn't intend for anyone to get hurt."

"Why were you away the weekend Aaron was shot?"

"We'd found out Zeta was back in San Antonio. Hector and I were both insane with fear. Hector told me to get out of town for a while."

"—so you couldn't be implicated. Hector was timing a murder."

"*No,*" Ines insisted. The word was a little shrill. "He swore to me. He didn't shoot Aaron."

"Then who?"

"God damn you, Tres. Leave it alone."

"Paloma knows," I said. "She was the witness."

"Paloma wouldn't talk to me."

"You must've guessed she was lying about Zeta being at your house that night. But you haven't pressed her too hard on that point, have you?"

Ines flattened her hands on the Formica. "No. I haven't."

"You knew she was lying to protect you. You figured if somebody had to go down for Aaron's death, it might as well be your husband."

"Zeta *isn't* my husband anymore. Why can't you see that?"

The waitress came to our table, sensed the tension, took a step back. She asked skeptically if we were finished with our food. We said we were. She slowly loaded our plates onto her tray. She smelled of black-eyed peas.

"I'll bring y'all the check." Before leaving, she shot me a chastising look. "Those are two cute boys over there."

The old couple at the next table had gotten up and were shuffling toward the door. The margarita-drinkers on the opposite side of the room kept doing their best to ensure prizewinning hangovers for the following morning.

Jem and Michael were making a pretty good dent in my quarter supply now. Their pockets bulged obscenely with prize capsules.

"I've told you the truth," Ines told me. "What now?"

"There's still the matter of my friend."

She frowned, not immediately understanding who I meant. That irritated me.

"George Bertón," I said. "He got himself shot poking around in your past after Zeta Sanchez was arrested. George talked to Hector, then visited your family farm. He must have found a photo of you there, used it to get an ID from the woman at the Poco Mas. He realized that the real story was *you,* but he didn't know all the details, and he was a little too soft-hearted to put a widow and her five-year-old boy in harm's way. So he set up another meeting with your brother. Probably George wanted to figure out a bargain whereby you could be spared discovery and Hector could give Del Brandon to the police on a skewer. It would've meant Hector getting jail time for the heroin, but this is the guy who'd got himself shot in the leg for you once. Hector would take the fall. Before that could happen, somebody interrupted his meeting with Bertón—murdered Hector, almost killed George Bertón."

"You're accusing me of that, too? Of murdering my own brother?"

"The police will wonder."

"I don't intend to talk with the police."

"Two people have died. Aaron. Hector."

"Don't you think I know that?"

"That's a lot of blood, Ines. A lot of blood even for a secret worth keeping."

She gazed across the room at her son, watching Michael's every move like she was trying desperately to memorize him. "Are you in love with somebody, Tres?"

The question struck me mute.

Ines raised her eyebrows—a gesture that reminded me powerfully of Ana DeLeon. "Are you?" she insisted.

"I—no." And then added inanely, "I don't think so."

That brought a dry smile. "Safe answer. Love's not the blazing epiphany some people imagine, is it? I didn't realize I was falling in love with Aaron until we'd been seeing each other for two months. When I started to fall out of love with him, the process was just as insidious. Now that he's gone . . ."

Streetlights on Broadway started to blink on as the sky darkened. The round window behind the 410 bar glowed, the glass liquor-bottle shelves that crossed it making it look like some sort of giant military insignia.

Ines fixed her eyes on the traffic outside. "Aaron so desperately needed to prove himself. He would've destroyed our family, endangered Michael, not even realized what he was doing until it was too late. That was his real inheritance from his father. Aaron and Jeremiah—they were like children. They both took what they wanted. No matter who got hurt. It took me a long time to understand that about Aaron. Hector—I'm not sure I ever understood my brother. To him, I was just some family banner he had to keep from getting trampled. All I'm really sure of now is Michael."

The kids used their last quarters. They began gathering up their loot.

"Don't destroy us, Tres." It was a whisper. Sandra's voice.

From across the room, Jem rolled open a Felix the Cat sticker for me to admire.

Our waitress came out of the kitchen with our check. She took one read of the situation—the boys with their loot, Ines and me still deep in conversation—then knelt down to intercept Jem and Michael before they could start back toward us. She gestured for the boys to climb onto the metal toadstool seats at the dining counter, questioned them about their stickers. Jem and Michael were happy to oblige.

I reached across the table, picked the crumple of packing tape from Ines' sleeve. "You don't have to talk to the police alone."

Her shoulders stiffened. "You said you would help."

"I will. But I can't be silent."

"The only reason I've been talking to you—" She swallowed back her anger. "Then we'll have to run. Michael and I."

"That won't help."

"I've done it before."

"You have a five-year-old now. Nobody's making you a new identity this time."

"Give me a one-night head start."

She tried to get up, but I caught her wrist.

Our eyes locked.

"What is it to you, Tres?" she demanded.

"People leave things behind by accident," I said. "But not you. Not that journal. Not the photograph George must've found."

She tugged against my grip.

"You left a trail," I said, "because you wanted to. You run again, you'll just leave another trail."

"Absurd."

"You said it yourself, Ines. You don't get away without a fight. You haven't had yours yet. Turn around and face what you left behind, take the consequences. Or you can run away again, talk tough about how you're somebody new, somebody who doesn't need help. If you're somebody new, then *maldición*. You and Sandra Mara would've gotten along just fine."

Her eyes flashed murderously. "I won't risk my child. You can't promise Michael will be safe."

"Look at your son. Tell me he's safe right now, in that cave he's been making."

"God damn you," she whispered.

"Nobody can guarantee Michael will be safe, Ines. You might as well realize it here, where you've got some friends."

"I—I can't, Tres. I wish—"

The sound of little sneakers hushed her. The boys crashed into us, showing off their spoils. Their arms glittered with holographic stickers.

I let go of Ines' wrist and forced a smile. I complimented Jem on his Felix the Cat. The waitress brought our check and left us with a few more admonishing comments about what nice boys we had.

Michael climbed onto his mother's lap. He was a little large for the task, but he just about managed a fetal position. He tucked his head against Ines' chest and began picking at a silvery low-rider decal on his wrist.

"I want to go home," he mumbled.

Ines stroked his hair. Sweat had plastered it into curls over his ears.

"We will," she promised. "It'll be like a sleep-over. In the new apartment. And tomorrow—"

Michael turned his face into her bright shirt, rubbed his nose back and forth, then looked up at her again. "No. *Home*."

"Sweetheart—"

"You took it down, I bet," he muttered. "You said you wouldn't."

Ines' hand closed over Michael's on her chest. Her mouth began to tremble.

"Michael," I said. "We're inviting you and your mom over to Jem's house, kiddo. You can have your sleep-over there. What do you think?"

Curled against his mother, Michael just looked at me, his eyes as pale blue as his murdered father's.

Jem, however, perked up instantly. He started filling Michael in on all the games they could play once they got into his room.

"Sweetheart—" Ines interrupted hoarsely.

But Michael didn't want to hear her. He was too busy listening to Jem's descriptions of Sega-Wonderland. The little frown didn't leave his face, but he kept his eyes on Jem.

I glanced at Ines. "If you can't beat them . . ."

She closed her eyes for one second, two. When she looked at me again, I couldn't shake the impression that her irises were dark, fractured prisms.

"Perhaps just for tonight," she said.

Jem and I rode together in the Barracuda, leading the way back toward Erainya's. Every few seconds, I checked the rearview mirror. Each time I was surprised to find Ines' headlights still behind us.

As we drove, Jem told me how super-funny Michael was. Jem wanted to make a sheet cave like his.

"I don't know if that's the best idea, Bubba."

Jem disagreed. He told me how cool Michael's setup had been inside.

He said Michael had been trying to make the cave bigger and bigger, so that someday he would never have to come back out again. Someday, Michael would close up the entrance and just disappear. It hadn't worked out that way, but Jem still figured it was a great plan.

"I don't know, Bubba," I told him. "I think maybe Michael's mom was right to take down the sheets."

Jem was unconvinced. He said that, according to Michael, that wasn't even his real mom. His real mom had disappeared down the sheet cave years and years and years ago. That's where Michael had been going—following his mom into the dark.

FORTY-THREE

Plans were discussed. Erainya cursed and slapped the air a lot. Jem and Michael were sent off to play video games. Ines was force-fed a platter of Greek food to make up for the dinner she hadn't eaten, then browbeaten into taking the main bedroom.

While Ines was changing clothes and the children were playing in Jem's room, Erainya broke out a Heineken and the keys to her gun cabinet.

"You," Erainya said to me. "*You* go home."

I insisted on checking the boys one more time.

Through his bedroom doorway, I watched Jem sitting at his PlayStation, engrossed in a 3-D jungle with flying, basketball-dribbling dinosaurs. Michael wasn't participating. He sat cross-legged a few feet behind Jem, a stack of Jem's old *Nickelodeon* magazines and toy-store circulars by his side. Michael was cutting out the pictures with safety scissors.

I drove slowly all the way home.

Back at 90 Queen Anne, I stared reluctantly at the phone for several minutes, then called Ana DeLeon's work number, got her voice mail.

I left a cryptic message—I had new information, I might be able to share it soon, but first we needed to talk. Preferably over another pitcher of margaritas.

DeLeon didn't call back.

I called Brooke Army Medical Center. No change in George's condition.

Then I lay down on my futon and burned my eyes out reading *The Woman in White*. By page 200, I still couldn't fall asleep.

Maybe it would've been easier if the Suitez family across the street had had another party and lulled me with the familiar sounds of Freddy Fender or Narciso Martinez. Or if Mrs. Geradino's Chihuahuas had yapped at the moon. Or if Gary Hales' upstairs TV had blared out a John Wayne movie on the night-owl theater. These noises I could've dealt with. But not dead quiet on a Saturday night in San Antonio.

Robert Johnson had no insomnia worries. He'd curled up happily on my crotch, closed his eyes, and proceeded to increase his body temperature by a hundred degrees.

I stared at the ceiling. I counted the inches that the moonlight advanced across my wall.

I thought about the ventilator in George's hospital room, about Zeta lying in his jail cell, looking out olive-green bars at more rows of olive-green bars, his eyes empty and maybe his thoughts just as hollow. I thought of Ana DeLeon the night before, in those few moments when the ice in her demeanor had melted. Mostly, I thought about Ines and Michael Brandon.

Finally I slid Robert Johnson as gently as I could off my crotch. I got up and dressed—black sweats, black T-shirt, black Nikes, a fanny pack with a few select tools.

The rumble of the Barracuda's engine seemed obscenely loud in the nighttime quiet. I headed down Broadway, past a group of low-rider Chevies in the Lions Club lot, a few teenagers smoking and talking outside Taco Cabana, the usual late-night crowd at Earl Abel's Coffee Shop. Otherwise, the town had shut down. I drove south, under I-35, past Southern Music, then turned right on Jones.

Unless Del Brandon had another nighttime transaction under way, I planned on resolving some unanswered questions tonight. If possible, I also planned on finding something I could use to nail Del Brandon's fat ass to his Super-Whirl.

RideWorks looked closed up, even the office. There were no cars on the street.

I parked at the gates, got out of the car, and was just examining the chain and padlock when headlights swung onto Camden behind me, about fifty yards back.

The obvious didn't occur to me—that I should get back in the Barracuda and get the hell out of there. Instead, stupidly, I squandered five or six seconds watching the white van pull up alongside the Barracuda. Before it had even come to a stop the side door slid open and five Latino men unloaded. One was Chicharron—still a Child of the Night in his black leather and silver, his trench coat conveniently covering the damage Ralph's fan-throwing practice had done to his arms. The self-confident burn in Chich's eyes told me he'd coked himself up just enough to make this encounter enjoyably bloody.

His four friends were the teenagers I'd met at the Poco Mas—Porkpie, with the hat and loose-cut *cholo* threads, his Taurus P-11 drawn with no preliminaries this time. The other three formed a right flank—all smooth young faces and wispy black beards, jeans, white tank tops, expensive sneakers. I focused on little differences—one had a hairnet. One a gold nose ring. The third held a length of bike gear chain. No visible guns except for Porkpie's. Not yet.

"I hear you're a professor." Chicharron smiled at me with what looked like artificially pointed teeth. "For a teacher, you learn slow."

I said nothing. With Porkpie's Taurus trained on me, there didn't seem much point. I chose to stay standing, back to the gate, arms free, George's car between me and them.

Chich kept smiling, measuring me. He wouldn't be sure

if I was carrying a gun or not, if I were alone or not. He'd want to be sure my situation was really as hopeless as it looked, that I'd truly been stupid enough to drive out here on my own, unarmed.

He gestured toward the Barracuda. "Nice wheels."

"A nice guy used to drive them."

Nosering cracked his knuckles. Hairnet and his friend with the gear chain both glanced over at the vampire, waiting for a signal.

"Funny," Chich said. "I start asking around, I didn't have no problem finding some people wanted to hurt you. Maybe we do you, then we go looking for your friend Ralph."

Porkpie said, "One round. Chest."

Chich held up his fingers for patience. His smile widened.

"You scared of the odds?" I asked him.

My only chance was to keep it close-range, keep them thinking I was a nothing job—blood sport. And then hope like hell to surprise them. The private eye as moron.

Porkpie chambered a round.

"Nah," Chich said. "Get him in the van."

The news that they preferred me alive failed to comfort me. It only meant they preferred the bloodstain to be somewhere of their choosing.

Hairnet and Bikechain went around either side of the Barracuda. Nosering pulled a blackjack. He opened my passenger's-side door, stepping onto the seat like it was a doormat.

Chicharron leaned against his van and watched. Porkpie's gun kept making a warm spot in my gut.

I had no intention of waiting to be surrounded on three sides. I stepped toward the hood of the Barracuda to meet Bikechain. He was the least prepared, his hands committed to the chain, probably thinking he would garrote me while I was busy with the others. Before he could change his strategy I feinted a punch at his face, forced his hands up, then shoulder-butted him in the sternum with my full body weight. I turned and ducked as his friend's blackjack slashed air next to my ear. I grabbed the blackjacker's pierced nose between my thumb and forefinger and yanked. The blackjacker screamed, dropped his sap. I dropped the bloody nose ring, then rolled the guy with the hairnet over my shoulder and onto the pavement.

I retreated, stepping over Bikechain, putting my back to the RideWorks gate, now fifteen feet away from the Barracuda. Porkpie's gun was still aimed at me. Chich was still smiling.

The guy who'd had the nose ring was making a hand-tent around his face, blood striping his chin and speckling his white T-shirt. The guy with the hairnet was getting up off the street. Bikechain limped forward, rewinding the chain around his fist. He scraped the gear links across the Barracuda's red paint job, then kept coming. His friends were close behind.

Then a metallic rumbling started in the RideWorks courtyard behind me—the warehouse door grinding partially open. I heard Del Brandon's voice, midconversation. My attackers froze.

A few footsteps, more of Del's voice—then nothing.

I chanced a look over my shoulder. Del and Ernie, the human boulder with the blond cornrows, were stopped in their tracks, both staring at the battle scene outside their gates. Ernie had his hand protectively on Del Brandon's shoulder. Del hadn't changed his clothes since dinner at the 410. If anything he was more disheveled, and a lot drunker.

Slowly, Del put his hand on his gun. Probably from his angle, in the dark, he couldn't see Vampire and Porkpie with the P-11—just me and the three homeboys at his gate.

"Well, well," Del called to me. "Fucking private dick

came back already. You figure I sleep? I don't. Not no more."

I glanced at the three *locos*. Still frozen.

"Listen, Del," I said. "Let's talk inside. You can beat the shit out of me there, okay? You and Ernie come on over."

Silence.

"Come on, Del," I called. "You want to prove you're on the good guys' team, this is your chance."

I was mentally running through wild possibilities—Del would walk over, I'd roll and run, they'd start an inadvertent crossfire, I would escape in the confusion.

Instead, Del laughed bitterly. "You hear anything worth listening to, Ernie? I didn't hear nothing. Must've been a dog."

Then their steps resumed across the courtyard. The stairs creaked. The office door slammed shut.

Two more seconds of miserable, heavy silence, then Bikechain and Hairnet charged. Hairnet grabbed my arm and found himself grabbed instead, his face yanked down and slammed into my upraised knee. My left hand intercepted Bikechain's punch and directed it aside, the chains raking the skin on the back of my hand. I slammed my other palm against his jaw, tried to step sideways. But Hairnet was up too fast, tackling my waist and sending me into the fence in a full-body slam. I landed a double chop on his ears that almost loosened his grip but Bikechain lunged at me too, knocking all three of us down on the pavement.

There is no greater terror than being completely prone, out of control, caught in a tangle of bodies.

It didn't last long—I remember gouging, kicking, elbowing, yelling, getting my head free of someone's choke hold just long enough to catch an image of the man with the bloody gash in his nose, raising the blackjack for a second try.

There was a *whish* sound, then my head turned to ice.

My eyesight faded. The pavement and feet walking around me became an afterglow in the darkness, like a television screen turned off in a dark room.

Somewhere, the bored voice of Chicharron was commenting to Porkpie—not about me, or the fight, but about George's red '70 Barracuda and how best to repaint it.

FORTY-FOUR

I was surprised to wake up, even more surprised to realize I had been awake for some time without my mind registering the fact.

My eyes burned from staring at a patch of yellow in the darkness. After a while I recognized the patch as a streetlight. I couldn't remember how to blink. There were moths fluttering around the streetlight. I stared at them for centuries.

Some part of me knew that I should be concerned, should move, but I couldn't remember exactly why. I just lay there on my back, anesthetized, waiting for the dental surgeon to start drilling, for the doctor to amputate my leg, my brain. Whatever. I had a nice streetlight to stare at.

The side of my head felt warm and wet, like a very affectionate leech had been attached there. I was pleased to have the company.

I'm not sure how many decades I lay like that. The sky had started lightening to gunmetal when I became aware of voices—two males, very close to me. They talked in conversational tones. Every once in a while their words were interrupted by the *ker-ploink* of liquor being tipped into a mouth and then settling back into the bottle.

I thought it would be just dandy to turn my head and look at the two men, but my head wouldn't cooperate.

Finally an upside-down face hovered above me in the

morning gloom. The young man had two beautiful nostrils. The rest of his face was shadowy but one eye seemed darker than the other. I could tell he wore a hairnet. I thought I'd seen him somewhere before.

The mouth under the beautiful nostrils scowled at me, then told someone in Spanish that my eyes were open. An offstage voice said it was probably time to drag me inside.

Hairnet's face went away.

The sensation of movement. I heard the sound of a body being dragged across gravel and after a time realized the body was mine. When we took an L-turn, my head lolled to one side and I saw the place where I'd been sleeping—a dirty blanket on the ground of an abandoned lot. Next to the blanket was a makeshift lean-to against the side of a warehouse—a gutted pink sofa slumped between two cardboard refrigerator boxes, a blanket draped over to make the top of a tent. A young Latino guy sat on the couch, drinking from a liquor bottle. Not far away, standing at the street curb under the lamppost, another Latino guy in a Raiders jacket was talking to a man in a station wagon. They seemed to be trading things.

Then I was dragged through a doorway and the scene disappeared in darkness.

My feet hit the ground. I heard footsteps receding, then a metal door rolling shut. I lay on my back admiring the blackness, wishing for more feeling in my body. None came.

Maybe I slept. When I opened my eyes again I could make out the outline of an air duct above me, thin lines of a corrugated metal ceiling. I got excited when my fingers twitched, involuntarily, and I could actually feel the scrape of the cement floor.

I started to be conscious of my own swallowing. I could feel my hands and my feet. The leech on my face started slithering around.

After a long, long time, I was able to make a fist. Light seeped into the high ceiling through constellations of rust holes. They made beautiful patterns—smiling faces, animals, monsters. Metal support beams started appearing out of the darkness.

I tried to lift my arm. I was scared when my hand actually appeared in front of my face.

I opened my mouth and a sound came out—nothing very human, but sound.

Whatever they'd drugged me with had a lot of staying power. I still felt no pain, just a greater heat—an invisible finger poking deeply into my rib cage over and over, trying to get my attention.

I was almost cocky enough to try sitting up when there was an explosion of sound, then light. The warehouse doors rolled open behind me and blinding sun poured in.

Men came in, talking. Some stepped around me. I saw flashes of faces—all Latino, most young and bearded, many with ski caps or bandannas.

Somebody told somebody else to move the pile of garbage. I recognized Chicharron's voice. Once I was jerked up off the floor and my vision twisted sideways, I realized the garbage was me.

I was shoved into a chair and promptly slid out of it again. Impatient hands dragged me back into a sitting position.

When my gyroscope readjusted itself, I saw a black leather executive chair with slash marks along the top. Chicharron sat in that chair, his legs crossed, his casual vampire-wear on—jeans, a billowy white shirt, lots of silver.

Other men moved around behind him—circling, watching me with predatory eyes. I recognized Porkpie, and the kid with the hairnet who sported a nasty shiner I devoutly hoped I'd given him.

Chicharron adjusted the folds of his shirt, then flicked his fingers toward me. "You got something to say?"

I worked my jaw and eloquently managed to reply, "Uh."

Chich looked at Porkpie, who moved a little closer, ever ready to serve and protect.

"Is he going to be like this permanently?" Chich demanded.

Porkpie said that I would come out of it eventually and they'd have to give me more of the stuff. "Unless we kill him." He said this hopefully.

Chicharron looked at me like I was a throwaway carpet sample in a color he didn't particularly care for. "You're still alive for three reasons."

I made a small noise.

Chich examined his fingers. His nails were as long as a classical guitar player's. "First, your name is Navarre. I'd rather not kill a guy who's got friends in the sheriff's department unless I have to. Second, you fight okay. I appreciate that. C, there's a little matter about some heroin."

He waited. I blinked, once maybe.

"You want to talk?" Chich asked. "Or you want to spend another night here with my boys, maybe be their mascot?"

"Another night," Porkpie broke in, "and he won't have no brain left, we keep him on this stuff."

"I can talk."

I think they were almost as surprised as I was that the croak was comprehensible.

I tried to say something else, failed, then realized that the more I concentrated on how to speak, the more I choked. "Chicharron—"

Chich made an X with his index fingers. "Nobody here by that name," he said. "You want any hope of getting out of this place still breathing, you'll remember that. Tell me what I want to hear, Navarre. Where's my heroin?"

I was watching his mouth move. When it stopped it took me a while to realize he needed a response. "Don't know."

"You really want that to be your answer?"

"Ask Del Brandon."

Chich glanced at Porkpie. "If we were to pull some of his fingers off, you think he'd feel it?"

Porkpie opined that I probably wouldn't.

Chich accepted this disappointment with a shrug. "Brandon's been talking to the police, Navarre. He's been in there all night, singing any song the cops tell him to sing. You know what he's claiming, Navarre? He's swearing Zeta Sanchez's wife is still around. He's claiming Mrs. Sanchez and Hector have been using RideWorks to move smack. *My* smack. He says his job was just to shut up and be silent about it. Says he doesn't have anything that belongs to me. And you know why I believe Del? I believe Del because Del's too fucking retarded to move heroin by himself. Are you hearing me?"

He snapped his fingers, which brought my eyes back from space, back to his mouth.

I said, "You know a lot about what Del Brandon is telling the police."

Chicharron's mouth crept up at the corner. "What I want from you—the only thing—is the heroin."

"Heroin's not important."

"Not important. My heroin's not important."

"Hector needed runaway money. So he ripped you off. But that's incidental."

"If it's so fucking incidental, think I'll just take it back."

"I don't have it."

"You got Mrs. Sanchez, don't you?"

A pain slid through my head like a shard of glass. I closed my eyes and heard myself whimper, hating myself for it.

When I forced my eyelids open again Chicharron had his hand raised, as if to signal his pals to be quiet.

"You fought well," Chich said. "I have three men who will not be healed for several days because of you."

"Good," I croaked. The intrepid detective gracefully accepts a compliment.

"Be a shame to kill you. Tell me where Sandra Sanchez is."

"I don't know."

"Let me kill him." The eager voice sounded like Porkpie's.

Chicharron thought about it for a full seven seconds. I know: I counted.

Then he stood up, nodded to someone behind me. Suddenly I was falling sideways—my chair'd been yanked out from under me. I lurched around on the floor, but it was like swimming through cement. The needle in the crook of my arm was the first sharp sensation I'd experienced since becoming conscious, and as the cement thickened around me I knew this needle would be the last.

"We'll visit again tomorrow," I heard Chicharron say. "If you have any brain left by then, you will be wise and use it for me."

As I went under, someone's voice muttered, "A shame."

Might have been my voice.

Then footsteps receded and the closing metal doors clanged shut like an earthquake.

FORTY-FIVE

I had a series of nightmares. In one my mother's house was on fire, and she was urging me and her muscular troop of Marlboro men to bucket-brigade armloads of knickknacks out the front door. My mother kept running back and forth down the sidewalk, her silk kimono on fire at the edges, imploring us to work faster. I would hand a basket of glass paperweights to the guy next to me, then a roll of Dia de los Muertos posters, then some Ghanaian burial masks. I was in the doorway and the fire kept intensifying until finally the knickknacks were being handed out to me by guys whose arms and legs were on fire and whose skin was melting from their faces.

Then I was on the playground at Jem's new school. I was frantically searching for Jem, but all the little kids looked exactly the same—little pastel polo shirts and khakis, black hair and brown skin, all with the face of Michael Brandon.

My eyes opened. The sky was dark. I focused on a fuzzy patch of yellow—my old chum the streetlight.

Other senses kicked in. I could smell dried urine and sweat and cigarette smoke. I was lying on something soft and bumpy—the broken-down couch in the vacant lot. I was covered with a blanket. Without much effort I turned my head and got a view of the street.

It looked like West Commerce, or one of the side streets around there. Two wide lanes, one way, moderately busy traffic. The warehouse where I'd been dragged the last time I was conscious rose to the side, a green cinder-block wall with a heavy door in the middle and a dumpster at the corner. Across the street was an old craftsman house, boarded up and ringed with cyclone fencing, vacant lots on either side. The street and the sidewalk glittered with broken bottles and syringes.

One of the young men who'd kept watch over me earlier was at the curb, dealing into a brown Chrysler. The young man collected cash, slipped something from the pocket of his jacket to the driver, then retreated to the lamppost and lit a match and a cigarette as the car pulled away. The next customer didn't take long to pull up, or the one after that. It was about the same frequency as the drive-through at Burger King.

A voice closer to me called over to the guy on the street. It asked, in Spanish, how the supply was. The guy answered: "Twenty dimes, five large."

The voice nearer to me said, *"Bueno."*

The speaker was probably leaning against the wall of the building, not two feet behind me.

A pager went off. At first I thought I was imagining the sound. Then Porkpie walked into my line of sight.

He was wearing the hat with a different ensemble today—baggy jeans, army-green-and-maroon shirt, leather bike-grip gloves, air-pump spaceman shoes. He checked his beeper and then took out a tiny cell phone, unfolded it, made a call. Meanwhile two more punks drifted in from down the street, shook hands with the dealer at the street-lamp, then walked over to the dumpster and hung out, talking casually, lighting each other's joint. Traffic continued down the street. Sometimes cars pulled up to the curb. Most just drove by.

I was lying not ten yards from a public street, doped to the gills, and nobody was paying me any mind. If anyone even noticed me, they probably figured I was just a wino, some derelict the punks had allowed to crash in their outdoor office. I wondered that no police cars went by, that they didn't rush in and find me and break up the dealing. But I knew better. If a police car had been anywhere close, signalmen armed with cell phones up and down the surrounding blocks would've been on to the threat instantly. Beepers would beep a warning code. The stash would get ditched in the dumpster and the kids would vanish down the side streets and I'd either get dragged back in the warehouse or, more likely, killed and left for the police to find—doped up and murdered, just another victim of another deal gone bad. Probably make an interesting feature on page A12, former sheriff's son OD'ed and killed at a West Side drug spot. The drug business would be back in swing on a different corner before my blood had even soaked into the stinking fabric of the couch.

Porkpie kept pacing back and forth. He glanced at me occasionally, but the fact that my eyes were open didn't seem to bother him. For all I knew my eyes had been open for days, glazed and useless while my brain had checked out.

I tried to wiggle my toes, got excited when I felt the fabric of my socks against them. I tried to move a knee. I couldn't do that. My arms were dead weight. My head throbbed. I swallowed, then ran my tongue back and forth in my mouth, got a sensation like licking a sand castle. I was not going to leap up right away and tackle anybody. But at least I could form the idea of doing so. The detective as philosopher.

I wanted to kill them all. I wanted to shove Porkpie's state-of-the-art cell phone down his throat.

Another car slid down the block and pulled over—a blue Impala, '83, pretty badly banged up. The car windows were tinted and the interior pitch-black.

The dealer disengaged himself from his two friends at the dumpster and took a wary step toward the Impala, his hand in his black coat.

The guy in the passenger's seat cracked open his window. "¡Azul rife! ¿Y qué?"

Old-style *cholo* greeting: *The Blue rules. What're you gonna do about it?*

The dealer and his friends relaxed. All flashed a hand sign at the Impala. The dealer walked toward the car's back window, which was just now rolling down.

Then the dealer's black coat exploded like an air bag.

The high-caliber shot launched him off his feet into a reverse jackknife, the back of his coat shredding away in a spiral of blood and fabric. He hit the ground just as a shotgun blast from the Impala's open passenger window slammed into his friends by the dumpster—scouring metal and brick and bodies with buckshot. Someone shrieked. Porkpie dropped his phone and ran. He made it over the fence at the back of the lot in two moves.

Then it was quiet except for the sound of two men in misery by the dumpster. One of them kept crawling around, screaming. The other just twitched. The dealer never moved. The dumpster and warehouse wall behind them were freckled with blood and shot.

Ralph Arguello stepped out of the passenger's-side door of the Impala holding a high-powered over-and-under Mossberg. Erainya Manos came from the driver's side, her .38 up next to her ear. Another guy I didn't recognize got out of the back. He carried the snub-nosed .45 automatic that had just drilled the hole in the dealer's chest.

The round lenses of Ralph's glasses glinted in the yellow streetlight like coins. He planted his boot on the chest of one of the guys who was still alive, then lowered the shotgun muzzle against the kid's face. Erainya snarled: "No!"

Ralph glanced back at her, had a brief staring battle, then raised the shotgun and made a golf swing with the barrel against the kid's face hard enough to roll him over. Erainya jogged over to me.

Her hair was a mess. She had red lines on her arms like junkie tracks. Her face was made up even gaunter and darker than usual. She was dressed in an old T-shirt and jeans. She passed very effectively for a strung-out user, a washed-up prostitute maybe, a woman like a hundred others who might visit this spot regularly.

She crooned, "Oh, honey." I'd never heard her sound so kind.

Then she got her arms around me and lifted me up. I was maybe seventy-five pounds heavier than she, but Erainya dragged me all the way back to the car.

I could see Ralph, training his shotgun lazily on the wounded second man. The gang-banger's face looked like a rust-eaten car hood—most of his left cheek scoured to blood, his left eye ruptured and the irreplaceable fluid dribbling down his cheek.

Ralph's helper, the man with the .45, was busy stripping the dead young dealer of his heroin.

Erainya got me in the car. Within seconds I was wedged between her and the man with the .45 and Ralph was in the driver's seat, speeding us silently away from the West Side. We heard a siren behind us, a long way off.

When Ralph spoke his voice was so taut with anger I hardly recognized it. He said, *"Mi pendejo rife. ¿Y qué?"*

FORTY-SIX

"Nobody passes a boosted red Barracuda in S.A. without me knowing about it." Ralph spoke somewhere in the darkness. "Fuck Chich, he thinks he can pull that shit in my town."

"I suppose I had nothing to do with this operation," Erainya griped.

"No offense, señora. You handled it pretty good for a gringa."

Erainya called Ralph some names in Greek. Ralph defended himself in Spanish. I knew neither could understand the other. That was probably just as well.

"I love you both," I mumbled. "Now shut up."

Astoundingly, they did.

I drifted to sleep to the sound of the Impala engine. Sometime during the ride, I think I recalled the mysterious .45 man, whom Ralph called Freeze, being dropped off. Freeze patted me on the shoulder and told me that for another hundred, he'd be happy to drill anybody for me any day.

The next time I woke up I was lying flat, staring at bare cedar rafters and an old ceiling fan. When I tried to move, cot springs clinked and clunked like a broken music box. The fan wobbled precariously.

A thickly accented woman's voice said, "Hol' still, damn it."

Dr. Janice Farn hovered over me, giving me a view of

curly white hair and bifocals and the Calvin Klein fedora
that Aileen the cow had once driven her hoof through.

I started to say something, but Farn cut me off. "Hol'
still and shut up."

I had no recollection of arriving where I obviously was—
the Navarre family ranch in Sabinal—but I held still. And
shut up. Dr. Farn's hand dabbed at my face.

"Had to cut a little to get at the infection in your cheek."
Her breath smelled distinctly of Jack Daniel's—not surpris-
ing, knowing Farn, but not a smell you wanted on someone
who was giving you urgent medical attention.

Farn must've been past eighty, tough as beef jerky, a
widow and a large-animal vet who'd leased most of her
neighboring wheat fields to the Navarre family for as many
years as I could remember. Now in her retirement, Farn no
longer made house calls unless it was for a sick cow she
really cared about. I supposed I should feel honored.

We were on the back gallery of the ranch. The early
morning air was bleeding through the screens. Outside,
ground fog was turning the yellow huisache trees into hazy
sketches. Charolais cows drifted across the pasture. The old
white water tank rose in the distance. The hay shed. Past
that, a hundred acres of stunted Texas wheat just turning
from green to gold. Pastoral.

Farn finished stitching me up, then checked the dilation
of my eyes and the IV that she had attached to my arm.
She yelled into the next room, "Arguello!"

Ralph came in, holding a snifter with my father's name,
JACK, printed on the side. Ralph's hair was freshly washed
and unbraided. It fell in a loose fan of gray and black.
With his huge white shirt untucked he looked like one of
the apostles, one of the very bad ones.

"Looking better, *vato*."

"Better than what?" I managed.

Farn closed up her kit, scowled down at me. "Yer lucky
as hell. Be all right—hell of a headache for a few days,

soreness all over. The drugs they gave you are going to leave you with the shakes, some nausea. Heroin mixed with some kind of prescription sedative, near as I can figure. You might black out once in a while."

"Yay."

"You're going to feel like you been run over on a West Texas highway and left to dry in the sun, darlin', but trust me—you're damn lucky."

"I want some water," I said.

Farn nodded. "Figures. I'll see y'all later."

She was replaced by Erainya, who stared down at me critically. She held a glass identical to Ralph's—one of the Jack snifters.

Ralph took the chair Janice Farn had been sitting in. He propped some more pillows behind my back.

Erainya drained her whiskey, then grimaced. "So, what—you think it's easy to get a baby-sitter for two days? You think Kelly wanted to give up a weekend to mind Jem and our guests while we bailed you out of trouble?"

"Our guests. Jesus Christ."

"Still at my house," Erainya assured me. "Little Michael . . ." She shook her head. "Poor *paidi*'s never even played Donkey Kong before."

"Can you imagine."

Erainya shook her head again. "Ines isn't too happy, either. She wanted to bolt out the door when she heard what had happened to you."

"Why didn't she?"

Erainya glared at me, giving me a taste of the scolding she had no doubt inflicted on poor unhappy Ines.

"Thank you," I said.

Erainya slapped the air. "She'll stay put for a few more days anyway."

"Long as you keep the television news turned off," Ralph added.

"The news?"

"Never mind, *vato*. Time for that later." Ralph drained the Jack glass.

I looked into the main house, through the mud-and-log doorway that had been the original front entrance in the 1870s. Beyond the archway, the living room was long and low, dimly lit. A fire was going in the old limestone hearth. Ozzie Gerson and Harold Diliberto, the ranch caretaker, stood looking down into the flames. Ozzie wore a side arm and Harold had a deer rifle nestled in his arm.

"Ozzie took early retirement as of today," Erainya informed me. "He says he'll be here as long as you need him. Diliberto says he won't put the rifle down until you tell him to. The old geezer told me anybody tries to get to you out here, he and Ozzie are going to use the tiger traps, whatever that means. I got my doubts about him."

My head ached. I rubbed my temples, discovered that was a major mistake. I tried to drink a little water from a paper cup Ralph handed me.

"I got to be going, *vato*," he said. "More than a couple of hours out here in redneck country, I start getting nervous."

"We wouldn't want that."

He grinned. "Give me a call when you want the Barracuda back, *vato*. I'll have it waiting for you."

"Thanks."

"There a back way to San Antonio?"

"Old Highway 90. Why?"

"I had to phone DeLeon, tell her what was up."

"Ines—"

"No, man. Not about that. That's your call. But Ana's coming out right now. She wants to kick my manly ass for the scene we pulled on Commerce. Some people are never grateful."

When Ralph was gone, it was just me and Erainya, watching the sun come up over the fields, the dew start to glisten on the leaves in the trees, the cows lining up for their daily trek down to the creek. Single file, heifer style.

Erainya stood over me, examining my face skeptically. "I thought we'd lost you, honey. Couple of times in the car, I put my hand on your chest, just to make sure you were still breathing."

I closed my eyes. My cheek had started to tremble. The trembling didn't stop.

"We didn't say anything to your mother," Erainya told me.

"Thank God for small favors."

"I figured it was better she didn't know."

"I've never been so scared, Erainya."

"I know, honey."

"I couldn't move. My arms—"

"I know. Here."

She came closer and helped me drink a little more water. Some of it dribbled out the side of my mouth and down my jaw, my neck, soaking into the collar of my shirt.

I lay back and shut my eyes, opening them again only with great difficulty.

Erainya was still there. She had her hand on my chest and her eyes were closed. I let myself drift into sleep.

FORTY-SEVEN

When I woke up again I was on the leather couch in front of the fireplace. The embers from the morning fire were just barely alive under the ash, and daylight was streaming through the windows.

The roaring of the water pipes in the old house told me that somebody was either taking a shower or locked in mortal combat with the toilet.

Harold Diliberto was still at his post by the fire, his coffee cup and half-empty bottle of bourbon on the mantel. In the crook of Harold's arm was his Remington 700—the decrepit deer rifle with the bent magazine spring dangling uselessly in front of the trigger.

I looked down at my feet and discovered they were resting in Ana DeLeon's lap. She was leaning back against the couch, her eyes small and dark and her face soft in thought. She was wearing jeans and a baggy black turtleneck. One hand rested on my ankle as if she'd long ago forgotten it was there. The other held the letter she was reading. I thought I recognized the distinctive block print—small, square, precise lettering. Ralph.

I said, "Hello." Ever the inventive conversationalist.

Ana started, looked at me, folded the letter, and put it aside.

"God damn you," she said. "When you're better I'm going to strangle you."

"Not the most loving thing I've heard all week. But

close." I looked at Harold. "How long have you been standing there?"

"It's Tuesday afternoon," he muttered. "They brought you in late Sunday night."

"Jesus. You can go to the bathroom now, Harold. Thanks."

He glanced distrustfully at DeLeon.

"Thanks, Harold," I repeated. "Take a rest."

He drifted off to do whatever it is drunk recluses do.

Ana squeezed my ankle. "You look like shit."

"Hotel Chicharron—no mints on the pillows."

When I tried to sit up, my head popped painfully back into its original shape. Ana slid my feet off her lap and onto the floor.

I looked down at myself. I was wearing boxers with little polo players on them, a T-shirt with a large Wild Turkey logo, and black socks.

"Whose idea of revenge was this?"

Ana shrugged. "You were like that when I got here. I'm still trying to figure out where *here* is."

I rubbed my eyes. "Welcome to the Navarre family ranch. Things get rough, I sometimes lay low out here. It's a hard place to get to. Hard for outsiders to come into Sabinal and make any trouble."

"Mmm." Ana didn't say more, but I wondered if she'd met some of our rancher neighbors, any one of whom would've given her more than a little polite trouble if she'd asked for directions.

"UTSA knows you're on sick leave this week," she said. "It's okay with Professor Mitchell."

"Probably has his professors abducted by drug dealers all the time."

"Mitchell should be relieved it was only that. I doubt the University's insurance rating could stand another fatality."

"Damn, you're cheery."

I listened to Harold clink around in the kitchen. I could smell butter sizzling in a frying pan.

"Can you talk about what happened?" Ana asked.

I did my best.

When I was done, Ana said, "Will you press charges against Chich?" Ever the cop.

"If you think it will do any good. But there's something else, before I change my mind. It's about Ines Brandon."

Once I got the truth out, I didn't feel a damn bit better. Apparently neither did DeLeon. She sat silent, staring at the embers in the fireplace.

"I didn't want to tell you," I said.

She flashed me an irritated look. "You want thanks?"

"Michael Brandon's only five years old. I don't want him to be the one who's punished."

"Tres—I already knew."

I stared at her. Vague memories started to form of my conversation with Chich. "Del Brandon."

"Kelsey and I played some hardball with Brandon on Saturday—hauled in one of his employees, man named Ernie Ragan."

"Big guy," I remembered. "Blond cornrows."

DeLeon nodded. "Turns out Ernest is wanted in three states—grand theft auto, agg. assault, rape. If you were him, would you want to be extradited to Mississippi? You ever been to one of their penitentiaries?"

"He decided to deal—give you his boss."

"Ernie would've given us his sweet old mother, we asked him to. So we chatted awhile, then brought in Del. Ten hours of questions, no lawyers. We told Del we wanted to ask him some questions about the murder of Hector Mara, mentioned how very cooperative Ernie had been. His employee in custody, the murder charges—that scared him. Del told us about Sandra Mara—Ines Brandon. Told us the whole thing was about her."

"The prick admit to anything himself?"

"He said he helped Sandra Mara change her name, then he threatened to give her up to keep Aaron from suing for the business a few years back. He says her brother Hector came to see him soon after that, intending to strong-arm him into silence, but they came to terms, decided to strike up a little business. Del admitted that there'd been some smack going through RideWorks, but he pinned the whole idea on Hector. He denied any knowledge of his brother's murder. Or Mara's."

"Del's lying."

"You can put that into past tense."

"What?"

"You can put *Del* in past tense."

My eyelids felt heavy, so I closed them. "How?"

"We didn't detain him overnight," Ana said. "Big mistake."

I thought about a big galoot in a loud shirt, gorilla hair, block face. I tried to remember why I'd hated his guts, but all I could picture was Del's look of pleasure when he spoke about well-constructed merry-go-rounds.

"Del went home about three in the morning Sunday," DeLeon said. "Walked inside and caught two rounds in the chest."

"Like his brother."

"Except a .357, this time. Silencer. Like Mara and Bertón. Del's neighbors, of course, saw and heard nothing."

"And the killer's still out there."

"Where's your friend Ines?"

"I don't know. But it wasn't her."

"You *are* going to bring her in."

"I didn't say I had her."

"Don't insult my intelligence, Navarre."

I rubbed my temples. "Give me some time, okay?"

"Time. Oh, is that all."

A quake started and it took me more than a minute to

remember that I no longer lived in California—that it wasn't the ground trembling but me.

I heard DeLeon say, "Go ahead and rest."

She put a quilt over me, lifted my feet back into her lap.

"Do me a favor," I said.

"Yes?"

"Don't disappear while I'm asleep. People keep disappearing on me."

And she didn't.

Sometime later, I opened my eyes in a haze and she was still there—pensive and beautiful, staring into the fireplace, Ralph's letter in her hand.

FORTY-EIGHT

I woke up flinching to the popcorn sound of distant gunfire—the ping of bullets on metal somewhere out in the fields.

A block of sunlight was glowing on my quilt. Ana DeLeon stood over me, snapping her Glock 23 into her Sam Browne holster. She'd changed into business clothes—blazer and skirt and immaculate white silk blouse.

"What's happening?" I asked.

"Your friend Deputy Gerson. That odd man, Mr. Diliberto. They're practicing on your target range."

"Since when does a line of beer cans constitute a target range?"

Ana checked her gun, straightened her blazer over it. "You want me to call them back in? I need to get to town. I'm already late."

"That's okay. Good luck with *Rey Feo*'s murderer."

Ana's eyebrows knit together. "What?"

I was hazy about how much I had told her the night before, or even if it *was* the night before when we'd talked, so I recounted my conversation Saturday with the bartender at the Poco Mas. I told her that the old man had seen Hector Mara arguing several weeks ago with a heavyset, dark-haired Anglo, a man Hector had derisively referred to as *Rey Feo*.

"It was Del," I said. "Zeta Sanchez had just gotten back into town. Del and Hector were meeting to figure out what to do."

DeLeon looked at the Army Corps of Engineers' map of Sabinal above the mantel. She seemed to be tracing the elevation lines, trying to separate them.

"Ana?"

She shook her head. "I'm fine. It's just—something Kelsey told me once. It rang a bell there for a second . . ."

Another round of gunfire crackled in the fields.

"Be careful when you go back. Chich knew you had Del. He knew exactly what Del was telling you. Chich has somebody in the department feeding him information."

Ana was silent.

"Kelsey was vice," I said, unnecessarily.

"Tres, he's my partner."

"As soon as you got into Chich's life, Chich was on the phone to Kelsey."

"Look, Kelsey may not be the best partner, but—"

"Ana, just tell me you'll be careful."

She hesitated, then slowly reconstructed her smile. "You're one to give advice. You sure you don't want me to get your friends?"

"Let the boys have their fun with the beer cans."

She kept her eyes on me a few seconds longer.

"What?" I asked.

"Nothing. You're going to be okay, is all. I'm glad for that."

"You make it sound like a good-bye."

DeLeon came over and gave me a swift kiss on the lips. Then she was gone.

I listened to her car engine start, the sound of gravel pinging under her wheels as she drove off.

After a few minutes I sat up, waited for the black spots to clear, then tried to stand. I felt like I'd just dismounted from an unfriendly bull. I looked down at the black socks and Wild Turkey T-shirt.

"No," I decided.

I made my way through the bedrooms until I found

some spare clothes I'd left on my last visit—jeans, a flannel shirt. After a year or two I managed to get dressed.

I checked the cupboard for something easy on the stomach and found nothing except ammo boxes and rat poison. The refrigerator held Budweiser and some cow drugs, massive syringes half full and dirty with blood from their last use. I settled for a large glass of tap water. On second thought, I didn't drink that either.

After finding my boots, I opened the front door and did a quick duck underneath the wasp nest forming there. Harold was as good about keeping up the property as he was at stocking the larder.

The morning gray had burned off. The air smelled of steamed grass and cow dung. A Mexican eagle circled over the trees that lined the creek in the center of the property.

The Navarre ranch isn't much of a spread by South Texas standards—250 acres, about the size of a King Ranch bathroom. The usually dry Apache Creek snakes through its middle, with wheat fields to the north and west, grazing lands and deer-hunting woods to the south and east. Where the land isn't cultivated it's choked with whitebrush and cactus, littered with limestone chunks, the topography around the creek gouged with sinkholes and gullies and washouts from years of unpredictable flooding.

I found Ozzie and Harold in a clearing where the mouth of the road dipped down into the trees between the creekbed and the man-made cow pond.

Ozzie was dressed in civilian clothes—jeans, white-and-red Hawaiian shirt, boots, white Stetson. A side arm and several extra magazines were spread across a table made from an old door and two sawhorses. Harold Diliberto stood next to him with the Remington 700.

The usual line of beer cans was set up on a hay bale fifty yards downrange. Ozzie had also set out a professional target—a small metal disk designed to rock back on its base when hit and make a resounding *ping*.

Ozzie grinned when he saw me walking up. "Well—it's alive."

I accepted his congratulatory pounding on my back, which was marginally less painful than an electric nail driver.

Harold Diliberto offered me a hit from his breakfast whiskey flask. I declined.

"Just getting my aim back," Ozzie told me.

His side arm was a .357 semiautomatic that had seen a lot of use. The muzzle was scored as if it had once been fitted with the wrong end sight.

I watched Ozzie aim at the metal target, then fire.

I flinched at the sound, even though I knew it was coming. There is nothing quite so loud as a gun fired by someone else.

There was no subsequent *ping* against the target. I kept my eyes on the gun.

"Used to be the recoil on this thing didn't bother me at all," Ozzie said. "You get stiff in one arm, even if it's not your good arm, it completely fucks you up. Give me that old rifle, Harold."

Harold looked from the rifle to Ozzie. "You serious?"

Ozzie took the Remington from Harold and clamped the stock under his bad shoulder, released the bolt with his good hand. The loading spring dangled uselessly underneath. It would be one shot at a time forevermore with the Remington.

With some effort, Ozzie pushed a .243 bullet into the magazine, slid the bolt forward to chamber the round, locked the handle down.

"Yeah," he said with satisfaction. "In the old days I could fire one of these with my good arm in a cast. Just prop it on a fence. I'm getting old. So, Tres—feel good to be done with the Brandon family?"

I looked down the reservoir road. Clouds of gnats floated over the little bridge of land between the creekbed and the water tank. I remembered a time in high school—coming out here with a half-dozen friends, getting together with some of the local kids who promised us dinner in exchange for beer. We'd set up a barbecue pit on that road, cranked up the truck radio, and watched the local boys shoot ring-necked doves out of the sky one after another, gutting and cooking them for us on the spot. I remembered Lillian, the girl I'd been with at the time, and what it was like trying to make out in the back of a truck with the constant fire of guns and dead birds falling all around us. I hadn't thought of that day in years.

"I don't feel much of anything," I said.

Ozzie nodded. "They doped you up pretty good. I'll give you a ride back to town this afternoon, you want it. I'm going to personally have a chat with Chich Gutierrez, let him know what's what. I'm a civilian now. I'm leaving town. I figure what the fuck—the bastard needs a talking-to."

Harold Diliberto sat back against the door-table and slurped his whiskey.

Ozzie brought up his bad arm carefully, used his forearm as a platform to stabilize the barrel.

"You figure Chich's men shot George Bertón and Mara?" I asked him.

"I mean to find out."

Ozzie sighted the target. A trickle of sweat wove its way down his cheek. His hatband was already stained brown as a coffee filter.

"The M.E. thought there was somebody else in George's house that night," I said. "A single shooter who came in the back. Maybe the shooter got out of the house before Chicharron got inside."

Ozzie shot and missed. He lowered the barrel, his eyes full of cool amusement. "The timing would be a pretty huge coincidence, kid."

"Not if the shooter choreographed it that way. Not if he knew Chich would be watching the house, knew that any witnesses would most likely implicate the guys in the white van."

Ozzie turned the vertical knob on the telescopic sight. "You ask Sandra Mara about that possibility?"

"Who says I could find her?"

Ozzie laughed, turned to Diliberto. "Dang, Harold. This five-by-thirty sighted for you? How you manage to hit anything?"

"Maybe you were right," I said.

Ozzie smiled at me. "Right about what?"

"Maybe the thing to do is just wait and ask George."

Ozzie turned the horizontal knob. "How's he doing?"

"Erainya says he's still sedated. But he's beat the infection. He's going to make it. Maybe another three or four days and he'll be able to talk."

Ozzie grinned. "That's excellent."

"Where are you and Audrey going? Cancun?"

Ozzie nodded, released the rifle bolt. The spent casing ejected, spiraling past Harold's ear. Harold Diliberto had finished his flask and was now looking for something else to do. He zeroed in on Ozzie's .357, picked it up, and began slowly, drunkenly, field-stripping it.

Ozzie just looked over and laughed good-naturedly. Diliberto liked taking things apart. Sometimes he even got them back together.

"I told Harold I'd leave that old .357 at the ranch for him," Ozzie said. "God knows he needs something better than this rifle. And yeah, kid. Cancun. If I was you, I'd tell Sandra Mara to clear out. They haul her in, they won't go easy on her."

"You're probably right."

"You know I am."

"Chich Gutierrez is still looking for those lost two kilos

of heroin," I said. "Sandra will be the one Chich holds ac-
countable."

Ozzie winced with effort as he reloaded the rifle. "I ever
tell you your dad was the first man I saw hunt with a handgun? That same .357 Harold's destroying right there."

Harold looked up like he'd just vaguely recognized his
name. He had unloaded the .357's magazine and was now
removing the chamber cover.

"Jack and I were out there"—Ozzie nodded toward the
creek—"looking at all the gravel in the riverbed. Your dad
always talked about selling it for people's gardens, you remember? And this huge buck just *appeared*. I couldn't believe it. Your dad borrowed my side arm and shot it on the
spot. Damnedest thing. We ate venison for months."

He brought up his forearm for a brace, rested the
Remington on it, and aimed.

Harold looked up sleepily from the half-disassembled
handgun. He was rubbing a finger over the irregular scoring
on the muzzle. "You been modifyin' for a silencer, Ozzie?"

Ozzie fired. Metal pinged. He smiled and lowered the
rifle. "Naw. Bought me a new sight, tried to fit it on the
barrel, turned out to be a bad match. You going to have
anything left of that gun when you're through?"

Harold blushed. He started collecting the pieces of the
.357 for reassembly.

I was hit with another wave of nausea.

"Whoa, son." Ozzie quickly put the Remington on the
table and caught my arm, guided me over to a flat piece of
limestone to sit. "You want us to walk you back to the
house?"

"I'll be okay in a second."

"Maybe we should take you back to town sooner than
later."

"No. It's all right."

Ozzie studied my eyes, seemed to be satisfied I wasn't in

immediate danger. "Couple more shots, then. Never like to leave before I'm fifty-fifty on the hits."

He stepped back to the table, began reloading.

"I guess you didn't recognize her," I said.

Ozzie glanced over, frowning, then turned his attention back to the gun. "Recognize who?"

"Ines Brandon. Sandra Mara. When she was at the river with me, when they pulled out the VW."

Ozzie finished loading the second chamber. "No. No, I didn't. I saw Sandra maybe once or twice back in the old days. She looked a lot different then—longer hair. Dyed black, I think."

"Four men were all shot by one gunman—Aaron Brandon, then Hector Mara and George Bertón, then Del Brandon. None of them fought back, except maybe Hector. None of them expected this guy to be their assassin."

"Argues that it could've been a woman."

"Except I know where Ines was the night Del was killed."

Ozzie prepped the gun for firing, but lowered it and sighed. "Chich Gutierrez, then. I told you, kid. You can't figure gang-bangers like that."

"Attila the rat."

His eyes glistened like ice over his smile. "Absolutely. Let them beat it out of Chicharron, once they haul him in. Or give them Sandra Mara if you really want. One of them will have the answers."

The nausea was starting to fade. I managed to get back on my feet. "A girl at the Poco Mas told me about a guy Hector Mara was arguing with a few weeks ago—big Anglo guy, dark hair, she thought his name was something like Branson."

"Del Brandon."

"That's what I thought too. Now I'm not sure."

Harold Diliberto had just about reassembled the .357, but the magazine wasn't going in right. It was jamming on something. Harold was listening to us with half his attention, trying to get the gun working with the rest, and his IQ divided by two projects yielded some pretty small numbers.

"Chich had an insider with the police department," I said. "I wondered if it was Kelsey."

Ozzie turned toward the target, examined it placidly. "Who's paying you to speculate, kid? UTSA isn't writing any more checks for this investigation."

Ozzie was right. I could've left it alone. Instead I kept wondering aloud, watching Harold's hands as they refitted Gerson's .357.

"Del Brandon wasn't smart enough to run heroin through RideWorks by himself. He didn't have the steel to set up his dad's murder, or his brother's, or anybody else's. He must've had somebody behind him telling him what to do, a silent partner. I'm thinking this silent guy went to Jeremiah Brandon first, back in '92. He had a great idea—use talent from the local gangs to help run drugs through the carnival circuit. Only Jeremiah wouldn't have anything to do with it. When Mr. Silent got insistent, Jeremiah flexed a little muscle and ruined this guy's day job. Mr. Silent held a grudge. He figured RideWorks would be a whole lot easier to profit from with somebody stupider at the helm. He helped set up Jeremiah's murder, told Del exactly how to do it. When the dust settled, he told Del how to pressure Hector Mara into the heroin deal. Later, when Aaron Brandon came back to town and got a little too hard to control, it was Del's partner who killed him and framed Zeta Sanchez. How does that sound so far?"

Ozzie had lowered the gun, apparently not happy with the sight. He made one more adjustment, lifted the rifle again. "I'd rest your mouth, kid. You're still weak."

"Hector Mara must've found out the gunman's identity. Or maybe Hector had known all along and hadn't been brave enough to do anything about it. After Aaron Brandon was murdered, Hector got scared for his sister. He started talking with George Bertón. Hector had two keys of Chich's heroin which he'd been planning to use as a get-away fund for himself and his sister. George persuaded him to bring it over instead, use it as evidence against Del. Unfortunately, Hector's partner got wind of what was happening. He went to Bertón's house to take care of things. He wanted to leave two corpses, but he screwed up. Chich's men moved in a little faster than he expected, or maybe it was a little harder to kill George than he'd figured. The gunman retrieved the heroin for himself, killed Mara, but he left Bertón alive, a loose end. The gunman figured Chicharron was good for the murder, but he couldn't wait around hoping that George would die before he ID'ed his shooter. Besides, Del was getting nervous. As dense as he was, Del was starting to realize he'd be the one on the spot if his partner cut out. So Del started talking to the police— not yet giving away his partner, but it was only a matter of time. So the gunman killed Del. Then he decided to cut his losses, take a little vacation with his winnings."

Ozzie laughed. "You definitely need to be out of the sun, kid. Let's ride back together."

"Not with you, Ozzie."

He still hadn't fired. Diliberto clicked the .357 magazine into place and was frowning back and forth between us like he wasn't exactly following the conversation.

Ozzie's pale eyes stayed on me. "What are you saying, kid?"

"I'm saying I'm not going anywhere with you because you might get a little trigger-happy, the way you did with George Bertón. That social cannibalism you talked about, Ozzie? Attila the rat? The end product isn't Hector or Del or even Zeta. The end product is you. Point the .357 at him, Harold. Now."

Harold, God bless him, did not hesitate. Like everything he'd ever done for me, he did it with unquestioning loyalty and the same completely good-natured incompetence.

Ozzie swung the Remington toward Harold's chest and Harold fired first—nothing. A click, a jammed load. The deer rifle blew a hole in Harold Diliberto's gut and flung him into the door and sawhorses.

I charged into Ozzie; I might've been made of paper for all the impact I made. Ozzie grunted, threw me off, and fumbled to manually load another .243 round.

I ran, made it fifteen yards when I heard the bolt action lock. I fell into a sideways roll as the blast turned a chunk of limestone on the ground to dust. Another five feet of blind panic and I hit the edge of the nearest washout—half rolled, half slid into the dry creekbed below.

Another shot cracked the air. I stumbled over river stones like marbles, scrambling to put distance between myself and Ozzie Gerson. My progress seemed insanely loud. My twisted ankle hurt like hell. I reached a turn where the washout joined the creekbed proper and stumbled on.

At a turn in the creekbed a massive live oak levitated against the clay bank on an octopus-shaped tent of roots. I flattened myself against the far side and scoped the ridge, saw nothing. The rattle of my breath was as noisy as a jet. I wanted to curl up inside the hollow underneath the tree and black out, but I knew I would merely be choosing my corner to die in.

Least you changed out of the boxers and the Wild Turkey shirt, part of me said. *Better to die in flannel.*

The rest of me told that part to shut up.

I forced myself to keep running.

I realized I was heading away from the farmhouse—away from the phone—then realized just as quickly that it didn't matter. Ozzie would expect me to double back to the house. He'd be able to shoot me before I ever made a call, much less got aid from one. Maybe going in the opposite direction had inadvertently bought me a few minutes.

Ozzie's rifle fired: a whiff of air puffed against my thigh. I launched forward, crashed into deadwood, got up, and kept running.

From somewhere behind me, up on the ridge, Ozzie yelled, "Bad way to play it, Tres. You think I wanted to shoot George? Don't do this. Don't force me like he did, kid."

I could hear him reloading. I staggered forward, around another washout, then another few yards before daring to scramble up the side of the bank and look back. I clung to live-oak roots and lifted my head just over the ridge. In his red-and-white Hawaiian shirt, Ozzie Gerson was easy enough to spot. He was thirty yards away, sideways to me, feeding another round into his rifle. I wondered if the women who gave out leis at the Honolulu airport had nightmares that looked like Ozzie Gerson.

"All I want is what's mine, Tres. You think anybody mourned the Brandons? Or a scumbag like Mara? Your lady friend Sandra, she should be thanking me. I just made her life a whole lot simpler."

Ozzie had the look of a man who was butchering a large animal—cultivating the inner deadness that was necessary to convince himself there was nothing repulsive about the hollowed-out intestinal cavity, the sinews, the exposed ribs.

I couldn't double back. Not enough room between us.

The nearest neighbor, Dr. Farn, was a half mile away over an open spread of wheat fields.

I clambered down the ridge, continuing along the creek bank, making enough noise for Ozzie to swing toward me and fire another shot over my head. I could hear him above me now, swishing through the whitebrush. Rocks skittered down the bank. Ozzie cursed as he lost his footing. Then he was up and following again. I'd gained a few feet.

The creekbed continued its labyrinthine turns. The dips and rises and heavy underbrush made visibility low. I crashed over a mound of deadwood and stumbled within feet of a rattler sunning itself on a rock. It didn't even have time to rattle before I was gone.

Twenty yards ahead, I saw the white shell of the old water tower. The tower was a leftover from one of my father's many failed ranch development schemes—a cone of pure lead as tall as I was, lying on its side and rusting in the sun. Just below the cone, in the creekbed, stood another stand of deadwood even larger than the rattler's. I ran to it, shed my shirt and snagged it against the top branch, then scrambled up the ledge to the water tank shell, flattening myself on the ground behind it.

Cicadas buzzed in the heat. A gnat did a kamikaze dive into my nostril.

Then I heard Ozzie's steps, very near. Grass scritched. Heavy breathing. I'd hoped for some luck, but he was on my side of the ridge, not more than fifteen feet away, the water tank shell between us. There was no way he couldn't see me.

I heard him lock the rifle bolt into place. Silence.

I waited to be shot.

Instead, I heard more skittering rocks, snapping twigs. Ozzie was slide-climbing down the ridge, toward the shirt on the deadwood.

His voice was aimed away from me when he called, "Come on, Tres. Let's talk."

I scrambled to my feet and pushed. All my strength wasn't much, but the water tank cooperated. It ripped free of its muddy moorings on the edge of the cliff and barreled down the ridge, bouncing once before Ozzie turned and yelled and the cylinder crashed into him with a very satisfying *bong*. I wanted to believe that Ozzie had been flattened into a redneck tortilla, but his loud curses of pain told me otherwise. I started running, on high ground now.

I could see barbed wire just ahead to the right and past

that two hundred acres of Dr. Farn's land, planted with Navarre wheat. Past that, Dr. Farn's farmhouse in an island of pecan trees, and fifty yards farther, the tiny shapes of cars and trucks gliding down the highway. The wheat fields between me and the road would be a killing zone hundreds of yards long with no cover.

As much fun as that sounded, I turned my back on the promise and veered left instead. I ripped through white-brush and cactus, heading back toward the farmhouse.

I bolted forward, tripped over a rusted coil of barbed wire and lost precious time getting my legs untangled. If I lived, I'd need a tetanus shot. When I fell out of the under-brush I found myself once again in the clearing—Harold Diliberto lying collapsed, facedown and unmoving in the weeds, the door-table tilted against one sawhorse like a lean-to. Blood soaked the grass.

The .357 was two feet away.

I'd just grabbed it when the rifle boomed and my left shoulder went cold. My legs gave out from under me. I fell forward, into Harold, twisting around with my face to the sky.

It was hard to breathe. Harder still to move my arms. The .357 was in my hands and my fingers kept trying to tighten around the trigger, trying to reload the magazine correctly. The cold was spreading from my shoulder into my chest.

Ozzie appeared from behind a tree, back by the ridge, just far enough away that I couldn't quite make out the color of his eyes.

His left shoulder, the one Zeta Sanchez had shot, was now bent at an odd angle. The shirt around it glistened with blood from the ripped-open wound. With his good hand, Ozzie still held the rifle.

He moved forward, talking in a monotone. "Could've been pretty simple. Sorry, Tres. You think I want to kill you?"

I aimed the .357 at him.

Ozzie managed a dazed smile. "Even if it wasn't jammed, kid—even then you couldn't."

He looked around, then took a step toward a small live-oak sapling. He raised the rifle barrel and set it with great care into the crook of two branches. He swung the muzzle toward me.

His eyes were drooping, heavy with pain and blood loss. But not heavy enough to prevent him from finishing. He sighted the gun.

When the shot came the volume was hideous. I convulsed and so did Ozzie Gerson. He raised his rifle barrel in slow motion while the rest of him lowered into a kneeling position. He looked down in disbelief at the hole I'd just shot in his hip, the bloody change that was dribbling out the front pocket of his jeans.

The terror of it sent me into a fit of giggling. I felt exhilarated. I loved the sound of the next .357 round that sawed off the live-oak sapling inches to the right of Ozzie's ear.

I don't know how I did it but I got to my feet.

I staggered forward, trying to aim the gun.

Ozzie had fallen on his butt. He was trying to tug the rifle up onto his bloody legs, to lift his knees so he could get the barrel high enough to kill me.

His face glistened with sweat. He managed a stuttering wheeze that might have been a distant cousin to a laugh. He muttered, "Well shit, kid. Well shit. That was good. Now come here a step—okay? Come here."

The little blood geyser kept bubbling up on the side of his pants. Ozzie's gun kept trying to slip off his knees.

I managed another step forward, just to be obliging. Anything for a friend.

Ozzie wheezed again, happily. He fired his last shot and something a long way off behind me went *ping*.

For Ozzie's sake, I hoped he'd finally hit that metal target. I raised my gun.

Ozzie let the rifle slip and held his hand over his pants pocket, trying to stop the blood.

Then an unwelcome voice snarled, "Put it down!"

I swung the gun to the left and found the muzzle of Ana DeLeon's Glock 23 pointing at me. Ana's skirt and blouse were scratched to hell from a trek through the foliage, her face as cold as the moon.

"You've got that aimed wrong," I heard myself saying.

Then I showed her what I meant. I turned the .357 back on Ozzie.

"I'll shoot you, Tres." DeLeon's voice was steady, louder than I thought it needed to be. "Put the gun on the ground."

I don't know how many chances DeLeon gave me to drop it, how many times she gave me that order. In the end, I was saved by Ozzie himself. He tried to sit up one more time and his face went silk-white. Then his head lolled back, hit the grass. His eyes squinted shut.

I lowered the .357, let it clunk into the tall grass. Then I crumpled into sitting position.

Ana DeLeon kept the Glock trained on me as she approached Ozzie, inspected him. I think she found him still alive. She tossed the deer rifle a few feet away, then knelt beside me. Her eyes burned with anger, but there was something else, too—alarm as she examined my shoulder wound.

"*Rey Feo,*" she said. "Kelsey's gang informants in vice used to call Ozzie Gerson that. You goddamn—you set yourself up for this. You *stupid* bastard."

"There's a doctor," I muttered. "Across the fields. Phone in the house."

"You wanted me gone while you handled this. If I hadn't come back—"

"I'm cold," I said.

Then Ana DeLeon was gone. I sat shivering in the spring sunshine, listening to DeLeon running toward my father's ranch house, cutting through the brush like a small tireless harvester blade.

FORTY-NINE

For the rest of that week, when I wasn't having night-mares, I was getting intimate with the acoustic ceiling tile in my semiprivate room at University Hospital, and with my roommate George Bertón's favorite talk shows.

Since George had been upgraded from critical and moved from BAMC, Erainya said it only made sense that he and I be roomies. Given our mutual experiences over the last few weeks, it was unlikely we'd end up shooting each other in ir-ritation, however much we might wish to.

George could only speak a few words at a time. These mostly consisted of "No cigars?" when the nurse visited and "Melissa" when he slept and "Bastard, Navarre" when-ever I tried to change the channel on him. The first thing he'd done when he'd regained consciousness was to de-mand his Panama hat. The second was to call Ozzie Gerson a son of a bitch.

While George was sleeping, which was often, I would watch the news and learn about what was happening out in the world.

A Bexar County deputy now faced indictment on three counts of capital murder for the shooting deaths of Hector Mara and the brothers Del and Aaron Brandon. The Brandon family maid had ID'ed Sheriff's Deputy Ozzie Gerson as Aaron's killer in exchange for charges of obstruc-tion of justice against her being dropped.

Gerson was charged on eleven other counts, including

drug trafficking. A raid on Gerson's home turned up two plane tickets for Brazil and two packed suitcases, one of which contained over $80,000 in cash. In Gerson's closet, in a locked gun box, police also found a substantial amount of black tar heroin. While Gerson made no comment about the other charges against him, he had happily offered up the name of Chich Gutierrez as his heroin supplier. Police now had a warrant out for Gutierrez's arrest. The reporter told us that prior allegations for drug trafficking in 1992 had resulted in Gerson's demotion at the sheriff's department. There was "widespread outrage" that this officer had remained on active duty for the past seven years. The sheriff's department was promising an immediate internal investigation.

Anthony "Zeta" Sanchez was still in jail on charges of shooting Gerson and resisting arrest, but was not expected to be charged with any higher crimes.

The SAPD brass and the D.A.'s office were praising the homicide detectives in charge of the investigation.

"This is a case where extra diligence paid off," their PR lady told TV viewers. "If we hadn't gone the extra mile, if the detectives involved had settled for the easy solution—"

A reporter interrupted, asking if SAPD detectives had ever settled for the easy solution before, if there'd been any pressure from the D.A.'s office to wrap up the Professor Aaron Brandon murder case quickly. The PR spokesman said, "Of course not."

A last strange twist on the case—Aaron Brandon's widow Ines had come forward and admitted to having a prior relationship with Aaron's supposed killer, Zeta Sanchez. She had, at one time, gone by the name of Sandra Mara-Sanchez. The local news was still chewing on that piece of information, not sure what to do with it, but they reported that Ines Brandon was not at present charged with any crime. After questioning, she had been released to be with her son. In the short clip they showed of Ines, I saw Erainya in the background, along with several high-powered defense lawyers.

I turned off the TV.

Harold Diliberto had failed to make the news, unless you count the early morning coffee crowd at the Sabinal General Store. Harold would live, and as Dr. Janice Farn succinctly put it, "He'll only be a little uglier than he was before."

The hospital room hadn't been quiet for two minutes when my mother appeared in the doorway with a wicker picnic basket. George was snoring, his Panama hat pulled down over his trach tube. Mother was dressed in a beaded denim dress, her neckline dripping with trouble dolls and Zuni fetishes. Her black hair was pulled back, also beaded. She looked like a Shopping Channel advertisement for the Bead-O-Matic appliqué kit.

"You look fine, dear." She sat down, hoisting the basket onto her lap. "You have a little color back."

"I feel colorful. And you don't have to whisper. When George sleeps, he *sleeps*."

She patted my wrist, then helped me raise the bed to a forty-five-degree angle. "You'll be ready for release this evening, I hear."

I tried to sit up and immediately regretted it. My bandaged shoulder screamed like it was being repierced with a hot glue gun. My not-very-funny doctor had asked me, after some successful minor surgery, whether I'd be wanting a stud or a dangle for the hole.

"Don't worry," my mother said. "This will cheer you up."

Out of a little lap table she brought a ceramic plate and soup bowl, a spoon and napkin, a vase filled with baby's breath and dried roses and incense—the whole Bohemian breakfast-in-bed kit. Then with a flourish she extracted a foam cup the size of a Bill Miller extra-large iced tea (which is to say, awfully big). The white top was scotch-taped in place, dripping with steam.

"*Caldo res* from El Mirador," she announced proudly.

I stared at her blankly. "But it's not Saturday."

One of the many absurd rules Texans learn to live with—El Mirador's famous soup cannot be had for love or money except on Saturday.

"I had a premonition," Mother told me. "I just knew I had to get an order to go this week. It reheated beautifully."

"Thank you."

Mother smiled, gratified. She spooned the concoction into my bowl, and watched, pleased, as I slurped it mouthful by greedy mouthful, spilling a good deal of it on my napkin.

Afterward I sat back, enjoying the warmth, even enjoying my mother's quiet company.

It seemed like hours before she said, "Jess isn't coming back."

Her jaw was set, her lips were pressed together in resolution. Her eyes were ever so slightly rimmed with red—from sleeplessness or anger or maybe crying—but she sounded confident, even upbeat.

"Apparently he came by and got the last of his things while I was doing my installation at the Crocker Gallery," she continued. "It's amazing—three years together, and amazing just how little he really made a mark on that house."

"That house," I assured her, "could never be anything but yours."

She nodded tentatively.

"And nobody makes a mark on my mama," I added.

She cracked a smile.

She gathered her things, replaced the items in her purse, and sat up in a glittery readjustment of denim and black hair and beads.

"I don't suppose I need to tell you," she said, "you scared me to death again."

"No, you don't."

We agreed on dinner next Monday.

Then Mother left me alone with the afternoon light growing long on the walls of the hospital room. I lay there for a long time, listening to George Bertón contentedly mumbling his dead wife's name.

FIFTY

To my knowledge, Ralph Arguello had never lived in any one location for longer than six months. He began life moving from shack to shack in the slums of Cementville, a factory-run shantytown where his father worked. After his father's death and his mother's success as a maid, they moved into a small cottage off Basse, behind the Alamo Gun Club, but Ralph, as much as he loved his mother, was constantly shifting from friend's house to cousin's house to God knows where, lying low when the cops were around, making money any way he could.

The habit proved hard to break once Ralph became a successful pawnshop king. Today, he would still move into the offices of acquired shops for a few weeks, to get a feel for the land, he claimed, and then move to another apartment or rental house. He had several homes in his name, several more in other names, but none of them were *his* home. He traded in and out of living quarters with the same kind of rootlessness the items in his pawnshops experienced.

Ralph's inseparable possessions were few.

This week he was living in the old Broadway Apartments in Alamo Heights. The units were dingy blocks, with narrow, perpetually shaded courtyards smelling of chinaberries and Freon and damp earth. The metal window frames had not been replaced since the Johnson administration. It was a place you could drive past a thousand times and never notice, which is exactly what appealed to Ralph, I was sure.

I paid off the taxi driver and walked through the courtyard of the nearest building. On the sidewalk, a couple of Anglo boys in striped shirts and corduroy shorts and paper Burger King hats were fighting over a Mr. Potato Head. There were fiesta leftovers scattered across the ground—colored eggshells and confetti from busted *cascarones*. A Night in Old San Antonio T-shirt was hanging over somebody's wall AC unit.

Ralph answered the buzzer at number five. He looked relaxed, his braid over his shoulder, his green Guayabera pulled sideways so his buttons made a diagonal line, his slacks wrinkled, his boots nearby on the carpet, and his feet in black socks. His glasses were in his shirt pocket, so his eyes again had that large, dark look that made me think of a night animal—a raccoon or a possum, something cute and silent and vicious.

"Come on in, *vato*."

The place had obviously come furnished. Brown shag carpet, white plastic furniture in seventies outer-space mod, an old Sony TV, a walnut veneer bookshelf that was mostly empty. The kitchen smelled like beer and fresh tamales and copal incense—three of Ralph's essentials.

I followed Ralph into the living room. The sliding-glass door was open and the small back porch was ringed in stone, furnished with an enormous jade plant and a hibachi grill, on which two pieces of flank steak were grilling.

Ana DeLeon sat on the stone wall, drinking a glass of red wine and watching me approach. She looked beautiful. Her short black hair was cowlicked on one side. She wore black leggings and one of her white silk blouses, untucked, the top two buttons undone to reveal the inward curves of her breasts. She was barefoot.

She said, "Tres."

I nodded.

Ralph said, "I'll get you the Barracuda keys."

He left for the kitchen.

"You didn't return my calls," I told Ana.

The steaks hissed. Music started up from Ralph's boom box inside—the bright guitar and basso of a *ranchera*.

"I don't owe you, Tres."

"That's right," I agreed. "No special privileges."

"It wasn't smart—you and me."

I let the idea hang between us until Ana's anger started to crumble.

"No," she decided. "That's the easy way out. The truth is I feel bad. But what happened out in Sabinal—"

"You won't have to live with it, Ana."

Ana stared into her wineglass. "I suppose my judgment is no better. I don't think I can explain to you why I'm here, Tres. Or explain it to myself."

She met my eyes. We had a silent conversation that lasted about five seconds and told me all I needed to know. There was no anxiety, no concern for career, no real desire for an explanation. Instead I recognized that kind of fractured heat—that reckless energy I had glimpsed in a few women before, and on a few very lucky occasions, seen directed toward me. But not this time.

"I'm sorry," Ana said.

The fact that she meant it, that she wasn't just being polite, hung awkwardly between us.

"SAPD won't hear anything from me."

She pursed her lips, nodded. Then the smell of bay rum intensified behind me. Ralph handed me a Shiner Bock and a set of car keys.

"Back lot, *vato*. I got a couple of Chich's boys to touch up the paint and wax it for you."

Ralph went to the hibachi grill and squeezed a lime over the flank steak with a wide arcing gesture like a priest using a censer.

He winked at Ana. "Quiet neighbors here, *chica*. I could like it."

She smiled. "You'd have to get better furniture."

"Don't need much," Ralph said. Then, out of nowhere, he quoted a stanza of Spanish love poetry—a few lines about a woman who fills a man's every empty room.

I looked at him. "I didn't know you read Neruda."

Ana fixed her eyes on the hibachi flames.

Ralph chuckled. "Can't survive on *American Gladiator* alone, *vato*."

We sat lined on the wall, Ana, Ralph, and I, drinking and listening to the *ranchero* music and the sizzle of flank steak.

"I got another one in the refrigerator," Ralph told me. "You want to stay, *vato*—it isn't every day the King cooks."

"Thanks. I should go."

"I'll walk you out." Ralph stood and fished for something in his pocket, then stopped, grinned at himself. "Ana's going to keep me from smoking, *vato*. How long you think that'll last, eh?"

"I'm not a betting man."

"But hey—you understand, *vato*, she ain't really here, right? She's *never* here."

"Of course," I agreed. "I understand that. See you, Detective."

Ana nodded silently, locking eyes with me with an intense message I couldn't read. Maybe I didn't really try.

Ralph walked me to the door. He patted me on the shoulder, smiled reassuringly.

"You still worrying. Don't, *vato*. It's all cool. Chich Gutierrez got so much heat on him now, he ain't going to have time or energy to fuck with you and me no more."

"Tell me something. How long you been impressing women with Pablo Neruda?"

Ralph looked surprised. "Ain't the poetry, baby. It's the

whole package, you know? Why—you got a woman in mind?"

He grinned at me, and then, when I didn't answer, waved and let the door close—shutting off the music, the dinner smells, the sight of Ana DeLeon so completely I had the feeling I was the one who'd never really been there.

FIFTY-ONE

The following morning, Ines Brandon, Michael Brandon, and I stood at the entrance to the Bexar County Jail.

Ines had stopped at the top of the steps, her fingers wrapped around the metal railing as if she hoped it would keep her stationary.

"I don't know if I can do this," she told me.

Days of worry had left her face drawn, her eyes underscored with shadows.

It wasn't the legal problems. Those were working themselves out. Thanks to the lawyers Erainya had recruited by cashing in favors, and Ines' cooperation with investigators, Assistant District Attorney Canright had apparently decided that bringing charges against a widowed mother who'd assumed a false identity for her own protection and that of her small son was not high on his political agenda.

The main battle was yet to come, and it wasn't legal.

"You're not alone," I told Ines. "You've got two studly guys for backup, remember?"

She gave me a weak smile.

Her hair was unwashed, tied back in a stiff ponytail that looked like the tip of a calligraphy brush. She wore rumpled black pants and a loose black denim shirt, both streaked with white dust. No makeup, no perfume. Nothing to indicate she'd slept, eaten, or changed her appearance since I'd seen her the night before for a pep talk.

Little Michael, by contrast, had received his mother's full

attention. Ines had dressed him in gray slacks, a newly ironed white button-down, a man's red-and-blue tie, probably his father's, that hung well past his belt. She'd made sure Michael's shoes were tied and his face scrubbed. Only his hair had resisted her ministrations. Michael's cowlicks had sprung back with an unruliness that reminded me of his uncle Del's.

The three of us stood on the jailhouse steps long enough for a silent prayer.

Finally Ines put her hand on Michael's head, then took a deep breath. "Let's go."

We walked into Visitors Receiving, through security to the room with the divided Plexiglas wall and the green chairs and tables.

The room was fuller than it had been on my previous visit. There was a large pasty blond woman talking to a skinny African American man on the other side. A young Anglo woman with two babies—one under arm and one in a chest-pack—was chastising her incarcerated boyfriend about somebody named Casey. The boyfriend's dazed expression mirrored the babies' perfectly.

Ines and Michael and I went to space "B" in the middle. There was one empty chair. None of us took it.

The longest five minutes in the universe followed.

Ines tried to smooth out Michael's hair with her fingers and didn't have much success. Her breath was shaky. Michael did small twists from his waist, swaying back and forth. He kept his eyes on the cement floor.

The large blond woman next to us vivisected her electric bill. The baby in the chest-pack on the other woman was making frustrated "ehh, ehh" sounds, kicking tiny feet at Mom's kidneys. The boyfriend seemed pretty upset about this person Casey.

Finally the prisoner's entrance buzzed open.

Zeta Sanchez emerged in his orange prison scrubs and plastic sandals.

His gold eyes zeroed in on Ines and stayed there as he walked toward us. His face was impassive. The beard had been shaved away, and his bare chin looked strangely pale, vulnerable. He'd cut himself shaving. One cheek sported a bandage, and that small bit of first aid seemed ridiculous next to the other damage on his face—the stitched and swollen lip, the fading black eye.

Zeta came up to the Plexiglas and sat on the table's edge. The guard at the door looked like he was thinking about walking over, telling Sanchez to use the chair, but he apparently decided against it.

Sanchez laced his fingers over his knee. "Sandra."

Silence.

Ines took in Sanchez with the same horrified fascination as a crime-scene novice taking in her first corpse. Her hands stayed on Michael's shoulders. Michael twisted his left thumb, seeing if it would come off.

When Sanchez failed to get a response, he looked at me. "Professor. What you told me on the phone true?"

"Talk to her, Zeta. Not me."

The golden eyes burned into mine, trying to find a challenge.

He looked back at Ines, turned his palms up in his lap, meditation style. "You got something to say to me?"

"You're shorter than I remember," she muttered.

Zeta's mouth spread into an uneasy smile.

"What you think I should do to you, Sandra? Huh? Tell me that."

His voice was thin, taut, dangerously dry. The fact that he kept smiling didn't help at all.

The strength in Ines' body seemed to be channeling down to her hands—into the fingertips that stayed on Michael's narrow shoulders. She said, "I'm tired of being scared of you."

Zeta laughed. "Don't get tired yet."

"That person you married seven years ago, Anthony—that was a different woman."

"Looked like you, Sandra."

She raised one hand and made a fist. "How long would it have lasted, Anthony? How long would you have put up with getting *nothing* from me? How long before you hurt me? If we'd had a child, *Dios me libre,* how long before you hurt him, too?"

Zeta ran a knuckle along his jawline. He seemed vaguely surprised to find his beard gone.

Next to us, the two babies started crying softly.

"I never lied to you, Zeta," Ines said. "I never forced you to kill anyone. But you can't take responsibility for any of it, can you? Couldn't be your fault."

Zeta curled his fingers into his palm, tightened them until they turned white.

"What do you want, Sandra? You come to apologize or yell at me?"

"I came to tell you I'm leaving you."

He laughed. "Thought you did that six years ago."

"I'm sorry. I was too afraid to say it then. I'm saying it now."

"And if I get out of here? If I come after you?"

Ines didn't flinch. She said, "I won't run anymore. I won't do that to my son."

I'm not sure which of us was caught off-guard most by the certainty in her voice.

Zeta focused on Michael for the first time. "Hey, *chico,* come here."

Michael didn't move.

Zeta cupped his hand inward, gesturing for the boy to approach the glass.

Michael stepped forward. He kept his head down. He hooked a finger under his collar and scratched.

Zeta crouched a little. "Show me your eyes."

Michael didn't.

Zeta looked at Michael, then Ines. His expression said, *Kid sure as hell ain't mine.*

"Somebody talks to you," said Zeta, "you need to look them in the eyes, little man. It's respectful."

Michael looked up.

Zeta's face was deadly serious. No smile for the little kid. He looked like he was trying to burn a message into Michael's mind and I had a feeling he'd be able to do it pretty successfully.

"What's your name, little man?"

"Michael."

"M-mml?" Zeta mimicked. "What's your name? Speak up."

"Michael."

"You scared, Michael?"

"My daddy had that, too."

Zeta frowned. "What?"

Michael pressed one finger to the Plexiglas, pointing at Zeta's face, then poked his own cheek. "Cut himself shaving. My daddy let me put the Band-Aid on for him. Yes. I'm scared."

Ines' hands made a tent over her mouth.

Zeta cleared his throat. "I got to tell you something, Michael. Okay?"

Michael shuffled.

"I want you to take care of your mom, little man. You hear me?"

Michael milked his red-and-blue tie.

"You hear me, Michael? Will you promise me that? That's a real important job."

"Okay."

"She gets scared, you're the man to protect her. You hear me?"

Michael nodded.

"How about a 'yes, sir.' "

"Yes, sir."

"All right, then."

Zeta gestured toward the visitors' exit. "Good-bye, Michael. *Adios,* Sandra."

Ines started to say something, then stopped herself. Closure was a bull's-eye she could've easily overshot. She nodded to Zeta Sanchez, then looked at me.

"I'll be there," I promised. "Go on."

She looked like she wanted to protest that, but her desire to get Michael out of the room was stronger. She held out her arms to reclaim her son. She took Michael's hand and led him toward the exit.

Zeta watched her go. "Shorter than she remembers," he murmured. *"Chingate."*

Sanchez wore the same expression I'd seen once on a lion on *Wild Kingdom*—right after the tranquilizer dart hit, the beast stumbling around in irritated bewilderment on the savannah, just before Marlin Perkins said it was safe to approach and the sleepy lion mauled the hell out of Jim or Bob or whatever the hell the assistant's name was. Marlin had had to cut to a Mutual of Omaha commercial pretty quick after that segment.

I said, "If word gets around you let her go—"

Zeta raised a cautionary finger. *"My* call. You remember that."

"You think Ines knows why you really came back to San Antonio? She wasn't the only piece of your past you needed closure on."

His eyes were getting sleepier and angrier by the second. "Go home, Professor."

"Your mother worked for Jeremiah Brandon until just after you were born. Jeremiah kept track of you as you grew up. Have you ever known for sure who your father was?"

Zeta didn't answer.

I strove to see some resemblance between Zeta Sanchez and the old photos of Jeremiah Brandon. I didn't see any.

"For what it's worth," I said, "you're more like him than Aaron or Del. You're the one who inherited his character."

I could tell that my words were no consolation. They simply sank in, probably joining the army of similar thoughts that Zeta had been amassing most of his life and still hesitated to put into the battlefield.

"You did something good today," I said. "Thank you."

Zeta stood. "I didn't do nothing, Professor. I'll be out of here sooner than you think. You wait until then before you decide to thank me."

Then he walked to the exit and disappeared back into the county jail.

I tried to convince myself that he'd needed to say those parting words to save face, that we'd come to a resolution despite that. I sat there listening to the crying babies and the fat woman grouse about her electric bill. But I kept watching the door Zeta had gone through, just to make sure it stayed closed.

FIFTY-TWO

Woodlawn Lake cuts a green, quarter-mile U through the near West Side.

The area had been affluent once. When my father was a kid back in the 1940s, the water had been pristine, the circular Casting Pond stocked with fish for children to catch. Dad once told me he'd beaten his friends in a rowing race around the lake's miniature red and white lighthouse, an idea I found incredulous, given Dad's massive beer gut in his later years. Neighborhood families had held their debutante parties and upscale Christmas *posadas* at the now boarded-up community center. My father and mother had gone to their first dance there.

Now the palm trees dotting the shore were dying. The Casting Pond was choked with watercress and cattails and old shoes. Most of the Spanish villas and Southern plantation homes fronting the water had long ago been divided into apartment blocks, their lawns gone to crabgrass and wild pyracantha.

Still, in the fresh light on a late spring morning, the place glowed with a kind of faded dignity.

Along the shore, joggers did their routes. Preschool-aged children toddled after the flocks of grebes and geese. The smell of roasted buttered corn filled the air from vendors' wagons.

We parked across from the old docks, in front of Ines and Michael's new apartment.

It didn't look like much—a two-story brownstone cube with white-framed windows and a briar patch of TV aerials on the roof. The first time I'd seen it, I'd been reminded of those buildings in atomic bomb test films, a few seconds before annihilation. I hadn't shared that observation with Ines.

On the doorstep, we found a wicker basket full of food, heavily cocooned in Saran Wrap. Ines' name was on the tag. Erainya's handwriting.

"Greek leftovers," I pronounced.

Ines hefted the new addition to her larder. "But she brought us a basket this big yesterday. We haven't even started—"

"Erainya is relentless," I warned her. "Now that you're on her list, she won't stop until your breath permanently smells like *gyros*."

I followed Ines and Michael upstairs to number five. Across the hallway, their neighbor's door was cracked open just enough to let out the sound of Spanish soap opera and the smell of cooking beans.

Ines unlocked the door to number five and Michael pushed through immediately, tugging at his tie as he disappeared around the corner.

Ines leaned against the doorway. She hugged the basket of food to her stomach and closed her eyes. Pain tightened in her face. I got the uncomfortable impression that she was passing through a labor contraction. *Congratulations, sir. It's a dolma platter.*

Finally she murmured, "I don't know what to do."

"Buy some fresh yogurt. A couple of bottles of ouzo."

She smiled wanly. "You know what I mean. I don't trust myself to stop moving. I'm afraid I'll fall apart."

"The worst is over."

She opened her eyes and looked straight through me, as if calculating the distance to the horizon. "Is it?"

She didn't sound like she expected an answer. That was just as well.

"You want me to stay for a while?" I asked.

She shook her head. "You don't have to."

"I could keep Michael company, if you want to take a nap or something. You look like you could use one."

She moistened her lips, tasting the idea, then asked almost timidly, "A hot shower?"

"A hot shower," I agreed. "Followed by several million calories of *spanakopita*. Just what Hippocrates ordered."

She laughed despite her weariness.

After Ines had disappeared into the bathroom, I unpacked Erainya's Greek food plates, put them with their brethren in the refrigerator, then walked over to the living-room windows.

The apartment was saved by its view—three wide picture windows looking out over Woodlawn Lake, just above the fronds of the palm trees. You could see the Y-shaped piers below, the lighthouse, the jogging trails, clusters of waterfowl, sunlight turning the water to hammered silver. On the eastern horizon, rising above the live oaks, the yellow-capped spires of Our Lady of the Mount gleamed. I could just make out the tiny iron Jesus who stared down at the Poco Mas Cantina.

I turned to the apartment's interior. Not as promising. The living-room wallpaper was blistered pink, the ceiling water-stained and fixed with a tiny glass chandelier. There were heaps of moving boxes everywhere. Despite Ines' cleaning efforts, the carpet still smelled faintly of cat urine.

On the right, master bedroom and bathroom. On the left was the kitchen, and the short hall that led to Michael's room. His father's silk tie was lying in a melted *P* on the floor just outside Michael's doorway.

I thought about it for a good three minutes. Then I walked over and peeked in.

No sheet cave. Michael's bed consisted of a stripped mattress and a sleeping bag. The walls were bare except for a little window that looked out on the trunk of a palm tree. Moving boxes were crammed into the tiny closet.

Michael sat cross-legged on the turquoise carpet, cutting out ads from a magazine.

He was still in his button-down and slacks but he'd pulled off his dress shoes and socks. His pale, bare feet were splotchy with chigger bites. He seemed completely focused on the toy advertisement he was cutting out.

When I'd visited the night before, Jem had come with me, bringing his PlayStation unit and a spare TV for Michael to borrow. Erainya had insisted.

Poor paidi *needs to learn these things.* Donkey Kong as a life skill.

Jem had done most of the playing last night himself, and the television was still on. As near as I could tell it was the same game. The basketball-dribbling dinosaur was doing continuous, pointless flips, waiting for someone to give it directions. Michael ignored it.

I rapped on the door. "Can I come in?"

Jem's PlayStation game kept cranking out the carnival music. I walked inside, sat down on the carpet, pressed ESCAPE on the gameset. It told me to enter my name. I was one of the high scorers. I punched in *T-R-E-S,* then shut off the TV.

Michael finished cutting out the picture. It was an advertisement for a G.I. Joe. He looked at it for a second, then added it to a stack of cutouts next to him.

"Hey, kiddo," I said. "You doing okay?"

"Uh-hmm."

He flipped a few more pages, set aside that magazine, and picked up another. "We don't have *Nickelodeon,*" he told me. "Jem borrowed me these."

"What're you doing?"

He shrugged.

"Can I look?"

He flexed his scissors thoughtfully a few times, then nodded.

The clippings showed action figures. Play-Doh kits. A Christmas tree that sang karaoke. Several other Christmas items. He must've found the December issue.

I thought about the little crumpled picture of a Christmas tree I'd found in Michael's cleaned-out room, two Saturday evenings ago, the last remnant of the sheet cave.

"Is this what you do when you're not zapping aliens with your ray gun?" I asked gently. "You collect art?"

Michael deliberated over an advertisement for an Erector set. "My wish list."

He looked as sleepy and grim as a late-night driver—no joy in his face, no indication that this toy-browsing was anything but deadly serious work.

He started to cut out the Erector set.

"You want all these things for Christmas?" I asked.

He pulled his head in, rubbed his ear on his shoulder.

"Mommy threw the old list away," he muttered. "It wasn't invisible. I have to start over now. Daddy said, 'What would you rather have for Christmas—a lot of toys or a new home in San'tonio? If you don't get it, you can put it on your wish list.'"

The house was strangely silent. A rustle of palm fronds outside the window. From the other bedroom, the faintest trickle of water from Ines' shower.

I focused on Michael Brandon's little fingers as they worked. I tried to remember if Jem's hands had even been that tiny.

"Do you want to know a secret?" I asked.

Michael's scissors stopped snipping.

"When I was younger," I said, "my father died, too."

There it was. Laid out in front of a five-year-old. Way to go, Navarre.

"I wasn't as young as you," I amended. "Not nearly. But it was very hard. For a long time."

Michael's pale, inscrutable eyes stayed on me for a heart-beat, then drifted back to the hole he'd cut in the magazine. "I'm making a wish list."

"I know," I said. "You want some privacy?"

He pondered that. He'd probably never had anybody ask him that question before. "No," he decided. "That's okay."

Then, almost inaudibly, he added, "Did you make a cave?"

I nodded. "A very big one. Called California."

Michael scratched a chigger bite. His fingernails left red streaks against the pale skin of his ankle. His lower lip started to tremble. "Daddy asked me what I wanted, and I said I wanted San'tonio."

He finished cutting another picture, flattened it on top of the other toy advertisements.

"And I'm sorry," he whispered. "Were you sorry?"

It took me a minute to get my voice to work.

"Yeah, Michael," I said. "Yeah, I was."

He pulled up one knee and rested his chin on it. He made the scissors do a one-bladed pirouette on his big toe.

"We need more Christmas pictures, Tres," he decided.

"It's April," I croaked. Then I realized how little that would mean to Michael—how the last four months in San Antonio had been one hellish Christmas present this little boy wanted with all his heart to put back in the box.

"More Christmas pictures," I repeated. "Yeah. All right. Hand me a magazine."

For the next thirty minutes, until his mother got out of the shower, Michael Brandon and I flipped through toy circulars, looking for things worth wishing for.

FIFTY-THREE

Final exam week at UTSA came too quickly. In all three of my classes, the students scrambled when they realized that there actually would be an evaluation for the term—that the chances of me getting blown away before grades were due were not as likely as they'd once thought.

Gregory the Radish Boy led the grad seminar in a rousing discussion of Marie de France. We decided that maybe Bisclavret's wife had gotten a bad deal, but they kept asking why Marie de France had chosen to tell such a depressing tale and why Aaron Brandon and I liked to teach it.

The last class before the final, Morticia Addams and the two housewives brought casseroles to class. Sergeant Irwin brought some pastries and made a big deal out of handing me a purple-sugar *pan dulce,* telling me it was my medal for combat wounds in my first term. The sergeant pounded me on the shoulder and said he was damn proud to have had my class.

Professor Mitchell sat in the back, smiling, taking notes, sipping a Sprite one of the students had given him, while we went through some last-minute questions from the study guide.

After the class broke up Mitchell offered to walk me back to my office.

"You're a hell of a teacher," Mitchell told me.

I refused to blush. I looked straight down the hallway of yellow bolted panels, thinking about the corridor as it had been a few weeks ago, filled with FBI and bomb-squad men and police.

"You should see me on semesters when I don't get shot."

Mitchell chuckled. As we walked he brought out some student evaluation forms, the kind they use to assess each class.

"I hope I get that chance," he said. "These reports are excellent—the dean was very pleased to see them after such a hard beginning to the term. There've already been quite a few questions about your classes for next fall."

"Next fall?"

"You're interested, I hope? Same arrangement? Same hours?"

"Dividing my time with Erainya Manos? You're willing to have a part-time P.I. on staff?"

Mitchell laughed. "Probably keep everybody honest when it comes to post-tenure review time, knowing I've got my own investigator. Absolutely, son."

We stopped at the door of my office. Mitchell patted me on the shoulder, grinned. His white sideburns inched back. "Well?"

"I'm on board," I said.

"You've got a future here, son. Unofficially speaking, I think you'll be around for some time."

"My landlord and creditors will be happy to hear that."

Mitchell patted me again, then said, "I'll see you at the department party?"

He turned without waiting for an answer and went whistling down the hallway.

I closed up the office and got home around one, just in time to change for my next engagement.

It was the first Friday in May. Some friends and I had a date. I put on one of my new dress shirts, some slacks, and a tie I had been able to afford with my first paycheck from UTSA. My tie was a springtime explosion of rose on yellow. I looked in the mirror and wondered if there had always been a little streak of gray above my left ear.

Around one-thirty, Erainya did her unsyncopated *rap-ta-tap* on the door. Jem and Michael burst in, followed by their mothers. The boys looked like miniature versions of me—slacks, white shirts, same rose-and-yellow ties, sawed off and hemmed to their sizes. They'd insisted on their own ties when they'd gone shopping with me a few days before. I told them we would look like a clown troupe if we went out in public together, but that just made them more determined.

Erainya and Ines, mercifully, had chosen their own clothes. Erainya wore her standard black T-shirt dress, black sandals, a black leather purse that looked like an S&M mask. Her only concession to the May Festival atmosphere was a single red plastic bracelet on her wrist. It somehow looked more like the remnant of incarceration than a spring fashion statement.

Ines wore white slacks and a blue Guatemalan shirt that made her red hair glow like neon. She gave me a kiss on the cheek, then went to rein in Michael, who was helping Jem capture Robert Johnson from the top shelf of the closet—his normal hiding place from children.

Erainya came up and straightened my tie. "You're how old? And you can't tie a tie?"

"I'm new at this formal dress business."

She sighed. "So you going to grace us with your presence at the office one of these days?"

"Tuesday," I promised. "Same day George'll be back. Things have just about settled down at UTSA. You close out the Brandon case?"

She stepped back and examined my outfit critically. "They sent the check. It didn't bounce. Things are fine."

"No more death threats to the English department?"

"Ah." She waved her hand. "Not unless you keep dressing like this. No."

Jem was raking Robert Johnson down the sleeves of my shirts. Michael was giggling.

We granted the poor feline a reprieve and told the boys to come on to the car.

As it turned out, Jem and Michael's new school was not going to be the one they'd visited together three weeks before. During the course of the police investigation, one of Erainya's lawyer friends who was representing Ines had learned that both women were looking into private education for their sons. The lawyer had put in a good word at his daughter's school on the North Side, which just happened to be short on boys' enrollment for the fall. Lo and behold, Jem and Michael received acceptance letters and half-tuition scholarships a few days later, along with invitations to visit for the annual Spring Celebration to meet their future classmates.

The school was just north of Loop 410 but it seemed a thousand miles from town—an isolated village of Spanish-style limestone buildings and courtyards and covered walkways nestled amid hundreds of acres of live oaks on the banks of Salado Creek.

Today the huge front lawn of the school was overrun with families and food booths. The trees were bedecked in ribbons. Hand-painted signs advertised Beanie Baby tosses, peppermint sticks in lemons, a dunking booth. In the breezeway by the theater, a junior school jazz band was foot-tapping their way through a tune that sounded like Miles Davis struck with baseball bats and strained through an organ grinder's box. Parents in suits and flowing white summer dresses floated along, smiles in place, tickets in hand, children in whirlwinds around them, faces painted like spiderwebs or rainbows.

Within fifteen minutes of our arrival, Jem and Michael were tugged into a group of kindergartners and taught to play fishing-for-treats with a stick and a glittery sheet.

Erainya was pulled into a conversation with her lawyer/

parent friend who wanted to introduce her to a state senator who might have some business for a good P.I. They walked off talking about the possibilities and eating Sno-Kones.

Ines Brandon smiled at me nervously. "What the hell are we doing here?"

"Pretending to be rich," I said. "Come on."

We walked along the periphery of the festival, trying our best to avoid little bodies. I glanced at Ines in her bright colors and tried to convince myself she really was the same woman I'd met just a few weeks ago.

We bought two lemons with peppermint sticks and sat in the shade of a live oak. Jem was showing some kids a trick with a yo-yo. Michael was betting the other kids a carnival ticket each that Jem couldn't do it three times in a row.

"I don't know about this new Jem/Michael alliance," I muttered.

Ines twirled her peppermint stick. Her lips were turning unnaturally red from the candy. "Hardly fair to the rest of the kids in the world, is it?"

We watched as Jem completed the third around-the-world/walk-the-dog combination with the yo-yo and Michael started collecting tickets, smiling for the first time I'd ever seen. He suggested the other kids try double or nothing.

The junior high band managed a drumroll and a horn crescendo, then unraveled into a very odd waltz arrangement of Glenn Miller's "String of Pearls." I got the feeling it wasn't really supposed to be a waltz arrangement, but I wanted to give them the benefit of a doubt.

"I'm wondering," Ines said. She had her legs crossed at the ankles, the tips of her loafers tapping the air with the music. "Should I thank you, or apologize for inflicting myself on you?"

"No apologies," I assured her.

"My problems almost got you killed, Tres."

"Technically speaking."

"And now I feel like I've been adopted. You and Erainya, George and Kelly, your other friends."

"It's an odd family," I admitted. "But our weirdness makes us strong. You'll fit right in."

She slapped my knee. "How can I thank you?"

"Feed Robert Johnson every day?"

"Guess again."

I smiled. Jem and Michael trotted over to us and plopped down on the grass, still counting their winnings. Jem appropriated my peppermint lemon and told me he was going to like this school.

The junior high band's waltz kept going. A daddy in a three-piece suit was now dancing with his little girl on his toes.

It looked like fun. "How about this dance?"

Ines smiled radiantly. "That's what you want as a thank-you?"

"It's one of the things on my wish list, yeah."

Michael let out a giggle, then caught himself. His mother looked at him, amazed. His ears turned bright red. She looked back at me and her eyes grew suspicious.

"What's the joke?" she demanded.

"You want to dance or not?"

"A dance. To *this* music."

I nodded. "Have to start somewhere."

She pointed her peppermint at me, daggerlike. "Someday, Tres Navarre, you'll regret saying that."

The hell of it was, I believed her immediately.

But when she stood and offered me her hand, I took it anyway.

If you enjoyed Rick Riordan's THE LAST KING OF TEXAS, you won't want to miss any of the novels in this sizzling, award-winning series.

And turn the page for a preview of Rick's mystery, COLD SPRINGS. Look for it at your favorite bookseller in hardcover from Bantam Books.

COLD SPRINGS

RICK RIORDAN

Chadwick struggled with his bow tie.

He was thinking about what he would say, how he would break the news that would end his marriage, when Norma came up behind him and told him about the heroin in their daughter's underwear drawer.

He turned, the bow tie unraveling in his fingers.

Norma wore only her slip, her bare arms as smooth and perfectly muscled as they'd been when she was nineteen. Her eyes glowed with that black heat she saved for lovemaking and really huge arguments, and he was pretty sure which she was planning for.

"Heroin," he said.

"In a Ziploc, yeah. Looked like brown sugar."

"What'd you do with it?"

"I smoked it. What do you think? I flushed it down the toilet."

"You flushed it down the toilet. Jesus, Norma."

"It wasn't hers. She was keeping it for a friend."

"You believed that?"

"She's my daughter. Yes, I believed her."

Chadwick stared out the window, down at Mission Street, where the Christmas lights popped and sparked under the sudden weight of ice.

He'd lived in this house almost all of his thirty-seven years, and he couldn't remember a November night this cold. The glass storefront of the corner *taquería* was greasy with steam. Lowriders cruised the boulevard billowing smoke from their exhaust pipes. Twenty-fourth Street station was swept clean of the homeless—all gone to shelters, leaving behind piles of summer clothes like insect husks. Next door, the Romos had turned up their music the way other people turn up the heater—the sorrowful heartbeat of *narcocorrido* pulsing through the townhouse's wallpaper.

Chadwick wanted to turn to steam and disperse against the glass. He wanted to escape from what he had to do, what he had to say. And now this—Katherine.

"The Zedmans will be here in a few minutes," he told Norma. "I've been home since yesterday."

She tilted her head to put on an earring. "What? I should've told you earlier? Last week I needed your help, you ran off to Texas. Maybe I should've told you at the airport, huh? Let you get right back on the plane?"

Chadwick felt his throat constricting. His Air Force buddy Hunter used to tease him about marrying Norma Reyes. Hunter said he wasn't getting a wife, he was getting a Cuban Missile Crisis.

He wanted to tell her why he'd really run.

He wanted to tell her that out there in the woods of Texas—for a few days—he had remembered why he'd fallen in love with her. He'd remembered a time when he'd been excited to have a woman half his size take him on so fearlessly, grab his hand like a toddler's grip on a shiny new toy and pull him onto the dance floor with a look that said, *Yeah, I want to marry an Air Force man. You got a problem with that?*

He had decided Norma deserved the truth, even if it destroyed them. But that had been at a distance of two thousand miles. Now, getting too close, the feeling was like a computer photo. Expand it too much, and it turned into pixels of random color.

He shucked his tuxedo coat, walked down the hallway to Katherine's room, Norma calling from behind, "I've already grounded her, Chadwick. Don't make it worse."

Katherine was on her bed, her back to the wall, her knees up to her chin—prepared for the assault. The Guatemalan fabric had fallen off her headboard, revealing the decorations Chadwick had painted when Katherine was two—rainbows and stars, a baby-blue cow jumping over a beaming moon. Kurt Cobain's picture sagged off the wall above, where Babar the Elephant used to be.

Sadness twisted into Chadwick's chest like a corkscrew. How the hell had Katherine turned sixteen? What happened to six? What happened to ten?

He tried to see something of himself in her, but Norma had dominated their daughter's genes completely. Katherine had her mother's fiery eyes, her defiant pout. She had the coffee skin, the lush black hair, the build that was both petite and combat-sturdy. As a child, Katherine would clench her fists and lock her knees and she'd be impossible to pick up—as if she were molded from stone.

"Heroin," Chadwick said.

She rubbed her silver necklace back and forth over her lips, like a zipper. "I told Mom. It wasn't mine."

"You went back." Chadwick tried to keep his voice even. "After everything we talked about."

"Daddy, look, a friend asked me to keep the stuff. A friend from school."

"Who?"

"It doesn't matter. It's over. Okay? I didn't want to piss him off. I was going to throw the stuff away, give it back, whatever. I didn't have time. Happy?"

Chadwick needed to believe her. He needed to so badly her words gained substance the more he thought about them, began to harden into a viable foundation. But goddamn it. After last Saturday . . .

He wanted to grab Katherine by the shoulders. He wanted to wrap his arms around her and hold her until she went back to being his little girl. He wanted to take her away from here, whether Norma liked it or not, put her on a plane to Texas, bring her to Asa Hunter's woods, teach her how to live all over again, from scratch.

It had seemed so simple when he talked to Hunter. Hunter saw things the way a gun did—narrow, precise, certain. Hunter had coached him, prepared him on what to say to Norma. He'd let Chadwick imagine Katherine walking those woods, free from drugs and self-destructive friends and pictures of asshole rock stars on her wall. He'd even offered Chadwick a job as an escort, picking up troubled kids from around the country and bringing them to the ranch.

This school I'm starting— It is the future, man. Get your family out of that poison city.

"Katherine," Chadwick said, "I want to help you."

"How, Daddy?" Her voice was tight with anger. "How do you want to do that?"

Chadwick caught his own face in Katherine's mirror. He looked haggard and nervous, a hungry transient pulled from some underpass and stuffed into a tux shirt.

He sat next to her on the bed, put his hand next to hers. He didn't touch her. He hadn't given his daughter a hug or a kiss in . . . weeks, anyway. He didn't remember. The distance you have to develop between a father and a daughter as she grew into a woman—he understood it, but it killed him sometimes.

"I want you to go to Texas," Chadwick said. "The boarding school."

"You want to get rid of me."

"This isn't working for you, Katherine. School, home, nothing."

"You're giving me a choice? If you're giving me a choice, I say no."

"I want you to agree. It would be easier."

"Mom won't go for it otherwise," she translated.

Chadwick's face burned. He hated that he and Norma couldn't speak with one voice, that they played these games, maneuvering for Katherine's cooperation the way a divorced couple would.

Katherine kept rubbing the necklace against her lips. It seemed like yesterday he'd given it to her—her thirteenth birthday.

"You can't baby-sit tonight," he decided. "We'll tell the Zedmans we can't go."

"Daddy, I'm fine. It's just Mallory. I've watched her a million times. Go to the auction."

Chadwick hesitated, knowing that he had no choice. He'd

been gone from work the entire week. He couldn't very well miss the auction, too. "Give me your car keys."

"Come on, Daddy."

He held out his hand.

Katherine fished her Toyota key out of her pocket, dropped it into his palm.

"Where's your key chain?" he asked.

"What?"

"Your Disneyland key chain."

"I got tired of it," she said. "Gave it away."

"Last week you gave away your jacket. A hundred-dollar jacket."

"Daddy, I hated that jacket."

"You aren't a charity, Katherine. Don't give away your things."

She looked at him the way she used to when she was small—as if she wanted to touch her fingertips to his chin, his nose, his eyebrows, memorize his face. Chadwick felt like he was melting inside.

Down in the stairwell, the doorbell rang. John Zedman called up, "Candygram."

"This isn't over, Katherine," Chadwick said. "I want to talk about this when I get home."

She brushed a tear off her cheek.

"Katherine. Understood?"

"Yeah, Daddy. Understood."

She made the last word small and hot, instantly igniting Chadwick's guilt. He wanted to explain. He wanted to tell her he really had tried to make things work out. He really did love her.

"Chadwick?" Norma said behind him, her tone a warning. "The Zedmans are here."

Little Mallory made her usual entrance—a blur of blond hair and oversized T-shirt making a flying leap onto Katherine's bed.

"Kaferine!"

And Katherine transformed into that other girl—the one

who could attract younger kids like an ice cream wagon song; the natural baby-sitter who always smiled and was oh so responsible and made other parents tell Chadwick with a touch of envy, "You are so lucky!" Chadwick saw that side of Katherine less and less.

She tousled Mallory's hair. "Hey, Peewee. Ready to have some fun?"

"Yesss!"

"I got Candyland. I got Equestrian Barbie. We are set to *party.*"

Mallory gave her a high five.

Ann and John stood in the living room, cologne and perfume a gentle aura around them.

"Well," John said, registering at once that Chadwick wasn't even half ready to go. "Grizzly Adams, back from the wild."

"The carnivores say hello," Chadwick told him. "They want you to write home more often."

"Ouch," John said, his smile a little too brilliant. "I'll get you for that."

Ann wouldn't make eye contact with him. She gave Norma a hug—Norma having dressed in record time, looking dangerous in a red and yellow silk dress, like a size-four nuclear explosion.

Chadwick excused himself to finish getting ready. He listened to Norma and Ann talk about the school auction, John flipping through Chadwick's music collection, shouting innocuous questions to him about Yo-Yo Ma and Brahms, Mallory setting off all the clocks on the mantel—her ritual reintroduction to the house.

When Chadwick came out again, Katherine sat crosslegged by the fireplace—his beautiful girl, all grown up, drowning in flannel grunge and uncombed hair. Mallory sat on her lap, winding the hands of an old clock, trying to get it to chime.

Chadwick locked eyes with his daughter. He felt a tug in his chest, warning him not to go.

"Don't worry, Dad," she said. "We'll be fine."

Those words would be burned into Chadwick's forehead. They would live there, laser-hot, for the rest of his life.

When the front door shut, Katherine felt herself deflating, the little knots in her joints coming loose.

She took Candyland down from the shelf. She joked with Mallory and smiled as they drew color cards, but inside she felt the black sadness that was always just underneath her fingernails and behind her eyes, ready to break through.

Katherine wanted a fix. She knew it would only make her depression worse—buoy her up for a little while, then make the blackness wider, the edges of the chasm harder to keep her feet on. Her therapist had warned her. Ann Zedman had warned her. Her father had warned her. They were all part of the educational team, all looking out for her best interests.

We're here to help you be successful again, Katherine.

Fuck that.

If there was anything worse than having a dad who was a teacher, it was having your dad at the same school as you. And not just for a couple of years. A K–12 school. A *small* K–12 school, so you had thirteen years of absolute hell, no breathing space, no room to be yourself. And if that wasn't bad enough, have your dad be best friends with the headmistress for a gajillion years—Ann Zedman always over at your house, peeking into your life.

That was why Katherine loved the East Bay. It was *hers*.

At least, it had been until last week—the stupid cops separating her out, scolding her, asking what the hell she was doing with *those* people. She remembered the ride home from the Oakland police station, her wrists raw from the handcuffs, her anger building as her father glanced in the rearview mirror, insisting that she *not* tell her mother what she'd been doing at the party because it would break her mother's heart. Katherine had snapped. She'd told her dad everything—to hurt him, to prove it was even worse than he thought. She did have a life of her own. Friends of her own.

Oh, Daddy.

She hated herself even more than she hated him. She'd told him. She'd ruined everything. Now he would send her away to goddamn Texas.

Mallory tugged at her sleeve. "Come on, Kaferine. You got a double red."

Katherine looked across the game board.

Mallory had been her dress-up doll, her pretend child, her toy self she could slip into whenever real life sucked too bad. But now that Mallory had started kindergarten at Laurel Heights, Katherine felt sad every time she looked at her. She never wanted to see them ruin this little girl, the way they'd ruined her. She never wanted to see Mallory grow up.

She forced a smile, moved her double red.

Mallory drew Queen Frostine and squealed with delight.

It was an easy skip from Queen Frostine to King Kandy. Mallory won the game while Katherine was still back in the Molasses Swamp.

"What can we play now?" Mallory asked. "Horses?"

"I have a better idea."

"No," Mallory said immediately. "I don't like that."

"Come on. It's our little secret."

"It's scary."

"Nah. For a brave kid like you?"

Katherine went to the secret panel in the wainscoting, the storage closet that her grandfather had constructed when the bottom level of the townhouse had been his shop. He was a clockmaker, her grandfather. He loved gears and springs, mechanical tricks.

The door was impossible to see from the outside. You had to press in just the right spot for the pressure latch to release. Inside, the space was big enough for a child to crawl into, or maybe an adult, if you scrunched. The back was still crammed with clock parts—copper coils, weights and chains, star-and-moon clock faces.

She remembered her grandfather telling her, "Never wind a clock backwards, Katie. Never." He had always called her

Katie, never Katherine. Her father said it was because he couldn't bear to think of his wife, whose smoker's lungs had shut down while she was waiting for her namesake to be born. "Winding backwards will ruin the clock. Always go forward. Even if you only want to go back an hour, always go forward eleven."

She wondered if her dad had been made out of clock parts, like the latch on the cabinet. She wished she could wind him backwards one week, to see if something would break.

She reached into the closet, to the little rusty hook only she knew about, and pulled out a copy of her Toyota key.

Ground me, Daddy. Go ahead.

She turned to Mallory, who was balancing Equestrian Barbie's plastic pony on her knee.

Poor little Mallory—the headmistress's daughter. She would have an even worse school experience than Katherine did. So what if she liked kindergarten? It was only a matter of time before she felt the walls closing in on her, that chasm opening at her feet. It sliced into Katherine's heart whenever she passed the lower school windows, saw Mallory wave a sticky hello to her, fingers covered in primary-colored gloop.

No, Katherine never wanted to see her baby doll grow up.

She smiled to cover the blackness. "Come on, Peewee. Let's go for a ride."

Laurel Heights School blazed with light. Luminarias lined the sidewalk. Arcs of paper lanterns glowed red and blue over the playground, transforming the basketball court into a dance floor nobody could use, thanks to the weather.

Inside, the two-story building was buttery warm with jazz music and candlelight, waiters bustling about with trays of champagne and canapés, parents laughing too loud, drinking too freely, enjoying their big night away from the children.

For an outside party brought inside at the last minute, Ann had to admit the staff and the caterers had done a great job. Cloths had been draped over the teachers' supply cabinets.

Banquet tables had replaced school desks. A hundred tiny articles of lost-and-found clothing had been taken off the coat hooks and stashed in closets, broken crayons and Montessori rods swept off the floor. Fresh-cut flowers decorated the music teacher's piano. The kindergarten teacher's desk had been converted to a cash bar.

The school was too small for so many people, but the cramped quarters just proved Ann's point, the purpose for the auction—the school needed to grow. They weren't the neighborhood school they'd started out as in the 1920s, with fifteen kids from Pacific Heights. They were busting at the seams with 152 students from all over the Bay Area. They needed to buy the mansion next door, do a major renovation, double the size of the campus. What better way to kick off the capital campaign than cram all the parents together, let them see how their children spent each day?

Despite that, despite how well the evening seemed to be going, Ann was a mess. The two glasses of wine she'd had to steady her nerves were bubbling to vinegar in her stomach.

She should have been schmoozing, but instead she was sitting in the corner of the only empty classroom, knees-to-knees with Norma Reyes on tiny first-grade chairs, telling Norma that marriage counseling was a great idea. Really. It was nothing to be ashamed about.

Hypocrite.

She prayed Chadwick would forget about their agreement—just forget it.

At the same time, she hoped like hell he had more guts than she did.

Norma kept crying, calling Chadwick names.

Parents streamed by the open doorway. They would start to greet Ann, then see Norma's tears and turn away like they'd been hit by a wind tunnel fan.

"I want to kill the *pendejo*," Norma said.

Ann laced her fingers in her friend's. She promised that Chadwick was trying his best, that Katherine would be okay.

Her therapist was sharp. There were good programs for drug intervention.

"Bullshit," Norma said. "You love this. You've been warning me for years."

Ann said nothing. She'd had lots of practice, diplomatically saying nothing.

For years, she had been the mediator between the family and the faculty, who would ask her—no disrespect to their colleague Chadwick—but why wasn't Katherine on probation? Why wasn't she taking her medication? When do they decide that they just can't serve her at this school? Ann endured the insinuations that if Chadwick hadn't been her friend for so long, if she didn't know the family socially, she would've jumped on Katherine's problems sooner and harder.

On the other hand, there was Norma, who had never seen the problem, not since seventh grade, when Ann had first pushed for psychological testing. Norma only saw the good in her daughter. Laurel Heights was overreacting. She'd never forgiven Chadwick for supporting Ann's recommendations for testing and therapy.

"You know what he's planning, don't you?" Norma asked.

Ann's heart did a half-beat syncopation. "What do you mean?"

"Come on. Me, he keeps in the dark. You, never. Asa Hunter. The school in Texas."

Ann's shoulders relaxed. "He mentioned it."

She didn't say that Chadwick had obsessed on it at length, been impervious to her reservations. A boot camp? Wilderness therapy? What was she supposed to say—yes, lock your kid up with drill sergeants for a year? Turn your back on everything Laurel Heights stands for—the child-centered philosophy, the nurturing environment—and give Katherine a buzz cut? The whole idea only underscored how desperate Chadwick was to be out of a failing marriage.

But she'd agreed to let him take time off for his trip to Texas, despite how hard it was to get a substitute around

Thanksgiving, despite the fact that the eighth-graders hated it when Chadwick—their favorite teacher—was gone. It was in Ann's interest to let Chadwick get his thoughts in order—about Katherine, about everything.

What bothered her most was that she had been tempted to endorse the idea of sending Katherine away. In a selfish, dishonorable way, wouldn't it make things easier?

"We both know," she told Norma. "He only wants what's best for Katherine."

"He wants to use her as a fucking guinea pig." Norma ripped another tissue out of her purse. "Christ, I must look like shit."

Oh, please, Ann thought.

As if Norma ever looked like shit. She had that petite figure Ann had grown up hating. She wished, just once, she could look like Norma. She wished she could cry in public and call her husband a dickhead and not give a second thought how it would affect her public image.

Okay. She was jealous. She hated herself for it, spent hours at night thinking, *That's not the reason. That's not the reason.*

John appeared at the door, a margarita in either hand. He surveyed the situation, smiled straight through Norma's tears.

"You'll never guess," he said. "The mayor thinks Mallory's panel is the best one on the kindergarten quilt. We're going to have lunch next week, go over some ideas for the Presidio."

Ann fought down a surge of irritation. She hated the way John skated across other people's emotions—so completely incapable of sympathy that he made it his personal mission to pretend bad feelings didn't exist. You could always count on John to be the first to tell a joke at any funeral.

"Lunch with Frank Jordan," Ann said. "Big prize, John."

He raised his eyebrows at Norma. "I get a piece of the biggest development deal in the city's history—you'd think that would please my wife. Lots of money. Lots of publicity. But what do I know? Maybe it's nothing special."

"Hey," Norma said, dabbing her tissue under her eyes. "Tonight is supposed to be fun. Remember?"

John handed her a margarita. "Your husband got stuck with that pretty blond Mrs. Passmore—had a question about her daughter's history project. Can't take him anywhere, huh?"

Ann wanted to slap him.

"We're about to start, honey," she said instead. "Why don't you go check with the cashiers?"

"Done, honey. Spreadsheet. Printer. Cash box. Don't worry about it."

He gave her a smug smile that confirmed what she already knew—letting John chair the capital campaign was the biggest mistake of her life. It was a pro bono thing for him, a good tax write-off, and since the school could hardly afford a full-time development director, Ann truly needed the help. But as she had been slow to figure out, the charity work made John feel superior, affirming his belief that Ann's career was nothing more than a hobby. Raising her $30 million would be his equivalent to helping her power-till a tomato patch or driving her to yoga lessons. *My wife, the headmistress. Isn't she cute?*

"I'll take Norma upstairs," he told her. "You go ahead. The faculty is probably paralyzed up there, waiting for your orders."

Ann contained her fury. She gave Norma's hand one last squeeze, then went off to join the party.

Upstairs, the removable wall between the two middle school classrooms had been taken down, making space for a main banquet room with an auction stage. Ann made her way toward the head table, past parents and student volunteers, waiters with trays of salads. Chadwick was talking to one of her sophomore workers, David Kraft, who sported a brand-new crop of zits. Poor kid. He'd been one of Katherine's friends until last summer, when Katherine gave up friends.

"Excuse us, David." Ann smiled. "Duty calls."

"Sure, Mrs. Z."

"You going to spot those high bidders for us?"

David held up his red signaling cloth. "Yes, ma'am."

"That's my boy."

She maneuvered Chadwick toward the faculty table.

"How's Norma?" he asked.

"She's right, you know. Your idea stinks. Boot camp school? It absolutely stinks."

"Thanks for the open mind."

"Things aren't complicated enough right now?"

They locked eyes, and they both knew that Katherine was not the foremost question on either of their minds. God help them, but she wasn't.

Ann wanted to be responsible. She wanted to think about the welfare of Katherine and Mallory. She wanted to think about her school and do the professional thing, the calm and steady thing.

But part of her wanted to rebel against that. Despite her wonderful little girl, her successful husband, her ambitious plans for Laurel Heights, part of her wanted to shake off the accumulated infrastructure of her life, the way she suspected Norma would, if their roles were reversed. Norma, who had become as much her friend as Chadwick was. Norma, the woman Ann probably admired more than anyone else.

Ann was thinking, *Don't say anything tonight, Chadwick. Please.*

And at the same time, she couldn't wait for the auction to end, for all four of them to get somewhere they could talk.

Ann felt like two different people, slowly separating, as if the Ann on the surface were a tectonic plate, sliding precariously over something hot and molten.

And right now, the Ann underneath wanted an earthquake.

About the Author

RICK RIORDAN is the author of the #1 bestselling young adult series Percy Jackson and the Olympians and the young adult series The Kane Chronicles, starting in 2010 with *The Red Pyramid*. He has published seven Tres Navarre thrillers: *Big Red Tequila*, winner of the Shamus and Anthony Awards; *The Widower's Two-Step*, winner of the Edgar Award; *The Last King of Texas*; *The Devil Went Down to Austin*; *Southtown*; *Mission Road*; and *Rebel Island*. He is also the author of the acclaimed thriller *Cold Springs*. Rick Riordan lives with his family in San Antonio, Texas.

www.rickriordan.com